P9-CEM-629

SOULMINDER

SOULMINDER

·

TIMOTHY ZAHN

OPEN ROAD
INTEGRATED MEDIA
NEW YORK

All rights reserved, including without limitation the right to reproduce this book or any portion thereof in any form or by any means, whether electronic or mechanical, now known or hereinafter invented, without the express written permission of the publisher.

This is a work of fiction. Names, characters, places, events, and incidents either are the product of the author's imagination or are used fictitiously. Any resemblance to actual persons, living or dead, businesses, companies, events, or locales is entirely coincidental.

Copyright © 2014 by Timothy Zahn

Cover design by Amanda DeRosa

978-1-4976-4620-9

Published in 2014 by Open Road Integrated Media, Inc.
345 Hudson Street
New York, NY 10014
www.openroadmedia.com

SOULMINDER

•

CHAPTER 1

●

I Pray the Lord My Soul to Keep

THE EVENING'S VISITORS to Mercy Medical Hospital had long since gone home, as had most of the day staff, and the hallway outside the small equipment-packed room was as silent as a grave. Across the room, behind the medical repeater displays, the old Venetian blinds clattered quietly to themselves as imperfect window seals let in small gusts of the increasingly turbulent air outside. Shifting stiffly in his chair, Adrian Sommer groped for his coffee mug, trying to shut out the oppressive feeling creeping over him. Late at night, with the extra blackness of a storm approaching, was a horrible time to have to watch a man die.

That the old man visible on the TV monitor would soon breathe his last, there was little doubt. The doctor preparing one last hypo of painkiller knew it—Sommer had seen that same stolid expression on over a hundred faces over the past three years, and knew all too well what it meant. The family gathered together around the pastel-sheeted bedside knew it, too, even those who only hours before had been struggling vehemently to hide it from themselves. Sommer had listened as the conversations, faintly audible through the door separating the two rooms, had gone from hopeful to angry to resigned.

And as for the old man himself . . .

Sommer sipped at his mug, his stomach burning with acid as the cold coffee reached it. *God*, he thought, *I hate this.*

Behind him, a chair squeaked. "I'm getting fluctuations," Jessica Sands announced quietly. "Won't be long now."

Sommer nodded. Pushing the morose thoughts away as best he could, he forced his mind back into work mode. "Mass reader is holding steady." He gave the instruments arrayed before him a quick scan. "Nothing showing on the Kirlian yet."

"Might want to switch the Mullner off stand-by," Sands suggested. "I still don't trust the Kirlian to give us enough warning." She paused as the blinds rattled again, louder this time. "Hope the lightning holds off until it's over."

"Oh, certainly," Sommer growled. "It'd be a shame for him to die without us getting any useful data out of him."

The words had come out with more bitterness than he'd intended them to, but for once Sands had the grace to let it pass without retort. For a long minute the wind and the drone of cooling fans were the only sounds in the room, and then Sands's chair squeaked again as she turned to look over her shoulder at him. "I've been thinking," she said. "After we've finished with this set, what say we move operations somewhere else for a while? LA or San Diego, for instance."

Sommer eyed her. "Something wrong with right here?"

"Oh, I don't know," she said too casually, and her eyes slipped away from his gaze. "It'd be a nice change of scenery, for starters. Climate's supposed to be better there, too."

Sommer felt his lip tighten. "Climate. As in they have fewer thunderstorms?"

Sands threw him a glare that was half resignation, half impatience. "What are you trying to prove, Adrian?" she demanded. "That you *like* the feel of knives twisting around in your gut?"

In his lap, Sommer's hands curled into impotent fists. "Running away isn't the answer," he told her stubbornly.

"I'd like to know what is, then," she countered. "Standing there and getting your feet knocked out from under you every time a thunderstorm moves through sure isn't doing you any good."

"I do *not* get my feet kn—"

"Hold it!" Sands cut him off, swiveling back to her instruments. "I think it's starting."

Sommer's eyes flicked to the main TV monitor, heart pounding in his ears. One look was all it took: the old man was indeed in his last moments. Flicking the selector on his other display to the Kirlian, he watched as the three-dimensional saddleshape began to flatten. "How's the Mullner?" he asked.

"Coming in strong," Sands said, a steady excitement creeping into her voice. "Fits the expected pattern: standard plus—oh, lots of embellishments."

Sommer squeezed the arm of his chair, a fresh wave of acid pain shooting through his stomach. *Embellishments.* As if the experiences and memories, the joys and sorrows of a lifetime had no more meaning than decoration. "Any anomalies?"

"You mean because of the Alzheimer's?" He sensed her shake her head. "No truncating of the memory traces or anything obvious like that. Something may show up when we run it through the computer, though."

On the monitor one of the old man's daughters, her back to the hidden camera, had taken his hand. Sommer blinked back tears, glad that he couldn't see her face. "It's starting to detach," he told Sands.

"Right," she said, an odd tautness in her voice. "Watch *real* closely, Adrian."

"What—?"

There was no time to complete the question. On the monitor the old man stiffened . . . and suddenly the Kirlian trace went flat.

Or, rather, almost flat. For a second it seemed to hesitate, and then, like a strong fish being drawn in on a line, the saddleshape began to reform. "Jessica!" Sommer snapped, eyes locked on the image. "What in God's name—?"

The question faded on his lips as the saddleshape again flattened. For good, this time.

The old man was dead.

"Damn," Sands muttered behind him.

Sommer drew a shuddering breath, a sudden sweat soaking his shirt as he turned to face her. "I thought we'd agreed," he said, his voice trembling with suppressed emotion, "that we weren't going to try the trap again until we had a better idea of what exactly we were doing."

She looked back at him unblinkingly. "We *do* have a better idea what we're doing," she said calmly. "Every death we record gives us a better picture of how the lifeforce is mapped out—"

"How the *soul* is mapped out," Sommer corrected her.

She shrugged fractionally. "The point is that we've identified fifteen new characteristic curves in the trace since the last trap experiment, and I thought it was time to give it another shot."

She had a point—Sommer had to concede that. But that didn't excuse her setting up the run behind his back. "You could have told me," he growled.

The hard set to her eyes softened, just a little. "The anticipation is almost as hard on you as thunderstorms are," she said quietly. "You know, I meant what I said before about taking this show on the road."

Or in other words, the subject of her unauthorized experiment with the trap was closed. Temporarily, at least. "We can't afford to move," he told her flatly. "Our equipment is here, our computer contract is here, all our financial support is here."

She gazed at him, studying his face. "We're close, Adrian. Real close. You saw what happened. We had a genuine grip on the life—on the soul—there."

"Except that it didn't look any better than the last attempt we made."

"Maybe, maybe not," she said. "We'll see what happens when the computer's chewed over it."

Sommer shook his head heavily. "It's not working, Jessica. Somewhere along the line we're missing something. Proximity requirements, pattern identification, power, trap design—*something*."

Sands's eyes flicked over his shoulder to the TV monitor. "Well, we're not going to be able to get the trap much closer than this. Not without putting it in someone's lap. But if it's pattern identification or one of the others, it's just a matter of time and experimentation."

Sommer sighed. "I know," he said. "It's just that . . . " He shook his head.

"I know; it's been a long road for you," Sands said quietly, her voice about as sympathetic as it ever got. "Look, I can pull all the packs and shut things down here. Why don't you go on home, okay?"

Sommer wasn't in the mood to argue. Outside, he could hear the rain beginning; the thunder wouldn't be far behind. If he got a sleeping pill down him fast enough, he could possibly be out before the worst of it hit. "Okay," he told her, getting to his feet. "See you tomorrow."

For a moment he paused, his eyes shifting one last time to the TV monitor. The family had left the room now, and the doctor was tiredly turning off the various monitors. Sommer focused on the figure beneath the sheet, and as it always did, David's old bedtime prayer whispered through his mind:

> Now I lay me down to sleep,
> I pray the Lord my soul to keep,

If I should die before I wake,
I pray the Lord my soul to take.

Blinking back tears, he turned away. Fumbling for the door-knob, he left the room.

He'd hoped to beat the thunderstorm home. The thunderstorm, unfortunately, won the race.

It was an especially violent one, too. The lightning flashed across the sky like a stuttering strobe light, blazing across the night and burning bizarre afterimage shadows into Sommer's retinas. The thunder stabbed at his eardrums and shook his car, while the wind turned the trees lining the road into crazed dancers.

And as he fought the wheel and winced every time a particularly deep puddle threw a blinding wash of water across his windshield, he thought about David.

It had been exactly this sort of night, with exactly this sort of terrible visibility, when the SUV had run a stop sign and slammed into the passenger side of their car. David had taken the full brunt of the impact, his little body half crushed, half torn by the wall of twisted metal as he was thrown sideways against his restraints.

And with the rain dripping through the cracks in the roof, Sommer had held his son in his arms and felt the life leave the little boy's body.

The life. The soul.

Could he have been saved? That was the question that had haunted Sommer's every waking hour in the eleven years since that night. David's body had been badly damaged, but even in the middle of a storm Sommer had been able to see that most of the injuries could have been repaired with proper medical care. Maybe all of them could have been.

But there had been no chance of that. Not that night. Not with the two of them trapped in the car, with the raging storm scrambling every cell phone in the area. And so Sommer had held his son, and watched David's last few minutes silently drift away into eternity.

He vividly remembered wishing over and over that there was a way to keep his son alive. To keep the child's soul attached to his broken body for a little longer.

Or if not to keep body and soul together, perhaps to capture and preserve that soul until the body could be repaired.

It was in the moments afterward, as Sommer laid his son gently back onto the cushions, that the idea of Soulminder was born.

Two months later, he resigned his position at the hospital and set off to make that desperate hope and dream a reality.

Everything he'd done since had been focused on that goal. He'd dug into the literature and discovered the work of James Mullner, who had investigated the long-forgotten fad of Kirlian photography and found an unexpected but intriguing link between a person's coronal discharges and his moods and personality. He'd found Jessica Sands, whose technical and electronics genius more than compensated for Sommer's own limitations in those fields. When the insurance settlement money ran out, he'd cobbled together enough loans and grants from friends, colleagues, and small professional groups to keep the work going.

Only now that work had hit a dead end. Possibly the final dead end.

Sommer snarled a tired curse under his breath as a particularly dazzling spear of lightning blazed across the sky directly in front of him. *No*, he told himself firmly. There'd been other roadblocks over the years, and he and Sands had always found a way around them. They'd find a way around this one, too.

Somehow.

Sommer had made a promise to himself, and to David, and to every parent, child, or friend who had ever watched a loved one die. And that promise was going to be kept.

One of the advantages of the sleeping tablets was that they kept him from dreaming. One of the disadvantages was that they nearly always made him oversleep.

It was nearly eleven before he opened the door to the tiny

office outside their equally tiny lab, to find that Sands had a visitor.

"'Morning, Jessica," he said as the two of them looked up at him. "Sorry I'm late."

"No problem," she said, a touch of grimness in her voice as the man rose to his feet. "Mr. Westmont, my partner, Dr. Adrian Sommer. Mr. Thomas Westmont."

Westmont offered his hand, a quietly calculating look in his eyes. "Pleased to meet you, Dr. Sommer," he said, nodding. His hand was cool, disengaging with practiced ease almost before Sommer had taken it. "I've just been talking with Dr. Sands about the possibility of offering some financial support for your Soulminder project."

Sommer studied him. "I was under the impression, Mr. Westmont, that our underwriters had agreed to keep Soulminder confidential."

Westmont waved a hand negligently. "Yes, well, you know how it is, Dr. Sommer. People have contacts, and those contacts sometimes let information slip."

"Those contacts being . . . ?"

"I hardly think that's important, Doctor. The point is that—"

"Excuse me, Mr. Westmont, but it's extremely important," Sommer interrupted. "We added those clauses specifically so that word of what we're doing wouldn't leak out. If someone's violated confidentiality we need to know about it."

Westmont gave a little snort. "Please, Doctor. The only reason contracts exist is so that lawyers will have a place to practice their jousting. As for privacy and secrets, please try not to be any more naïve than you absolutely have to. You should be thanking me, really."

"I should?"

"Of course," Westmont said. "Because it's clear that you and Soulminder are rapidly running out of money. Fortunately, I have access to a great deal of that precious commodity."

Sommer looked at Sands. Her expression was even more

wooden than it had been a moment earlier. "It sounds wonderful," he agreed. "Where's the hook?"

Westmont's eyes went politely wide. "There's no hook, Dr. Sommer. All we ask is that we be kept abreast of your progress and that we be allowed to share in the various side discoveries you pick up along the way."

Sommer held his gaze. "Any particular side discoveries you had in mind?"

"Little things, mostly," Westmont said with another shrug. "Any relationships or correlations you might have picked up between the shape of this soul-image of yours with, say, personality or intellect or whatever."

Somewhere in the back of Sommer's mind, the name belatedly clicked. Thomas Westmont, chief legal bulldog of flamboyant Congressman Mula Barnswell. The architect of the Congressman's latest attempt to slip one of his blatantly ethnically-slanted bills under the legal barriers that had been set up to catch such things. "I see. You're *that* Thomas Westmont, are you?"

Westmont smiled, without even a trace of embarrassment or guilt. "I'm flattered that you recognize me."

"The bill you're pushing for Congressman Barnswell is hardly back-page news at the moment."

"Yes, but most of the media fascination is with the chanting idiots out in front of the Capital," Westmont said, lip twisting with contempt. "Anyway, that's beside the point."

"Is it?" Sommer demanded. "Do you really expect us to believe that our data wouldn't show up in your documentation the day after tomorrow if we handed it over to you?"

Westmont cocked an eyebrow. "Are you saying your data *does* support the Congressman's views?"

"I'm saying nothing of the kind," Sommer said. "But I know that a collection of raw data can be twisted to support nearly any preconceived notion if you use a big enough wrench on it."

Westmont shrugged. "Perhaps. But, really, that's not the Congressman's interest in your project. In fact, if you'd like, I'd be happy to stipulate that Congressman Barnswell wouldn't release any of your data without discussing it with you first."

"In one of these jousting-field contracts of yours?" Sommer asked pointedly. "You'll forgive me if I say the Congressman and his associates don't inspire that kind of confidence in me. Don't forget, Mr. Westmont, that any misuse of our work is ultimately our responsibility."

Westmont's eyes narrowed. "Let's not bleed quite so much, Doctor. A renewed sense of ethics may be all the rage among scientists these days, but the simple fact is that none of you is qualified to even *see* the long-term implications of your work, much less make any decisions concerning it. In a democracy that's the job of the elected officials, the men in tune with the country's needs and wishes."

"Like Barnswell?" Sands put in, heavily sardonic.

Westmont glanced at her, turned back to Sommer. "The bottom line, Doctor, is that you need money. You know it and I know it, so let's table the ethical posturing." Across the desk, Sands snarled something under her breath. "I can have five million dollars in your account by this afternoon," Westmont continued, ignoring her. "You would then have three days to collect your data into reasonably readable form and send it to Congressman Barnswell's office."

"You'd be wasting the taxpayers' money," Sommer told him firmly. "The data is limited and raw, and any conclusions you tried to draw from it would be completely useless."

"Indeed?" Westmont cocked an eyebrow. "Are you saying there *are* indications there that you'd rather not be made public?"

"I'm saying nothing of the kind," Sommer growled, backpedaling from the edge of the verbal trap. "I'm saying that at the moment there's nothing solid anyone can draw from the data. On *any* topic."

"Of course," Westmont said, almost soothingly. His hand slipped beneath his suit coat, withdrawing a slender wallet. Selecting a card, he flicked it onto the desk. "Think about it, Dr.

Sommer, Dr. Sands. And consider the fact that you're down to your last shoestring on this. Without our money, Soulminder is finished." He nodded toward the card as he put the wallet away and gathered his topcoat from the back of a nearby chair. "Call me when you've made your decision."

The door closed behind him, and Sands spat a curse. "*Damn* him," she snarled. "Damn him, damn Barnswell—*double* damn the idiot who let this leak."

"Try to ignore him," Sommer said. The confrontation-induced adrenaline was draining away, leaving behind a growing depression. Pulling over the chair Westmont had been sitting in, he sank into it, wincing at the residual warmth.

"Ignore him how?" Sands retorted. "In case you missed it, Adrian, Congressman Bigot-Lunatic Barnswell and his brain-dead fringe know about us. How long do you suppose it'll be before they break the wonderful news that there are distinct and measurable differences between the souls of different races and genders?"

"The differences are between individuals, not races or whatever."

"*I* know that," she snapped. "You think such subtleties aren't going to be lost once people like Barnswell get their grubby hands on it?"

"So what do you suggest we do?"

Some of the steel went out of Sands's back. "I don't know," she admitted. "We could release it ourselves, but Barnswell and everyone else with an axe to grind would jump on it and the final result would be the same. Not to mention that the publicity would probably scare off any potential renewals by our underwriters."

Something in her voice . . . "You aren't seriously considering Westmont's offer, are you?" Sommer asked, frowning.

She took a deep breath, her eyes meeting his with visible effort. "He was right, Adrian," she said softly. "Soulminder *is* on its last shoestring here. Besides, we'd have three days to run the data through some more analysis—maybe decorrelate it beyond even Barnswell's ability to distort it."

Sommer stared at her. "Jessica, maybe to you this is just another job—"

"You know better than that," she snapped. "Soulminder is just as important to me as it is to you. But all the sentiment in the world isn't going to change the facts. A, that we're broke, and B, that Barnswell has money."

Sommer locked eyes with her. "I am not," he said, biting out each word, "going to let people like Barnswell get their filthy hands on Soulminder. Period; end of discussion."

For a long moment they glared at each other in silence. Sands blinked first. "I don't much like it, either," she sighed. "Look. That stuff about moving to LA last night wasn't all froth. I've got some feelers out to the police department there, trying to get them interested in the possible forensic applications of our Mullner-trace work. Why don't I fly out there and see if I can squeeze some money out of them? It would at least postpone any decision on Barnswell's offer."

"The decision's already been made," Sommer told her stubbornly.

Her standard patient expression began to look a little strained. "Sure," she said. "All the more reason for me to shoot over to LA."

Sommer got back to his feet. "Yeah, go ahead," he told her tiredly. "Has last night's data been chewed over yet?"

"I got it running before Westmont arrived," she told him, reaching for her terminal. "It'll be done soon if it isn't already."

"Thanks," he nodded.

She was studying one of the consolidated airline websites as he stepped through the back door of the office into the lab.

Keying off the last page of the correlation analysis, Sommer leaned back in his chair, reaching wearily for his coffee cup. Sands's gut-feeling statement the night before had been correct: the basic kernel of the old man's soul-image was indeed the same as all the other hundred-odd Mullner traces they'd collected over the last three years. Just the same, without any new correlations the analysis could detect.

In other words, the deathwatch had been a total waste of time and effort.

As had been the one before, and the one before that, and the one before that. The last five samplings combined, in fact, had yielded only a single new correlation factor; even with a hundred samples to do comparisons of, they still didn't have the slightest clue as to how the incredible tangle of embellishments could be interpreted, read, or otherwise made use of.

Soulminder wasn't just running out of money. It was also running out of steam.

"Nothing, huh?" Sands said from over at her own terminal.

Sommer shook his head. "Not a drop. I think we've finally hit the wall, Jessica."

She grunted deep in her throat. "Well, no one ever said this was going to be easy. Have you tried doing a similarity analysis on the embellishments yet?"

"The program's still running, but I'm not expecting anything. If the computer can't even distinguish Alzheimer's patients from normal people, it's sure not going to be able to find anything more subtle."

Sands swiveled her chair around to frown at him. "Last night must have hit you pretty hard. You usually bounce back from blind alleys better than this."

"Maybe I've bounced off one blind alley too many. Maybe the whole concept of Soulminder is just one massive blind alley."

"No," Sands said firmly. "It's going to work—we're going to *make* it work. We just haven't got the right handle on it yet. And we're not going to find it sitting around feeling sorry for ourselves."

Sommer took a deep breath, exhaled it between tightly clenched teeth. She was right, as usual. "All right," he growled. "Let's run it by again. We've proven the existence of the soul—or at least that there's *something* that leaves the body at death," he corrected himself before she could do it for him. "We can make a trace/map of this thing, show it consists of a common kernel plus embellishments, the complexity of the latter correlating slightly with age. We can even trap the soul for—how long did you have hold of it last night?"

"Two point three seconds. Up two-tenths of a second from the last time."

He nodded. "And *that* gain represents three generations of trap upgrades, to the tune of eight hundred thousand dollars, *and* setting the trap directly beneath the patient's bed." He waved his hands helplessly. "So where do we go from here?"

Sands's lips compressed briefly. "We stall for time," she said. "We find something else of commercial or scientific value in the Mullner traces and peddle it to interested customers in exchange for fresh money."

He eyed her suspiciously. "Like Congressman Barnswell, for instance?"

"I didn't say that," she said. But there was a distinctly defensive set to her mouth. "I don't especially want his hands on our data either, you know. Do bear in mind, though, that there's absolutely no evidence in our Mullner traces to support his small-minded opinions. All he'd do would be to make a fool of himself if he tried it."

"A fool, or a martyr," Sommer said sourly. "He may be smart enough to play the one into the other. And don't forget that there are a lot of people out there whose brains shut down when they're faced by loud people waving scientific data."

Sands's eyes slipped from Sommer's gaze and came to rest on the trace printer—a highly sophisticated piece of equipment that they still owed nearly ten thousand on. "All right, Adrian," she said. "There's no point in discussing it anyway until I get back from LA. Which reminds me"—she glanced at her watch—"I really ought to get home and pack."

"Will you need a ride to the airport?" Sommer asked as she keyed off her terminal and got to her feet.

"No, thanks—I've got an airport shuttle coming to get me. Oh, here"—she scooped up a folder and handed it to him—"If you get a chance, you might want to file this into the database."

Sommer accepted the folder and glanced at the first page. The psychological profile and history of the man they'd watched die last night. "Sure," he sighed, tossing it onto his desk.

"Okay. Be good, and I'll see you tomorrow evening."

For several minutes after she left he just sat in the quiet room, staring at the display before him. So close . . . and yet so very, very far.

Sands didn't understand. How could she? She was an electrical engineer, unschooled in the formalized ethical training that physicians like him had been run through in school and often needed to call upon. For all her enthusiasm she still saw Soulminder as little more than an intriguing challenge, and perhaps the road to future wealth and fame. A scientific and technological breakthrough, to be treated on a scientific and technological level.

Not as a way of saving lives. Certainly not as a memorial.

For a minute Sommer teetered on the brink of self-pity. But there was work to do . . . and anyway, he'd traveled that road all too often in the last eleven years. Taking a deep breath, he picked up the folder Sands had left him and opened it up.

It wasn't as depressing as he'd feared it would be. There was the heavy sense of a wake about it, certainly, leafing through the facts and figures of a man now dead. But on the other hand, the man *had* been old, and had lived a full and rich life before the effects of aging and Alzheimer's had sapped his strength and memory. Sommer turned the pages, scanning the records of the man's childhood and youth, a copy of his marriage certificate, the beginnings of his family—

A hand seemed to close over Sommer's heart. *First-born son, Harold*, the line read. *Died 8/16/51, five years old.*

The page dissolved into a blur as fresh tears rose to Sommer's eyes. The same age as David had been.

Except that, in this man's case, life had continued on afterwards. He'd pulled himself back together, kept his wife, had had more sons and daughters. He hadn't let his son's death become an obsession . . .

Angrily, Sommer rubbed the moisture and self-pity from his eyes. "It's not like that," he snarled aloud to the empty room. He *wasn't* just doing it for David, but for every child who'd ever had to die unnecessarily. For every parent who'd ever had to face such a crushing trauma—

Abruptly, his train of thought froze on its rails. *Trauma*: an injury or shock to a person's body or psyche. And, perhaps, to the pattern of embellishments making up his soul-trace?

And if so, would similar events cause similar changes?

He looked up, glancing around the room. Their main Mullner setup was still back at the hospital, but they had a secondary one that Sands was forever tinkering with. The recording itself would be no problem—he could skip the data pack and just run it directly into the computer's memory. If Sands wanted something of commercial value, this might just do it.

For a moment he hesitated as natural caution reasserted itself. They hadn't hooked a living person to the Mullner since the very first calibration readings, and Sands had boosted both the power and read-density a hundredfold since then. Besides that, basic safety rules said never to try something new alone.

But it could easily take a day or more to find the proper correlation between his soul-trace and that of the old man. And if Sands came back from LA empty-handed, she might not be willing to wait that long.

The thought of Barnswell's bigots with their hands on David's memorial made up his mind for him. Pushing his chair back against the Mullner computer feed, he got to work.

The first time he'd gone under the Mullner, Sommer had been struck by the dreamlike qualities the device seemed to induce. Now, after Sands's improvements, the effect was even stronger.

Sitting alone in the lab, the walls of which seemed to fluctuate between too close and too far, he listened to the hum in his ears and brain.

And dreamed of David.

David's birth, and the sixteen-hour labor that Sally had had to go through to bring him into the world. David's first step, ten months later, which had careened him headfirst into the corner of the coffee table. David at his daycare center when he turned two, at first impossibly shy and then turning completely around to become the world's shortest tyrant.

David on the night of his death.

Sommer had relived that night a hundred thousand times in the past eleven years, and though the emotion surrounding it had subsided from an exquisitely sharp pain to a dull background ache, the wound had never entirely healed. Would never heal.

The accident, and David's death. The funeral, and his frustrated sublimating into the burning need to find a way to keep such unnecessary deaths from ever happening again. His growing obsession with the Soulminder project—yes, he could admit now that it had been an obsession. Sally's inability to understand his drive and reliving of the past. Ultimately, her inability to put up with it and him any longer.

David would have been sixteen this year. Sommer tried to envision him as a teenager, but he couldn't. The small, five-year-old face kept intruding, and eventually he gave up the effort. The face faded, and he drifted off into other, less painful dreams . . .

It seemed to take him a long time to find his way back to consciousness, and when he finally became aware he discovered that that, at least, hadn't been an illusion. His desk clock read six-twenty: two hours and four minutes exactly since he'd activated the Mullner. Blinking aching eyes, he worked himself out of his chair and limped over to the computer. Even with the relatively low read-level he'd set the Mullner on it shouldn't have taken nearly that long.

Sure enough, the time indicator showed the Mullner had finished its trace two hours and two minutes earlier and had been waiting patiently ever since then for new instructions.

Frowning, Sommer keyed for storage and duplication of the trace and then took a moment to stretch stiff muscles. Knocking him out for two hours was a new trick, something the original Mullner model hadn't been capable of, and for a minute he wondered uneasily if he was in for a long night of equally unexpected side effects. But aside from fatigue and a few muscle twinges he felt all right, and dismissed the worries as being overly paranoid.

Besides, he'd been pretty exhausted lately. Maybe all that had happened was that his body had seen the opportunity for a quick nap and taken it.

His stomach growled, reminding him it was dinnertime. Taking a deep breath, rib cage creaking with the effort, he sat down at the terminal and began to set up the comparison program. There would be plenty of time to run over to the deli down the street after the computer was chugging away.

As he worked he thought about the dreams. And wondered whether the Mullner apparatus induced similar ones in the dying.

"It's amazing the tricks one's mind plays when one starts getting old," Sands said conversationally, her fingers dancing nimbly over the relevant sections of the two Mullner traces, Sommer's and the old man's. "Take me, for instance. Thirty-six is hardly approaching senility, and yet, I would have *sworn* I could take off cross-country for a day without worrying that my partner would do something damn-fool stupid."

"Guilty as charged," Sommer said, mentally urging Sands on. "Except that anything that works isn't stupid, is it?"

"You're thinking of treason," she corrected him absently. "'For if it prosper, none dare call it treason.' Stupid risks are always stupid risks." She hissed between her teeth, a sound that was as much thoughtful as it was deprecating.

Sommer could stand it no longer. "Well? What do you think?"

Sands hesitated, then shrugged. "I don't know, Adrian. I really don't know."

"Why not?" he demanded. He jabbed a finger at the spots where her fingers rested. "The exact same curl on both Mullner traces? What else could it be?"

"You're assuming—again—that it's the topography of the embellishment tendrils that's significant," she reminded him tartly. "We don't *know* that that's true. Besides which, you'll note that the two curls aren't in anywhere near the same area. How do you explain *that*?"

Sommer sighed, feeling the excitement of the discovery beginning to fade and slip from his grasp. "I don't explain it," he told her tiredly. "I presume it's related to the differing circumstances of our sons' deaths—timing, emotional impact, life afterwards; that sort of thing. *Yes*, there's a lot more work that'll need to be done on it. But it *is* a start. Isn't it?"

"Of course it's a start," she soothed him. "And anything that helps us understand the lifeforce certainly qualifies as progress." She waved a hand helplessly. "But whether it's enough to shake more money out of our underwriters is something else entirely."

Sommer clenched his hands into fists. "Did the people in LA give you any kind of timeframe for their response?"

"If you mean can we get this written up and sent to them before they make a decision, yes. Whether it'll affect that decision, I don't know." She hesitated. "And at any rate, we need to be thinking about long-term funding, not these last-minute, stopgap things. I don't know about you, but I don't focus well when I'm wondering where my next circuit board is coming from."

"Barnswell is not getting his hands on Soulminder," Sommer said flatly.

Her lip twisted, just a bit, before she could smooth it out. But it was there long enough for Sommer to read the impatience. "Look, Adrian, I know how you feel—"

"No, you don't," he cut her off brusquely. "We both know what Barnswell would do with the data. He'd tear it apart until he found something he could use as evidence for his petty little prejudices. And in the process he'd destroy Soulminder."

"Oh, come *on*," Sands snorted. "Aren't you getting just a little melodramatic here?"

"Am I?" Sommer countered. "You really think potential underwriters will want their names and corporations associated with us after that?"

For a moment Sands was silent. "Maybe we can get some guarantees from him up front," she said at last. "A written promise not to release any of the data without our permission. Westmont more or less offered that, you know."

"Westmont also all but said that contracts were made to be broken," Sommer countered. "What do we do if he reneges? Sue him for breach? It would be a useless gesture—the damage to Soulminder would already have been done."

Sands looked him straight in the eye. "Five million dollars is a lot of money, Adrian," she said softly. "A hell of a lot of money."

"No."

For a long moment they just stared at each other. Then, reluctantly, Sands broke the contact. "All right," she said. "I guess I understand. Well . . . " Getting to her feet, she headed for the door. "I guess I'll go back to the hospital and pick up the trap."

"I thought Dr. Samuels had another volunteer patient lined up for the room."

"He does, but the prognosis gives her another two to four weeks to live, and I thought I'd see what else I could do with the trap. Maybe boost the range or focus—it's got to be one of those that we're missing out on. See you later."

She left, and Sommer turned his attention back to the two Mullner traces spread out on the desk. Somewhere here was the evidence they needed to bring fresh money into Soulminder.

Five million dollars.

Tears blurred his eyes, and he sank down wearily into his well-worn chair. Five million dollars. Five million filthy dollars. From a filthy little man with a filthy little mind.

And Sands was probably on her way right now to get it for them.

"Damn!" he swore viciously, uselessly, to the empty room. Sands didn't care a burned-out diode for his vision of Soulminder. Only for Soulminder itself. Coldly determined to make Soulminder work, willing to sell her own mother to see it work.

An iron-ringed, single-minded goal . . . without which, Sommer knew full well, she would long ago have left him to carry the burden alone.

He sighed, hearing defeat in the sound of rushing air. Sands would sell their data to Barnswell—if not today, then tomorrow or the next day. And there was nothing he could do to stop her. Even if he'd had the strength of will left to fight her; even if she didn't really have as much right of ownership to the data as he did. She would sell out, and Barnswell would give her his assurances . . . and as soon as her back was turned he would do what he damn well pleased anyway.

His eyes drifted to the file cabinet where the hard copies of their precious Mullner traces were stored. Little more than complex curlicues of ink on paper, as people themselves were little more than a collection of exotic chemicals. Each trace—somehow—the record of an entire life. The life of someone who'd allowed him to share in the very private moment of death . . . and had trusted him to respect that privacy.

Sommer clenched his hands into fists and took a deep breath. "All right," he said aloud, getting to his feet. It would probably make Sands furious when she found out—and was almost certainly unethical to boot—but right now his tacit promise to the souls he'd traced mattered a lot more than either consideration.

The project took nearly an hour to complete. Repeating the operation on the duplicate computer files was considerably easier, taking less than a quarter of that time, and when he was done he sat back in his chair in vaguely guilty satisfaction. Barnswell could now have the data, and if he misused it he, and not Soulminder, would be the one to suffer most.

Or so Sommer hoped. At the very least, the individuals who'd let him take their soul-traces would be unaffected—

He paused in mid-thought as something suddenly occurred to him. Something so obvious that he couldn't believe he hadn't thought of it before.

For a long moment he just sat there, gazing off into space, feeling an old fire he thought he'd lost forever begin to burn again within him. Leaning forward, he attacked the computer keyboard.

A minute was all it took to hit the first wall. Muttering under his breath, he scooped up the phone and punched for Sands's cell.

She answered on the third ring. "Hello?"

"Listen, do you remember where the data on the Mullner trace recognition pattern is stored?" Sommer asked.

"Uh . . . try a file called FITTER.CV," she suggested. "Or something like that—I'm sure FITTER is part of it. What do you want it for?"

"I think it's time we took another shot at that approach," he told her, struggling to keep his voice calm.

"What, you mean tailoring the trap to the individual soul? I thought we proved way back when that even a supercomputer wouldn't be fast enough to record the Mullner trace and configure the trap fields in the time available."

"Right," Sommer agreed, "*if* we wait until the moment of death to take the reading. What if we instead take the initial trace beforehand, like I did last night."

There was a long silence on the other end of the line. "I don't know," Sands said at last, slowly. "It's not exactly the way we wanted Soulminder to work—you plug your average accident victim into the Mullner and you're likely to kill him right there and then. You saw what it did to you."

"So find a way to modify the Mullner," Sommer ground out, beginning to be annoyed at Sands's attitude. "Make it gentler but still able to take the entire trace. At least it's something to try."

"I agree," Sands said. "I'll see what I can do when I get back.

Meanwhile, you might call Dr. Samuels and see if he can scare us up a guinea pig. Best bet is probably someone who's reasonably healthy right now but needs some risky surgery."

"Uh . . . right," Sommer managed, thrown off-balance a bit by her abrupt switch to his side of the argument. "I'll do that. See you later."

"'Bye."

They worked late into the night, Sommer on the computer software and Sands on the trap itself, until a throbbing headache forced Sommer to call it quits. Sands remained behind, and when he arrived the next morning there was a note from her telling him that, as of five-thirty a.m., the hardware modifications to the trap were complete. The note wished him luck with the software, and suggested he not expect her in too early.

Sommer got to work, but before he did so he took a moment to check the flag he'd planted in the Mullner-trace computer files.

The files had indeed been copied, just after he'd left the evening before.

Not unexpected, though it still hurt that Sands would go behind his back and against his wishes like that. But, oddly enough, even such duplicity was unable to dampen the growing enthusiasm within him, the gut-level sense that this time they were indeed on the right track. With any luck, Barnswell's money would take them far enough along that track that they would never again have to deal with him or his kind.

It took four more days to finish the software modifications, and another two after that to complete their limited repertoire of simulation tests. At that point, there was nothing to do but wait for Dr. Samuels to locate a likely patient.

Three days later, he did.

"You have to understand," Dr. Dian Janecki said gently, "that with this type of operation the chances of success are directly proportional to the immediate risk involved. The more of the medulloblastoma we can clean out of your son's cerebellum, the better his long-term chances of survival. At the same time, the deeper we go and the longer we stay there, the greater the dangers of the operation itself."

"We know that, Doctor," Peter Coleman said impatiently, the strain of his son's long illness etched on both his and his wife's faces. "If you're going to suggest more chemical treatments, don't bother. All they do is make Danny sick, and they aren't helping him a damn."

Janecki nodded her agreement. "I know that. And my colleagues and I agree that we can't put off surgery any longer." Her eyes flicked to Sommer. "What I'm going to offer you is—well, maybe it's an unexpected bit of hope. Dr. Sommer, if you and Dr. Sands would care to explain your proposal?"

Sommer mentally braced himself. "What we have, Mr. and Mrs. Coleman, is—maybe—a way to give Dr. Janecki that extra time she wants while still minimizing the risks of the surgery itself."

They listened in stony silence while he explained how Soulminder could—in theory, at least—hold their son's soul in safety while the surgeons removed the cancer and gave his body time to recover. He finished, and for a long moment both parents were silent. Sommer held his breath . . .

Coleman shook his head. "No," he said firmly. "Out of the question."

Huddled beside him, his wife threw him a startled look. "Peter—?"

"Out of the question, Angie," he repeated, more emphatically this time. "It's unnatural, it's unworkable"—he threw Sommer a suspicious glare—"and I'm not sure that it's not downright blasphemous right along with it."

"All surgery is unnatural," Sands pointed out calmly. "So is all medical treatment, if you want to come down to it. As for unworkable; yes, we freely admit that we can't guarantee success. But if we don't keep trying, we'll never succeed."

Coleman sent her the same glare he'd just given Sommer. "You are *not* going to experiment on my son," he growled.

Angie's hand tightened its grip on her husband's. "Peter, if there's even a *chance* it might help, why not try it?"

He looked down at her. "Why? I'll tell you why." He looked back at Sommer. "Tell me, Doctor, what happens if your Soulminder gizmo works but winds up damaging Danny's soul in the process? Or what if you can't get it back into Danny's body afterwards? Or can't get it out at all?"

They were, Sommer had to admit, good questions. "I don't know," he conceded. "Releasing the soul from the trap shouldn't be a problem—shutting off the power will do that much. But as to the rest of it, we just don't have any answers yet."

"They can't hurt Danny's soul," Angie said, a new trace of firmness creeping into her voice. "There's nothing this world can do to a person that God won't heal in the next life."

"And what if God rejects Danny because he was part of something blasphemous?" Coleman countered. "What makes you people think you can stuff a human soul into a machine, anyway?"

"You could argue that the human body is nothing but a biomechanical machine," Sands pointed out. "Yet *it* manages to hold onto the soul quite adequately."

Coleman visibly clenched his teeth, shifting his eyes to Janecki. "What's *your* opinion of this, Doctor?" he demanded. "You really believe they can do it?"

"I don't know," Janecki told him. "All I can say is that in my lifetime I've seen a lot of medical advances, some of which sounded a lot less plausible than this one. It's your decision, of course . . . but in my opinion I don't see any reason not to give it a try."

"So that you can go in as deep as you want?" Coleman snapped. "Is that it? So you can play with your scalpel and hope that this half-baked idea will cover any mistakes you make in there—?"

"It doesn't matter," Angie spoke up, with a sudden strength in her voice that made her husband pause and look at her. "Dr.

Janecki is going to try to get as much of the tumor out as she can, whether we use Soulminder or not." She blinked tears from her eyes as she looked at her husband. "Danny's going to be healed thoroughly," she said quietly, "or he's going to die. Right here, right now."

Coleman licked his lips, concern replacing the antagonism in his face. "You don't mean that, Angie. Where there's life there's always hope."

"Not any more, Peter," she said, an infinite weariness in her voice. "Not for me. Not for Danny. Can't you see that he's been through enough hell already?" She looked at Janecki. "He's not going to spend the next five years of his life in and out of hospitals, Doctor, and then die anyway," she said. "Heal him completely . . . or let him go on to God."

Janecki nodded, her own eyes a little moist. "I understand, Mrs. Coleman. I'll do everything I can." She glanced at Sommer. "About Dr. Sommer's proposal, then . . . ?"

Angie looked up at her husband. Coleman's face was tight . . . but when he broke from her gaze and looked at Sommer there was no resistance left. Only resignation. "Go ahead, Doctor," he said.

Sommer nodded, a swirl of sympathetic pain and dark memory tightening his stomach and throat. "Thank you," he said quietly. The newly reworked Soulminder's first trial run . . . with a five-year-old boy as its subject.

Unbidden, David's face rose up accusingly before his eyes, and the ache in his stomach grew worse. *A five-year-old boy*, he thought morosely. *God, why did it have to be a five-year-old boy*? "We'll have to do a tracing to map the Kirlian and Mullner patterns of his soul," he forced himself to say. "With your permission, I'll go ahead and set up for that right away." He got to his feet, wondering how he was ever going to face the boy in there—

"I'll handle that," Sands put in smoothly, standing up beside him. "You can go with Dr. Janecki and start setting up the equipment in the operating room. Mr. and Mrs. Coleman, perhaps you'd like to come and watch me—the procedure's completely painless, but I imagine Danny would like your reassurance of that."

They nodded. Getting silently to their feet, they followed Sands from the lounge.

"I hope, Doctor," Janecki commented into the silence, "that you're right about all this."

Sommer took a deep breath. "I do, too. I know what they're going through, Dr. Janecki. I lost a son myself eleven years ago."

"I'm sorry," Janecki said, her eyes locking onto his. "What I meant was that I hope you're right about Soulminder not doing any . . . damage."

Sommer felt his stomach tighten. "I hope so, too," he said quietly.

The boy's face was painfully thin, a thinness that his shaved head and the size of the operating table beneath him only served to emphasize. Watching the small monitor screen as they prepared him, Sommer felt a fresh ache in his heart. Danny was so young . . . just as David had been. *If I should die before I wake . . .*

"Adrian?" Sands's voice came from the speakerphone beside him. "Things underway there yet?"

With an effort, Sommer forced the memories back. "They're just getting ready to start," he told her. "You getting everything all right?"

"Coming in clear and clean," she assured him. "The trap here is set and running."

"Same here," Sommer said, wondering if this particular elaboration had really been necessary. If the trap set up beneath the operating table failed to catch Danny's soul, after all, there was virtually no chance that the backup duplicate Sands had going in their lab would be able to do so. But on the other hand, distance might not be the significant factor, and the more sophisticated computer back there might be able to feed Sands's trap a better Mullner trace than could the portable machine humming along at Sommer's side.

Besides which, it was probably better that Sommer be here

alone. Already he could tell that it was going to be a morning filled with thoughts of David, and Sands's presence would only be an intrusion. "Kirlian and Mullner both look strong," he added.

"Same here," Sands confirmed. "By the way, I noticed a few minutes ago that the trap software was doing a continual scan of the entire Mullner-trace file. Is it supposed to be doing that?"

Sommer cursed under his breath. "Not really. I put that in as a secondary system in case the primary targeting flag got confused and lost hold of its target trace. I guess it did."

"Fixable?"

"Not now," he sighed. "I'll have to tear the targeting software apart and completely rebuild it. Damn—I *knew* we were going to have trouble with that."

"Well, no harm done," Sands assured him. "This is only here for backup anyway, remember. As long as it doesn't latch onto one of the already departed and yank them back from heaven, that is."

"Not funny, Jessica," Sommer growled.

"Sorry. They started there yet?"

He peered at the scene. "Looks like they've just finished putting him under," he told her.

"Good. Be sure and keep a close watch on the EEG trace—if something starts to go wrong, we'll want as much warning as possible."

"Sure," he said between stiff lips. There was an odd note of anticipation in Sands's voice, a quiet eagerness that sent an unpleasant shiver up his back. On some level, he realized, she was actually hoping Danny would die this morning.

The operation began.

For Sommer, it was an exercise in tense boredom. The camera had been positioned with convenience rather than a clinical view in mind, and it was rare when he got even a glimpse of the operating field beyond the wall of green surgical gowns. The surgeons' voices, when he was able to hear them over the beeping of monitoring instruments, were calm and businesslike: the voices of people accustomed to holding human lives in their hands. Beside the TV monitor the bank of repeater instruments punctuated the minutes with the monotonous constancy of a steady heartbeat. The minutes stretched into an hour; into an hour and a half; into an hour and three-quarters.

And precisely an hour and fifty-two minutes into the operation, it abruptly fell apart.

"Adrian!" Sands snapped over the phone.

"I see it," Sommer gritted, fists clenched in agonized helplessness. *If I should die before I wake . . .* "Looks like neurogenic shock—no blood's getting to his tissues. The EEG . . . God, Jessica, they're losing him."

"Steady, Adrian," she said tightly. "This is going to work. Everything reading ready?"

Sommer gave the Soulminder instruments a quick scan. "It's all set," he told her, stomach churning. He'd fought to hold onto some semblance of professional calm through this, but now he could feel the professionalism boiling away like an ice cube on a hot burner.

Eleven years later, he was once again watching helplessly as David died. "No," he half whispered, half groaned.

Once again, hope and wish proved inadequate. Two minutes later, it was all over.

"Adrian!" Sands barked. "What the hell's happening?"

"He's dead," Sommer said mechanically, his eyes on the flat EEG trace. "It was . . . it all happened so quickly."

"Never mind that," Sands bit out tautly. "What about the trap?"

Sommer broke his gaze from the EEG, recognizing even as he did so that he was afraid to look at the Soulminder instruments. If it hadn't worked . . .

The trap registered active.

He tried twice before he could get the words out. "It's got him," he breathed at last. "Jessica, it worked. It's really *got* him."

Sands's shuddering sigh whistled through the phone speaker. "Okay," she said. "Good. Great. But we're not out of the woods yet—we still have to get him back in his body—"

"Hold it," Sommer interrupted her. On the monitor Dr. Janecki had stepped up to the camera's microphone. "Dr. Sommer?" she called. "Should we continue with the operation?"

Bracing himself, Sommer switched on his intercom. "Yes," he said. "The first stage seems to have worked."

Even on the small monitor screen, he could see relief smoothing the lines around her eyes. A cautious and almost disbelieving relief. "I understand," she said.

She turned away and began issuing instructions, and Sommer flipped off the intercom. "Dr. Janecki's going to continue the operation," he told Sands. "They're getting the heart-lung machine set up—looks like they've got a hypo of neuropreservative, too." He shivered at the thought. Neuropreservatives were still highly experimental, and what they did for dying brain and nerve cells was usually more than offset by the hallucinations and associated emotional trauma they inflicted.

But, of course, Danny wasn't there to feel any of that.

"Well, she's the doctor," Sands grunted. "Probably knows what she's doing. You think I should go ahead and shut down the backup trap?"

"No, leave it running," Sommer said. "There's no guarantee this one will keep going long enough, and if we really have Danny's soul here I don't want to lose it now."

"Good point," she agreed. "Keep an eye on the readouts, and if anything changes let me know right away."

"You'll be the first," Sommer assured her, a trace of humor seeping through his fading tension. Leaning back in his chair, he took a deep breath, his eyes drifting to rest on the trap. A big, ugly conglomeration of hardware, sophisticated electronics, and software.

And now the temporary resting place for the soul of a five-year-old boy.

Or at least, he hoped that was what was there. It could, he reminded himself soberly, just as easily be nothing more than an echo of Danny's Mullner trace, or a secondary trace made of Danny's now-gone soul, or something else entirely.

Only time would tell. Time, and a successful attempt to return the soul to Danny's body. Only then would they really know.

For now, all he could do was wait. And hope that Sands's off-handed comment about pulling someone else back from heaven had been only a joke.

The operation was a success, with as much of the boy's tumor removed as the doctors could manage.

The surgery was followed by two days of recovery. Not nearly enough, in Sommer's opinion, given the complexity of the surgery. But it was as much as anyone was willing to allow.

And it was time.

"Well," Janecki said heavily, "I guess this is what they call the moment of truth."

Sommer grimaced, blinking uselessly against the grit that seemed to have become a permanent feature of his eyes during the past two days. "I hate that phrase," he growled. "Truth is an ongoing reality. It doesn't come in moments."

Janecki threw him an odd look, and he shook his head. "Sorry," he muttered, making one final adjustment to the wave-guide cable arrangement connecting the Soulminder equipment to Danny's body, motionless except for the slow rise and fall of the boy's chest with the rhythm of the heart-lung machine. "I'm a little nervous, I guess."

"Probably short of sleep, too," Sands commented, peering closely at the contact band circling Danny's head. "I've never found hospital cots to be all that comfortable, myself."

Sommer nodded silently. In point of fact, he'd hardly had any sleep at all the past two nights, and the short naps that exhaustion had forced on him had been filled with nightmares. "What do you think, Jessica?" he asked. "We ready to give it a try?"

She straightened, and for the first time he noticed the tension lines about her mouth. "As ready as we're ever going to be," she said.

"Dr. Janecki?"

She stepped over to the controls of the heart-lung machine. "I'm ready."

Sommer looked over his shoulder, to where Danny's parents stood silently against the wall. Then, setting his teeth firmly together, he turned back and reached for the trap release. *If I should die before I wake . . .*

He touched the switch.

The lights indicating the soul's presence flicked out, and for a single, terrible, split-second eternity he was sure he had failed. David; now Danny—

And suddenly Danny's body twitched violently. "Mommy!" he croaked. "Mommy!"

She was there in an instant, her husband half a step behind her. "Danny!" she gasped, enfolding him in her arms.

And even as his eyes blurred with tears, Sommer felt his knees go weak. Turning away, he groped his way to a chair and collapsed into it.

"You okay?"

He blinked away the tears to find Sands squatting down beside him, her face shining with disbelief-tinged triumph. "We did it, Jessica," he said.

"I know," she said, taking his hand and squeezing it. "Congratulations."

"You too," he breathed. It was over. After eleven years, it was finally over.

No. It was just beginning. "We still need to check Danny over," he told her quietly, forcing back the growing euphoria. "Make sure he's undamaged; make sure"—*it really is him*—"his memory and everything else is all right," he said instead. The thought that someone other than Danny might have somehow been drawn into the trap still gave him the shakes.

"Dr. Janecki'll take care of most of that," Sands assured him. "She's got a whole row of psychologists and brain specialists lined up ready to go to work."

Behind them the door opened, and a nurse looked in. "Dr. Sommer?" she said, an odd expression on her face. "There's a group of reporters down in the lobby who want to talk to you."

Sommer cocked an eyebrow at Sands, got a puzzled shrug in return. "Not me," she said. "Maybe Janecki or the parents called them."

"Jumped the gun a little, didn't they?" he grunted. Still, since it *had* worked out all right— "I'll be right down," he told the nurse. She nodded and disappeared, and he got to his feet. "You want to come down and get red-eye flashed to death?" he asked Sands.

She made a face. "I'll pass, thanks. If it's all the same to you, I'd rather go back to the lab and start analyzing the trap readings."

"Yes, well, be sure and leave both traps running," he warned, digging out his comb and wishing he'd taken the time to shower earlier. "Those neuropreservatives could still drive Danny into shock, and after all this we sure don't want to lose him in extra innings."

"Right," Sands nodded. "I'll just pull the packs and leave everything else intact." Her lips twitched in a mischievous smile. "You'd better get down there and give them their lead story. And be sure to save something for your Nobel acceptance speech, okay?"

He stuck his tongue out at her, gave her hand a final squeeze, and left the room.

The nurse had, if anything, strayed on the conservative side: the mass of reporters resembled a mob more than they did a simple group. A dozen minicams swiveled toward him like gun barrels as he entered the lobby; twice that number of directional microphones were right behind them. Sommer stepped to more or less the focus of the semicircle, raised a hand for silence—

"Dr. Sommer," a voice called, "how do you respond to the allegations made this morning by Congressman Barnswell's attorneys that you have proved the existence of the human soul and of distinct racial differences in that soul?"

For a long moment Sommer just stood there, hand still raised, as the universe seemed to gently tilt around him. Barnswell—Sands's secret sale of their Mullner-trace data to him—the work of the past two weeks had completely driven all of that from his mind. "Ah—yes," he managed at last. "It was my understanding that Congressman Barnswell would discuss any implications of our work before he released it."

"Do you confirm his results, then?" someone else asked, clearly uninterested in anything as common and un-newsworthy as betrayed trust.

"I confirm that our work has proved the existence of a human soul—or a lifeforce, if you prefer," he added, remembering Sands's own reluctance to use the more theologically loaded term. "But as to whatever these racial implications are that he thinks he's found, I would say they are at the very least exceedingly premature, and more likely a whole-cloth fabrication of his followers' prejudices."

"*Are* there, then, different types of souls?" someone pounced.

Sommer gritted his teeth. "There are differences in souls, certainly," he said. "Each one of us is a distinct individual—how on earth could our souls not be different? Again, though, there is absolutely no evidence at this point that there are any significant differences between racial, ethnic, or any other sort of group."

"Dr. Sommer, it sounds as if you haven't actually seen Congressman Barnswell's conclusions yet. Is that true?"

"It is," Sommer nodded.

"May I ask, then, how you can dismiss them out of hand?"

"Simple." He glanced around the battery of minicams, a small fraction of his mind wondering just how Barnswell was going to take this. "As I said, Congressman Barnswell's representatives promised not to release our data without our permission. To make sure he didn't go back on that promise"—he took a deep breath—"I took the liberty of scrambling the personal profiles and Mullner traces of our subjects. Whatever patterns the Congressman's people think they see, therefore, simply don't exist."

There was a moment of stunned silence. Then, the whole mob seemed to explode at once into a blizzard of shouted questions. Once again Sommer held up his hand; eventually, the wordstorm dwindled and died. "Ladies and gentlemen, as far as I'm concerned, Congressman Barnswell and his theories are old news, and not very interesting news, at that.

"Now, if you're interested in a *real* story . . ."

It was, he thought more than once during that long day, as if he'd dropped a tactical nuke into the middle of the news industry. The shock wave of his announcement utterly shattered their neatly prepared list of events and stories to be covered, sending them scrambling for background and interviews and commentary. By early afternoon the shock wave had reached the political arena, prompting instant speeches from both ends of Pennsylvania Avenue and assorted foreign capitals. And as afternoon shaded into evening the wave jolted the nation's religious leaders into statements of their own, ranging from reflexive denunciation on one extreme to cautious wait-and-see acceptance on the other.

Most of the sound and fury Sommer got only second-hand, mainly in the form of references within the never-ending stream of questions thrown at him by successive shifts of media people. Local media interviews, long-distance phone calls from the international news services, live network interviews on the evening news, late-evening commentary programs—he was put through the entire gauntlet. Occasionally he was asked about Barnswell, but it was clear that the Congressman's big bombshell announcement had been completely lost in the glare of the Soulminder story, and by the evening commentary shows all such questions had disappeared.

Finally, just after midnight, it was finally over.

"Is that it?" Sommer asked as the red light on the camera went out and the monitor showing his face went blank.

"That's it, Doctor," the station manager nodded, stepping forward to help him unfasten the mike from his coat. "*Nightline* was the last one on your schedule."

"*Your* schedule, you mean," Sommer reminded him wearily. "None of this was *my* idea, if you recall."

The other smiled. "You should have thought of that before you became famous," he joked. "Anyway, the morning programs start at six—"

"Do me a favor and tell them I died overnight, will you?" Sommer told him, digging his knuckles into his eyes. "Death by overexposure, or something."

The manager chuckled. "Don't worry about it, Doctor—everyone's got enough of you on file to cover half a dozen programs if they have to. Not to mention a hundred people standing in line to comment on your discovery. You have a car here?"

Sommer shook his head. "I left it back at the hospital. Probably got fifteen parking tickets on it by now."

"No problem." The other caught the eye of one of the security guards, beckoned him over. "Blake, Dr. Sommer needs a ride home. Make sure he gets there all right, and fend off any late-night vultures and paparazzi, okay?"

"Sure, Mr. Hardin," the guard said genially. "My car's out front, Dr. Sommer."

Sommer swallowed as the other led the way through the maze of cameras and cables and lights. The thought that reporters and commando photographers might be lurking in wait for him at all hours was one that hadn't occurred to him before, and it sent an unpleasant chill down his back. To lose all chance of a private life in a single day—

No, he told himself firmly. *It's just a temporary notoriety. That's all. Nothing that'll last past the end of the month.*

Still, he felt his stomach tensing as he and Blake headed across the lobby toward the big glass doors. No one was visible, but there were lots of places out of view where the paparazzi could be hiding. They stepped out into the cool night air . . .

No flashes went off. No one jumped from behind the low shrubs shouting questions.

"This way, Dr. Sommer," Blake said, leading the way across the circle drive toward the front parking lot.

Sommer followed, feeling relief and, paradoxically, a faint stirring of disappointment. He scowled at the latter; he was not—was *not*—going to be one of those who became addicted to fame—

He'd reached the middle of the circle drive when, fifty feet away, a pickup truck suddenly lunged away from the curb and headed toward him.

He paused, feeling his emotions re-mix themselves. So there *had* been a reporter lying in wait for him . . .

And with fatigue and resentment dimming his brain, it was another second before it registered that the truck wasn't slowing down. Was, in fact, still accelerating.

Directly toward him.

He tried to run. But it was far too late for that. Dimly, through the sudden rush of blood in his ears, he could hear Blake's shouts as the other sprinted back in a futile attempt to help. Could hear the screams of the driver, slurred and angry and obscene.

Could feel the awful impact as the truck rammed into him, sending him hurling into darkness.

He seemed to be in a long tunnel, a tunnel that glowed with a dim but uniform light. For a moment he wondered where he was, and then he remembered. The truck, the impact, the darkness.

And it occurred to him that he was dead.

Dead.

For a moment he studied the word, and the concept behind it, waiting for the inevitable emotional reaction to hit him. To his mild surprise, there was none. Apathy, he thought at first, or perhaps a completely mind-numbing despair. But it was obvious that neither label even came close to describing how he felt. It was, he decided, more like a deep and restful peace, one that permeated his being so thoroughly that it filled every corner, leaving no visible edges by which it could be defined or even really noticed without a deliberate effort to do so.

Ahead—a long way ahead, so it seemed, though he could sense that distance didn't have much meaning here—he could see the end of the tunnel he was traveling through. Beyond it was a bright light; bright, yet not in any way hurtful . . . and it was from the Light, he suddenly understood, that the sense of peace radiated. He willed himself forward; in response, though there was no sensation of movement, the tunnel walls increased their silent speed past him.

So gradually that he didn't notice at first, the movement of the walls slowed. Slowed, and then stopped.

There was no way to tell how long he waited there, hovering motionlessly in the center of the tunnel—time, like distance, seemed to have lost all of its meaning. Ahead, the Light beckoned to him; not insistently, like a siren being deprived of her victim, but like a friend, waiting with patience for him to finish the journey. Once, he tried explaining that the delay wasn't his doing, but even as he searched for a way to make himself heard at so great a distance he could sense that the Light already understood what had happened.

By the time the walls again began to move, Sommer understood, too . . . and so it was with no surprise at all that he found the walls were moving in the wrong direction. The Light faded as he moved, disappeared entirely—

And abruptly pain flooded in on him.

He gasped, feeling the sensation of inrushing air as something almost alien. A blinding stab of fresh pain lanced through his chest as he did so—

"Adrian!" a familiar voice almost barked in his ear. "Take it easy, Adrian, it's all right. You're here. You're safe."

His eyelids were heavy, but with a supreme effort of will he pried them open. Sands was leaning over him; behind her, an unfamiliar face frowned at something outside his field of view. "Heartbeat looks good," the man said. "He's breathing on his own." He peered at Sommer as if at a laboratory specimen. "I wouldn't have believed it if I hadn't seen it."

Sands threw him an irritated glance before turning back to Sommer. "How do you feel?" she asked. "Can you talk?"

Sommer worked saliva into his mouth. "How long?" he croaked.

She understood. "That drunken idiot ran you down six days ago," she told him, eyes flashing with anger. "One of Barnswell's more brainless supporters, I gather, who didn't much like you making a fool out of his idol on international television."

"How's Danny?" The words came out easier this time.

"Making a rapid recovery," Sands said, and there was no mistaking the satisfaction in her voice. "Dr. Janecki says that aside from an occasional moody thoughtfulness, there don't seem to be any aftereffects at all from his stay in Soulminder."

Sommer thought about his own experience, and about the Light. "Maybe he wishes he hadn't been brought back," he murmured.

Sands's forehead furrowed for a moment. "Yes, well, I'm sure that'll pass," she said. "Janecki also says that because of Soulminder they were able to get nearly the entire tumor out. She figures that a couple of months of chemical treatments ought to clean out any residue, and that'll be the end of it." Her lips twitched in a smile. "I don't know about you, but I think that's a pretty good memorial for your son. Wouldn't you say?"

Sommer closed his eyes. A fog was rolling in over his consciousness . . . "Yes. It's finished now."

He heard Sands's hesitation, felt her hand squeeze his carefully. "You'd better get some rest," her voice came distantly. "We've still got the lab's trap running, so there's no danger we'll lose you. You're pretty lucky it was still doing that complete file scan when you got run over."

"Lucky," he echoed, his own voice sounding even more distant than hers. His last thought before he fell asleep was of the tunnel . . . and of the Light.

It was another two weeks before they would let him return to work.

To work . . . but not to his lab.

"Well, what do you think?" Sands asked, gesturing proudly around her.

Sommer stared at the huge room, and all the gleaming electronic equipment laid out on long and uncluttered lab tables. "It looks like a Hollywood movie set," he growled, an uncomfortable feeling beginning to gnaw at the pit of his stomach. "May I ask just who is footing the bill for all this?"

She waved her hand. "Oh, we've got backers coming out of our ears now. Everyone from basic electronics people like Hewlett-Packard—that stuff over there's from them—all the way up to good old Uncle Sam himself."

Sommer grimaced. "Oh, great. The government. How to screw something up, in one easy lesson."

She gave him an odd look. "Maybe you haven't got it yet, Adrian. No one's moving in to take over—the only thing Washington's concerned with at the moment is renting a set of Soulminder units to protect top government officials. *We're* the ones in the driver's seat. And that's the way it's damn well going to stay."

Sommer shook his head, the movement sparking a twinge from his neck. "It won't last, you know," he reminded her. "The minute you apply for a patent on the trap there'll be a hundred copycats making their own versions."

"Which is why there won't *be* any patents," she told him. "We'll put our money into keeping the Soulminder design and process a complete, black-hole secret. It shouldn't be all that hard—thanks to you, we now know that Soulminder can handle a subject from at least ten miles away. We'll be able to keep everything of value safely locked away in our own buildings, with our own security web around them."

Sommer nodded tiredly. "Well, I wish you luck with it. Just make sure—"

"Whoa," she frowned. "What's this *you* stuff? We're in this together, you know."

"No, I don't think so, Jessica. I've done everything I set out to do. Soulminder exists, it works, and according to you, it has a good chance of surviving. It's over now."

She snorted. "Hardly. There's a tremendous amount of work yet to be done. Research on better neuropreservatives, regrowth of damaged tissue, bioengineered organs and limbs—maybe even entire replacement bodies—"

"Wait a minute," he interrupted her. "What on earth are you going on about?"

She took a deep breath, eyes blazing into his with a dark fire he'd never seen there before. Or perhaps only never noticed. "You see Soulminder as a holding tank for critical patients," she said quietly. "I see it as mankind's ticket to immortality. *My* ticket to immortality."

For a moment he stared at her. To have worked with her for three years, without ever recognizing what it was that was driving her . . . "That's not realistic, Jessica," he said gently. "Death is a part of life—"

"So was smallpox, once," she said tartly. "I've heard all those arguments, Adrian. Every one of them is either nonsense or rationalization."

"Death is a part of life," he repeated, louder this time. "It's as much a passage to what lies beyond as your birth was a passage into *this* world."

She snorted, a sound that was at the same time contemptuous and oddly nervous. "What lies beyond. You mean all that stuff about tunnels, do you, and bright lights and passages and friendly voices?"

"Why not?" he demanded, even as her tone made him wince. "Don't forget that I was there. I *saw* it."

"Saw *what?*" she retorted. "Something real, or something totally imaginary? Can you *prove* it wasn't a psychovisual reaction or a forced memory of birth or even a side effect of Soulminder itself? Come on—you know that a mind in that state can't be trusted."

He swallowed, gazing into her eyes. Hostile eyes: eyes that showed she had already made up her mind. "It's your life, Jessica," he sighed at last. "If you want to spend it chasing a rainbow, that's your business. But count me out."

Something in her face changed. "I'm sorry, Adrian. But I can't."

"Jessica, I don't *want* to be immortal."

"I know." She pursed her lips, and a flicker of pain crossed her face. "But for the moment . . . I can't let you have that choice."

He stared at her, something cold running straight through him. "I don't understand," he said carefully. "Are you trying to say that my Mullner pattern can't be erased from Soulminder's files?"

"I'm saying," she said, "that your pattern *won't* be erased from the files."

"Then I'll go in and do it myself."

"No," she said quietly. "You won't."

He just looked at her silently, and after a moment she sighed. "I can't let you die, Adrian," she said, the words coming out with difficulty. "All this medical research is going to cost money—*lots* of money. I need Soulminder to be as big and as powerful and as rich as it can possibly be . . . and you're the key to that. *You*—Dr. Adrian Sommer—are the symbol of Soulminder. The man they couldn't kill; the man whose resurrection machine has fired imaginations all over the world." She took a deep breath. "The only man who can keep those imaginations fired."

"That's crazy," he breathed.

"Yes, it is," she admitted, an odd weariness in her voice. "But it's happened. And until Soulminder is firmly on its feet, I have no choice but to take advantage of it."

"And if I refuse to be Soulminder's mascot?"

Her eyes were almost pleading. Almost, but not quite. "Soulminder is your child, Adrian, as much as David ever was. You can't turn your back on it—who knows what kind of monster it might become without you?"

He looked her square in the eyes. Jessica Sands, once his co-worker . . . now with literally the power of life and death over him.

The power of life *without* death. "I think," he said quietly, "that it's already becoming that monster."

She winced, but remained silent, and after a moment he turned away. A hundred small lights flickered at him as he did so, reflected from the gleaming new instruments surrounding him. *What is a man profited*, he quoted tiredly to himself, *if he shall gain the whole world, and lose his own soul?*

He had no answer to that. But one way or another, it looked as if he was going to find out.

CHAPTER 2

●

Judgment Call

THE CIRCUIT TRACER BEEPED notification that it had completed its task, and for a moment the computer paused, mulling over the numbers. Raising his coffee mug for a cautious sip, Adrian Sommer rubbed one eye as he kept the other on the monitor. *Please let it have worked,* he pleaded silently with the computer. If this latest design bottomed out like the last two, his partner was likely to either throw an angry fit or else drop into a dark-brown depression, and Sommer was far too tired to deal with either. *Please . . .*

Abruptly, the software finished its ruminations and sent the cursor skittering across the screen, scattering amber letters and figures in its wake. "Well?" Jessica Sands asked from over the paperwork pile on her desk, dark anticipation in her voice.

"Hang on," Sommer told her, keeping his mental fingers crossed as he waited for the screen to scroll to the end. "Bottom line is . . . um. Well, bingo, I guess. Nearly a four percent reduction in baseline power requirements. We're definitely on the right track."

She grunted. "Maybe," she said, without noticeable enthusiasm. "Remember that it also requires twenty percent more circuitry and at least that much more space than the original trap."

"But theoretically more than doubles our assumed three-thousand-mile range," Sommer pointed out, annoyance beginning to percolate in his stomach. Sands had been tinkering with the basic Soulminder trap design for months now, but even though she was making somewhat jerky progress on streamlining the device, each improvement seemed to make less and less of an impression on her. A phlegmatic attitude which, unfortunately, didn't also extend to her failures. "At the moment, I'd think boosting our national coverage to something that's effectively continental should be more important than any gains in overall efficiency."

"Certainly if you're talking such niggling gains as four percent," Sands agreed sourly. Looking at her watch, she tossed her pen onto the desk and then tiredly cracked her shoulders backwards. "I suppose we ought to throw everything back into the safe. Your junior watchdog could be here any time now."

For a moment Sommer just looked at her, his eyes tracing the new lines and shadows in her face and the hardness around her mouth. Soulminder had burst into existence barely eight months ago—had been handling commercial operations for only half that time—and already the strain was visibly aging her.

Was aging both of them. "Look, Jessica, I understand how you feel," he said quietly. "But you know as well as I do that it has to be done. There's just no way on the face of this Earth that we can keep handling all the core Soulminder work ourselves. Somewhere along the line, sooner or later, we're simply going to *have* to let other people in."

The lines tightened a bit further. "Yes, well, someone like

Frank Everly wouldn't exactly be at the top of *my* invitation list. If you want me to be undiplomatic about it."

"When have you ever been otherwise?" Sommer countered dryly, and was rewarded by a slight and almost unwilling smile. "I understand your reservations, but now is *exactly* the right time to hire a professional security consultant. And Everly comes highly recommended, by people I've always been able to trust."

Sands sighed. "I'm sure he's capable of being part of the solution," she conceded. "I'm equally sure he could be a major part of the problem."

"We have to trust *someone*, Jessica. We can't continue to do all this alone."

"Why not?" she demanded. But there was little fire in her voice. The argument was pure reflex, a bare shadow of the knockdown fights they'd had on the subject throughout the last month. "All right, so Soulminder takes off slower than everyone wants it to. Would that be so bad? We're still the only game in town, and if people have to wait a little while for us to increase our capacity, then tough."

"You don't mean that, and you know it," Sommer told her. The counter-argument, too, was little more than automatic reflex. Both of them were deathly tired. "You push our current pedestal of popular support too far and it'll get knocked right out from under us."

"I'm willing to take that chance," she muttered.

"It's not a chance you can take," he told her bluntly. "Period. You want Soulminder to be the money machine that'll maybe give you a shot at immortality someday. If you keep trying to do everything yourself it won't matter *how* rich Soulminder ultimately becomes, because you'll be dead from the stress inside of five years."

Her reply, whatever it would have been, was interrupted by a ping from the intercom. "Dr. Sommer, Mr. Everly is here," the receptionist in the outer office reported briskly.

Sommer glanced at all the equipment strewn about the lab

tables, some of it utterly top secret, as he leaned over the speaker on his desk. "Show him into the office, Rita," he instructed the receptionist. "We'll be out in a minute."

"Yes, sir."

The heavily reinforced door that led between the lab and their office was at the far end of the room, beside a control board and a pair of flat screens. Sommer was halfway there when, on the leftmost screen, the office door opened and Rita ushered Everly into the room. The door closed behind him; with a casual glance around, he chose a chair in the conversation area between the two desks and sat down.

"Doesn't look like much," Sands commented from over Sommer's shoulder.

"We're not hiring him for his looks." Reaching over, Sommer keyed the right-hand screen for a scanning of the detectors that had studied Everly on his way down the hallway leading to Rita's desk. X-ray, infrared, metal detector, explosives sniffer . . . "Looks clean enough," he told Sands. "Shall we go in?"

Even without looking, he could sense that Sands was bracing herself. "Might as well," she growled.

He nodded and began unlatching the deadlocks that sealed the lab from the inside. By the time he had the door open, Everly was on his feet again. "Mr. Everly," Sommer greeted him, crossing the room to offer his hand. "I'm Adrian Sommer."

"Pleased to meet you, Dr. Sommer," Everly nodded. His grip was the kind Sommer liked in a handshake: firm and clean, with a strength behind it that the owner felt no need to demonstrate. "You too, Dr. Sands," he added, releasing Sommer's hand and taking Sands's.

"Likewise," she said with noticeable coolness. "Please, sit down."

"Thank you." Everly resumed his seat.

"You've compiled quite an impressive resume for someone who's barely reached his forties," Sommer commented as he and Sands took seats opposite. "CIA, FBI, security adviser to the

Secret Service, head of security for Apple's Brainchild Project. And that's just the high points."

Everly shrugged slightly. "I'm good at what I do."

Beside Sommer, Sands stirred. "You have a high opinion of yourself, Mr. Everly."

Everly cocked an eyebrow. "Would you prefer false modesty, Dr. Sands?" he asked calmly, with no trace of irritation or defensiveness that Sommer could detect.

Her lip twisted, just a bit. "No, I suppose not," she admitted.

Everly turned his attention back to Sommer. "You've seen my resume, and probably sifted through whatever dossiers on me you could get hold of, so I expect my credentials really aren't in doubt here."

So Everly was the direct type. Sommer liked that, too. "True enough. I suppose the only real questions are why you'd want to work for Soulminder, and what you think you can do for us."

"Second one's easy enough." Everly waved a hand back toward the reception area. "For starters, I'd toss out that stop-gap hallway detection gear you've put together and install a *real* system. I could name you at least five weapons, right off the top of my head, that your net wouldn't catch."

"I thought our little gauntlet was reasonably unobvious," Sands said, a touch of challenge in her tone.

Everly shrugged. "It is. Reasonably. I just happen to know what to look for. Second, I'd run a fine-tooth over the rest of the building—with emphasis on your main lab back there—and see what else has to be done to make this place secure. Third, I'd take a look at the plans of your new building and correct any problems *now*, before it actually starts going up and you wind up having to knock out walls to fix things. Fourth, I'd get some people in here to start a complete—and I mean *complete*—screening of all current and prospective employees. Especially those who'll be working with the main Soulminder equipment itself."

"Sounds like a lot of work," Sands said. "Especially when you'd be doing it all for considerably less than Apple's already paying you."

He looked at her. "True," he agreed. "Which leads us back to Dr. Sommer's first question. The answer's simple: I want to work here because I think what you're doing is a hell of a lot more important than anything else going on in the world today. I can see the possibilities you've got here—some of them, anyway—and some of the ways all the good parts could be killed outright or perverted or bureaucracied to death." Something behind his eyes seemed to harden. "I've seen all of those happen, and to projects that weren't anywhere near as ambitious as yours. I don't want to see Soulminder go down that road."

For a long moment the room was silent. "I don't really trust you," Sands told him at last. "I don't suppose that comes as a surprise."

"Not really," Everly said, again without irritation or defensiveness. "In your position, I wouldn't trust a lot of people, either. Soulminder is the kind of prize that makes grown men salivate down thousand-dollar ties. You're soon going to have people trying their damnedest to beg, buy, cheat, or steal it out from under you. If they aren't doing it already."

"You sound as if we're going to be under siege," Sommer said, his throat suddenly tight.

Everly shrugged. "Actually, it's not quite that bad. You hit the ground running, with a nuke-sized blast of instant publicity that caught everybody flatfooted. That, plus the floodlit microscope you've been living under since then, will have scotched all the more overt snatch schemes, at least for the moment. If we move fast—and if we're lucky—we can get the lid screwed down tight before anybody gets any quiet espionage schemes going."

"And if you're one of those quiet schemes?" Sands challenged.

Everly looked her straight in the eye. "If I am," he said, equally bluntly, "I already know enough about your setup to break in and steal Soulminder out from under you."

He shook his head. "I can't prove I'm on your side, Doctor. But somewhere along the line, you're going to have to trust *someone*. If you don't, you'll lose by default."

Sommer stole a glance at Sands. Uncertain eyes, tight mouth . . . but behind it all, a grudging but growing acceptance. "Adrian?" she asked tentatively.

And behind the word was capitulation.

Sommer took a careful breath. Sands was not, he knew, simply being paranoid. This was nothing less than a win-or-lose throw of the dice . . . and if Everly wasn't what he claimed to be, then he and Sands had just lost everything. "Well, Mr. Everly," he said, fighting against a tremor in his voice. "Welcome to Soulminder."

Behind the hum of the computer's cooling fans, Sommer could hear that the singing from the TV had ended. Hunching forward, he wrapped himself closer about the keyboard, hoping that maybe Sands wouldn't notice that he wasn't paying attention.

It was a futile hope. "Adrian!" she called, turning up the TV's volume a couple of levels. "Come on—he's ready to start spouting."

Sommer straightened with a sigh and turned to look. On the screen a scrubbed and brushed and impeccably dressed middle-aged man was just stepping up to the pulpit, his face ablaze with righteous fervor. "God bless you; God *bless* you, my friends," he said, the fervor in his voice exactly in tune with his face. "Release your spirits to *hear* the Word of the Lord."

Sands turned to glance at Sommer. "Come *on*, Adrian," she called again, more emphatically this time.

"I've seen all I want to of the Reverend Tommy Lee Harper, thank you," he sniffed. But even as he said it he found his eyes attracted almost irresistibly to the man on the screen. By anyone's definition of charisma, Reverend Harper definitely had it.

"Hey, this was *your* idea, remember?" Sands reminded him tartly. "Know thy enemy, and all that?"

"I meant to keep tabs on people like Harper through the web and news channels," Sommer retorted. "Not in person. Or whatever this is."

"Quiet," she shushed him.

With a sigh, Sommer got up and rolled his chair over, and resigned himself to the inevitable.

It was, he had to admit, an electrifying performance. The Reverend Harper was almost a caricature—or cynic's portrait—of a TV evangelist: slick without appearing too Hollywood, dogmatic without overt smugness, careful of appearances, and adept at measuring the direction of the social winds. He'd been on the national scene for barely six months, but in that time he'd already established himself as one of the dominant figures of the new breed who were beginning to turn around a decade-long erosion in televangelism's viewership and cash flow.

Though of course a large part of that reversal was directly traceable back to Soulminder. Even while the nation's religious leaders continued to debate the morality of the technology and its applications, they couldn't escape the fact that positive proof of the soul's existence had sparked huge revivals among their congregations.

Harper's included . . . which was more than ironic, given the man's attitude toward Soulminder.

"—and in those End Times, God warns us to watch for—to *beware* of—the Antichrist."

Harper paused and seemed to straighten as his face hardened in an expression of firm resolve. "Here it comes," Sands muttered.

"Who *is* the Antichrist?" Harper continued. "Is he yet to come, for our children or grandchildren to wrestle with? Or is he here now, walking God's Earth and plotting the destruction of all those he can ensnare in Satan's web?"

Again he paused, and in the silence Sommer heard the pinging from the hallway alert system. Swiveling around in his chair, he squinted across the room at the wall monitor. "Frank Everly's coming," he announced.

"I told him to stop by after he finished at the building site," Sands said absently. "Shh!—there's more."

"My friends, I'll tell you right up front that I don't know," Harper said, his face and voice in a homey I'm-just-one-of-you-folks mode. It seemed to be a favorite expression among the wealthy and powerful; Sommer had seen copies of it a hundred times during the long and tedious Capitol Hill hearings that continued to take up an inordinate percentage of his working days.

"It may be one of those mysteries of the End Times that God won't be revealing to anyone," Harper continued, "except perhaps to the Two Witnesses who'll preach for him against the Beast. But then again—" his gaze hardened. "Then again, maybe it's all right there, right in the open, staring us in the face from our morning news. *Let him who has ears to hear, let him hear,* our Lord said—and may I add, let him who has eyes to see, let him see."

The bank of sensors was triggering now, feeding onto the second and third screens a series of images of Everly, each less recognizable as a human being than the one before, each clearing him of yet another weapon or potential threat. By the time he reached the outer office and Rita's desk, he'd been sifted so thoroughly that the Soulminder security computers probably knew as much about him as his own doctor.

"When God set us on this Earth, He set guidelines for our behavior—guidelines for our behavior, and walls about our earthly kingdoms. *Render unto Caesar that which is Caesar's, and to God that which is God's.* Those were our Lord's own words. *And yet...*"

Abruptly, Harper leaned over the lectern, a finger jabbing accusingly at the camera. "*And yet,* there are people *right now* claiming they can command the human soul—that they can hold it in their hands, that they can do with it what they please.

"The human soul. Think about that, my friends. *Think* about that—think about what it truly means."

On the monitor Sommer watched as Everly pressed both hands against the glass ID plate outside the lab door. The light flickered once, and as Everly removed his hands a chemically treated roller swept over the glass, wiping it clean. Apparently, there were ways an intruder could trick the system by using the trace oil residues left on the glass by the last person to use it. Everly had been just slightly vague on exactly how he'd discovered that trick.

"If there is *any* part of creation that is unarguably God's own, my friends, it is the human soul. That quality that sets us apart from the animals; that unique bit of God's own nature, given to Adam as the greatest gift the Creator of the universe could bestow on his children. It is *not for us to meddle with!*"

The vault-like door swung easily on its balanced hinges, and Everly stepped into the room, giving it his usual quick once-over before sealing the door behind him. "Join the party, Everly," Sands waved him over, her eyes still on Harper. "Sackcloth and ashes for everyone—put it on Soulminder's tab."

"Harper, huh?" Everly commented as he came up. "Puts on a good show—I'll give him that much. Got good writers, too."

"He doesn't write all this himself?" Sommer asked.

"Oh, he does some of it, and rewrites the rest into his own style. But all the more flowery stuff comes from professionals." Everly nodded toward the TV. "I did a check on him five months ago, when he first latched onto Soulminder."

Sands frowned up at him. "You hadn't even *joined* us five months ago."

Everly shrugged, his eyes on the screen. "The Brainchild Project will be almost as controversial as Soulminder if it ever pans out. You're ahead of the game if you can identify your opponents before they know whose side they're on."

"My friends, I don't have to tell you the state America's in today. Abortion on demand, atheists in the highest positions of power, the systematic destruction of the family—God's people are *losing* this country, my friends. Losing it to the false pride of modern-day Pharisees who think they have more wisdom than God-fearing men and women. Losing it to the arrogance of would-be tyrants who want to run our lives from halfway across the country. Losing it to the sterile, self-appointed morality of people who claim that the world is changing, that there's no place for God in our schools, our legislatures, or our hospitals. All of them will try and tell you that *they*, not God, are the ones who should set the moral standards for our nation."

"A little hyperbole never hurt ratings, did it?" Sommer growled.

Everly shrugged. "He acts like he believes it."

"Oh, right," Sands said sourly. "And it's pure coincidence that in picking on Soulminder he just *happened* to strike a major ultra-conservative nerve?"

"It's a major nerve because there's a large chunk of people who really believe we're evil," Everly reminded her. "Who's to say he isn't one of them?"

"Awfully charitable of you," Sands said with a snort. "I still think he's just playing games." She looked at Sommer. "His people still nagging you to come on his show and defend our side of it?"

"We get a registered letter from them about once a week," Sommer told her, grimacing. "We've got a form-letter refusal I keep sending them. Can we turn this off yet? I've about had all I can take."

"Yeah, he's probably finished flaying us for today," Sands said, reaching for the switch and pausing a moment to listen. Harper had segued into a condemnation of welfare money intended for the poor instead simply disappearing into the bloated welfare bureaucracy; turning off the set, Sands settled back into her chair. "I'd sure like to find some way to shut that guy up."

"We'd probably do better to ignore him," Sommer told her, listening to his heartbeat slow down. Harper's accusations got far deeper under his own skin than he cared to admit. "Starting right now, in fact. So tell us about your trip to the new building, Frank. Everything going all right?"

"Oh, the work itself is coming along okay," Everly said. "But I think we're going to have to tighten things among the employees.

We've got what looks like four or five CIA men who've infiltrated the concrete crew."

"What?" Sands sat up straighter. "What are they doing, scoping out the floor plans?"

"More likely looking for good places to plant bugs," Everly said. "They would have had a complete set of the blueprints months ago."

Sands hissed a curse between clenched teeth. "What about Soulminder's own employees? Your people finding any moles there?"

"Oh, sure," Everly said. "At the moment we're up to about seven, all in low-level, non-critical positions. More or less the sort of deep-mole gambit we expected. I'm having them watched until we're sure we have everyone, at which point we can throw the whole group out at once."

"Are they all CIA?" Sommer asked.

"No, actually they're a mixture of military and civilian intelligence types," Everly told him. "From what my contacts have said there seems to have been a kind of jurisdictional struggle when you first hit the scene, which the Secret Service apparently won. My guess is they invited these other people into their Soulminder task force to help soothe any feathers that were still ruffled."

"So the CIA people in the construction crew are really on temporary Secret Service duty?"

"Or else they're the CIA keeping its own hand in," Everly said dryly. "They can be sore losers sometimes."

"Wonderful," Sands growled. "Just wonderful. On one side we've got Congress trying to legislate and oversight-committee us into their own box, and *now* we've got the Executive Branch doing *its* best to put us on strings. What's next, the Supreme Court?"

"Oh, they'll find a way into it eventually," Everly agreed. "But I doubt it's the Administration that's behind this mole operation, at least not directly." He waved a hand, the gesture encompassing the lab. "Remember that you have a hell of a lot of *very* important lives in the palm of your hand here, and no one in government is ever happy at leaving that kind of power under private control."

"But they always have that problem, at least potentially," Sommer pointed out. "You get the President visiting some out-of-the-way place and having a heart attack, and they're going to be stuck with local doctors."

"And they don't like it one bit, which is why the Presidential party always includes an Army doctor," Everly said. "But flukes like that they can't control. Soulminder they can." A faint smile twisted at his lips. "Or so they think."

Sands looked at Sommer. "We've got to head them off," she said. "Go public with this, maybe, and let the country know what they're up to."

"I'd strongly recommend against that, Dr. Sands," Everly said, shaking his head. "There's a loud chunk of the populace that thinks all health care should be under government control, and another chunk who don't trust *any* form of big business. If you force the issue into the open, you're likely to get both groups of people calling for a government takeover."

"They try it and they can all go straight to hell," Sands said, her voice icy. "I'll destroy Soulminder before I'll let anyone take it away from us."

Sommer swallowed. *Do I feel that strongly about it?* he wondered uncomfortably. If push really came to shove, would he be willing to sacrifice all the potential good in Soulminder for . . . was it really anything more than pride?

"I wouldn't worry about any serious takeover bids, at least not at the moment," Everly said, saving Sommer from having to say anything. "Mr. Porath's people downstairs have good reputations—they could tie anything overt into legal knots with their eyes closed." He nodded toward the blank TV. "Actually, people like the Reverend Harper are some of your best allies right now."

Sands gave a snort. "You *are* kidding, I presume."

"Not really. His followers may feel uneasy about Soulminder, but they *damn* well don't trust the government."

"Ah," Sommer nodded as understanding came. "If they think Soulminder is potentially evil *and* that the government is controlled by atheists, it would be utterly disastrous if the government took us over."

"Right," Everly said. "And there are a lot of people who'd react that way, with or without Harper's religious overtones."

"So we're back to your floodlit-microscope theory, are we?" Sands commented, her voice growing thoughtful.

Everly shrugged. "Light *does* tend to keep the rats away."

"In that case, maybe we should turn up the rheostat a little." Sands looked at Sommer, an odd glint in her eye.

"What?" he demanded suspiciously. He'd seen that look before.

"I was just thinking," she said, "that maybe you ought to accept that head-to-head with Harper, after all."

"Now *you're* kidding," Sommer growled. "Why don't you just stake me out over an anthill and invite the media in?"

"It might not be a bad idea, actually," Everly said. "It would help keep the pot stirred, as well as showing them that you're not some shadowy government bureaucrat they can't even find, much less confront. It'd make Soulminder more human."

Sommer glared at him. Sands was already way too good at talking him into things he really didn't want to do. The last thing he needed was someone else feeding her ammunition. "So one of *you* do it," he growled. "If you think I'm going to be turned into dog meat on Harper's own show—"

"Well, now, of course you wouldn't want to face him on his own ground," Sands soothed. She must have sensed victory, Sommer thought sourly; she'd shifted into conciliatory mode. "I meant neutral territory. One of the Sunday talking-head shows or something. Maybe a prime-time debate special—we're big enough news to pull something like that."

"You could require that other religious leaders be invited in, too," Everly suggested. "It would give a more balanced view of the questions involved, besides giving you a chance to bring in some allies."

"Sure," Sands said, nodding. "It wouldn't be any harder than going up to Capitol Hill and facing Barnswell and his crowd." She hesitated. "And it's something only you can do, Adrian. You're the public image of Soulminder, not me."

A fact that she'd been reminding him of and pushing him with ever since Soulminder's creation. How much of that, he wondered, was public hero-worship, and how much merely Sands's own self-fulfilling prophesy?

And did it really matter?

As a theoretical matter, perhaps. As a practical matter, not at all.

With a quiet sigh, Sommer pushed his chair back to his worktable and reached for the phone.

" . . . but as the initial euphoria about the breakthrough itself ran its course," the reporter droned on, "questions and doubts began to appear . . . "

His eyes on the monitor, Sommer took a deep breath and willed calm into his throat. Why the producers had felt it necessary to recap Soulminder's brief history for the viewers he couldn't imagine—there couldn't be any adult in the Western Hemisphere who hadn't heard the story over and over again in the past year.

But it hadn't been worth arguing about. So he sat and suffered the pre-broadcast jitters, and wished they could just get on with it.

As, he suspected, did at least three of the other four guests. Rabbi David Kaufmann was puckering his lips in and out as he stared the monitor, while the Reverend Robert Edgington's hands rubbed back and forth endlessly across his chair arms and Father James Barry ran a finger inside his clerical collar as if trying to loosen it. Even the host of this circus, Barbara Leach, was staring down at her notes as if seeing them for the first time, a tight set to her mouth. Only Harper, at the far end of the semicircle, seemed totally at ease.

The taped history lesson was coming to an end. Sommer took a deep, calming breath; he sensed the others doing the same. A shadowy figure behind the lights raised a hand and counted off the seconds—

And by the time the red light on the central camera flicked on, everyone in front of it was calm and collected.

"Good evening to you," Leach said into the lens, her voice gravely polite. "Welcome to this special edition of *Focus*. For any who tuned in late, my guests this evening are, to my left, Dr. Adrian Sommer of Soulminder; beside him, Father James Barry and Rabbi David Kaufmann. To my right, the Reverend Robert Edgington; beside him, the Reverend Tommy Lee Harper. Gentlemen, welcome. As we just heard, the creation of Soulminder has raised a number of complicated ethical questions—not only questions about how the technology is to be applied, but concerns about the very nature of what Soulminder does. Rabbi Kaufmann, let me begin with you. Tell us what concerns, if any, you have about Soulminder."

"Oh, one must always have concerns about new inventions and technologies," Kaufmann said. "That's not to say we should automatically oppose them, of course, but that we *should* give them close and careful scrutiny. As you indicated, there are certainly questions that need to be asked: access to Soulminder for the poor, for instance, and at what stage in a person's life Soulminder would represent just one more unrealistic attempt to prolong a life that's ready to cease. But bear in mind that we've been wrestling with such issues for a good portion of the past hundred years. In that sense, Soulminder merely joins the list that already includes open-heart surgery, chemotherapy, and organ transplants."

"Does the idea per se of separating the human soul from its body raise any moral issues?" Leach persisted.

Kaufmann raised his eyebrows slightly. "If you mean by that whether or not I consider it blasphemous—" he shrugged. "No. At least not at the moment, though I consider it my prerogative to change my mind if further study convinces me otherwise. God gave the Earth into mankind's hands, and I don't believe that anything mankind can learn or invent is in and of itself outside that dominion. However—" His face hardened. "As Auschwitz and the Nazi horror experiments so graphically showed, there are things that *can* be done that should *not* be done. Whether or not Soulminder falls into that category, we'll just have to wait and see."

Leach nodded. "Thank you, Rabbi. Father Barry? Your comments?"

"In many ways the Church's views parallel those of Rabbi Kaufmann," the priest said. "We expect to be continually reminding Dr. Sommer and his colleagues that Soulminder must not become the province only of the rich and powerful; on the other hand, let me add that we recognize the realities of this world, that Soulminder's start-up costs will probably keep the service out of reach of the average person for the short term. We *do* expect that to eventually change, though." He gave Sommer a significant look.

"We're already looking for ways to increase our capacity while at the same time lowering maintenance fees," Sommer told him. "There are also several unions and corporations who are exploring the possibility of adding Soulminder service to their general health benefits package, which may bring us into reach of at least a part of the general population even sooner."

Barry nodded. "As to theoretical questions of splitting the soul from the body, Barbara, the Church has historically held that the soul doesn't leave this world until irreversible damage to the body has taken place. In that light, you could easily make a case for putting Soulminder in the same class as the temporary surgical removal of the heart."

Leach nodded, and Sommer found his breath coming a little easier. The producers hadn't allowed him to have any input in choosing the other three guests, but it was beginning to look as if Soulminder had some strong allies on the panel.

And it was going to need them. At the far end of the semicircle Harper was watching Sommer steadily.

"Since your feelings about Soulminder are well known, Dr. Sommer," Leach said, a touch of dry humor in her voice, "I'd like to pass you up for the moment and move on to my other guests. You'll then have the opportunity to answer any questions they might bring up."

Sommer nodded acceptance, and Leach turned to her right. "Reverend Edgington?"

"My views are pretty much in line with those that have already been aired," Edgington said, his voice deep and resonant and verging on the pompous. His church was in the forefront of what he and his colleagues liked to call "modernization," which seemed to involve throwing out most traditional beliefs and teachings. "I'd like to add one thing, though, to Father Barry's equating of Soulminder with other surgical techniques. While organ transplants have been with us for decades, it's only been in the past couple of years that the invention of ultra-efficient heartlung machines and neuropreservatives have made many types of transplants even possible. Bodies can now be kept healthy and free from decay for weeks or even months until the proper recipient for a given organ can be found. Soulminder actually does nothing more, except that instead of preserving a body for the benefit of others, it preserves it for the benefit of the original owner." He smiled. "There's really no way you can argue against saving lives, Barbara."

He nodded slightly, signaling he was through . . . and, unconsciously, Sommer braced himself. It was Harper's turn.

"Reverend Harper, you've been one of the most outspoken critics of Soulminder since its invention," Leach said, "first in your own congregation and, since then, on your syndicated television show. Tell us why."

Harper paused, cocking his head slightly to the side. "First of all, Barbara," he said, his voice even and polite but with heat smoldering beneath it, "let me say that I join Father Barry and Rabbi Kaufmann in wondering if Soulminder will indeed wind up perpetuating the social injustice that continues to drive wedges between the rich and the poor of this world. At the same time"—a hard edge began to creep into his voice and his gaze drifted from Leach to settle onto Sommer—"I also think that they and Dr. Sommer have all either missed or deliberately ignored Soulminder's basic flaw: the fact that by its very nature the artificial removal of a human soul from the body is blasphemy."

Beside Sommer, Father Barry shifted in his chair. Harper's eyes flicked to him, then returned to Sommer. "The soul simply isn't part of mankind's realm," he continued. "It isn't for us to hold or deal with; it *certainly* isn't ours to keep back from God when He's summoned it home."

"And yet isn't all of medicine in a sense the holding back of a soul from God?" Leach interjected. "People used to die who can now be routinely saved."

"That's exactly my point," Harper told her, his eyes still on Sommer. "We keep people alive—asleep under anesthetics, sometimes, or in comas—or we let them die. Life"—he held a hand out, palm upward—"or death." He held out the other hand beside it. "Those have always been our only two choices. And properly so, because life and death are the two states of existence that were ordained for mankind in the beginning. But Soulminder does more, and in doing more it goes beyond any comparison with normal medical treatment. It creates a *third* state of existence— a state that's neither true life *nor* true death. A disembodied existence: conscious, with all human desires and ambitions and needs, yet completely and utterly cut off from participation in, or communication with, the rest of creation." His eyes flicked to Father Barry. "A man-made purgatory, Father?"

"Perhaps," Barry said evenly. "On the other hand, in a lesser sense, don't we all have some control over each other's existence?

Over their souls, if you will? Isn't that really what government or even community means?"

Harper shook his head. "You can't equate social influence—not even the heavy coercion of a tyranny—with the one-hundred-percent control exerted by Soulminder over those in its power. That's not what was intended for mankind."

"And if God had intended man to fly, He would have given us wings?" Edgington suggested sardonically. "Inventions and technology are never evil in and of themselves, Mr. Harper. It's what we do with them that's important."

Harper sent him an icy look, and Sommer swallowed. The arch-conservative, seated next to the arch-liberal. Fleetingly, he wondered if Leach had deliberately put them next to each other, and decided she probably had. *He* certainly wouldn't have wanted to sit in the crossfire between them. "I trust, Mr. Edgington," Harper said, his voice as cool as his look, "that you haven't forgotten that the Earth and everything in it is in a fallen state. Nothing that man can invent is untouched by that taint. For that matter, I can name you a set of inventions that *is* evil in and of itself."

"And that is . . . ?"

"Instruments of torture," Harper told him. He held Edgington's eyes a moment longer, then looked back at Sommer. "I'd like to ask you a question, Dr. Sommer, if I may." He paused a split second, as if waiting for Leach to step in and stop him, then continued, "You claim that Soulminder is to be used for medical purposes only, that once the body has been repaired it will be reinsouled."

"That's correct," Sommer said, wondering uneasily where Harper was going with this.

"Let's assume for the moment that we all find that particular usage acceptable," Harper said. "So. Assume the body is now repaired. What if you then change your mind and decide to continue holding the soul and body apart?"

"That would be unethical, of course," Sommer agreed carefully. "A timely insertion of the soul has always been our policy."

"Ah—timely." Harper arched his eyebrows. "What does timely *mean*, Doctor? An hour after the doctors declare the body is sufficiently healed? Six hours, just to be on the safe side? A week? Two weeks?

"Five years?"

"Of course not," Sommer insisted. "Timely is—well, it's an individual thing, something that has to be decided between our people and the person's own physician."

"Remarkably similar to the language of free abortion," Harper said. "But suppose the doctor doesn't feel the patient is yet ready, even after you do? For that matter, what if the body can't actually *be* repaired at present? How long do you hold the soul in your electronic limbo on the off chance that *someday* that body might be useful again?

"Where do you draw your lines, Doctor?"

Sommer took a deep breath, but before he could speak he was rescued. "Much as I hate to interrupt good drama," Leach said gravely, "we do have to take a break here. When we return, we'll have Dr. Sommer's response, and further debate."

She held the pose a moment . . . and then the camera light went out, and she exhaled loudly. "Two minutes, gentlemen," she said, standing. "If any of you want to stretch, this is your chance."

Sommer wondered briefly if his knees were up to standing. "Don't let him get to you," Father Barry murmured beside him. "A lot of his arguments are pure smokescreen."

"And a lot of them aren't," Sommer said heavily. "This is all too reminiscent of those college bull sessions on situational ethics and morality that used to keep me up nights."

The priest shrugged. "I remember those, too. But until and unless God grants us omniscience—"

"Dr. Sommer?" a stagehand loomed before him, silhouetted by the lights. "Phone call, sir, from Dr. Sands. She says it's urgent you call her."

"Thank you," Sommer said, turning his cell back on and punching in Sands's number.

She answered on the first ring. "God, I'm glad I got you," she said, her voice tight and urgent. "We've got trouble. The minute you're done there get straight over to St. Elizabeth's Hospital."

Sommer's stomach hardened into a knot. "What's happened? Someone get hurt?"

"I wish it were that simple," she said grimly. "One of our clients died there an hour or so ago—heart attack or something. The trap caught him okay, no problem there. But the hospital's declared him dead and are getting ready to start carving him up for spare organs."

"They're *what*?" Sommer demanded. "No—they can't do that. What about the hold-and-suspend protocols?"

"Either he never filed them, or they got lost somewhere in the system," Sands said. "Porath's trying to get an emergency injunction, and one of his staff's gone to the hospital to try and reason with them. But he's not going to have nearly the stalling power you will."

"Agreed." Behind the cameras someone called a one-minute warning. "I've got to go, Jessica. I'll get out there as soon as I can. Where are they?"

"Room 258. At least that's where they were ten minutes ago—I presume they haven't moved him. I'll see if there are any strings I can pull from here in the meantime." She hesitated. "I trust you can see just exactly how much is riding on this. If our big expensive safety net can lose someone this easily . . . "

"I get the picture," Sommer told her. "I'll be there when I can."

The rest of the debate remained forever afterward little more than a fuzzy blur in Sommer's memory. He remembered answering Harper's arguments, though with a vague accompanying sense that he hadn't really done a very good job of it. He remembered a polite verbal free-for-all in which everyone basically ganged up against Harper, with occasional jabs at each other, while Leach sat back and allowed herself just enough control to hold things together without ruining the spontaneity of it all. But the details remained lost to him. There was too much on his mind.

He didn't remember much about the drive to the hospital, either, except that, like the debate, it seemed to take forever.

He expected to find a crowd of reporters jamming room 258 and the surrounding corridor. Thankfully, the media apparently hadn't yet been alerted.

Standing just outside the room, his back to the door, was a young man Sommer recognized as one of Murray Porath's legal staff. Facing him were half a dozen medical types and a youngish man in an expensive-looking three-piece suit. Their voices were too low for Sommer to make out the words as he approached, but from the tone it was abundantly clear that the conversation wasn't a friendly one.

"Good evening," Sommer nodded, coming up to the group and scanning their faces as they turned to face him. Concern— awkward concern, even—from the medical people; quiet anger and suspicion from the man in the suit, who wasn't quite as young as he'd looked from a distance. "I'm Dr. Adrian Sommer of Soulminder," Sommer continued. "What seems to be the trouble here?"

"It's called illegal restraint," the suited man bit out before any- one else could speak. "Your people are preventing, by threat of force, the lawful performance of legitimate medical duties, and in doing so are threatening the well-being of at least four other people."

Sommer cocked an eyebrow. "I take it you're a lawyer."

He hadn't intended it to sound like an insult, but the other apparently took it as one, anyway. "My name is Tyler Marsh," the other said coldly. "I doubt that that means anything to you, but yes, I *have* had a certain amount of legal experience. Enough to know that you have no right to interfere with the carrying out of a deceased man's last wishes."

"Mr. Ingersoll is not yet deceased," the Soulminder lawyer interjected. "That's the whole point of—"

"Then what is *this*?" Marsh cut him off, waving a paper in his face.

"What *is* that?" Sommer asked him.

One of the doctors cleared his throat. "It's a death certificate, Dr. Sommer," he said.

Sommer regarded him. "Signed by . . . ?"

The other sighed. "Me."

"And it's perfectly legitimate," Marsh put in. "By every legal and medical definition in the book, Wilson Anders Ingersoll is *dead*."

Sommer pursed his lips and turned to the Soulminder lawyer. "Mr. Walker, why don't you fill me in."

"Yes, sir." Walker took a deep breath. "Mr. Ingersoll came down from New York two days ago on business. Early this morning he suffered a heart attack at his hotel and was rushed here in critical condition. Dr. Raines"—he nodded to the doctor—"was in charge of the team who treated him. They succeeded in repairing the damage to the heart muscle. Despite that, two hours ago his heart abruptly stopped again—"

"And Mr. Ingersoll died," Marsh put in.

"And Mr. Ingersoll's EEG trace went flat," Walker corrected, an edge to his voice. "Dr. Raines declared him dead and filled out a death certificate, and the body was put on neuropreservatives and a life-support machine."

"He was carrying an organ donor card," Raines explained. "Liver, lungs, and corneas. Dr. Bartok, here"—he indicated the woman standing beside him—"has been assigned to remove the organs."

Walker nodded to the door behind him. "The nurse in there monitoring the body called us, and Mr. Porath sent me over here to prevent any irrevocable action from taking place. That's about it."

"Death is as irrevocable as you get," Marsh snorted. "All you're doing by your grandstanding is preventing Mr. Ingersoll's last wishes from being carried out and denying four sick people the organs they so desperately need."

"Maybe we shouldn't be quite so quick to dispose of Mr. Ingersoll's property," a new voice came from behind. Sommer turned to see Murray Porath stroll up, dapper as always in a three-piece suit of his own. "Especially since he may not be done with it yet."

Marsh glared at Porath, and for an instant Sommer had the sense of two fighters sizing each other up. "You're with these other ghouls, I take it?" Marsh asked.

Porath raised polite eyebrows. "That's hardly the term I would use," he said calmly. "At least, not for us. I'm Murray Porath, chief legal counsel for Soulminder. Tell me, Mr. Marsh, did you know Mr. Ingersoll was on file with us?"

"Mr. Ingersoll's been into a lot of fads," Marsh said shortly. "Cryogenics, crystal healing, sub-sonic bio-feedback—you name it, he was probably into it at one point or another. Usually he'd go through all the motions, read all the literature, even sign the papers; then his interest would fade, he'd let his memberships lapse, and that would be the end of it. As far as Soulminder was concerned, he told me at least twice in the past month that it was a waste of money and that he was going to dump it."

His eyes and face were hard, the very essence of righteous anger and honesty. *Liar,* Sommer thought.

"Indeed," Porath said. From his tone, Sommer guessed that he thought so, too. "I don't suppose there were any witnesses to this conversation?"

"Not that I recall," Marsh said, his tone frosty. "Are you questioning my memory? Or just my word?"

"Oh, heaven forbid," Porath said soothingly, almost as if he really meant it. "It would have been nice to have some corroboration, but we all understand how these things are. Incidentally, if you'd rather have your lawyer present before you answer any more questions, by all means give him a call."

"I don't want a lawyer," Marsh snapped. "And I don't want any more of these stupid and totally irrelevant questions. Mr. Ingersoll was more like my father than my boss, and I'm damn well not going to sit by and let him be robbed of the respect and dignity that he deserves. He's been certified as dead, I've officially claimed the body, and *that* is *that*. The funeral home in New York has been notified and the service has been scheduled, and I want whatever organ removals he specified to be done *now*." He glared at Bartok and Raines. "Or else I'm going to go in there and shut down all that hardware and take him out myself."

Raines took a deep breath, glanced at Bartok, and took an uncertain step toward Walker and the door behind him—

"Funeral already scheduled, eh?" Porath said interestedly, moving smoothly past Sommer to stand beside his subordinate. "That's fast work, I must say, Mr. Marsh. Almost as if you were expecting his death. Hmm?"

"This was his third heart attack," Marsh grated, "and he died two hours ago. He set up the funeral arrangements himself, incidentally, over two years ago. Not that you seem to have much respect for personal wishes. Dr. Bartok?"

"Tell me, Dr. Raines," Porath said, "didn't you notice that Mr. Ingersoll was wearing a Soulminder ID bracelet before you signed that death certificate?"

"It would have been hard to notice something he wasn't wearing," Raines growled, irritation beginning to shade into the uncomfortable defensiveness in his voice. "There was no Soulminder bracelet. Not here, not in the ambulance."

"It was seven-thirty in the morning," Marsh put in, "and Mr. Ingersoll was still getting dressed when he had his attack."

"And you didn't think to mention to the paramedics that he was on file with Soulminder?" Porath asked pointedly.

"I told you, I assumed he'd dropped his registration." Marsh took a long step forward, his hand coming to rest, not quite heavily, on Porath's shoulder. "And I am *finished* with your stalling. The law is on my side, Mr. Porath. You know it and I know it. And you're going to move aside, or I'm going to *move* you aside."

"There's no need to get dramatic," Porath said calmly, his eyes flicking over Marsh's shoulder. "No need at all. James! Over here!"

Sommer turned to see a young man striding toward them,

an envelope clutched in his hand. "Mr. Porath?" the other asked tentatively.

"Right here." Porath raised a finger. "That goes to Dr. Bartok—that lady right there."

"What is it?" Bartok asked . . . but it seemed to Sommer that some of the tension in her face smoothed out as she accepted the envelope.

"It's a temporary injunction," Porath told her, his eyes steady on Marsh. "It bars you or anyone here from releasing the body of Wilson Anders Ingersoll—to anyone—and from taking any surgical action on it. So that, at least for the moment, is that." He looked at each of the medical people in turn, then nodded briskly and turned to Sommer. "Well, Dr. Sommer. Shall we go in and see how our client is doing?"

The media were on the story less than an hour later, and for the next day and a half Sommer found himself besieged by reporters and news services in a blitz strongly reminiscent of that following the original Soulminder breakthrough. Then, it had been a floodlight he'd been totally unprepared for. Now, with concerns of prejudicing the case weighing heavily on each word, it was no less difficult.

Finally, late in the afternoon on the second day, the flurry began to fade and he was able at last to sit down with the others and find out what had been happening in the background while he'd been facing the cameras.

"The preliminary deposition dates are all set," Porath said, readjusting his feet on his desk and sipping at a cup of tea. "We've got Marsh, Ingersoll's executive secretary, Doctors Raines and Bartok, the head of the hospital, and the nurse whose call originally got us onto this in the first place."

"I never did hear just exactly why she did that," Sommer told him.

Porath shrugged. "She just had a hunch, I gather. She told me that something about Marsh's manner just popped the thought into her head."

"Just one more bit of proof that Marsh knew damn well that Ingersoll was still on file," Sands growled. "As if we needed it."

"Hunches hardly qualify as proof, Dr. Sands," Porath reminded her. "We're almost certainly not going to be able to prove that Marsh lied about that, incidentally, so abandon any thoughts you might have of nailing him to the wall. Keep your eyes on the main point—getting Ingersoll back together again—and be glad that he had the blind luck to draw a nurse willing to play her hunches. Otherwise, Marsh would have just waltzed out with the body, and we'd have been left literally holding the bag."

Sommer shuddered. To be left with a hopelessly disembodied soul in their care . . . "Blind luck, or an act of God."

"Better call it luck," Porath said wryly. "Events defined as Acts Of God have a peculiar status in the law, and they almost always wind up working in your opponent's favor in court."

"If this ever gets to court," Sands said.

Porath snorted. "Oh, it'll get to court, all right. Marsh isn't likely to give up now."

"Not even when he's lost?" Sommer asked. "I mean, couldn't the judge just handle it on a pre-trial basis?"

"He could, but he probably won't. You see, Dr. Sommer, as a strictly legal matter, I have to tell you that Marsh has a pretty strong case."

"He *what*?" Sands growled.

Porath shrugged. "Look at the facts. By all accepted medical and legal definitions, Ingersoll died when his EEG trace went flat. Everything else flows directly from that: the death certificate, Marsh's claiming of the body, the card authorizing the hospital to remove Ingersoll's organs—all perfectly legitimate. *We*, not him, are the ones walking on loose sand here."

"That's crazy," Sommer told him. "Haven't erroneous death

certificates been issued before? People who eventually recovered, or even just clerical errors?"

"Oh, it happens all the time," Porath agreed. "But in every one of those cases, the supposedly dead person is able to get up off the table and announce that he is, in fact, alive. Ingersoll can't do that, and unless and until he does, Marsh has legitimate claim to the body."

Sands muttered something under her breath and shifted her attention to the fourth person in the office. "Everly? What have you dug up on Marsh?"

Everly shook his head. "Hints and innuendoes, but nothing solid. He started out as a lawyer at Drummond Information Services about fifteen years ago, quickly became Ingersoll's protégé, and has been his heir apparent for about three years. There was a certain amount of low-key friction between them earlier this year, centering on whether Ingersoll was keeping Marsh on too short a leash, but that seems to have faded away a few months back with Marsh accepting the limits set for him."

"And then came Marsh's lucky break," Sands said sourly. "Ingersoll has his fatal heart attack on an out-of-town business trip, with a doctor who doesn't know he's on Soulminder." Abruptly, she sat up a little straighter. "Unless . . . ?"

"Don't even think it," Porath warned her. "You start even *thinking* that Marsh might have committed murder here and we'll all wind up on the short end of a major defamation suit."

"Unless we can prove he actually did it," Sands countered.

"He's not stupid enough to take that kind of risk," Everly said. "Especially when there was no need for it. The handwriting was on the wall—Ingersoll had already had two heart attacks and was bucking for a third. All Marsh had to do was to bide his time and not rock the boat."

"Agreed," Porath nodded. "The police will be looking into that, but it's almost certainly just blowing smoke rings. Regardless, we need to stay totally clear of it."

"So where does that leave us?" Sommer asked.

"Like I said, walking on loose sand," Porath conceded. "The original injunction will keep Ingersoll on life-support as long as the court is mulling it over, and the follow-ups will keep Marsh away from the body—just in case he *does* intend anything," he added, nodding to Sands. "So that's one for our side. On Marsh's side is the fact that Soulminder's own position in this case is fairly ambiguous—we're not Ingersoll's next of kin or his corporate partners or his heirs, or anything else that comes in a neat legal package."

"Friend of the court?" Everly offered.

"I've already filed us in as a trustee," Porath told him. "After all, we *are* holding something in trust for him."

Sommer shivered. "Yeah. Himself."

Porath nodded, and for a second the logical legal facade seemed to bend a bit. "Yes, well . . . anyway, the judge is still considering what status to grant us."

"Can't we simply show that a Soulminder trap does indeed hold a person's lifeforce?" Sands asked Porath. "We've done, what, six successful transfers?"

"Eight, if you count Dr. Sommer and the Coleman boy," Porath said. "I've filed them as part of my petition to have the judge turn Ingersoll's body over to us, on the grounds that Soulminder is a life-saving technique and that its use wouldn't in any way violate any of his last requests. But again, the judge is under no particular obligation to consider the data, just as he might not give much weight to the overall statistics on some surgical procedure in a particular malpractice suit."

"But it's not like that," Sommer objected.

"It's not like *anything*." Porath spread his hands helplessly. "I'm sorry, Dr. Sommer, but it just isn't. We're breaking virgin legal ground here, and there just aren't any obvious precedents."

"And I'll just bet the judge is just smacking his lips over it," Sands growled. "His big chance to write trail-blazing law. Well, you called it, Adrian—the judicial branch has just officially gotten into the act."

Sommer grimaced. "Yeah. Swell."

Everly cleared his throat. "That reminds me. We've finished identifying all the assorted Spook Central infiltrators now. Any particular way you'd like to have them bounced?"

"Quick and clean and final," Sands told him. "No publicity, unless they want to squawk about it to the media themselves. And you might have them tell their respective bosses not to bother trying again."

Everly cocked an eyebrow. "That could easily be construed as a challenge," he warned.

"So let them try," Sands said grimly. "The sooner they find out we have no intention of becoming U.S. Government property, the better."

"Maybe we ought to try talking to whoever's in charge before we start waving red flags," Sommer suggested cautiously. Sands had a bad tendency to lose her sense of proportion when she latched onto something like this. "We really don't have the energy to waste on a full-scale intelligence war. We've got at least a hundred American cities and foreign capitals clamoring for Soulminder facilities, and if Frank's people have to spend all their time guarding our backs here, we may never get another adequately secure building built. Anywhere."

"And what are you going to say to them?" Sands scoffed. "Pretty please let us alone?"

"Depends on what they want," Everly told her. "If they're after Soulminder itself and aren't going to stop at anything less, then you're right, talking won't do any good. But if all they really want is to make sure a Presidential soul transfer will be secure, then we might be able to convince them that we've got things under control."

"I think it's worth a try, anyway," Sommer said. "Frank, can you get me the name and number of the man to talk to?"

"No problem."

"Good," Sommer said. "And I'll want to talk some more with

you about this later. There are some thoughts and scenarios I want to get your reaction to."

"Just let me know when you're ready."

"Then let's get back to Ingersoll," Sommer said, glancing around the table. "If the judge—"

He broke off as he saw a new and oddly intense look on Porath's face. "Murray?"

Slowly, Porath's distant gaze came back to focus. "I was just thinking . . . no. No, it's crazy."

"Everything about this is crazy," Sands said. "Come on, Porath, out with it."

Porath's fingers probed through his beard. "I was just thinking that—well, presumably the government wouldn't try to influence the judge himself. But on the other hand, they might be able to get the *type* of judge they want assigned to the case."

"And what type of judge might they want?" Sands persisted.

"A type who could be expected to rule against us," Everly said quietly.

All eyes turned to him. "Then it's *not* just a crazy idea," Porath murmured.

Everly shook his head. "If Marsh wins Ingersoll's body, you can probably say goodbye to ninety percent of our prospective clientele. No point in spending that much money when the courts won't guarantee you'll get a return on your investment. We'd either have to attract private funding somehow—and I don't know offhand what we could offer them—or else find another source of money."

Sands swore. "And there would be the United States government with a bag of cash in each hand."

"Something like that." Porath exhaled thoughtfully between his teeth. "It may be just fever-dreaming, but it would be stupid to take chances. I'll get in touch with one of the judicial watchdog committees, see if I can get a list of voting records and find judges we definitely *don't* want."

"We'll need to do more than that," Sommer said, his stomach knotting. Of all the ironies about this whole mess... "We need to get this in front of the public—put your famous floodlit-microscope theory to work, Frank. If we're lucky maybe we can scare off the trial-fixers before they get going."

"May I ask how you intend to do that?" Sands asked. "Without looking like *we're* trying to fix the trial, that is?"

"I really don't know." Sommer hesitated. "Frank, would you happen to know if Tommy Lee Harper is still in town?"

"He is," Everly said without hesitation. "He's been making a tour of Capitol Hill, trying to drum up opposition to a couple of bills that are under consideration."

"Why do you want to know?" Sands asked, a trace of suspicion in her voice.

Sommer got to his feet. It had been an exceedingly long three days, and the worst part was probably still to come. "Because," he told her, "I'm going to ask him for his help."

"I must say, Dr. Sommer," Harper said, coolly polite as he waved Sommer to a chair and closed the hotel room's door behind him, "that you were probably the last person I expected to call me this evening."

"Proves that miracles still happen," Sommer said, sinking into the chair and glancing around. It was one of the best suites in one of the most expensive hotels in Washington.

Harper must have caught the once-over. "You'll excuse the luxury, I trust," his tone a bit defensive. "The *Focus* people made all the accommodation arrangements for us, and since I'm taping another interview with the network tomorrow they went ahead and booked me for the entire week. I would have preferred something less ostentatious, myself."

"Ah." To anyone else it would probably have sounded like a rather feeble excuse. To Sommer, who'd had abundant dealings of his own with network guest liaisons, it sounded only too typical. "Yes, I've run into that mindset myself on occasion."

"I expect you have." Settling into a chair across from a coffee table patterned with stone mosaic, Harper gave Sommer a measuring look. "So. On the phone you said something about a truce. I don't know what you could possibly have in mind, but I'm willing to listen."

"I appreciate that, sir," Sommer said. "I suppose *truce* is really the wrong word, but I couldn't come up with the right one. I presume you've been following the Ingersoll flap?"

Harper's lip twisted. "Oh, yes. A man trapped helplessly in your machine. A pity it couldn't have happened a day earlier—I could have used that at the debate. The perfect example of just what's wrong with the whole Soulminder concept."

"It's not our fault Ingersoll's soul hasn't been restored to his body," Sommer said, fighting down a rush of anger. "It's Tyler Marsh and his card-house of legal technicalities that's got him stuck, not us."

Harper sighed, and some of the tension faded from his face. "I know that, Doctor." For a moment he studied Sommer's face. "In fact, I'll go so far as to say that I believe you, personally, are a decent person. That you really *believe* Soulminder can be made into a force for good. But don't you see? This is exactly the sort of twisting of good intentions that always comes about when you set up shop in a fallen world."

"So we shouldn't ever try to make anything new?" Sommer countered. "Never even *try* to create something good in the midst of all the ugliness?"

"Of course we should," Harper said. "And sometimes we succeed, despite ourselves. But a machine like Soulminder raises the stakes too high. We're not dealing with the potential for abuse that's inherent in the automobile, say, or even in the mass killing frenzies modern warfare makes possible. We're dealing with the human soul, Doctor—the *human soul*. Can't you see the terrible atrocities that could come out of your line of research?"

Sommer closed his eyes briefly. "*It's not out of bad mice or bad fleas you make demons,"* he quoted quietly, *"but out of bad archangels."*

"You and C.S. Lewis make my point for me," Harper nodded. "Soulminder is an archangel, Doctor, so far as earthly creations go. I'm very much afraid that it'll be beyond your ability to keep it from becoming a demon."

"You may be right," Sommer agreed quietly. "All the more reason for you to help me protect it."

He gave Harper a rundown of Soulminder's tenuous legal standing in the Ingersoll case, along with Porath's fears that a victory by Marsh might inevitably drive Soulminder under the protective wing of the Federal government. Harper sat silently until he'd finished, his face an unreadable mask. "An interesting bind you find yourselves in," he commented. "So what exactly do you want from me?"

"Nothing more than that you publicize the Ingersoll case," Sommer said, the knot of tension in his stomach easing fractionally. To be talking joint strategy with Soulminder's most vocal enemy . . . "I need you to keep it in the public spotlight, to make sure that the basic unfairness of what's happening doesn't get lost amid the flurry of learned discourses on law and public policy that are bound to flood the media when this gets a foothold. Above all"—he hesitated—"I need the kind of pressure from you and your followers that'll make sure the lawyers and judge don't try to drag things out."

Harper snorted. "Lest the influx of customers and their money into Soulminder drop off?"

"That's part of it, yes," Sommer said without embarrassment. "But it's as much for Ingersoll's sake as it is for ours. A trial like this, even at its speediest, could take months . . . but we've never kept anyone in a Soulminder trap for more than five weeks at a stretch. Certainly not an old man whose heart's going to need proper exercise if it's ever going to heal. Time is on Marsh's side, and I doubt he would mind losing the verdict if Ingersoll subsequently died when we tried to return him to his body."

For a long minute Harper gazed past Sommer, at the lights of the city stretching to the horizon. Then, slowly, he shook his head. "I'm sorry, Dr. Sommer," he said, "but I can't help you."

The knot in Sommer's stomach retightened. "Why not?" he asked, fighting to keep his tone polite. "You see the evil in what Marsh is doing—"

"But you ask me to support one evil to keep another from happening," Harper interrupted him. "I can't do that."

"Then you lose everything," Sommer snapped. "You think this could kill Soulminder? Is that it? Because it won't. Even if the government doesn't take us over—even if you *shot* Jessica and me tomorrow—Soulminder wouldn't die. You can't destroy a known technology, Mr. Harper. Not ours, not anyone's. Somebody, *somewhere*, will eventually reinvent it."

He stopped, embarrassed by his outburst. But oddly enough, Harper didn't seem angry. "I know all that, Dr. Sommer," he said quietly. "I know that I'm losing—*Focus's* choice of guests on our debate was a graphic illustration of just how solidly the liberal media is on your side, and they're not the least of the forces arrayed against me. But ultimately, it isn't my job to *win* against you, anyway. That decision is God's, and His alone, and I wouldn't think of dictating to Him just how He should shape the future of this world. *My* job is simply to take the stand I think right, no matter how unpopular or hopeless or even ridiculous the cause looks, and to have the courage to act on my beliefs. No matter what the consequences turn out to be."

Sommer swallowed, a wave of quiet shame coloring his frustration. "I see I've been guilty of believing the popular image of TV evangelists," he conceded, the words coming out with some difficulty. "I apologize."

Harper smiled lopsidedly. "I've gotten used to it, I'm afraid," he said. "In my experience, there are very few people—in *any* profession or ethnic group—who actually fit the caricatures others build up around them. Unfortunately, many people live their entire lives without realizing that, and those that find out differently are usually unwilling to admit their error." He stood up. "I respect you for that, Doctor, and for other things. In a way I'm almost sorry I can't help you."

"I'm sorry, too," Sommer said, getting to his feet. Harper beside him, he walked to the door . . . and there he paused. "One last thing, Reverend Harper. Do you truly believe I'm the Antichrist?"

"You, yourself? No, not really. But you may well be his unwitting forerunner. The Bible speaks of a mark on the foreheads of the Beast's followers . . . and the equipment with which you make your soul-traces *does* include a band that wraps around the forehead."

Sommer stared at him, a cold chill running up his back. For a moment he'd almost forgotten that this was a man who saw the world far differently than he himself did. "I see," he said carefully. "I'll do my best to make sure Soulminder doesn't come to that end."

A grim smile touched Harper's lips. "So," he said, "will I."

Sands was back in the lab when he returned, poring over a pile of folders in a little pool of light from her desk lamp. "How'd it go?" she asked, straightening up tiredly and running a hand through her hair.

"He isn't going to help us," Sommer told her, dropping into his own desk chair.

"Didn't think he would," she grunted. "It would ruin his image forever among the rabid faithful if he did."

"I almost wish it were that simple," Sommer shook his head. "No, I don't. It may be people like him who'll help keep us honest." He nodded toward the papers before her. "What are you working on, the local facility requests?"

"What else?" she growled. "I'm starting to feel like a millionairess sorting through marriage proposals. You wouldn't believe the tax breaks and incentives some of these cities are throwing at us. You'd think we were a major league franchise or something."

"It's nice to be wanted," Sommer murmured. "Just remember

that we don't have enough security monitors to set up more than three or four offices at a time."

"I'm not likely to forget," she countered sourly. "If it weren't for that one small bottleneck I'd have stamped every one of these things *approved* and been done with it. Speaking of security, Everly left you the name and number of the man he says is probably in charge of the Secret Service's worm squad."

Sommer craned his neck to scan his desk, located the slip of notepaper. "Douglas Grein. *Four* numbers?"

"One public, one private, home phone, and cell," Sands said. "Everly doesn't do things halfway. What are you smiling at?"

"Sorry," Sommer said. "I was just thinking how I had to practically twist your arm off to get him hired."

She snorted, but it was a self-deprecating sound. "Yeah. Well, none of us is right all the time. I'm glad it was my turn to be wrong on him."

Sommer looked down at the paper with Douglas Grein's name on it, the brief flicker of cheer already fading from his mind. "Maybe we were both wrong. Maybe it's a waste of time and effort to try and keep Soulminder to ourselves."

Sands peered hard at him. "This is a rotten time to be thinking about throwing in the towel, Adrian," she said. "You show any hesitation and they'll eat us alive. Hang in there—we're going to win this."

"Maybe," he said. "Harper would say that winning wasn't the most important thing."

"Then Harper's a bigger fool than I thought," Sands said coldly. "Or else knows damn well he's going to lose."

Sommer didn't answer. Yes, Harper knew he was going to lose—he'd as much as admitted it tonight.

And yet, that knowledge didn't seem to matter in the least to his determination to keep fighting. *My job is to take the stand I think right*, he'd said, and that had somehow been enough for him. Vaguely, Sommer wondered if he himself would have the courage to fight that way for his convictions.

Or had he already had the opportunity . . . and failed?

It was a question that had bothered him greatly during Soulminder's first months, one which the recent crises had allowed him to push to the back of his mind. But now it came roaring back to life, like a pile of burning leaves stirred with a stick.

Because what he was fighting for here was *Sands's* vision of Soulminder, not his.

He hadn't originally wanted Soulminder to remain a dark and private secret. Had never really agreed that a monolithic corporation would necessarily be the best way to use their invention to save people from unnecessary death. Had certainly never believed that Sands's single-minded quest for human immortality was a proper goal for such a corporation in the first place.

So what had happened? Had he been convinced otherwise? Or had he merely conformed his thoughts to hers?

What *was* he fighting for, anyway?

His eyes drifted around the room . . . and came to rest on the lab table to Sands's right, where her latest trap design was lying scattered about in a dozen pieces like a dissected electronic frog. The Soulminder trap. The heart of their whole technique—the device that actually held a person's soul in safety while his or her body was being repaired. From which the soul could be restored when the process was complete.

And *that* was what he was supposed to be fighting for. Not security, not legal rights, not even Soulminder itself.

He was supposed to be fighting for life.

My job is to take the stand I think right, no matter what the consequences might be . . .

"Has Frank gone home yet?" he asked Sands.

She was still looking at him, he discovered, as he focused again on her. "No, I think he's in his office doing paperwork," she said, her face and voice both frowning. "Why?"

"I need his help," he told her, scooping up his phone and punching Everly's number. "I'm going to show Harper that we can play the game the same way he does."

"I like it already," Sands said, a slightly grim smile on her face.

No, you don't, Sommer thought to himself. But he remained silent. There would be time enough to tell Sands later what he really had in mind.

What he had in mind, and how much it might cost.

There was a man outside the room, of course, lounging in a padded chair that had clearly been swiped from the waiting/visiting area down the hall. Arms folded across his stomach, chin resting on his chest, and legs extended and crossed at the ankles, he looked for all the world like a man whose response to graveyard-shift guard duty had been to fall asleep and hope nothing happened. Sommer kept his eyes on the man's face as he walked quietly toward him, an unreasonable hope simmering within him. If the man was, indeed, asleep . . .

He got to within five yards, and the head came smoothly up, eyes focusing and then widening slightly with recognition. "Dr. Sommer, right?" he asked.

"That's right," Sommer confirmed, getting another couple of steps closer before stopping.

"Nice to meet you," the guard said. His voice was pleasant enough, but there was a note of wariness in his face as he glanced at his watch. "Three in the morning. You keep strange hours, if you don't mind my saying so." Reaching down to the floor on the far side of his chair, he picked up a gently steaming coffee cup and took a sip.

"One of the prices of fame," Sommer told him. "How's he doing?"

The guard shrugged; as he did, Sommer's peripheral vision picked up a man in hospital whites pushing a heavily laden equipment cart into view around a corner and start toward them. "He's okay, as far as I know," the guard said, replacing the cup on the floor. "'Course, they don't exactly keep me up to date on these things."

"Me, neither. Unfortunately." The intern and his cart were getting closer, now, the sounds of the wheels just becoming audible. "I don't suppose you could let me take a look for myself."

"Sorry, Dr. Sommer," the guard said. He sent a brief glance at the approaching cart, then turned back to Sommer. "Judge Billings's order was very clear: none of the principals are allowed access to Mr. Ingersoll's body until the case is over."

"I wouldn't have to get anywhere near Ingersoll himself," Sommer said. The cart was almost abreast of them now. The intern's right hand briefly left its grip on the push bar—

And then he was past Sommer, continuing down the corridor behind him. "I could see the instrument readouts from the door, and you'd be beside me the whole time."

"Sorry, Doctor, but the answer's no," the guard repeated, his voice beginning to harden. "Look, I let you past that door and my butt is lunchmeat—pardon my language."

Sommer felt his stomach tighten. "I understand," he said. "I just wish—well, never mind. Sorry to have bothered you."

"That's all right," the other said, his tone softening again as he realized Sommer wasn't gearing up for a major argument. "The judge is the guy you have to talk to if you want to get in."

"Yeah. Thanks. Well . . . good-night."

"Good-night," the other said, reaching again for his coffee cup.

Feeling the guard's eyes on the back of his neck, Sommer headed back down the hall, turning at the cross corridor leading to the elevators.

Everly and his equipment cart were waiting for him just around the corner. "You do it?" Sommer asked, heart thudding in his chest.

Everly nodded. "No problem. I used to bull's-eye cups smaller than that one, and from further away. The pellet dissolves practically instantly, of course."

"Of course." Sommer took a deep breath. They were committed now. Totally. "How long before he's asleep?"

"A man that size?" Everly squinted thoughtfully into space. "Half an hour. Maybe less."

"All right." Dropping his gaze to the cart Everly had been pushing, Sommer did a quick scan of the portable life-support gear piled there. If any of it turned out to be defective . . .

My job is to take the stand I think right . . . "Let's find a safe place to wait," he told Everly, fighting to keep his voice from trembling. "I'd hate to get caught now."

"Right," Everly said, his own voice glacially calm. "There's an empty storage closet down this way. While we wait, maybe we can have that conversation you mentioned earlier."

Sommer nodded, his stomach achingly tight as he followed Everly down the corridor. *No matter what the consequences might be.*

The guard fell asleep on schedule and later awoke without, apparently, attaching any significance to his nap. With Sommer's gimmicking of the monitors, the theft of Ingersoll's body remained undiscovered until the shift change at six o'clock. Ten minutes after that, the police were on their way to the Soulminder building, arriving just in time for the news conference.

Wilson Anders Ingersoll, it turned out, was an excellent speaker.

"Just don't think you're out of the woods yet," Porath warned Sommer, not waggling a finger at his employer but looking very much like he wanted to. "Billings can be a really vindictive sort, and he could very well slap you down for this."

"Slap us down for what?" Everly asked with a shrug. "Kidnapping? Body snatching? Theft of evidence?"

Porath made a face. "Well, yes, this *does* sort of fall through the cracks in the law," he conceded. "He *could* still nail you with contempt charges, though."

"He won't," Sands said, shaking her head. "Judges are just

as subject to public opinion as anyone else. He wouldn't dare throw Soulminder's figurehead into jail, certainly not for cutting through legal red tape to save a man's life. I presume that's why you went there yourself, Adrian, instead of just sending Everly?"

"More or less," Sommer nodded, going with the simple answer. Sands probably wouldn't understand Harper's philosophy that a person should accept direct and personal responsibility for his actions.

"Just remember that we really didn't gain anything but some time with this," Porath said, clearly determined to be gloomy. "Soulminder's still in legal limbo, and eventually someone else will bring a court challenge."

Sommer shook his head. "I doubt it. Long before anyone else has the nerve to try another end run around us our status will have been properly defined. Congress and the states were caught napping, but they're scrambling to write laws that'll cover us."

Porath made a face. "That'll take months. A new lawsuit could be filed tomorrow."

Everly stirred in his chair. "No. Ingersoll will be done with his checkup by this afternoon."

Porath frowned. "That wasn't nearly as clear as you probably thought it was."

"I talked to Ingersoll for a minute after the press conference this morning, while Dr. Sommer was shooing out the reporters," Everly explained. "He told me that as soon as he can get hold of his lawyer he's going to have an attempted murder charge filed against Marsh."

Sands's eyebrows went up. "You mean Marsh was responsible for that heart attack after all?"

"Oh, I doubt that. But he *was* responsible for trying to destroy Ingersoll's body while his soul was locked up here, and there's a fair chance he was the one who made sure the hold-and-suspend protocol paperwork never got filed. Add those together, and you're awfully close to attempted murder."

Porath whistled tunelessly between his teeth. "It'll never stick," he said thoughtfully. "But you're right, it ought to scare the vultures away long enough for the legislatures to get moving."

Beside Sommer, the intercom buzzed. "Yes?" he called toward it.

"Dr. Sommer, there's a Mr. Douglas Grein on the phone for you," Rita announced.

Sands sat up straighter. "Grein? The Secret Service man?"

"I called him this morning," Sommer told her. "Told him we needed to talk. Rita, go ahead and send that press release out on the wire now."

"Press release?" Sands asked suspiciously. "Adrian, what are you up to?"

"You'll find out in a minute." Bracing himself, Sommer keyed for speakerphone and punched the button. This was it. "Mr. Grein, this is Dr. Sommer," he said. "Thank you for returning my call."

"I've been looking forward to talking with you, Doctor," the other said. His voice was gentle and cultured, but there was steel beneath it.

"So have I. Let's get right to the point, shall we? You're trying very hard, on behalf of the Federal government, to steal Soulminder's secrets out from under us. I'd like to know why."

There was a slight pause. "I would, of course, deny any such allegations in court," Grein said. "However, between us and whoever you've got listening in, I can tell you that we simply can't leave the possible future safety of the President and other top people in non-government hands."

"And you think you'd have better security if the Secret Service or CIA or Marines were running it?"

"That *is* a reasonable assumption, yes," Grein said dryly, "given the government's vastly superior facilities. You obviously disagree."

"Obviously," Sommer said. He glanced at Everly, got a nod and a silent thumbs-up. "And I'll show you why. Consider the following scenario: you've broken into our technology and have

Soulminder units of your own. The Mullner soul-traces of all government people are recorded in your own files, and you have your own traps and equipment in the White House basement. Now: what happens if the President is shot?"

"We get him to the White House basement, of course."

Sommer shook his head. "Wrong. Because the minute you have Soulminder everyone else has it, too. That's the flip side of your superior facilities: with that many people on the payroll you have no way on earth to keep it totally clean of spies and traitors. And one properly placed spy would be all it would take. Six months after you have Soulminder traps, so do Iran, China, and possibly even the North Koreans.

"Now suppose they also get hold of a pirated copy of the President's Mullner trace?"

He paused, but Grein didn't speak. "You see what that means, I trust," Sommer continued. "If the President is shot under those circumstances you will literally have no idea whatsoever where his soul is. He'll have been kidnapped, right from under your noses, and there won't be a single way you can protect him against it. Is that *really* the situation you want, Mr. Grein?"

From the phone came a hiss: Grein taking a thoughtful breath. "There are ways to safeguard the data."

"Yes, there are," Sommer agreed. "And the simplest *and* safest is for you to leave the secrets of Soulminder right where they are: here, with us. To leave them here, and to cooperate with our security people instead of fighting them. Oh, and there's one other thing you should know. As of three minutes ago Soulminder has gone international. We've accepted the Swiss government's request to build a facility in Geneva."

Across the room, Sands's mouth fell open. "We've *what*?" she breathed.

"That means any attempt by the U.S. government to take us over will become an international incident," Sommer continued, ignoring her.

"It also means ample opportunity for someone else to steal your precious technology," Grein retorted.

"Not if you work with our people in creating security for the new building," Sommer reminded him.

There was a long pause. "Even if you were right about all that," Grein said at last, his voice stiff but cautious, "we still couldn't allow you to handle the soul-tracings and transfers of the President and other sensitive people."

Quietly, Sommer let out a breath he hadn't realized he was holding. "You won't have to," he told the other. "We can designate one wing of our new facility for private government use. You can staff it with military doctors and Secret Service personnel and anyone else you want."

"An interesting proposal," Grein said after another short pause. "I'd need to discuss it with certain other parties, of course."

"I understand," Sommer agreed. "Just be sure and impress on them that anything but the current status quo will cost you considerable time and energy . . . and in the end will leave you far less secure than you are right now."

"Good-bye, Dr. Sommer," Grein said politely. With a click, the line went dead.

"He doesn't like it," Porath commented as Sommer also hung up. "Not a bit."

"But he'll go along with it," Everly said quietly. "The thought of foreign access to Mullner-trace files should ensure that. For now, anyway."

"Geneva, huh?" Sands said, turning arched eyebrows to Sommer.

"You disapprove?" he asked mildly.

She snorted. "Not really. It would have been nice if you'd told me, that's all."

"Especially since major judgment calls aren't a proper part of a figurehead's role?" he suggested.

She had the grace to blush. "I didn't mean it that way, Adrian," she said. "I just meant that you were the public image of Soulminder, that's all."

"I understand," Sommer said. But she had caught the message, all right. He could see that in her eyes. No longer would he be content to sit back and smile for the cameras and let her single-handedly run the whole show.

Which was as it should be. And should have been from the very beginning.

CHAPTER 3

●

Justice Machine

FOR A LONG TIME—LONGER than he thought he had any business being there—he floated in the middle of the long tunnel. Around him all was gray. Behind him, the gray turned to black; ahead of him, far down the tunnel, was the Light.

He tried not to look at the Light. It bothered him, the way the Light seemed to see right through him, right down to the middle of his mind. It bothered him a hell of a lot worse the way the damn thing made him start thinking about the way he'd lived his life.

But that was okay. He'd spent that life fighting everything that got in his way, or whoever didn't like the way he did things. Eighty-four years' worth of fights, everything and everyone from street hoods right up to big-shot Federal prosecutors. One friggin' hell of a lot of fights, and he'd won every damn one of them.

Every one that mattered, anyway. And he'd damn friggin' well win this one, too.

Besides, fighting back against the damn Light and the damn friggin' way it was trying to make him feel about himself was something to do. Something besides wondering if he'd been double-crossed.

And finally, he started to move again. Not toward the Light, but back along the tunnel away from it. So Digger hadn't double-crossed him, after all, and the damn Light was out of luck. Maybe forever. He sent the Light one last nasty smile—

And gasped as sensation suddenly flooded back in on him.

"Digger!" he managed to get out. The room was spinning around, everything blurry. He squeezed his eyes shut, shivering as his whole body felt like it was burning up with a cold fire—

"Right here, Mr. Cavanaugh," the familiar voice came. Familiar, but like his eyesight, there was something friggin' strange about it. "Hang on—the doc's gonna give you something."

He felt the stab of a needle somewhere on his arm. Clenching his teeth together, he waited.

A minute later the room seemed to settle down. Carefully, he opened his eyes again. Things were still blurry, but the double images were starting to disappear. He could see now that Digger was standing over him, the lined face pretty worried. Turning his head, he searched out the doctor on the other side of the table. "Well, Emerson?" he demanded.

The doctor shrugged. "Naturally, I can't be one hundred percent sure—I warned you about that going in, if you'll remember—"

"Forget the goddamn friggin' warnings." The words felt funny in his mouth, almost like it was the first time he'd ever sworn. "Cut the crap. Is this gonna take, or isn't it?"

"I can't tell for sure, Mr. Cavanaugh," Emerson repeated. "Try to remember that you're pushing Soulminder's known limits—"

"The boss asked you a question," Digger cut him off.

The doctor grimaced theatrically. "If all the side effects are gone within twelve hours," he said, "and they stay away for at least a week, I'd say it worked. Of course"—he nodded his head back behind him—"even if something goes wrong, you're not in any danger. Your Mullner trace is still on file, and I've set the readouts to alert me if you come back in."

Come back in, he said. *Die*, he meant. If Cavanaugh died and went back into Soulminder . . . where the Light would be waiting. "Thanks, but I'll pass." With an effort, he swung his legs over the edge of the table, feeling Digger grab his arm as he did so. His whole body still felt funny, but not as bad as it'd been a minute ago. He pulled himself up into a sitting position . . . and found himself staring at his hand.

His hand. A real, flesh-and-blood hand. After being a loose spirit rattling around Soulminder, he couldn't believe how good it was to be alive again.

Alive for now. Maybe alive forever.

The steady drizzle that had ruined most of the weekend had finally gotten a grip on itself and become a full-fledged rainstorm, hammering at the triple-glazed, security-wired windows with drops that sounded like small hailstones. Glowering out at the soaked Washington scenery and the uniformly gray sky beyond it, Adrian Sommer tried to remember the last time he'd seen the sun. "I hate living in Washington," he growled.

"You don't live in Washington," Jessica Sands corrected absently from her desk across the room. "You work in Washington. You live out in Chevy Chase. There's a big difference."

"To whom?" he retorted.

"To everyone else in Chevy Chase, I presume." She shrugged. "You finished looking over the New Orleans progress report?"

"As finished as I intend to be," Sommer told her. "Looks like the office will be ready to go just about the time the annual August steam bath rolls in. Naturally, you're going to want me to go down there for the christening?"

She looked up at him, a patient look on her face. "Do we have to go through this every time a new Soulminder facility opens up? As long as you're the one the TV cameras are crazy to focus on, we haven't got any choice in the matter. Steady profits or not, Soulminder is still dependent on favorable publicity—and I, for one, would hate to have come this far and then lose everything we've built."

Or everything you've *built*, he corrected her silently. Co-creator of the Soulminder miracle and—on paper, anyway—the director of the entire corporation, Sommer had long since noticed that, once again, more and more of his time was being taken up by public relations froth instead of real policy work.

Not that his policy opinions had ever much mattered. It was Sands, not him, who had the shining-bright vision of what it was she wanted from Soulminder; Sands, not him, who had proven to have the skill and the drive to bend the corporation in the direction she wanted it to go.

Sands, not him, who desperately wanted to live forever.

"You make it sound like the opening of a new Soulminder facility is front-page news these days," he grumbled.

"It is to the city involved." She peered across the room at him. "What are you so surly about today, anyway? Just because Barnswell wants to use us for target practice again?"

He snorted. "What's this *us*, paleface? *I'm* the one who has to sit at these stupid hearings and act polite."

Her face softened a little. "I know, Adrian, and I'm sorry. Just remember that every time he acts like the bigoted idiot he is, he alienates his colleagues just that much more. And with every single one of them on file here . . . " She shrugged.

"They're starting to take attacks on Soulminder personally," Sommer said. "Yes, I know. I'm not sure I like *that* trend, either. Unanimous praise for *anything* makes me nervous."

"I'm sure Barnswell's crowd will do their best to keep the praises from being sung *too* loudly," she said dryly.

"I'm sure they will."

For a moment the room was silent, as Sands went back to

whatever she was working on and Sommer skimmed through the comprehensive schedule for the day's work—not just his own list of activities, but every meeting, test, or upgrade that anyone in Soulminder had planned.

He was only about halfway through when the intercom buzzed. "Dr. Sommer, the Capitol just called," Rita reported from the outer office. "The limo will be here in fifteen minutes."

"Thank you," Sommer said. An item on the schedule caught his eye; punching keys, he called up the full file. The list of names . . . "I'll be waiting at the security entrance," he added to Rita. Flipping the intercom off, he got to his feet and scooped up his briefcase. "If you need me I'll be down in the parameter test lab," he told Sands as he headed for the door.

"Now?" she called after him. "Adrian—"

"Don't worry, I won't keep the Congressmen waiting," he called over his shoulder.

Even after a solid four years in operation, there was still a great deal no one knew about Soulminder.

Its ultimate range, for one thing: how far a dying person could stray from the computer/trap arrangement that held his Mullner soul-trace on file and still be safely captured. Or what was rather vaguely called the timeline question: how often a person needed to update his Mullner trace to ensure that the trap could successfully recognize and lock onto his soul.

There were theoretical models that could hint at the answers. Unfortunately, the only way to know for sure was to experiment . . . and since by necessity such experiments would eventually lead to death, it followed that those being experimented on needed to be expendable.

The pool was, unfortunately, a large one.

Six of them were waiting quietly in a row of chairs along the wall just inside the lab complex, their handcuffs glinting in the bright lights. The one on the end— "Hello, Willie."

"Well, hi, Dr. Sommer," the thin young man said, a touch of surprise in his face and voice. "How you doin'?"

"I'm fine," Sommer told him. "What are you doing here?"

Willie blinked. "I'm helpin' out, 'course. Like always."

"Yes, but—" Sommer broke off as a familiar face came around a corner. "Tom, come over here a minute, will you?"

"Dr. Sommer," Dr. Thomas Dumata nodded, looking as surprised to see Sommer as Willie had. "I thought I saw you listed for a stint on Capitol Hill today."

"What's this man doing here?" Sommer demanded, pointing at Willie.

Dumata glanced at Willie. "He's part of a mid-range timeline experiment," he said guardedly.

"And how many times has he been run through Soulminder?"

"Ah . . . I'd have to look that up—"

"I'll save you the trouble: the answer is five. He's died and been transferred back five times. So I'll ask you again: what's he doing here?"

"Dr. Sommer—?"

"Quiet, Willie. Well?"

"Dr. Sands gave the timeline studies an exemption from the standard policy," Dumata said reluctantly. "It seemed to make more sense to keep going with the same individuals than to start new batches all the time and have to fiddle with the intervals we're using."

With an effort, Sommer held onto his temper. "And are you aware that the ACLU is running a major court challenge against these tests at the moment?"

"They're all volunteers—"

"Who signed up for five tests each. *Five.* Not ten or twenty or thirty."

"I understand, Dr. Sommer. But—"

"But nothing. Come on, Tom, we barely got this protocol through by the skin of our teeth as it was. All we need is for people to find out you've got prisoners signing blank checks as to how we use their bodies and souls."

"Prisoners have the legal right to volunteer for risky scientific experiments," Dumata said doggedly. "If they insist on doing so more than five times, the ACLU can complain to *them* about it." He gestured toward the line of prisoners. "Go ahead—ask him if we twisted his arm."

Frowning, Sommer turned back to the line of prisoners. "Willie?"

"I 'preciate what you're tryin' to say, Dr. Sommer," Willie said. "But, really, I want t' do this. I gotta"—he shrugged—"lotta stuff to make up for 'fore I die. I mean, die for real."

Sommer stared at him. He'd seen Willie when he first came to Soulminder. Remembered what he'd been like. "What sort of stuff is that, Willie?" he asked.

Willie grinned, self-consciously. "Come on, Dr. Sommer— you know what I did. Shot down those four people for nothin'." The smile disappeared. "I wish I could do somethin' for 'em. Somethin' t' make up for it. But I can't. So"—he gestured with his manacled hands—"I come here."

Sommer looked at Dumata, then back at Willie. "You've certainly changed, Willie," was all he could think of to say.

The dark eyes looked back at him steadily. "You don't look at that Light in there without it makin' some changes in how you see things."

A gentle chill ran up Sommer's back. He remembered the Light, too. "No," he agreed soberly. "You don't."

"Dr. Sommer?" the lab's receptionist called. "Security says your limo is here."

Sommer took a deep breath. "All right. But I'll be having a talk with Dr. Sands about this, Tom." He turned to Willie. "Good-bye, Willie. And . . . thanks."

Turning, he hurried out of the lab wing and down the hall toward the security entrance. As Sands had warned, the Congressmen wouldn't be pleased if he were late, and with the rain outside the trip was likely to take longer than usual.

He rather hoped it would. He had a lot to think about.

The hearing went about the way Sommer had expected it to: powder-puff questions from most of the committee, hardball ones from Congressman Barnswell. No big surprises, no real substance, and most of it territory that they'd already gone over before.

Until the very end.

"Now, there's just one more thing, Dr. Sommer," Barnswell said, his almost lazy tone contrasting sharply with the glint in his eye. "You've stated several times before in front of this committee that your people have got safeguards all over your fancy Soulminder equipment—in fact, I believe you once said that there was no way at all that anyone could abuse or manipulate Soulminder for illegal purposes. You remember saying all that?"

A quiet alarm bell went off in the back of Sommer's mind. "Of course, no security system's completely airtight, Congressman," he said cautiously. "On the other hand, I think we can claim to have arguably the best arrangement anywhere in the country."

"Uh-huh," Barnswell grunted, his voice abruptly turning icy. "Then maybe you'll tell me, Dr. Sommer, how it is that less than twelve hours ago a man wanted by the FBI—wanted very badly, I might add—managed to die, get locked up in your Soulminder traps, *and* get put back into his body without your fancy security system blowing the whistle on him.

"You want to tell me how that could happen, Dr. Sommer?"

He reached the office, still seething, to find that Sands had a visitor.

"Adrian—good, you're back," she said, relief evident in her voice. "This is Special Agent Peter Royce from the FBI."

Sommer nodded briefly to Royce. "I don't suppose there are any prizes for guessing why you're here."

"Not really." Royce looked at least as annoyed as Sommer felt. "I gather you've heard all about Cavanaugh's little sleight-of-hand trick last night?"

"I had the high points thrown in my face, yes," Sommer told him sourly. "None of the details. I wonder how the hell Barnswell found out. Operational details like that are supposed to be strictly confidential."

"In this case, it's probably just as well someone leaked it," Royce pointed out. "You know anything about Mario Cavanaugh?"

"Barnswell said he was the head of one of the East Coast's biggest independent mobs. Nothing more."

"Semi-retired head," Royce corrected him. "Eighty-four years old, in poor health. And, at the moment, in deep hiding."

"From you or his own people?"

"Possibly both. We've finally gotten something solid we can nail him to the wall with, but given the choice we'd rather peel the skin off his organization. He knows it, they know it; hence, the vanishing act."

"So how does Soulminder figure in?"

"Cavanaugh was one of the first people to sign up when we got the office going," Sands interjected. "When the indictments came through our flags picked up on his name, and the FBI directed us to set up a red light in the event the file was ever accessed."

"So why didn't it trigger?"

"For the simple reason," Royce said heavily, "that Cavanaugh didn't get reborn here. He did it out in Seattle."

Sommer stared at him. "In *Seattle*?" He looked at Sands. "He had *two* traces on file?"

"You got it," Sands sighed. "The Seattle one under a false ID. Somehow, the background profile check missed that."

Sommer shook his head, a shiver running up his back. "That was one hell of a risk for him to take," he murmured.

"What, that you wouldn't spot the duplicate?" Royce asked, frowning.

"That having two functioning traps trying to grab him at the same time wouldn't do something terrible to his soul."

Royce's lip twitched. "I never thought of that," he admitted. "I assumed that the one nearest him would automatically do the grabbing."

"Obviously, it did," Sommer said. "But we've never done that experiment ourselves with either of the last two generations of trap design. He could have wound up with his soul ripped in two."

Royce hissed between his teeth. "That sounds like Cavanaugh. He always was the type to take big gambles."

With an effort, Sommer shook the image of a bisected soul from his mind. "So what can we do?"

Royce nodded at the computer terminal behind Sands. "It occurred to us that if Cavanaugh managed to get himself on file in two places, there's no particular reason he can't be on file in every one of your offices. Might be locking the door after the car's been stolen, but then, it might not."

Sommer looked at Sands. "I hope you're doing more than just checking names."

"Don't worry, we're doing it right this time," she said grimly. "We're comparing Cavanaugh's Mullner trace with every single one we've got on file."

Sommer felt his eyes goggle. "You and whose nested super-computer?"

"The NSA's," she said, sounding distinctly unhappy about it. "They generously lent us some of their spare capacity."

Sommer swallowed. "I see." The thought of a hundred thousand confidential soul-traces being sifted through a government computer . . .

On the other hand, Sands was far more paranoid about the possibility of government encroachment than he was. The fact that she was going along with this meant either she'd decided there simply wasn't enough worthwhile data to be gleaned from the traces—which was certainly true—or else she'd already argued the point with Royce and lost. Either way, probably a good topic to steer clear of. "We have anyone talking with the Seattle office directly?" he asked Sands instead.

"Everly's been burning up the line to them for the past half hour. He's ready to go out there in person if it seems useful."

"Good. Well, then—"

The phone beside Sands trilled. Snorting under her breath, she snatched up the handset. "This better be important," she warned.

And as Sommer watched, the lines around her eyes tightened. "Damn," she breathed.

"What?" Royce demanded.

She shook her head briefly, shifting the phone to speaker. "How long since the trap was triggered?" she asked.

"Almost twelve hours," the monitor's voice came from the speaker. Sommer could hear a slight tremor beneath the words. "His name's Jonathan Pauley, twenty-six years old, from Bethesda. I've just finished checking with all the area hospitals and morgues—nothing."

"What is it?" Royce murmured.

"One of our clients has triggered a trap," Sommer told him grimly, "except we don't know where his body is."

Royce swore gently under his breath. "And it happened twelve *hours* ago?"

"It's not necessarily that bad," Sands told him. "A lot of hospitals keep terminal patients on life-support and neuropreservatives even if they're not wearing Soulminder bracelets. Just in case. Have you alerted security, Hammond?"

"Yes, Doctor. They've got some people doing a backtrack on him."

"All right. Keep us informed."

Sands keyed off the phone, and Sommer could see her brace herself as she looked up at Royce again. "There's a good chance they'll find him," she said. "This has happened before."

"Ever lost one?" Royce asked bluntly. "Accident, or suicide?"

Sands didn't flinch. "Not because we lost the body. There've been a few accidents where there was too much damage for the doctors to do anything, but that doesn't really count."

"At least, we weren't blamed," Sommer murmured.

"Which is as it should be," Sands said. "We've had a few close calls—accidents in out-of-the-way places. Luckily, we were able to get to all of them in time. As to suicides, right now the service is expensive enough that potential suicides don't typically sign up."

"I'm sure we'll lose someone eventually," Sommer said. "The rate we're growing, it's pretty much inevitable."

"Well, you'd better hope it's not today," Royce said. "All you need is something like that on top of the Cavanaugh fiasco."

Sands drew herself up in her chair. "Pardon me, Special Agent Royce, but I hardly think we can claim full credit for the Cavanaugh mess. We set up our computer red light precisely the way *your* people told us to."

"The media may not notice the distinction," Royce pointed out.

"You're going to release it?" Sommer asked him. "I'd think it would be to your advantage to let Cavanaugh think he's still flying under everyone's radar."

"I agree," Royce said with a grunt. "But that decision's pretty well out of both our courts. Even granted that Congressman Barnswell has excellent information sources, if *he* knows, the blogs can't be far behind. Still"—he added, levering himself out of his chair—"the media *does* have a history of being gentle on you people. You've got my number, Dr. Sands—keep me informed."

He left, and for a moment Sommer and Sands just looked at each other. "They won't be nearly so gentle," Sommer said at last, "if it turns out we've lost a client."

"No," Sands agreed soberly. "They won't."

There was nothing about it on the midday news, not even a hint in the afternoon web updates, and by the time six o'clock rolled around Cavanaugh was starting to get more than a little edgy.

Brilliant and gutsy though his plan might have been, it was pushing things way too far to think it had been *so* surreptitious as to sail totally past Soulminder's notice.

Unfortunately, the only other options were either that he'd become so important that the government had slapped a secrecy lid on the whole thing, or else that he'd become so *un*important that they didn't even care anymore what he did. Neither alternative was especially pleasing.

But then came the evening news . . . and life was back on a reasonable footing again.

It was a short report, hardly more than a minute long, but in that brief time they managed to hit the high points. The notorious criminal Mario Cavanaugh had managed to escape death, thanks to Soulminder, and then disappear before anyone thought to notify the authorities. The FBI wouldn't speculate as to his whereabouts, but there were suggestions that an old man who had gone through Soulminder once was highly likely to do so again, and the next time they would be waiting.

The news turned to the start of the baseball season, and Cavanaugh clicked off the set with a grunt of satisfaction. He'd pulled it off, and the Feds were both furious and helpless. All in all, better than he'd dared to hope.

And yet . . .

Sipping at his beer, Cavanaugh frowned unseeingly at the blank TV screen. For just a minute, there, the satisfaction had been tinged with something else. Something he hadn't felt in over fifty years. Something that had felt disturbingly like guilt.

He scowled. It was the Light, he told himself firmly. The damn Light he'd seen while he was stuck in Soulminder. That was all it was, just some crazy hangover from that crazy ride. A few days, and it would be gone.

It was nearly ten o'clock, and Sommer had just decided to give up for the night, when the long-awaited knock came on the door. "Come in," he called, pushing the lock release.

It was Everly. "Dr. Sommer," he nodded in greeting, walking into the office with his usual easy grace. "The telltale board said you were still here, and I thought you might want to hear this."

"You've got some news about Jonathan Pauley?" Sommer asked hopefully.

Everly's lip twisted. "News, yes. Good news, no. We still haven't had any luck locating his body. And I'd say chances are good we never will."

"Why not?"

"There are still some leads we have to run down," Everly said. "But at the moment it looks like Pauley disappeared nearly three days before he showed up in Soulminder."

Sommer felt his stomach tighten. "What do you mean? Disappeared how?"

"All we know is that he didn't come into his office on Friday and that they tried all day to get hold of him. His mail for Friday, Saturday, and Monday hadn't been picked up, and his neighbors haven't seen him since Thursday night. No Internet use, either. Could be he decided to go on a quick vacation and got in trouble."

"Or maybe he was kidnapped?" Sommer asked.

"There's been no ransom note. Besides, he wasn't exactly the classic kidnap profile." He pulled out a well-worn notebook, found the right page. "He'd been a realtor for the past five years—good one, too; got his picture in the paper about a month ago for racking up the highest sales numbers in the D.C. area. Not exactly rolling in money, though. He was a good solid Catholic—went to Mass at least twice a week, his priest told us, and was involved with a lot of their other activities."

"Hardly the type to be involved in shady activities," Sommer commented.

"Not even close," Everly agreed. "Unmarried, parents living comfortably but without extra cash on hand; ditto for one brother and two sisters. And that's about it for now." He offered Sommer the notebook.

"I wish you wouldn't keep talking about him in the past

tense," Sommer growled, glancing over the notes. In his mind's eye he saw Pauley's battered body lying off the road in a ravine somewhere . . . "We have *got* to get that satellite system going," he muttered. "Running the heartbeat screamer through the cell network still loses us too much territory."

"Oh, that's the other thing," Everly said with a grimace. "His officemates said he usually didn't bother to wear his bracelet. Thought it looked too elite and upper-class-snobby. The only reason he was on Soulminder at all was that his company bought slots for all their top salespeople. Sort of a bonus."

Sommer tossed the notebook back onto the desk. "That probably finishes it, then."

Everly nodded. "Yeah. Well . . . we'll check his finances and all that—see if he might have had some reason to pick up and run. But I'm not expecting anything to turn up. He sounds like the original model citizen." He slid the notebook back into his pocket. "A shame we can't talk to people while they're in the traps. We could ask *him* where his body is."

"Tom Dumata's been working on that since about ten minutes after he joined us," Sommer said. "So far he hasn't made even a dent in it." Thoughts of Dumata sparked a memory of the morning— "Incidentally, Frank, as long as I've got you here . . . have you noticed any changes in the death-row prisoners we've been using for our distance and timeline experiments?"

Everly's forehead creased slightly. "Afraid you'll have to lead the witness, Doctor."

Sommer pursed his lips. "I talked to one of them this morning—Willie Kern—and I was struck by how much calmer and more polite he was than the first time he came through here. It started me wondering if the experience of going through Soulminder might have some overall rehabilitating effect."

"Um," Everly grunted. "Cute idea. You're talking about the tunnel-and-Light routine, I suppose?"

Sommer shrugged, not entirely comfortably. "It's not an experience you can just toss off."

"So I hear." Everly pursed his lips. "I can't say I've noticed any massive repentance going on, but then I don't see as much of them as the line guards and test people do. I'll have someone ask around, see if anyone else has noticed it."

"When you get around to it," Sommer told him. "It's not exactly top priority at the moment."

"Yeah." Everly hesitated. "What are you going to do about Mr. Pauley?"

Sommer sighed, their earlier conversation with Special Agent Royce flashing back to mind. *Inevitable . . .* "We'll hold him as long as there's even a chance of finding his body in usable state. If we don't, we'll have no choice but to release him."

"What about the media? You going to try and keep it quiet?"

Sommer thought about Sands and her ambitions for Soulminder. About her fierce opposition to anything that reflected badly on the corporation. "Again, we have no choice," he said. "If we don't release it, it'll look like a cover-up."

"I suppose." Everly got to his feet. "Well, I'm off for the night. You might want to go home, too."

"I will soon. Incidentally, do you have a copy of that newspaper article on Jonathan Pauley that you mentioned?"

"Yeah, we've got one downstairs. You want it?"

Sommer nodded. "I'd like to know as much about him as possible. It might be helpful when we release the story to the media."

Everly's eyes bored into his face for a moment. "Okay," he said. "Just be careful not to get too involved with the guy. When you can't do anything to help, all it does is tear up your gut. Take it from one who knows."

"I'll be careful," Sommer said, trying for a smile. "Goodnight."

Everly left. Alone again, Sommer found his eyes drifting to the window, and the street-lit Washington skyline beyond. For decades now, he thought morosely, physicians had had to deal with the problem of when and how to pull the life-support plug on hopelessly terminal patients. Now, barely four years after its creation, Soulminder was going to have to do the same.

Sommer's hope had been that his creation would be a way to prevent needless deaths. Sometimes, no matter how much everyone tried, death happened anyway.

With an effort, he focused again on the papers facing him on his desk. It wouldn't take more than another hour or so, he estimated, to clear this stack out of the way. Might as well do it now as put it off until morning.

Besides which, there really wasn't any point in going home yet. With the image of Jonathan Pauley's uselessly trapped soul hovering like a ghost before his eyes, sleep was at least another hour away. Possibly longer.

With a tired sigh, he got back to work.

"I was just about to call you," Sands greeted Sommer as he trudged into the office the next morning. "You all right?"

"I was here till nearly one-thirty this morning," Sommer said, dropping into his desk chair and rubbing his eyes.

"Yeah, I saw the logout," she grunted. "You may be wishing very soon that you'd taken the whole day off. Our friendly neighborhood FBI agent is on his way up."

Sommer frowned. "Royce? I thought you and he settled things with the Mullner files yesterday."

"We did," she said grimly. "This one is worse. It seems Frank's people have found indications that the Soulminder doctor who handled Mario Cavanaugh's transfer in Seattle may have been suborned."

Sommer felt his mouth fall open. "*What*?"

"You heard me." She held up fingers, started ticking them off. "One: the computer's autorecord shows that Dr. Uriah Emerson handled the transfer alone—totally forbidden except in extraordinary circumstances. Two: all the external recording instruments were shut down, or else erased afterward; forbidden under *any* circumstances. And three . . . he seems to have disappeared."

Sommer shook his head. "Hell."

"Yeah, we really needed something like this," Sands agreed sourly. "Give me a hand here, will you? Royce wants everything we've got on the man."

They had the appropriate files assembled and copied onto a flash drive by the time Royce made his appearance. "I trust," he said after perfunctory greetings, "that I don't have to tell you how this is going over down at the Bureau."

"I trust," Sands countered, "that you're not going to blame the whole corporation for one man's actions."

"And how do we know it *was* just one man's actions?" Royce demanded. "How do we know more of your people weren't involved?"

"They weren't," Sommer said. "If they had been the computer's autorecord of the transfer would have been tampered with."

Royce frowned at him. "Explain."

"If Cavanaugh had gotten to a computer specialist or possibly even one of the transfer techs he could have had the autorecord altered or erased, too," Sommer explained. "If he'd done that, we might still not know he'd been through Soulminder at all."

Royce grimaced. "Yeah, all right. Point. You got that file?"

He copied the file onto his tablet, and for a few minutes read through it in silence. "So Emerson's been with the Seattle office since it was opened. Sent there from *this* office." He snorted gently. "That sounds like Cavanaugh, all right. Suborns a pigeon, swings out there and gets a duplicate trace made, and then just leaves things on hold for two years until he needs it."

Somewhere in the back of Sommer's mind, an odd thought clicked into place. "Jessica, is Emerson's old Washington address listed in here?" he asked, scanning the file.

"It's right here," Royce answered for her, flipping back to the first page and pointing. "Bethesda. That's another thing—we know Cavanaugh was living in Bethesda two years ago too."

"It's also where Jonathan Pauley lived," Sommer said slowly. "The man in Soulminder whose body is missing."

Royce and Sands exchanged glances. "Are you suggesting a connection?" Royce asked.

"I don't know," Sommer admitted. "But the only reason we assumed he hadn't been kidnapped was because there was no ransom note. That, and because he didn't have any serious money."

"But if he was picked up because he knew something he shouldn't?" Royce suggested thoughtfully. "Knew, or saw something?"

"That's a horrible thought," Sands murmured, shivering.

"Yeah, but it happens," Royce said grimly, getting to his feet. "I'll get some people started looking for connections." He headed for the door, then turned back. "One other thing. Do you have Emerson's Mullner trace on file?"

Sommer looked at Sands. "We should," she said. "All senior Soulminder people are supposed to be protected."

Royce nodded. "You might want to call Seattle and make sure he hasn't shown up in one of the traps. Cavanaugh's not the sort to leave loose ends dangling." Turning again, he left the room.

"Great," Sands muttered, sitting back down at her desk. "Just great. A suborned Soulminder doctor. This thing just gets better and better. Barnswell and his crowd are going to have a field day when this gets out."

Sommer shrugged. "One bad apple in four years is hardly a record of failure."

"It's still one more than we should have had," she snapped. "Everly's going to have to tighten the screws on the employee screening process a couple of turns, that's all. Which reminds me," she interrupted herself, "I was talking to him before you arrived, and he tossed out an odd comment about having assigned Hillyard to your rehabilitation project." She arched her eyebrows slightly. "May I ask just what it is you're intending to rehabilitate?"

In the sound and fury of the Cavanaugh thing, Sommer had almost forgotten. "It's something I came up with yesterday morning, before all of this hit the fan." He gave her a quick summary of the possible effects a trip through Soulminder might have on the criminal mentality. "It also makes sense financially—"

"No," she cut him off.

He blinked. "I beg your pardon?"

"I said no," she repeated firmly. "We're not going to get mixed up in something like that."

A wisp of anger began to drift across Sommer's vision. "May I ask why not? If Soulminder really *can* be used to rehabilitate criminals—?"

"You're out of step with the nation," she said icily. "No one believes in rehabilitation these days. Prisons are for keeping dangerous people off the street, and that's all."

"Really," Sommer shot back. "And it's costing the taxpayers billions of dollars a year to do it. Whereas with Soulminder imprisonment, you could have your felons stacked on cots like cordwood, with fewer security requirements than the average department store. Have you considered *that*?"

"We are not," she said, biting out each word distinctly, "going to allow the name Soulminder to be associated with prisons, or prisoners, or punishment. Period."

For a long moment they glared at each other. "Jessica," Sommer said at last, "I understand your concern for Soulminder's public image. But I told you what's happened to Willie. If we can help people understand that what we do in this life matters beyond it—"

"Soulminder is not some kind of justice machine," Sands said in a voice that accepted no argument. "And it isn't going to become one."

And there was clearly no point in arguing about it further. At least, not now. "Will you at least look over the results of Everly's survey when it comes in?" Sommer asked. "We could always set up a new corporation, without using the Soulminder name."

She hesitated, then gave a reluctant nod. "I suppose it couldn't hurt. Not that Everly should have any spare time to waste on that at the moment," she added archly. "Now, can we get back to one or the other of the more immediate crises at hand?"

"Sure." It wasn't exactly the way he'd hoped she would react to the idea. But then, the war was hardly over, either.

She'd come around to his point of view in the end. He was sure of it.

It was like a one-two punch, Cavanaugh thought as the second story broke the next morning. First Soulminder's embarrassment over his own trick maneuver, and now the much grimmer matter of Jonathan Pauley's entrapment in limbo.

A matter that Cavanaugh found just as disturbing as they did. Though for far different reasons.

Disturbing and infuriating both. How in blazes was he supposed to have known that Pauley had been on file with Soulminder? The man hadn't been wearing one of those stupid bracelets; Digger hadn't picked up on it—

Digger. Right.

For a moment Cavanaugh's vision seemed to swim as he contemplated doing awful things to Digger for fouling up like that. But revenge wasn't going to do him any good. The big question now was whether or not Pauley could still pose a threat to him. If there was any way that they could talk to a trapped soul, for instance; or if they could read all those tangled Mullner-trace curlicues, the way Gypsies could read tea leaves. If there was any way at all that they could find out how Pauley had spent his last days . . .

But then, if there was, then the authorities should already have closed in on him.

Cavanaugh took a shaky breath, feeling his pounding heart start to calm down again. Too much imagination, he scolded himself. There weren't any loose ends here. Pauley was mute now, just as mute as if he were finally and properly dead.

Strange, though, how the image of Pauley trapped in Soulminder almost made him wince. Again, probably just too much imagination.

It was the middle of the afternoon when Royce's call finally came. It wasn't what Sommer had hoped for.

"What do you mean, no connection?" he asked the agent.

"Just exactly that: no connection," Royce said. "Jonathan Pauley and Mario Cavanaugh have never done business together, have never attended the same clubs or meetings or social functions together, have never lived closer than four miles apart. As far as we can determine, they've never even seen each other. Period; end of file."

Sommer squeezed the phone handset tightly. "There has to be a connection. There *has* to be. The timing is too close to be just coincidence."

"What timing?" Royce retorted. "Your own numbers show that six other people were in or out of Soulminder traps around the country that same night. Not to mention that DC and Seattle are about as far apart as you can get."

"But there's no way to tell where Pauley actually was when he died," Sommer argued. "He *did* disappear three days before that, remember, and the trap could grab him from anywhere in the country."

"Can you prove he was in Seattle?" Royce asked pointedly. "Or that Cavanaugh had anything to do with his disappearance? If not, it's still just speculation. Loose speculation, at that."

Sommer clenched his teeth. "May I ask a favor, then? Could I make copies of all the public record material in Cavanaugh's file?"

There was a long silence. "What for?" Royce asked at last.

"I don't know. Maybe I can see something that your people missed. Maybe there's some kind of cross-generational thing—Pauley's grandfather going to school with Cavanaugh or something. I just don't want to let it go yet."

There was another long pause. "I don't suppose I can stop you from poking around," Royce conceded after a minute. "The public record stuff you could always go out and dig up for yourself."

"I could," Sommer agreed. "But that would take a lot of time and manpower. And since you already have it all together there . . . ?"

Royce snorted. But behind the snort Sommer could hear the recognition that Soulminder was the darling of official Washington. For darlings, the rules could always be bent a little. "Yeah, all right. Not exactly standard policy, but what the hell. I'll copy the files—you're in charge of getting someone over here to pick them up."

"Thank you. I'll have a messenger there within an hour."

"Yeah. And keep in touch—we still want to find that missing doctor of yours."

"So do we. Good-bye."

Sommer keyed off the connection. A punch of a button got him an inside line, and a minute later the messenger had been given his instructions and was on his way. Replacing the handset in its cradle, Sommer looked up.

To find Sands's eyes on him. "Something?" he asked.

"We're branching out into the detective business now?" she suggested coolly.

"If there's anything at all we can do to clear this up—"

"Do *how*?" Sands demanded. "Pauley is *dead*, Adrian—you know it, I know it, the whole world knows it. Hashing endlessly through it isn't going to do either him or us any good."

"Won't it?" he countered. "Then let me point out something that may not have occurred to you yet. Are you aware that, for possibly the first time in history, we know the *exact moment* an unwitnessed murder was committed?"

Sands opened her mouth . . . closed it again. "We don't know it *was* a murder, though," she said, a little uncertainly.

"I think it was," Sommer said. "But even if it wasn't, the point remains that this is a side benefit of Soulminder that no one's ever thought of."

Sands's lip twisted. "One way or another, you're determined to make Soulminder into a justice machine, aren't you?"

"And that bothers you?"

She looked hard into his eyes. "You know how important image is to people. Soulminder's image is that of hope and health and life. The noble side of this world, not the dregs. We're an extension of doctors and hospitals—not prisons or homicide departments. That's the way I want to keep it." She snorted. "For that matter, that's the way *you've* always wanted to keep it."

"And Jonathan Pauley?" Sommer asked quietly. "His company paid good money to make him a part of the Soulminder safety net. If he was murdered, don't we owe them at least the courtesy of doing what we can to find his murderer?"

For a long moment they just stared at each other. Sands dropped her gaze first. "Just keep it quiet, all right?" she muttered, turning back to her terminal. "The negative publicity we're getting already is bad enough. I don't want it any worse."

"Right."

For a moment he gazed at her profile, at the hard determination there. Yes, Sands was the drive behind Soulminder: the drive and the spirit and the mind. Leaving Sommer as little more than the public image.

And, perhaps, the conscience.

Sitting to one side was the newspaper article on Jonathan Pauley that Everly had sent over. Picking it up, Sommer leaned back in his chair and began to read.

The package from Royce arrived an hour later . . . and Sommer found himself astonished at just how much stuff the FBI had managed to collect on Mario Cavanaugh.

As well as just how thorough they'd been. There were photocopies of Cavanaugh's school attendance records, from third grade right through college. His high school and college yearbook photos, as well as a listing of some of the clubs he'd belonged to. A summary of his Korean War military service, including suggestions that he'd been involved even then with black market and other illegal activities. Two sets of wedding pictures, copies of two divorce decrees. Ads and official papers from each of his various legitimate businesses, and from some that it was hinted had been little more than fronts for money laundering and smuggling operations.

There was more. Much more.

Fascinating reading. But it was a fascination that for Sommer became increasingly tinged with regret and even impotent anger. The Mario Cavanaugh reflected in the records was a brilliant and driven man, the sort of man who would probably have been a success in any field he'd chosen to apply himself to. For all that to have been twisted to the acquisition of power and illegal money struck Sommer as a tragic waste.

"You going to stay late again tonight?" Sands asked into his thoughts.

Sommer looked up, vaguely surprised to discover it was already nearly six o'clock. Absorbed in his reading, he hadn't noticed the time passing. "Probably not," he told her with a sigh.

Sands nodded, coming over and surveying the boxes and papers scattered around his desk. "So, any names jump out at you yet?"

He blinked. "Come again?"

"You told Royce you were hoping to find a connection between Cavanaugh's childhood chums and Jonathan Pauley." She picked up one of the high-school yearbook pictures. "Randall Peterson, Rosemary Phelps, Aubrey Raystone," she read off the surrounding names. "Seems to me we've got a Phelps with Soulminder— Los Angeles office, I think."

"San Francisco," Sommer corrected her. "I've already run the check; they don't seem to be related."

Sands looked at the piles again, shook her head. "You're really going to wade through all this stuff?"

He shrugged. "Until I find something, or prove to myself that there's nothing there to find, or collapse. Whichever comes first."

"I'd vote for collapse, myself," she said, gazing again at the photos in her hand. "Certainly had that solid-citizen look back in college, didn't he?" she commented, handing the page back. "I wonder what went wrong."

"I don't know," Sommer sighed, looking at the picture himself. She was right: with his dark hair and thin, intensely earnest face, Cavanaugh should have been a future business or political leader. Not a—

Abruptly, Sommer's thoughts broke off. There was something about that face . . .

He looked up. Sands was already at the door— "Hold it, Jessica," he called.

She paused, her hand on the knob. "You find something?"

"I don't know," he frowned, digging carefully through the pile. "Come here a minute, will you?"

He'd found the newspaper photo of Pauley by the time she reached the desk. "Take a look," he said. "Tell me what you see."

Frowning, she looked at the two pictures. The frown deepened, and she held them side to side. "They could be brothers," she agreed. "Almost twin brothers, for that matter. I hope you're not suggesting Pauley and Cavanaugh are related—Royce would have to be an idiot to have missed something that obvious."

Sommer swallowed hard. "No, not related. Not exactly."

She stared into his face . . . and slowly, her puzzlement dissolved into a look of horror. "Oh, my God," she whispered, her face turning almost green. "You're not suggesting that Cavanaugh . . . ?"

Sommer felt a little sick himself. "Why not?" he asked.

"But it's—" she floundered. "It's *impossible.* Isn't it?"

"I don't know," Sommer said grimly. "But I think we'd better find out."

Sands hissed between her teeth, her expression of repugnance vanishing into dark determination. "Damn right. Let's get to it."

Royce frowned at the photos for what seemed like a long time before finally laying them down on the desk. "Yes, I agree that

Pauley looks a lot like Cavanaugh when he was a young man. I hope that's not all you dragged me over here for."

"That's just the starting point," Sommer said, a mild wave of dizziness shooting through him. Four cups of coffee on top of less than four hours of sleep was already starting to take its toll, and he wished they could have put this off a little longer. But with Pauley's life hanging in the balance . . . "The pictures were what got me wondering if maybe Cavanaugh threw a curve none of us were expecting."

"That being?" Royce asked with clearly forced patience.

"Last night we did a complete examination on the computer autorecord of Cavanaugh's transfer," Sands said. "We discovered a couple of anomalies that no one had paid attention to before."

She leaned over to hand Royce the hard copies. "I've combined the event timelines from Seattle and the office here," she continued. "Note that Cavanaugh entered Soulminder at precisely twelve fifty-one last Monday morning, and was transferred back at three-fourteen."

"Two hours twenty-three minutes," Royce shrugged. "So? You've kept bodies alive a lot longer than that."

"With full life-support," Sommer agreed, "and with the use of neuropreservatives. Without them, the brain cells start to degenerate within a few minutes, and for most people irreversible damage begins well within an hour. For a man Cavanaugh's age, it would happen even faster."

"So he had black market neuropreservatives."

Sommer shook his head. "That's just the point: he didn't. No black market neuropreservatives; no neuropreservatives of any sort. The body was brought in, connected to Soulminder, and the soul transferred. A quick in-and-out operation."

"That's not just a guess," Sands added. "The autorecord gives a complete procedural timeline. There was no flushing of neuropreservative residue."

Royce had a strange, almost pained expression on his face. As if he saw what they were driving at but didn't want to believe it. "So why isn't he dead?"

Sommer took a deep breath. "Because he didn't transfer into his own body. He transferred into Jonathan Pauley's."

He'd expected Royce to be amused, angry, or just plain disbelieving. But the other passed up all the obvious reactions. For a long minute he just looked back and forth between them, his eyes seeming to measure them. Then, still silent, he looked back down at the combined timeline Sands had prepared. "I presume you've double-checked all these numbers?" he asked at last.

Sands nodded. "Against two independent clocks. Pauley entered the Washington Soulminder at exactly six-eleven. Three-eleven Seattle time. Three minutes before Cavanaugh was transferred."

Sommer shivered. "He must have died right there on the transfer table."

Royce's fingers worried gently at the edge of the paper. "It's an interesting theory," he said. "But that's all it is: a theory."

"There are other indications," Sommer told him. "Emerson did the transfer alone, remember—*and* he had the video cameras off. Why would he do all that if it was Cavanaugh's own body they were transferring into?"

"To keep us from knowing Cavanaugh had been through Soulminder?" Royce suggested doubtfully.

"Except that the computer autorecord would tell us that," Sommer reminded him. "Besides, he could easily claim ignorance that he'd done anything wrong—the Seattle system didn't have your red light on it."

Royce shook his head. "This is crazy. A soul isn't just some"— he groped for words—"some interchangeable computer card or something. You can't just pull one out and plug another one in."

"Cavanaugh did it," Sommer said. "Dr. Sands and I are convinced of that."

"Well, I'm not," Royce said doggedly. "It's still just a left-field theory. And with all the witnesses having so conveniently disappeared, that's what it's going to stay: a theory."

Sommer glanced at Sands. "Except," he told Royce carefully, "that not *all* of those witnesses have disappeared."

Royce stared, and Sommer could see in his eyes that he understood. "You're not serious."

"Deadly serious, Special Agent Royce." Sommer braced himself and got to his feet. "If you'll come with us . . . we're going to ask Jonathan Pauley what happened to him."

The preparations were already complete, and they entered the experimental transfer facility in the lab wing to find five uncomfortable-looking people waiting for them: a doctor, three transfer techs . . .

And a quiet, dark-haired young man.

"Special Agent Royce, this is George Gerakaris," Sommer did the introductions. "One of our research people."

Royce and Gerakaris exchanged nods. "Why him?" Royce asked.

"We did a computer comparison of all our employees' Mullner traces," Sands explained. "Mr. Gerakaris's came out the closest to Pauley's."

Royce eyed Gerakaris. "And they asked you to do this?"

Gerakaris smiled, a smile that didn't wholly relieve the tension around his eyes. "I volunteered, Special Agent Royce," he said, his voice showing just a trace of an old Greek accent. "I'm a scientist, after all. How could I pass up a chance to take part in such an experiment?"

Royce shifted an uncomfortable frown back to Sommer. "You realize, I hope, that what you're about to do is technically murder."

Sommer realized it. Realized it exceedingly well. "Mr. Gerakaris has signed a release," he told Royce, keeping his voice even.

"Which may not be worth a damn, legally," Royce growled.

He looked at Gerakaris, then back at Sommer. "Have you discussed this with your legal department?"

"They're not exactly happy about it," Sommer said candidly, "but they say the release will cover us reasonably well. They also talked a lot about the right-to-die statutes, but I wasn't sure exactly how those applied."

Royce snorted gently. "They don't apply at all. Not really. This is nuts, Sommer. You're putting your personal and corporate necks—not to mention mine—on the block here without even a scrap of proof that Cavanaugh tried this. Let alone that it worked."

"Oh, it worked," Sands said. "It had to. Otherwise, why did Emerson disappear?"

"Because Cavanaugh didn't want him to talk, of course."

"Naturally," Sands agreed. "So why hasn't Cavanaugh gone ahead and killed him?"

Royce started to speak . . . paused. "You tell *me*," he challenged.

"Because Cavanaugh knows that souls can be transferred to different bodies," Sommer said. "With Emerson on file at Soulminder, killing him would just put him back in our reach."

"By that logic, Pauley was a lousy choice," Royce argued. "Even if I grant you that Cavanaugh was vain enough to try to get back his youth when he saw Pauley's picture in the paper, he wasn't stupid enough to let vanity get in the way of common sense."

"Except that Pauley seldom wore his Soulminder bracelet," Sands reminded him. "Cavanaugh probably never knew he was on file here."

"And what if Emerson disappeared because Cavanaugh died on the operating table and the doctor's taken his guilty conscience into hiding?" Royce countered.

Sommer opened his mouth. But it was Gerakaris who answered. "It's a calculated risk, Special Agent Royce," he said firmly. "But all of us are willing to take that risk."

"If you want," Sands offered, "you can wait outside until it's over."

Royce sent her a glare. "If it doesn't work, I'm still accessory to murder," he said shortly. "It's not going to matter a damn where I'm standing at the time." He jerked his head toward Gerakaris. "Get on with it."

It was as close to assent as they were going to get. Turning, Sommer gave the nod to the others.

And watched as they prepared Gerakaris to die.

It was a simple enough procedure. Gerakaris got onto the transfer table, settling himself as comfortably as possible as the techs wheeled the instrument tray and backup life-support gear into position. Last came the waveguide cable and headband electrodes that would—if all went well—provide the path for Jonathan Pauley's soul to enter Gerakaris's body.

"You all set, George?" the supervising doctor asked, leaning over the table to look at Gerakaris.

Gerakaris's hand lifted from the table, made a surreptitious cross: forehead, heart, right chest, left chest. Eastern Orthodox style, Sommer noted. Pauley, he remembered, had been a solid Catholic. How much of the similarity in their Mullner traces, he wondered distantly, had come from the two men's religious convictions? "I'm ready," Gerakaris said, dropping his hand to his side again and closing his eyes.

The doctor looked at Sands, got a confirming nod, and picked up the hypo. With just the slightest hesitation, he gave Gerakaris the injection.

Gerakaris inhaled sharply, and Sommer found himself unable to watch. Turning his head, he found himself staring at the medical readout panel . . . and even as he watched, the life signs disappeared.

Sommer swallowed against the lump in his throat. It didn't seem to help. "How long?" he murmured.

"A few minutes," the doctor said, his own attention on the instruments and his assistants' work. "I'm going to give him a small dose of neuropreservative, just to be on the safe side, and we'll have to wait until we can flush out the residue."

The minutes ticked slowly by, and at last they were ready. "All right," the doctor said, reaching for the panel. "Here goes." He touched the switch—

Abruptly, Gerakaris body gave a violent twitch. Sommer felt his heart jump in sympathetic response. "Pauley!" he called, tension putting snap into his voice. "Are you there?"

"Mother of God," Gerakaris gasped. "I—oh, God in heaven, I can't see. Where—where am I?"

"You're in the Soulminder office in Washington, D.C.," Sands told him. "How do you feel?"

"I'm burning up," the other managed. His body shivered violently. "I can't see—everything's just a blur. Have I gone blind?"

"Don't worry about it," the doctor advised, his eyes on his instruments. "This sometimes happens, and it's always temporary."

Off hand, Sommer couldn't remember such a side effect ever happening before. But the assurances seemed to help, and Gerakaris calmed down a little.

No. Not Gerakaris.

Pauley.

An icy shiver ran up Sommer's back. It had worked. It really had worked. A man's soul had been transferred into another man's body . . .

He turned to find Royce gazing rigidly at the man on the table. "Royce?" he prompted quietly.

Royce threw him a sharp look, took a careful breath. "Mr. Pauley," he said, the name coming out with noticeable difficulty. "Are you—I mean, you *are* Jonathan Pauley?"

"Yes," the other said. "Why do you . . . ? I feel strange, Doctor. Is this how it's supposed to feel?"

"What happened to you, Mr. Pauley?" Royce put in before the doctor could reply. "You disappeared last Friday morning. What happened to you?"

Gerakaris's head turned, eyes squinting in Royce's direction. "They came to my house—right into my house—and pulled me out of bed. I don't know why—they never told me. Can I have something to drink?"

Sands gestured, and one of the techs hurried off toward the prep room. "What did they do to you, Mr. Pauley?" she asked.

"Uh . . . " Pauley frowned in thought. "I really don't know. They put something over my mouth. When I woke up I was in the back of a van." He shook his head, blinking his eyes as if to clear them. "But they kept giving me stuff, and I kept falling asleep. But then—"

The tech returned with a paper cup of water. The doctor got a hand under Pauley's head, raising it enough to let him take a few sips. "Go on," Royce prompted.

Pauley's eyes suddenly looked haunted. "There was a man," he whispered. "An old man. Very—" He swallowed. "He came up and looked at me. Asked me some questions."

"What sort of questions?" Royce asked, keying his tablet.

"He asked . . . whether I had any health problems," Pauley said, his voice vaguely confused. "It didn't make any sense."

"Is this the man?" Royce asked, stepping close to Pauley and holding up the tablet.

Pauley squinted. "Yes. Oh, Mother of God, yes." His hand came up, crossed himself shakily. Forehead, heart, right chest, left chest. "He was . . . evil. I could feel it. He said . . . he said I would do just fine. And then they took me back to the van and drove me around—"

Abruptly, Gerakaris's face twisted with emotion. "And then they—*they killed me!*"

The words seemed to ring in the room. Pauley groped for the doctor's arm, found it and gripped it tightly. "Soulminder," he breathed. "It's just like purgatory. You're dead, but you can't get into heaven."

The doctor looked at Sommer. "Dr. Sommer?"

Sommer glanced at Royce, got a confirming nod. "Mr. Pauley," he said, trying desperately to find the right way to say this,

"I'm afraid we're going to have to put you back into Soulminder for a little while. There's—" He looked at Sands helplessly.

"There's a problem with your body," she said. "A medical problem. Nothing serious—probably why you're feeling so strange. Okay? You'll be out again soon, I promise."

Pauley's face stiffened. "You're going to kill me again?" Again, the quick up-down, right-left swipe of hand across chest. "Oh, please. Please, Doctor—"

"I'm afraid it's necessary," the doctor said firmly. "Don't worry, it'll be all right." He picked up the hypo, set it against the arm—

And Pauley raised his hand in front of his eyes, eyes that were suddenly filled with confusion and horror. "My *hand*—" he gasped.

Sommer braced himself for the reaction.

A reaction that never came. Without a sound, Pauley's eyes closed, the hand fell back onto the table.

And for the second time in ten minutes, the instruments registered death.

The doctor reached for a second neuropreservative hypo, injected Pauley's body with it as the hum of the life-support equipment started up again. "It'll be another couple of minutes, Dr. Sommer."

Sommer nodded and took a shuddering breath, feeling his sweat-soaked shirt clinging to him as he did so. It had worked. It had actually worked.

And he'd been right. Cavanaugh had indeed stolen another man's body.

The thought made Sommer's stomach want to be sick.

A subtle breeze brushed over his skin as Royce moved up beside him. "Congratulations, Dr. Sommer," he said quietly, a sour tinge to his voice. "You and Soulminder have just created a brand-new crime. Body theft."

"I hope you're not going to try and blame *us* for this perversion of Soulminder's capabilities," Sands growled.

"Why not?" Royce countered. "It's your machine, isn't it?"

"It doesn't matter whose fault it is," Sommer verbally stepped between them. "The question is how we're going to keep it from happening again."

"Dr. Sommer?" the physician at the table spoke up. "We're ready to transfer Gerakaris back."

"Go ahead," Sommer told him, turning back to Royce. "It seems to me that what we're talking about is a stronger security arrangement for both the initial Mullner tracings and the transfer rooms themselves. We'll get Frank Everly looking into what would be appropr—"

"Adrian!" Sands cut him off.

He spun back to the table. One look at the instruments was all he needed. "What is it?" he snapped, taking a long stride to Sands's side.

"It's not taking," the doctor said tightly, hands hovering uncertainly over the control board. "Gerakaris's soul isn't remelding with his body."

Sands swore under her breath, stepping around the table and elbowing the doctor aside. "Can you tell what's causing it?" Sommer asked her.

She shook her head. "This has never happened before," she gritted out.

"Could Pauley have done something to the brain chemistry or Mullner topography while he was there?" Sommer suggested.

The muscles in Sands's cheeks tightened visibly. "I hope to hell that's not it. Because if it is . . . "

She left the sentence unfinished. Consciously unclenching his own teeth, Sommer shifted his eyes to the bank of readouts. "Let him go," he said quietly.

Peripherally, he felt all eyes turn to him. "We've got no choice," he said into the silence. "All we're doing is building up to massive physical trauma in the brain. We'll put the body on full life-support, let it rest a while, then try again."

Sands took a deep breath. "All right," she said, reluctantly but clearly with no better option in mind. "Here goes."

The readout lights changed, turning from green to amber to red . . . and the body again died.

"Neuropreservatives," Sands ordered. The doctor moved to comply, and Sands stepped away from the table to the computer terminal off to the side. Sommer held his breath . . . "The trap caught him," she confirmed, straightening up. "He's back in Soulminder."

Sommer nodded, turning back to find Royce's eyes on Gerakaris's motionless form. The eyes of a man seeing *accessory to murder* on his record. "Don't worry, it'll work," he assured the agent, trying hard to sound confident.

With a visible effort, Royce broke his gaze away from the body. "I hope so, Doctor," he said, looking Sommer square in the eye. "Because if it doesn't—if you can't put a soul back into a body after someone else has been there—then finding Cavanaugh won't buy us anything but the chance to hang another murder on him. Pauley will still be dead, and he'll stay that way."

Sommer felt his stomach tighten. "I know."

The Soulminder file on Jonathan Pauley was slender, consisting of nothing more than the usual information taken from those who were willing to pay large sums of money for the security of Soulminder's safety net. Sommer had gone over both the file and Pauley's newspaper article three times and was midway through a fourth reading when the call finally came.

Sands was ready to try the Gerakaris transfer again.

He arrived downstairs to find the same team assembled as before, along with Tom Dumata and a handful of Soulminder's other top people. "Adrian," Sands nodded to him as he strode into the room. "Anything new come up on the Mullner analysis?"

Sommer shook his head. "The computer's still checking over the third-order effects, but there was nothing on first or second. I think our original analysis was valid, that there were no inherent incompatibilities between Pauley and Gerakaris."

Sands grunted satisfaction. "Good. That gives that much more weight to the physiological analysis."

"The neuropreservatives?"

She nodded. "It's looking more and more like that's the culprit. The simulations still go crazy when we try putting two doses of the stuff in that closely together, even when the usual flushing procedures are followed."

Sommer felt his throat tighten. "Possibly just one more of the lovely psychological side-effects neuropreservatives create."

"Yeah," Sands grunted. "Instead of completing the transfer into that emotional snake pit, the soul simply refuses to reconnect."

"Or can't do so even if it wants to," Dumata put in from the readout panel. "I think we're ready, Dr. Sands."

Sands looked at Sommer, seemed to brace herself. "Let's do it."

It was, for Sommer, a distinct and welcome anticlimax. On the table Gerakaris's body jerked and gasped . . . and then the Soulminder indicators went out, and he was back.

"Mr. Gerakaris?" Sommer asked as the other blinked his eyes against the overhead lights. "How do you feel?"

"O—okay," Gerakaris grunted, his voice sounding strained. "That was—God above, that was strange. How long was I in there?"

"Longer than we originally planned," Sands said soothingly. "But it worked out all right."

Gerakaris squinted at her, suddenly tense. "There was a problem?" he asked, his hand tracing a surreptitious up-down, right-left across his chest.

And Sommer found himself staring at that hand. Staring at the imaginary cross Gerakaris had just traced across his chest.

Staring at the mental image of that same hand, and that same motion, an hour earlier . . .

Someone was calling his name. "I'm sorry," he said, bringing his thoughts back with an effort and focusing on Sands. "What did you say?"

Sands was frowning at him. "I asked if you wanted to ask any questions before we took him to the examination room," she repeated.

The question spinning through Sommer's mind almost came out . . . but this wasn't the time or the place to bring it up. Even if Gerakaris had any chance of answering it.

But perhaps there was someone who could. "No," he told Sands. "There'll be time enough to talk about the experience after we're sure he's all right. Go ahead and start the exam. I'll join you in a few minutes."

Sands's frown deepened, and he could tell she very much wanted to ask him what was bothering him. But she too knew better than to press the point in front of Gerakaris. "All right," she said, striving to keep her voice casual. "Give me a hand here, Doctor?"

Sommer left, breaking into a jog as soon as he was out of the room. Back in his office, he read one last time—very carefully— through both Pauley's Soulminder file and the article. Then, just to be sure, he called up the videotape of Pauley speaking through Gerakaris's body.

There was no mistake.

He sat silently for several minutes, thinking it through. Then he reached for the phone and punched a number.

A neutral voice answered on the third ring. "FBI."

"This is Dr. Adrian Sommer at Soulminder," Sommer identified himself. "I'd like to talk to Special Agent Royce. Tell him it's important."

"One minute."

The phone went blank, and Sommer had just enough time to pick up the Pauley article again before Royce came on. "This is Royce." The agent sounded tired.

"We just got Gerakaris out of Soulminder," Sommer told him. "We're checking him over to be on the safe side, but it looks like the transfer was completely successful."

"Yeah, your man Dumata just called to tell me that," Royce

grunted. "Congratulations, and I'll tell you right now that you were damn lucky."

"No argument," Sommer agreed soberly. "How's the search for Cavanaugh going?"

He could almost hear Royce shrug. "Way too early to tell. We've sent Pauley's photo to the Seattle authorities, but we can't make too much fuss or we're likely to spook him."

"I understand." Unconsciously, Sommer braced himself. "If I may offer a slightly long-shot suggestion . . . I think there's a place—or, rather, a group of places—that might be worth staking out."

He explained where. And then, of course, he had to explain why.

The two men were waiting by the door as he filed out with the others. Young men, Cavanaugh saw, with the look of FBI agents stamped all over their faces.

For a brief moment he considered trying to flee. But the thought was pure reflex, without any real force of will behind it. Their eyes were locked on him, now; they'd identified him, and there was no point in making a fuss.

The game was over, and he'd lost.

The young men moved forward together as he approached, coming to stand directly in front of him. "Mario Cavanaugh?" the elder of the two asked quietly.

Again, there was nothing to be gained by lying. "Yes."

"FBI," the other said, holding his ID cupped in his hand. "Will you come with us, please?"

"Of course." Cavanaugh glanced around at the others milling about. But if any of them had overheard the brief conversation they made no sign of it. "Thank you for not—for doing this quietly."

The agent cocked a slightly puzzled eyebrow at that. "No problem," he said. "This way, please."

Walking between them, Cavanaugh stepped through the large

ornate doors and out into the sunlight. The game was over, and he'd lost. And yet, he felt none of the angry frustration he should have felt at such failure.

Instead, his mind was filled with genuine relief. Relief that the lie was finally over. And mild surprise that he should feel that way.

Sommer hung up the phone, and for a long moment the office was silent. "Well?" Sands asked at last.

"They're finished with their interrogation," Sommer told her. "Royce will be bringing Cavanaugh back here in about half an hour. For his execution."

The word hung heavy in the air. "He destroyed his own body, Adrian," Sands reminded Sommer gently. "He doesn't have any claim to the one he's using now."

"I know." Sommer sighed. "It just seems . . . I don't know; *wrong*, somehow. Execution without due process, or something."

"It can't be helped," Sands said, a touch of impatience creeping into her voice. "Pauley has rights, too. And a lot better claim to those rights than Cavanaugh has."

Sommer grimaced. "You sound like Congressman Barnswell."

"Well, maybe for once he's right," she growled. "Even Barnswell can't be wrong *all* the time."

"I take it you haven't seen the bill he's preparing to introduce into the judicial committee."

"As a matter of fact, I have," Sands said calmly. "I think it's a good idea."

Sommer stared at her. "I thought you were the one who didn't *want* Soulminder used as a justice machine."

"No, no—I was the one who didn't want it to be a prison substitute," she corrected him. "Offering maimed victims the temporary or permanent use of their assailants' bodies is something else entirely. *That's* justice, Adrian. More to the point, it's justice that fits the mood of the country."

The justice of judicial vengeance. *An eye for an eye, a tooth for a tooth.* "Oh, it fits the mood, all right," Sommer admitted wearily. "Fits it perfectly. The only problem is that it won't work."

"Well, of course it'll take some overhauling of the legal system—"

"No!" Sommer snapped. "It *won't work.* Period. Royce was right, Jessica—the soul isn't some kind of standardized module you can pull out of one body and plug into another. Habits, memories, temperament—they're all locked into the brain and body chemistry, as much as they are into the soul itself." He took a deep breath. "When Pauley was in Gerakaris's body, he crossed himself, twice. But he did it Eastern Orthodox fashion, not Catholic. The way *Gerakaris*, not Pauley, would have done it."

Sands's eyes were steady on him, the lines around her eyes tight. "That may not be all that significant," she suggested slowly. Carefully. "Maybe a small habit like that . . . I mean, they *are* both very religious men, after all."

Sommer closed his eyes briefly. "Do you know where they picked up Cavanaugh?"

"No, I didn't read the—"

"They picked him up in a church. St. James Cathedral, to be exact. Attending Sunday Mass."

For a long minute the room rang with silence. A strangely horrified silence. "Are you suggesting . . . ?" Sands's question faded away unfinished.

Sommer nodded. "There doesn't seem to be any doubt about it. A totally amoral criminal boss attends church . . . and according to Royce, was actually eager to clear his conscience of all the slime he's participated in.

"Tell me, Jessica: what do you think would happen to a normal person transferred via justice machine into the body of a psychotic killer?"

"Oh, my God," she whispered, very quietly.

133

CHAPTER 4

●

The Hand That Rocks the Casket

THE AIR WAS DRY but comfortably warm as Dr. Adrian Sommer stepped out the door of the unmarked plane and started down the steps, his two companions close behind him. The warmth was a distinct and welcome change from the 747's over-enthusiastic air-conditioning, and an even more welcome change from the January blizzards taking place five thousand-odd miles to the north. It was, he decided tiredly, precisely the right time to vacation in South America.

Some day he would have to try it. A vacation might be nice.

He'd asked that the reception committee be kept small, and for a wonder the Chilean government had taken him at his word. The man in military dress uniform waiting at the foot of the stairway stood there alone, with only a single stretch limousine waiting a discreet distance behind him on the tarmac.

Such willing cooperation was a good sign. Sommer could only hope it would continue.

"Welcome, Dr. Sommer," the man awaiting him smiled as Sommer reached the tarmac. The other's English held just the slightest trace of an accent, one composed of what seemed to be equal parts Spanish and British. It was a combination Sommer hadn't run into before. "I am General Miguel Diaz, Minister of the Interior. On behalf of General Jose Santos and the Chilean government and people, allow me to welcome you to our country. It is an honor to have one of the co-inventors of the Soulminder visit our humble country."

"It's an honor to be here," Sommer told him as they shook hands. "My colleague, Dr. Sands, asked me to thank you personally for your invitation to her, and to send her regrets at being unable to accept."

"I understand fully," Diaz assured him. "The day-to-day management of your Soulminder empire must leave Dr. Sands very little time for traveling."

"It certainly doesn't," Sommer agreed. "May I introduce my staff: this is Mr. Samuel Alverez, my technical adviser."

"Señor Alverez," Diaz nodded, offering his hand as Alverez stepped eagerly past Sommer to take it. "If I may say so, you look very Chilean to me."

"You have a good eye," Alverez said, smiling with a twenty-five-year-old's standard youthful enthusiasm. "My parents came to the United States from Santiago during the height of the Pinochet regime. This has been my first chance to see their land—I'm very much looking forward to it."

"Your interest does our country great honor," Diaz smiled. "Perhaps you'll have time to take a proper tour. If you're interested, the resources of my office are at your complete disposal."

"I'll look forward to it," Alverez said.

"And this," Sommer said, gesturing to his other side, "is Mr. Frank Everly."

"General," Everly nodded, offering his hand.

For just a second Diaz's eyes narrowed. Then his face smoothed out again, and he took the proffered hand. "Señor Everly," he nodded. "The same Frank Everly, I presume, who oversees security for all of Soulminder?"

"You're well informed, General," Sommer commented, trying to read the other's face.

"I'm always interested in men of outstanding abilities," Diaz said, his eyes still on Everly. "To handle security so successfully for so important a corporation as Soulminder is a great achievement indeed."

"It's not that hard," Everly said with easy modesty. "The secret's in finding the right people to do all the real work."

Diaz favored him with a slightly stiff smile. "You're too modest." He looked back at Sommer, eyebrows raised slightly. "There are no others, Doctor?"

"None who'll be coming with us into the city," Sommer told him. A true statement, but misleading: the rest of Everly's twenty-man security team was, in fact, already in Santiago, having quietly infiltrated the country as tourists and businessmen over the past two weeks. Members of the team would be moving with them from now on, an invisible defense perimeter augmenting whatever security the Chileans themselves provided. "And speaking of the city . . . ?" he added, surreptitiously stretching his shoulder muscles.

"Yes, of course," Diaz agreed, waving the limo forward. "It *is* a long flight, isn't it? I remember the first time I flew to the United States—I don't think I'd ever before had a true feeling for just how *long* South America really is."

"I had the same thought," Sommer nodded. "Somewhere over Peru, I think."

Diaz smiled. "Well, you'll have a couple of hours now to recover from the trip."

"I thought nothing was happening until the formal dinner tonight," Sommer said, frowning.

"It is," Diaz said, a slightly sour look on his face. "But the great dog Media proved harder to put off than even the most impatient of our own government officials. I'm sure you're familiar enough with media sorts, Doctor: if you take their bone away from them one place you must give it back elsewhere or suffer their incessant howling." He shrugged. "In this case, the only way to keep them from the airport was to promise a news conference at the Ministry this afternoon."

Unless you just decided to shut them all down for the duration, Sommer thought with a touch of fatigue-driven cynicism. Unfair, really—for all the tendencies to excess inherent in military rule, the recently established government *did* seem to be working hard at tolerating its detractors. "No problem, General," he assured the other. "When did you schedule it for?"

"Four o'clock." The limo pulled up beside Diaz and a smartly dressed sergeant jumped out to open the rear door. "Exactly"— Diaz consulted his watch—"two hours twenty minutes from now."

"That'll be fine," Sommer nodded, ducking his head and climbing into the limo.

"Your communications said you wouldn't require more than the one suite," Diaz continued, ushering Everly in beside Sommer and pointing Alverez to the seat facing them, "but we have nevertheless reserved three more suites for you, in the event that you changed your mind."

"That won't be necessary," Sommer told him. "We brought only a handful of other people with us, and they'll be staying aboard the plane. It's quite comfortable," he added as Diaz seemed about to protest. "A sort of scaled-down version of Air Force One."

Diaz shrugged and got in beside Alverez. "As you wish, Doctor. The offer will remain open, though, for the duration of your stay." He leaned forward. "To the hotel."

"Yes, sir," the driver nodded.

"I have to confess," Sommer commented as they started across the tarmac toward a distant security fence, "that I was a little surprised to learn that the Soulminder facility here was under the Interior Ministry's jurisdiction. In most countries we work directly with the Health Ministry."

"Ah, but in most countries the Soulminder is reserved for the rich and powerful," Diaz countered. "In Chile, it's open to all, so who better to operate it but Interior?"

It was a vague logic, one that several weeks of thought on Sommer's part had failed to really penetrate. "I see," he said. "I wonder, General, if you'd tell me just what exactly your vision is for Soulminder in this country."

Diaz frowned. "You were sent our full proposal."

"Proposals are written by bureaucrats. I want to hear it in your own words."

The general's face cleared. "Ah. I see." Turning his head, he gazed out the window, and for a moment he was silent. "As I mentioned before, Dr. Sommer," he said at last, his voice low, "in most countries—including the United States—your Soulminder safety net is available solely to those who can afford to pay the price. The very rich, the very powerful, and their friends."

"And the middle class," Everly murmured.

"Many countries have no middle class," Diaz said, showing a brief spark of annoyance at Everly's interruption. "And even in those that do, there are still many others who are too poor to afford the Soulminder's protection."

Sommer nodded, an echo of old frustration sending wisps of acid pain through his stomach. It was a problem that had haunted the edges of his thoughts for nine long years, ever since the very beginning of Soulminder's commercial existence. If the Chileans had finally solved that problem . . .

"Regardless," Diaz continued, "in Chile we saw that happen—saw the inequity, saw the unfairness—and resolved that it would not happen here. And so, when you granted us our first Soulminder facility, we set out to find a way all could share in it."

He turned back to Sommer, a new fire in his gaze. "*That*, Dr. Sommer, is our vision," he said quietly, earnestly. "A nation with every single man, woman, and child protected against unnecessary and premature death. A nation whose people are allowed to live out their full lives . . . and, perhaps, even beyond."

An unpleasant shiver ran up Sommer's back. *To live even beyond.* "Soulminder is a medical tool," he reminded Diaz firmly. "If it allows people to live out their natural lives, that's all we can expect from it."

"Of course, Doctor," Diaz said easily. "I was referring merely to the vast research you and others are putting into medical advances. Advances we can hope will push back by a few years the death which is, of course, inevitable."

"Of course," Sommer echoed. But the words were polite and meaningless, and both men knew it. Like Jessica Sands, Diaz was looking to Soulminder's future . . . and what he saw there was the dream of immortality.

A dream that already possessed Sands. Sommer could only hope it didn't do the same to Diaz. The future, he knew from bitter experience, could all too easily swallow up the present.

The hotel suite wasn't the most luxurious that Sommer had ever been in, but it was easily in the top ten. Extending over the hotel's top two floors, the levels connected by a wide spiral staircase, the place looked like it had been designed to sleep an entire presidential entourage. The three of them, Sommer thought more than once, were going to feel just a little bit lost.

Their luggage arrived from the plane while they were still looking around the suite, a promptness that pointed to an extremely perfunctory customs inspection. Leaving Everly and Alverez to unpack, Sommer took a quick nap, setting his alarm to leave him enough time to shower and shave before the news conference. His timing was right on the money, and he'd just finished choosing his tie when the front desk called to say that General Diaz had arrived.

The news conference itself was a virtual replay of hundreds of similar ones Sommer had endured over the past nine years. Though there were a handful of questions about the technical aspects of traps and Mullner traces and a few about his own personal involvement with it all, the bulk of the questioning centered on the social implications of Soulminder for the people of Chile. Most of the questions he'd heard many times before, in a variety of different contexts, and he could probably have answered them in his sleep. Others were new, and actually required a certain amount of thought before he could respond.

And there were others—the more pointed political questions in particular—which were conspicuous mainly by their absence.

The news conference lasted until nearly five o'clock, after which it was back to the hotel for a quick change into black tie and a drive to the presidential palace for the formal welcoming dinner. What with the meal itself, the required round of glowing speeches, and the post-dinner mingling and conversations, it was after midnight before they finally made it back to the hotel.

"Well, that was fun," Alverez commented, heading over to the suite's wet bar as Sommer shrugged off his jacket and shoes and flopped down onto an ornate but nevertheless comfortable couch. "You always get wined and dined this well, Dr. Sommer?"

"Not always," Sommer said, working at freeing his windpipe from the strictures of his tie. "It usually depends on how badly the hosts in question want something from me."

"In which case the generals must want that second unit pretty badly," Everly commented, pulling a portable bug-detector from his suitcase and beginning a leisurely stroll around the room. "You'll notice that among all the glitter and glitz they keep finding ways to remind you of how democratic and egalitarian they're being these days."

"You're a born cynic, Everly," Alverez called, carefully measuring out a small nightcap.

"Cynics aren't born, they're trained," Everly countered.

Sommer eyed his security chief thoughtfully. "Back at the airport, Frank, General Diaz seemed to recognize your name. Does he know you?"

Everly shrugged. "Probably only by reputation. I spent a couple of years here in 2001, during the Escobar administration. The government and I had some differences."

"I don't doubt it," Alverez commented, wandering back to the center of the room with his drink. "Weren't you still with the CIA back then?"

"Actually, the CIA was generally supportive of the regime," Everly said. "I just had a bad habit of thinking for myself, which didn't exactly endear me with anyone. Actually—"

He broke off as the cell phone Sommer had set on the end table beside him trilled gently.

"Uh-oh—they heard you," Alverez said, not sounding entirely facetious.

Sommer glanced at the ID and thumbed it on. "Hello, Jessica."

"About time," Jessica Sands's familiar voice came. "I've been calling every twenty minutes since ten o'clock. You forgot to turn on your cell after dinner again, didn't you?"

"Guilty as charged," Sommer said, feeling a sense of relief. He hadn't really expected it to be the Chilean police. But still . . . "You *can* leave messages on this thing, you know."

"And *you* know I hate doing that," Sands said. "How'd the evening go?"

"About as expected," Sommer told her. "You really ought to join in these things sometime."

"No, thanks. Anyway, you're the one they all want to meet."

Sommer rolled his eyes. But she was right. For most of the world, Dr. Adrian Sommer was still the image and heart of Soulminder. "Lucky me," he murmured. "I hope you didn't call just to make sure we were getting to bed on time."

"Actually, I called to give you some news that may have not filtered down there yet. The Supreme Court verdict on Arizona v. White finally came in this afternoon. The law was upheld, six to three."

Sommer took a deep breath, let it out slowly. "Well. Not exactly unanimous, but I suppose it's better than a five-four split."

"It's a shade better than losing entirely, too," Sands countered. "Especially given that there are at least sixteen more states with Professional Witness statutes of their own in the pipeline who've been waiting to see how Arizona's stood up."

"No stopping them now, I suppose."

He could sense Sands shrug. "The people want this, Adrian. I don't know if you heard about it, but an NBC poll taken last week showed up to eighty-five percent positive in some parts of the country."

"At least until the first case of fraud is proven," Sommer reminded her sourly. "At which point the egg is likely to hit the fan at an extremely high rate of speed."

"Luckily, that won't be our responsibility," Sands said. "It's the legal establishment who'll be in charge of screening their Pro-Witnesses for honesty, stability, and sanity."

Sommer snorted a sudden laugh. "What?" Sands demanded suspiciously. "Come on, Adrian, let's have it."

Sommer sighed. "Sanity. A person *volunteers* to let us kill him and put his soul into storage, so that a bodiless murder victim can be transferred out of Soulminder into *his* body and testify at the person's own murder trial. What part of that comes under the heading of *sanity*?"

"That's not fair, and you know it," Sands growled. "Just because it makes *you* cringe doesn't mean everyone who joins a Pro-Witness program is a ghoul."

"I still think there's trouble ahead," Sommer said. "But thanks for calling in the update. Sorry we were so late."

"No problem—I was cleaning up some paperwork, anyway. I'll go ahead and send copies of both the majority and minority opinions to the plane—you might want something to read on the flight home."

"The way I feel right now, I'll probably be sleeping most of the flight home."

"Hint heard and understood," Sands said dryly. "Go toddle off to bed. Let me know how it goes tomorrow."

"I will. Good-night, Jessica."

Sommer keyed off the phone and looked back up at the others. "Arizona v. White came in?" Everly ventured.

Sommer nodded. "Six to three in the People's favor."

Everly grunted. "Not exactly unexpected. Anything unusual in the opinions?"

"You can read them yourself later—she's going to send them to the plane," Sommer said. "If you get impatient, they can probably download it to you before we get back."

"I'll think about it," Everly said.

Alverez drained the last of his glass and set it down on the coffee table. "And on that note, I think I'll turn in."

"Probably a good idea all around," Sommer said, pulling himself vertical with an effort. "We've got a lot of work ahead of us."

"I'm looking forward to it," Alverez said. "Good-night, sir." With a nod to Everly, he disappeared into one of the bedrooms.

"I remember when I could be that enthusiastic after midnight," Sommer commented to Everly.

"Quiet pride works as well as enthusiasm," the other said. "It's easier to maintain, too."

"Good point." Sommer gestured. "You might as well turn in, too. If anyone planted any bugs while we were out, they're not going to learn anything tonight."

"Yeah." Everly paused. "You didn't seem all that pleased that the Pro-Witness program's gotten the green light."

Sommer shrugged. "The whole idea of a person making a career of loaning out his body still bothers me. I'll get used to it eventually."

"Not all that different from surrogate mothers, really, if you want to be strictly technical about it." Everly rubbed his cheek thoughtfully. "You know, sir, it occurs to me . . . I don't know if the numbers have been made public yet, but during the time that the Arizona program's been going there's been a significant drop in violent crime rates. Especially against people wearing Soul-minder ID bracelets."

"I'm not surprised," Sommer grimaced. "Knowing that even murder won't cover your tracks probably makes the average armed robber stop to think a little."

"As well as the average rapist, the average home breaker, and the average kidnapper," Everly nodded. "The numbers are down in all those categories. But now"—he waved a hand, the gesture encompassing the city around them—"we have the Chilean government proposing to put everyone in Santiago on file with Soul-minder in the next five years. If the Arizona pattern holds, we could get something here worth taking a close look at."

Sommer pursed his lips. No premature deaths, a steady increase in lifespan, and now a drastic reduction in violent crime. Paradise restored to Earth, courtesy of Soulminder and the Chilean government. It sounded too good to be true.

Far too good to be true.

"Agreed," he said grimly. "Let's just make sure it's a *very* close look."

There were, by prior arrangement, two cars waiting for them when they came down the next morning. One, with Alverez inside, headed off to the Interior Ministry, where he'd been assured by General Diaz that he would have carte blanche to examine any records relating even remotely to Soulminder's fiscal operations. Sommer and Everly, riding in the second car, headed the opposite direction, arriving ten minutes later at the modern building housing Soulminder itself.

General Diaz was waiting in the medical section anteroom as they entered. "Ah—Dr. Sommer, Señor Everly," he greeted them. "I trust you both slept well?"

"Very well indeed, General," Sommer assured him. "I didn't expect to see you here today."

Diaz shrugged, smiling almost shyly. "And let someone else show off my Soulminder facility to you? Pride is, I'm afraid, one of my many weaknesses. Come—we can start with the tracing rooms."

Sommer had visited dozens of Soulminder facilities throughout the world, and was always fascinated at the myriad of ways variations could be played on what was, essentially, a common theme. The tracing rooms, where clients underwent the recording of their Mullner soul-traces, were here little more than narrow booths, an efficiency of space that had enabled the Chileans to squeeze eighteen tracing stations into a space that would normally have been occupied by ten. "As I recall, General," Sommer commented, looking down the rows of doors, "your proposal included the expansion of this facility to first thirty and then fifty Mullner tracers. Where on earth do you intend to put them?"

Diaz gestured toward the window at the end of the hallway. "We would need to expand, of course. Our plan would be to purchase the building across the street and move all the tracing facilities there, leaving the transfer operations and Core in this building."

Sommer nodded, wondering if the reference to purchasing had been solely for his benefit. There were certain elements of the regime, he'd heard, who believed that private property was merely state property that the government hadn't yet found a use for. He made a mental note to have the local Soulminder staff confirm that a fair price was paid when the purchase went through.

Or rather, *if* it went through. Shaking thoughts of local politics from his mind, he paused outside one of the tracing booths, peering through the window and getting his mind back on the subject at hand.

The tracing procedure had been greatly improved since the first crude Mullner device he and Sands had first started recording soul-traces with, but there were some limits that further research had failed to budge. Even as he watched, the operator finished the final adjustments to the client's headband and touched the recording switch—

And the client's eyes closed, his face stiffening in a look of sheer terror.

"Bad dreams," Diaz murmured at Sommer's side. "They affect perhaps half of those who undergo the procedure."

"I know," Sommer nodded, stomach tightening. His own first-hand experience with the tracer hadn't been very pleasant, either. He watched as the man's face smoothed out and he drifted into a deep sleep.

Two minutes later, it was all over. The operator touched another button and began unstrapping the headband. By the time he'd finished, two orderly-types with a wheelchair had arrived, brushing past Sommer with muttered apologies to enter the booth and manhandle the client out of the recording chair and into the wheelchair. "Recovery room?" Sommer asked.

"This way," Diaz pointed. "If you'd like, we can simply follow this client there."

"That would—"

"Hold it," Everly cut him off, the other's eyes drifting with concentration. "Listen."

Sommer held his breath . . . and then he heard it, too: the thin wail of an ambulance.

Getting louder.

He looked at Diaz, but the other had already guessed the question. "Yes," he nodded, "it sounds like someone on his way here. Come—we'll find out which transfer room has been prepared to receive him."

They were waiting when the man was brought in—a younger man, wearing middle-class clothing. "What happened to him?" he asked.

One of the ambulance men rattled off something too fast for Sommer's limited Spanish to follow. "Frank?" he murmured.

"He was murdered by a terrorist gang," Everly translated.

Sommer looked at him sharply. "He was *what*?"

"Señor Everly is correct," Diaz said, his voice dark and angry.

"Radical terrorists are once again becoming active throughout Chile."

Sommer frowned across the room, trying to see the patient around the physician and transfer techs moving between him and the table. "I don't see any sign of bleeding."

"Oh, they don't use firearms for this sort of thing," Diaz snorted. "They seem to find it more amusing to use a more local form of death: curare-tipped airgun darts."

"Quieter and harder to trace," Everly said. He glanced meaningfully at Sommer. With a quiet sigh, Sommer nodded back.

So much for the elimination of crime.

At the table one of the techs inserted a needle into the victim's arm and hung the attached IV bottle to a hook. "What's the IV for?" Sommer asked.

"It's a glucose drip," Diaz answered. "It's standard procedure for all transfers here."

"I see," Sommer murmured, trying to remember if he'd seen any references to that in the Chilean reports. It seemed a totally superfluous addition to usual Soulminder procedure. The doctor had a hypo now, and was injecting it into the patient's neck. "I presume he was given neuropreservatives in the ambulance?"

"I would presume so," Diaz said. "That, too, is standard procedure."

Sommer nodded. The doctor's hypo, then, would be flushing solution, designed to remove the remnants of the neuropreservative from the patient's system. That, at least, *was* standard Soulminder procedure. The other finished the injection, stepped back to the control board— "Wait a minute—he can't start the transfer yet," Sommer said, starting forward.

Diaz's hand caught his arm, bringing him to a halt. "I'm sure he knows what he's doing, Doctor," the general said soothingly.

Sommer wasn't nearly so sure. He'd seen first-hand what would happen if a soul transfer was tried before the neuropreservative was completely flushed. Namely, nothing at all. The soul wouldn't remeld with the body under such conditions, and trying to force it would do nothing but put added strain on the brain chemistry. If the attending physician was inexperienced enough to try it anyway . . .

He wasn't. His interest in the Soulminder control board was apparently merely a double-check of the equipment's readiness, and after a careful inspection he turned back to the table and settled in to wait.

Sommer clenched his teeth, feeling rather foolish. "I didn't realize the insurgency problem had started again," he said, more to change the subject than anything else.

"It was never entirely gone," Diaz said. "We've made great strides toward reform, but for some people nothing is enough."

"Odd that they'd pick on a man clearly wearing a Soulminder bracelet," Everly commented.

Diaz shrugged. "We think it's their way of harassing the government. Forcing us to go through the trouble and expense of reviving one of our citizens; perhaps hoping to prove we don't really care for the common people at all."

"So how many of Soulminder's clients *have* they picked on?" Everly persisted.

"A fair number, I know," Diaz said. "I'd have to look up the exact figures."

"If they were all attacked with the same curare darts, the numbers will be trivial to retrieve from the main Soulminder records," Sommer pointed out. "As soon as we've finished with the perimeter facilities, Mr. Everly and I will be going into the Core. I can dig out the stats then."

Diaz's snort was just barely audible, but Sommer knew what it meant. "I'm sorry, General," Sommer continued, "but my hands really *are* tied on this. I'm sure you can understand the reasoning behind it."

"I understand," Diaz said, his voice under careful control. "You will understand, in turn, if I find it insulting that you refuse to allow Chilean nationals into the Soulminder inner sanctum."

"It's not just you," Everly put in before Sommer could reply. "Every country's treated the same. Security considerations dictate that *only* specially chosen people be allowed access to the main Soulminder equipment."

Diaz locked eyes with him. "To you, perhaps, it is security," he said softly. "To many of us, it is little less than a form of economic imperialism."

"It's protection of a trade secret," Everly countered, his quiet voice a match for Diaz's.

For a split second there was genuine hatred in the general's eyes . . . but even as Sommer braced himself for an explosion the general took a careful breath and relaxed fractionally. "Call it what you will," he said stiffly. "It's still in many ways a slave's collar around our nation's neck."

Across the room, the man on the table twitched abruptly and gasped something. Sommer spun back, relieved that the awkward confrontation had been interrupted but simultaneously annoyed that he'd missed the crucial parts of the transfer procedure. Unlike the Soulminder people behind the Core's security wall, all the personnel out here *were* Chilean, most of them trained locally along Soulminder guidelines, and nothing could replace first-hand observation as a method of evaluating how closely those guidelines were being followed. "I'd like to watch another transfer," he told Diaz.

"Of course," the other said, his eyes on the revived man, the anger of a moment earlier replaced by an almost grudging sense of wonder. "It never ceases to amaze me, Dr. Sommer. That a man could be brought back from the dead . . . " He shook his head.

For a moment they watched in silence as the doctor completed the final check and one of the techs helped the patient off the transfer table. A little wobbly, but otherwise clearly recovered from his ordeal, he was helped into a wheelchair and guided toward the door.

And on his face, as he passed them, was an oddly absorbed expression. The expression, Sommer knew, of a man who had taken a look beyond earthly life. Who had waited, all alone, in the gray Soulminder tunnel.

Who had faced the Light.

"A miracle, indeed, General," he said, a gentle shiver running up his back at the memory.

"Yes," Everly put in. "Kind of puts national pride in perspective, wouldn't you say?"

Diaz threw him a look that was almost a glare, but merely nodded. "Perhaps. If you're ready, Dr. Sommer, I'll escort you to the Core."

And with that, the spell was broken, the miracle gone. Now, it was back to straight, hard-headed business again. Perhaps, Sommer thought, that was precisely what Everly had been going for. "Lead on, General," he said.

From the very beginning Sands had decided that the secrets of the Soulminder equipment would remain solely with her, Sommer, and what would eventually become the corporation's inner circle. The result was that the central chamber—the Core—of each Soulminder facility always reminded Sommer of a cross between Fort Knox and NORAD's old Cheyenne Mountain fortress.

For Everly and him, of course, the entrance procedure was reasonably straightforward. Sommer had sent their official clearances via layer-encrypted satellite signal a week earlier, and the counter-checks had also already gone through. At that point all that remained was for the two of them to provide handprints, hold still long enough for the computer to run surface facial and bone structure comparisons with the clearance records, and submit to the standard multi-spectrum scan for concealed weapons, microphones, electronics, dangerous chemicals, and whatever else Everly's security experts had set up the equipment to look for.

In nine years no one had yet managed to penetrate a Soulminder Core. Sands and Everly intended to keep it that way.

"Dr. Sommer, Mr. Everly," a smiling young man greeted them

as they came through the final screening and passed through the vault-like inner door. "Welcome to Soulminder Santiago. I'm Martin Van Proyen, in charge here. I don't know whether you remember me, but I was one of the people you met with in London two years ago when the Italian government went through that corner-cutting fiasco."

"Of course," Sommer assured him, offering his hand. "You were assistant head of the Rome office, as I recall. Congratulations on your promotion."

"Thank you, sir," Van Proyen nodded as he shook hands with Sommer and then Everly. "Actually, I'm not sure I *have* been promoted—officially, I'm still listed as an assistant head, temporarily in charge here until someone a little more senior is found. But since that assignment was a year ago—and since they're giving me full Station Chief pay and benefits—I think I can assume the promotion came through."

Sommer made a face. "Probably can, yes. Sorry about that—what with all the countries clamoring for Soulminder facilities, the personnel office has been sort of buried lately. I'll look into it when I get back."

"I'd appreciate that, sir. Well—" Van Proyen waved around him. "This is it. What can I show you?"

Sommer looked around. The Core of each Soulminder office was always the same: a half dozen small offices and work areas surrounding the central section, where the computers and actual soul-trap equipment were kept. "I'd like to start with the financial records," Sommer told him. "I'm particularly interested in how the costs per Mullner tracing and soul transfer compare to other Soulminder offices around the world."

Van Proyen's forehead furrowed. "We can take a look, but I'm pretty sure they're comparable," he said. "Our operational costs aren't anything special, either high or low. The Chilean government's certainly been paying the standard fees, and we've been forwarding them to Washington faithfully."

"The money's all been coming in," Sommer assured him. "My

interest is in how exactly the Chileans plan to put everyone in Santiago on Soulminder for the price they're proposing."

"Ah," Van Proyen nodded. "That. You've got me, Dr. Sommer. All I can suggest is that they're somehow cutting their own bureaucratic costs."

"Or else they're cutting quality," Sommer countered grimly. "In which case, your records ought to show a pattern of incompetence or inexperience from the Chileans working out there in the Periphery."

"I haven't noticed anything obvious," Van Proyen said. "But I'm hardly a walking statistician, either. Let's go to my office and we can start digging. Oh, before I forget, there was a phone call for you earlier this morning. Archbishop Manzano asked if you might call him whenever you got the chance."

Sommer stared at him. "The Archbishop called *me*?"

"And called here?" Everly murmured, his tone thoughtful. "Interesting."

"What's so interesting?" Van Proyen shrugged. "He probably wasn't able to get in touch with you at the hotel."

Sommer eyed Everly, an uncomfortable feeling beginning to gnaw at the pit of his stomach. "We haven't been *that* hard to find," he said slowly.

Everly nodded. "I agree. I'd guess he called here because our phone lines are more secure than the hotel's would have been."

The uncomfortable feeling grew stronger. "You know the Archbishop, Mr. Van Proyen?"

"Not personally. He's something of a local hero among the people, though—he was a strong supporter of democracy before the Santos government was elected, and he doesn't hesitate to speak out against governmental injustice and reform foot dragging."

Sommer nodded. The Archbishop's exploits as the people's unofficial advocate had received a fair amount of international media coverage over the past year or two, but Sommer never quite trusted media darlings to live up to the hype surrounding them. Apparently, this one did. "Did he leave a number?"

"Yes, it's on my notepad. This way."

Van Proyen's desk was as cluttered as Sommer's own workspace, but like Sommer the younger man seemed to know exactly where everything was. He reached beneath a fat printout, pulled out a notepad, and handed Sommer the top sheet. "I think that's his residence," he added. "He said he'd be there all morning."

Sommer nodded. Pulling the phone over, he punched up the number. One ring . . . two— "*Hola*," a man's voice answered.

"This is Dr. Adrian Sommer," Sommer said, belatedly wondering if the Archbishop even spoke English. "I have a message to call Archbishop Manzano."

"Ah—Dr. Sommer," the other said, switching to thickly accented English. "I am Archbishop Manzano. Thank you very much for returning my call."

"No problem, your Excellency," Sommer said, trying to keep his voice casual through a dry mouth. On Van Proyen's phone a red light had begun flashing, alerting him that the call was being monitored. Not all that surprising, really, if the Archbishop was as much a thorn in the government's flesh as Van Proyen had indicated. "What can I do for you?"

There was just the briefest hesitation on the Archbishop's part, and then, strangely, the wiretap indicator flickered once and then went out. "I mainly wanted to add my voice to those urging you to allow the expansion of our Soulminder facility," the other continued. "I'm sure you realize that the greater part of the Soulminder is reserved for government officials and the upper and technical classes. Only if the program is expanded can the poorer of our people be so protected."

Sommer frowned at the phone. "Ah . . . yes, your Excellency, I'm aware of that. It was my understanding, though, that a sizeable fraction of the Soulminder facilities already here were reserved for the poor."

"That is true," the other agreed. "But the fraction is not nearly sizeable enough."

"I understand, sir," Sommer said. There was something off-key here, but he couldn't put his finger on it. "Perhaps we could meet later and discuss what's being done for Santiago's poor."

"I would look forward to such a meeting," the other said. "I'm sure your schedule is very heavy, but if you find a free hour please let me know."

"I'll do that, your Excellency," Sommer assured him. "Thank you for your call. I hope we'll be able to make connections while I'm here."

"Good-bye, Dr. Sommer, and may God continue to bless your work."

"Good-bye, sir."

Sommer lowered the handset carefully back into its cradle. "Trouble?" Everly asked.

"I'm not sure," Sommer told him.

"Let's find out." Pulling Van Proyen's chair out from the desk, Everly sat down, keying a handful of commands into the computer. "Probably should start by getting both sides of the conversation."

Sommer leaned over his shoulder as the screen filled with a transcript of the conversation. "It wasn't anything he specifically said," he told Everly. "More like the *way* he said what he did."

"Uh-huh," Everly grunted. "That and the fact that the tap on his line got lost?"

"Well, now that you mention it . . . " Sommer paused as Everly keyed in some more commands, and to the right of the transcription a cryptic column of numbers and letters appeared. "What's all that?" he asked.

"Tonal information," Everly told him. "Plus . . . well, well, well. What a surprise." He looked up at Sommer. "The wiretap light went out because the line got switched on us."

Sommer exchanged glances with Van Proyen. "You mean the government cut us off?"

"That's it," Everly confirmed, tapping a spot on the screen. "Right here, just after you asked what he wanted. Shunted you to a prepared line where they had either a good mimic or an electronic parrot waiting. Let's see if we can find out which."

"How?"

"Voiceprint analysis—there's a nice little package of programs around for that sort of thing," Everly told him, fingers skating across the keyboard. "Standard issue at Soulminder ·ffices— you'd be surprised at the stuff foreign governments and industrial spies try and pull on us. There we go . . . and the winner is electronic parrot. Damn good one, too. Let me get a deep-probe going on it, see if we can figure out whose design it is. Might tell us where they got it."

Sommer chewed at his lip. "You think it's worth trying to call the Archbishop back?"

Everly shook his head. "No. They were somehow caught flat-footed by his earlier call here, but they won't miss again."

Sommer looked past him to Van Proyen. "I suddenly don't think," he said quietly, "that we want to wait for Frank to finish here before we get started."

"Agreed," Van Proyen nodded, his expression tight as he started toward the door. "Come on, let's go scare up another terminal."

Sommer had expected the search to take perhaps half an hour. It took, in fact, nearly two hours.

And at the end they found nothing.

Van Proyen keyed to the last page of the analysis and leaned back in his chair. "It's not here," he announced unnecessarily, reaching back to massage his neck muscles. "Wherever it is the Chileans are saving money, it isn't with basic Soulminder functions."

Sommer glared at the display. "You absolutely sure we didn't miss anything?"

Van Proyen shrugged. "We looked at the Mullner tracings,

transfer operations, non-hospital paramedical work, baseline storage and power costs, and worker efficiency. That's all there is."

"It's got to be in the way the government's handling their end of things, then," Sommer growled. "Paying drastically reduced salaries, maybe?"

"Could be," Van Proyen said doubtfully. "But remember that that's one of the things the Italians did when they were trying to cut costs—and in *that* case, there was a big jump in worker turnover and general inefficiency. There's nothing like that here—average stay for the low-level workers was, what, fifteen months?"

"Something like that."

"And even the physicians are staying an average of a year or so," Van Proyen reminded him. "Physicians down here are notorious for jumping jobs if their pay doesn't suit them."

Sommer chewed at his lip. "Maybe the prestige of working for Soulminder makes up for starvation wages."

Van Proyen raised his eyebrows politely. "Would it make it up for *you*?"

"I doubt it," Sommer admitted, getting to his feet. "Well, whatever they're doing, at least we know for sure now that the difference is coming out of their half of the pie. I suppose that qualifies as progress."

"Probably." Van Proyen got to his feet. "Your man Alverez probably has it all scoped out by now. Assuming, of course, it isn't buried too deeply."

Sommer grimaced. "That's what bothers me. Why it should be buried at all."

General Diaz had left, they found as they emerged from the Core, but he'd left his car and driver and a message to phone him whenever they were ready to continue their tour.

"Is there anything else to see?" Sommer asked Van Proyen.

"Not really," the other said. "There's some administrative stuff, mostly concerned with the Chilean staff and supplies and all, and I suppose if you really wanted to you could hang around and watch another transfer." He stepped to the Core receptionist's desk, tapped out a command on her computer. "There's one going on now, and four more scheduled later today—accident victims, all of them, who've spent the last few weeks healing in the hospital."

Their bodies technically dead, with only full life-support keeping the biological functions going. The whole concept still gave Sommer the shivers if he thought about it too hard. "No point to it," he told Van Proyen. "We already know that the savings aren't coming from the transfers. In fact, some of the things they've added to the standard procedure are actually boosting the cost."

"Those silly glucose IVs," Van Proyen snorted. "Well, the medical part is their business. I've known hospitals in the States that were always throwing glucose at their patients, too." He spread his hands. "In that case, I guess the tour is over."

"Appreciate your time, Mr. Van Proyen," Sommer said as they shook hands. "Do me a favor, will you, and keep sifting through those records of yours."

"It might be interesting," Everly put in, "to check the Chilean records against those from Argentina, say. Someplace comparable."

"Good idea," Sommer nodded. "I'll talk to Jessica later, see how much trouble it would be to collect those records and download them to you."

"You get them here, and I'll run them through the grinder," Van Proyen promised. "You've got me fully intrigued now, Doctor. Good luck, and happy hunting."

The rest of the day was of the sort that Jessica Sands often referred to as a cotton-candy day: full and rich, but with little substance to it. Rejoined by General Diaz, they made a quick walk-through of the teaching hospital where Soulminder physicians and transfer techs were given the necessary specialized training. Then it was off to a luncheon of Santiago's business and civic leaders: good food and what turned out to be politely meaningless conversations. Afterwards came a tour of the mainsprings of Chile's economic revival, including a plant busily turning Chilean copper and yttrium into superconducting ceramion, a computer chip facility using that ceramion, and a technical institute for teaching young Chileans the science and technology they'd need to keep the boom going.

It was a long tour, made even longer by the need to periodically pose for the crowd of tagalong photographers who seemed determined to record the entire thing on film and disk, and it was nearly five-thirty before they were finally able to return to the Interior Ministry and pick up Alverez.

One look at his face was all Sommer needed.

"Well?" Sommer demanded when they were back in the hotel room and Everly had done his maddeningly slow search for microphones. "What did you find?"

"Actually, it's more negative information than anything else," Alverez said. "But I guess it still counts as progress. The savings are definitely coming from the actual Soulminder operations."

For a long moment Sommer stared at him, and the satisfied look on Alverez's face slowly faded as he belatedly realized he wasn't getting the reaction he'd expected. "What's wrong?" he asked carefully.

"You checked the Chileans' own costs?" Sommer asked him. "Including the salaries they're paying their people?"

"Of course," Alverez said, starting to look a little flustered. "With a fine-mesh sifter. Their costs are completely compatible with a Soulminder operation this size."

Everly rubbed his cheek thoughtfully. "Curiouser and curiouser."

Alverez looked at him, then back at Sommer, his expression now guarded. "Do I take it," he asked, "that you'd already decided that it was the Chilean side that had the whittled end of the stick?"

"You take it right," Sommer said wearily, dropping down onto the couch. "The station chief assures us that everything looks normal from where *he's* sitting, too."

Alverez glared off at nothing for a moment. "Well, then, they're shifting money from somewhere else," he said. "That's the only explanation. They're fiddling the records, making their Soulminder activities look cheaper than they really are."

"Then why are they keeping it a big secret?" Sommer demanded. "They have the perfect right to subsidize Soulminder if they want to. Why all the smoke about having a cheaper way of doing it?"

"Perhaps," Everly said slowly, "it's because they don't want us to know where the money's coming from."

Sommer's stomach tightened. "As in, it might be coming from some kind of illegal activity?"

"Military governments have a tendency toward that sort of thing," Everly pointed out. "Alverez, did you happen to check out their copper production records?"

Alverez frowned. "I glanced at the figures. The industry's booming, of course, but don't forget that the unions have the miners' wages set at a pretty reasonable rate these days. I can't see them pulling all of the Soulminder shortfall from there."

"I was thinking more along the lines of whether they might be siphoning off some of that copper," Everly told him. "Maybe to unlicensed superconductor or chip manufacture. They've got the facilities, that's for sure, and they certainly wouldn't want us to know about it."

"But why pour the money into Soulminder at all?" Sommer asked. "It just doesn't seem consistent for them to steal money and then use it for altruistic purposes."

"Maybe they want to go down in history as the first nation to offer Soulminder protection to all its citizens," Alverez suggested. "I can see them doing it for ego."

Peripherally, Sommer saw Everly stiffen a bit. "Dr. Sommer," the security chief said carefully, "do you remember the list of people the Chileans already have on Soulminder? It was mostly the military and political leaders and educated classes, but it also included people like Archbishop Manzano who are outspoken critics of the government."

Sommer nodded. "It was one of the reasons we decided to take their expansion proposal seriously. It implied a commitment to keep their use of Soulminder non-political."

"Does it?" Everly asked. "What it implies to *me* is that they want everyone—including their enemies—to have a Mullner trace on file."

For a long minute Sommer stared at him. "Are you suggesting that they've found a way to pull personal information out of Mullner traces?"

Everly's eyes bored into his. "I think," he said quietly, "we'd damn well better find out."

A cold chill ran up Sommer's back. The vast and intricate tangle of embellishments that made up a human Mullner trace had so far defied every attempt at all but the broadest interpretation. Or at least it had in Soulminder's own labs. If the Chileans had found a way to crack the code . . . "Well, whatever's going on, we can't do anything about it now," he said reluctantly. "General Diaz will be picking us up for dinner in an hour, and I don't want to try to call Washington from here, even with our encrypted cells. Maybe after dinner we can make up an excuse to drop by the Soulminder office and use their satellite link—"

He broke off as the phone trilled. Frowning, he picked up the handset. "Hello?"

"Dr. Sommer?" a familiar voice said. "Hi, this is Martin Van Proyen at Soulminder. Awfully sorry to bother you, sir, but I'm afraid that when you and Mr. Everly finished using the terminals this morning you left them locked into your personal codes. Would it be possible for you to come by sometime tonight and unlock them?"

Sommer's mouth went suddenly dry. Neither he nor Everly had a personal computer code capable of doing any such thing. But the government people presumably tapping his phone wouldn't know that. "Sorry about that," he said, striving to sound casual. "We'll stop by on the way to dinner tonight, all right?"

"That would be fine, Doctor. Sorry for the inconvenience, but it's kind of vital that we get the terminals freed up."

Vital. "We'll be there in forty-five minutes," he said. "Good-bye."

"Sorry to have dragged you back here," Van Proyen apologized as he escorted the three of them through the Core's security gauntlet. "I hope the cloak and dagger approach didn't worry you—after that thing with Archbishop Manzano this morning I thought I should make this sound as harmless as possible. Though, actually, the truth sounds pretty harmless even taken straight. This way, please."

The Core was nearly deserted, with only a few staff people on hand to keep an eye on evening operations. Van Proyen led them to what turned out to be the main records office. "I was shuffling through the files like you'd told me to," he said, busying himself with one of the terminals, "when totally by accident I ran into a real puzzler. Let me first tell you that virtually every physician in Santiago is on file with Soulminder."

"No big surprise," Everly murmured. "The government's been concentrating on the educated classes."

"Right," Van Proyen nodded, "and that didn't bother me. What *did* bother me was that nearly sixty percent of the doctors who are now involved in some way with Soulminder have themselves been through the procedure."

"They've *what*?" Sommer frowned.

"Died and gone to Soulminder," Van Proyen said grimly. "Like I said, I'm not sure what it means, but it sounded crazy enough to bring to your attention."

"Crazy and a half," Sommer agreed uneasily, hunching his chair closer to the terminal display. "What about the other, non-medical workers? Can we check on those?"

"Already did." Van Proyen punched up another set of numbers. "You can see that there's an almost linear progression of percentages from the menial workers up the line to the more skilled, topping off with that sixty percent of the doctors. That number down there"—he indicated it—"is the overall percentage of Santiago citizens who've gone through Soulminder."

A number, Sommer noted, that was reasonably comparable with the percentage of menial Soulminder employees who'd used the facility. "Again, that may not be all that significant," he said slowly. "The more skilled the employee, the more likely he'd be on file in the first place."

"Yes, but sixty percent is still way too high," Alverez said, shaking his head.

"Agreed," Sommer nodded, thinking back to their conversation back at the hotel. "Can you get me an overall salary schedule?"

"Sure." Van Proyen bent again to the keyboard. "Remember, though, that the schedule is just a guideline—all the Chileans are being paid directly by the government."

The salary schedule appeared on the screen. Sommer frowned at it, trying to make a quick estimate in his mind—

"You thinking blackmail?" Everly asked.

Sommer shrugged. "Why not? If we assume that the government's learned how to read a person's innermost secrets from their Mullner trace, blackmail becomes trivial."

"Except that all they have to do then is hire people who are on file," Everly pointed out. "Going through Soulminder itself would be a waste of money."

Sommer wrinkled his nose as the idea evaporated beneath the logic. "You're right," he admitted.

"Besides," Alverez put in, indicating the numbers, "even if you put everyone who works here on starvation wages the savings wouldn't add up to more than twenty or thirty percent of the shortfall they've got in Soulminder costs."

"Well, it was a thought," Sommer said.

"On the other hand . . . " Alverez said thoughtfully, his voice fading away.

Sommer looked up at him. "Something?"

Alverez was frowning off into space. "On the other hand," he repeated, "it might be instructive to run a quick check on the other Soulminder patients. See what's happened to them afterward."

"You'd need access to Santiago's city records for that," Van Proyen pointed out.

"I know," Alverez said. "I don't know about the whole city, but I think I can get you into the government employment roster."

Van Proyen cleared his throat. "Yes," he said, striving to sound casual. "Of course, breaking into their files is highly illegal." He looked questioningly at Sommer.

Sommer pursed his lips, then stood up and gestured Alverez into the chair. "Try not to get caught," he said.

Visibly bracing himself, Alverez sat down in the vacated chair and got to work. "I just hope they haven't changed any of the passcodes since this morning . . . no, I guess they haven't."

"It's getting late, Dr. Sommer," Everly reminded him. "The driver's going to wonder what's going on."

Sommer glanced at his watch. "Yes. I suppose we should get going."

"If you don't mind, sir," Alverez said, his eyes still on the screen, "I'd like to keep going on this."

"All right," Sommer said. "I'm sure we can make up some excuse for you. Frank?"

"Yes, sir," Everly said. "But I'd like to make a quick call first, if I may. To the States, on the satellite link."

"There's a phone in the next office," Van Proyen offered, pointing.

"I'll wait for you in the car," Sommer said.

"I'd rather you wait here," Everly said, his voice oddly dark as he headed for the door. "If I'm right . . . I'd rather you weren't out of my sight, sir."

Sommer swallowed. It took a lot to make Frank Everly nervous. If he was nervous, it was probably time for Sommer to be nervous, too. "All right," he said. "Make it fast."

The dinner and its accompanying niceties fit easily into the same lavish mold as had the previous night's dinner. But now, with the mystery of the Soulminder employees nagging at him, Sommer found that his perception of the Chileans' activities had drastically changed. The luxury of the meal was an attempt to put him subtly in their debt, the complimentary speeches a trick to lull him into complacency, the round of social events themselves a means of keeping his attention off the real purpose of his trip. He could feel his conversation becoming guarded, his eyes and ears probing for nuances and hidden meanings in even the most casual of remarks. He was acutely aware of General Diaz's movements and comments, and nearly had a heart attack when the other was called from the room for a few minutes.

Only when the general returned and nonchalantly resumed his meal did Sommer finally realize just how far into paranoia he had slipped. It was a sobering thought, but it did little to help.

Eventually, the festivities came to an end.

"Perhaps you'd like to join me for a tour of Santiago's night life," General Diaz suggested as he guided Sommer and Everly down the steps toward the waiting car. "We're very proud of the variety of entertainment available here, and I think you would find it most enjoyable."

"Thank you," Sommer told him, "but I'm afraid business once again calls. I need to get back to the Soulminder office—there's some kind of flap going on up in Washington, and I need to sit down and get the complete story."

"I understand," Diaz said, with no hint of suspicion Sommer could detect. "There'll be a car waiting whenever you're ready to return to the hotel."

"Thank you, but that won't be necessary," Sommer said. "One of the Soulminder employees can give us a ride."

"I insist," Diaz said firmly. "You're our guests—we'll not have you hitching rides like peasants."

Sommer gave up. "In that case, thank you."

Van Proyen had been alerted by the main reception desk and was waiting for them at the entrance to the Core. "Get a grip on your vitals," he warned as he ushered them in. "This one's going to bounce you off the ropes."

The security clearance seemed to take forever, but at last they cleared the inner door. Alverez was waiting in the records office, looking both tired and oddly disillusioned. "I think we've found it, Dr. Sommer," he said, waving vaguely at the terminal in front of him. "Take a look."

With Everly at his side, Sommer stepped over and peered at the screen. "What is it?"

Alverez pointed to the top of the screen. "That first number is the overall percentage of government workers who've been through Soulminder. This is the breakdown by profession and current position, with real salaries before and after entering government service. And *this* is the record of how many of those switched to their government jobs only after going through Soulminder."

For a long minute Sommer stared at the numbers. "There's no chance of a mistake?" he asked at last.

"I don't think so," Van Proyen said quietly from behind him. "The Chilean government is giving its citizens free access to Soulminder . . . in exchange for turning them into slaves."

"At least," Everly said into the silence that followed, "it isn't any blackmail magic with the Mullner traces. I suppose that's something."

Sommer nodded, still staring at the numbers. Physicians, transfer techs, copper mine engineers, chip designers—all high-demand professionals, all working now at what was probably a tenth of their marketplace salaries. "So what do they hope to gain by extending the program to the less educated classes?" he asked.

Van Proyen and Alverez exchanged glances. "I don't know," Van Proyen answered for both of them. "Unless they want to maintain a pool of unskilled labor they can throw into the copper mines without having to pay union wages to."

"The forced government service may only be temporary, too," Everly pointed out.

"More like an indentured servitude than actual slavery," Van Proyen agreed. "If that's the case, they'll need to keep replacing them."

Everly rubbed his chin thoughtfully. "There may be more," he said, stepping over to the phone and punching a long series of buttons. "It's a little soon, but let me see if my friends have come through yet," he added, touching the speakerphone button and replacing the handset.

The phone was answered on the first ring. "Dr. Sands."

"Doctor, this is Frank Everly," Everly identified himself. "Have you had any response on that request I asked you to place?"

"Yes, indeed," she said, and from her tone Sommer could visualize a sour look on her face. "Is Adrian with you?"

"Right here, Jessica," Sommer called. "Along with Mr. Alverez and Station Chief Van Proyen. What's this all about?"

"I'm not exactly sure myself," she growled. "And I don't especially like playing blind-man's messenger, Frank. Anyway, here's the list: South Africa, Bulgaria, Central African Republic, Nicaragua, and Russia. So what does it mean?"

Everly hissed gently between his teeth. "Those are the countries secretly helping the Chileans fund their Soulminder experiment."

"Odd combination," Van Proyen murmured.

"Not when you consider that all of them have a certain problem with dissident elements," Everly said grimly.

"Why do I get the feeling," Sands said, "that I'm missing some of the pieces here?"

"The missing piece," Sommer told her, "is that we've uncovered indications that the government's using Soulminder to put its citizens into effective slavery."

"Those unfortunate enough to die at the right time, anyway," Alverez muttered.

Abruptly, Everly seemed to stiffen. "Van Proyen—get on that terminal. You have access to news/media databases?"

"Of course," Van Proyen said, stepping to the terminal as Alverez hastily vacated it. "Chilean and international both."

"Chilean will do," Everly told him. "Do a search for the names of well-publicized dissidents and correlate it with the Soulminder records. Find out how many of them have gone through Soulminder and then disappeared into some obscure government post up in the mountains somewhere." He pursed his lips. "And check on how many of them went through Soulminder because of curare poisoning."

Sommer stared at him, a cold knot gripping his stomach. "Are you suggesting . . . ?" His tongue froze, unable to say it.

"That the government's own death squads are behind the curare murders?" Everly said it for him. "Why not? It's certainly the simplest way for them to handpick the people they want."

Sommer took a shaky breath. "Well, then . . . that's that."

"That's *what*, Adrian?" Sands asked suspiciously.

"That's it for Soulminder Santiago," Sommer told her. "If Frank's right about government death squads, we're pulling out of here."

"On what grounds?"

Sommer stared at the phone. "On what *grounds*? Are you serious, Jessica?"

Her sigh was a snake hiss from the speaker. "Adrian, I understand how you feel, and I sympathize. But the Chileans have an operations contract with us, a contract they've done nothing to break."

"What about the misuse of our technology?" Sommer demanded.

"How do you prove that?" Sands countered. "Legally, I mean?"

"She's right," Van Proyen murmured. "The stuff we got from their database wouldn't be admissible."

Sommer threw him a glare. "They're using us to defraud their own people," he snarled. "They're paying Soulminder employees intern wages. They're *murdering* people, damn it!"

"All of which are internal affairs," Sands said icily. "I'm sorry, but they are. We have no legitimate excuse for canceling our contract."

"How about in the name of ordinary humanity?" Sommer shot back. "Or doesn't that count in business dealings?"

"Adrian, look," Sands said, her tone switching to a combination of cautious and soothing. "We are not in the business of crusading for truth and justice. We're in the business of preventing unnecessary death. If we try to pull out of Chile without a legitimate reason, the government will take us to court, and even if we win the legal fees and damage to our reputation will kill us. You know that."

Fleetingly, Diaz's remark about economic imperialism flashed through Sommer's mind. Other nations undoubtedly felt that way, too, and would likely be on Chile's side, no matter what atrocities the government was committing. "I understand," he said. "But we still can't just sit by and let Soulminder be used this way."

Beside Van Proyen the intercom beeped, and the other bent to speak quietly into it. "I'm open to suggestions," Sands said. "If you can find a way to make *them* break or cancel the contract, we'll be out of there so fast it'll make your head spin. But otherwise, I think we're stuck."

Van Proyen looked up, an odd expression on his face. "Dr. Sommer, the front desk reports that General Diaz is on his way back."

"Oh, *is* he?" Sommer said, starting for the door. "Good. I have some things to say to the man."

"Take it easy, Adrian," Sands called. "Don't do anything hasty."

"I'll talk to you later, Jessica," Sommer called as he yanked the door open.

"She's right," Everly's voice said quietly from behind him as he strode down the hall. "Bullying him isn't going to help."

"We'll see," Sommer said.

Diaz was waiting in the deserted anteroom just outside the Core entrance when Sommer and Everly emerged. "Ah—Dr. Sommer—"

He broke off, his eyes hard on Sommer's face as his own expression went tight and oddly sour. "I see," he continued, in a changed tone of voice. "So you've figured it out. And I can see you don't approve."

"I doubt that comes as a surprise," Sommer said evenly. "The game's over, General. As of right now."

Diaz's eyebrows lifted politely. "Or else . . . ?"

"Or else I'll pull Soulminder out of Chile. Forever."

The eyebrows remained lifted. "Indeed. I take it you're not overly familiar with the concept of specific performance?"

"I'm perfectly familiar with it, and I don't give a damn. No one will force us to continue operations here once this gets out."

Diaz smiled . . . and in that smile Sommer could see that his bluff had been a waste of time. "I beg to differ, Dr. Sommer," the other said. "When you lose the case—and you *will* lose it, because we've violated nothing in our contract—when you lose, then the courts will have no choice but to order you to fulfill the specific performance clause." Diaz's eyes hardened. "You can waste Soulminder's time and money, Doctor, and you can gain yourself a reputation for trying to bully small countries. But you can't stop us."

With an effort, Sommer unclenched his jaw muscles. "Why are you doing this?"

Diaz studied him, shrugged slightly. "It's very simple, Doctor. People whose lives have been miraculously spared are grateful. Grateful enough to devote a year of their lives repaying such a favor."

"At starvation wages, of course."

"As I said: they're grateful."

"And the pseudo-terrorist gambit? Or did you get the inspiration for that one from South Africa and Bulgaria and the others?"

Diaz's eyes flicked to Everly. "I see you've maintained your old CIA contacts," he said, a touch of bitterness in his tone. "As a matter of fact, no, that was our idea entirely. It occurred to us that perhaps that marvelous Soulminder gratitude might extend even to those who were critical of their leaders."

"And has it?" Everly asked.

Another flick of a glance. "Not as much as we'd hoped," Diaz acknowledged. "That part is still being evaluated. Of course, the indenture by itself gives us the opportunity to put them somewhere out of sight for a year."

"In a place of your own choosing, of course," Everly pointed out coldly. "High-risk, if at all possible."

Deliberately, Diaz turned his attention back to Sommer. "What it ultimately boils down to, Dr. Sommer, is that everything we're doing—certainly everything that you can prove we're doing—is no more illegal or unethical than the things any other government does with and to its people."

"The world community might not agree," Sommer countered.

"And you plan to tell them?" Diaz asked blandly. "You're at liberty to do so, but I'd advise against it. There are far worse slaveries in existence in a dozen other countries, slaveries that don't draw so much as a spot on the evening news. And *we*, at least, make servants only from those who would otherwise be dead." Abruptly, his gaze hardened. "Remember that, Doctor. What's a year of service to a man brought back from the dead?"

And in that moment, Sommer realized he'd lost. Diaz was right—there were too many atrocities being committed in the world for the general public to take all that much notice of this one. If it hadn't involved Soulminder, Sommer had to admit, he might not have noticed it himself.

But it *did* involve Soulminder.

"You don't need to drag us into it," he told the general, trying one last time. "People are effectively being brought back from the dead all the time. Most major medical procedures being done today qualify as life-saving."

Diaz shook his head. "You miss the point. Medical procedures can be done by anyone, in any place, and the fees for the doctors' work can be subsidized or forgiven by any of a thousand charitable organizations.

"But there is only one Soulminder. And in Chile, it's under *our* control." He favored Sommer with a brief, brittle smile. "The cradle is passé in today's overcrowded world, Doctor. It is now the hand that rocks the *casket* that rules the world."

For a long minute Sommer stared at him, searching for a way to refute that. But he couldn't, and both of them knew it. "I'm going to stop you," he said at last. "Soulminder is mine, not yours, and I'll find a way to get it back from you."

Diaz shrugged. "Perhaps. Perhaps not." He straightened. "And now, if you're finished here, I'll drive you back to the hotel."

"We're not finished," Sommer said through stiff lips. "And send your car home—we'll find our own way back."

Diaz sighed theatrically. "There's no reason to be awkward, Doctor. One of my jobs at the moment is to act as your escort and liaison, and I intend to complete that job."

"Good-night, General," Sommer said. Turning his back on the other, he stalked back through the security door into the Core.

Where, out of Diaz's sight, he paused, clenching his hands into painful fists as he swore the tension out of his chest.

Behind him, Everly slipped through the door to join him. "They're not going to get away with it, Frank," Sommer snarled at him. "They're *not.*"

Everly's eyes were steady on him. Eyes, Sommer saw, that had the same frustrated anger he himself was feeling, but under considerably better control. "Are you suggesting we interfere?" he asked quietly.

"You have a better suggestion?"

"Yes. Leave it to the Chileans themselves. People like Archbishop Manzano, who aren't afraid to speak out against the government. They know what's going on, or will soon." Everly's cheek twitched. "The only way there's going to be any permanent change here is when the people decide it's time for that change."

"And how many slaves will they make before that happens?" Sommer demanded. "How many other countries will decide the experiment is a success and initiate servitude projects of their own?"

"And how many people will die when they revolt against the junta?" Everly added heavily. "It's not easy to sit by, Doctor, when people are hurting. But the quick fixes never really fix anything. Especially quick fixes from outside."

Sommer sighed. "I suppose you're right. We can't single-handedly make Chile over into the American dream. But Diaz was also right: there *is* only one Soulminder. And no matter who has control over it locally, the ultimate responsibility for its use and misuse is still ours."

For a long moment he and Everly stared at each other. It was Everly who finally nodded. "You'll want a surgical operation, then," he said. "Something that'll affect the junta's use or control of Soulminder and nothing else."

Sommer nodded grimly. "*Surgical* is exactly the right word, as a matter of fact. Come on—let's get back inside. I need to find out from Van Proyen if what I've got in mind is feasible."

The last notes of the song ended, and for a moment the echoes reverberated through the cathedral. Sommer took his seat again, feeling his heart pounding in his chest. Archbishop Manzano would be speaking next.

"I trust you realize," General Diaz murmured at his ear, "that the Archbishop almost certainly won't be giving one of those fiery and impassioned speeches against the government which the international media so dearly loves. That type is usually reserved for when there are cameras focused on him."

"I understand," Sommer said between dry lips. "You're welcome to leave if you think it'll be boring."

He looked over to find Diaz glaring suspiciously at him. "Just what is it you expect to learn here?" he demanded in a harsh whisper. "That the Archbishop is unsatisfied with the progress of our reforms? You know that already."

Sommer forced himself to meet the other's gaze. "Perhaps," he said, allowing his voice to carry just a bit, "I'll find out what it was he wanted to tell me a few days ago. When he called me at Soulminder and your people substituted an electronic mimic for his voice."

A few heads turned their way, and Diaz actually winced. "This is neither the time nor the place—"

"Shh!" Sommer cut him off. Archbishop Manzano had risen to speak.

Sommer's grasp of Spanish was far too limited to allow him to follow what the Archbishop was saying. But from the very beginning it was clear that Diaz had been wrong on both counts. The Archbishop's homily was as impassioned as any Sommer had seen on the evening news back in Washington, and its target was most definitely the government.

Beside him, Sommer felt Diaz squirm uncomfortably in his seat. "The shoe fit too closely, General?" he murmured, not bothering to turn.

He could almost feel the heat of the other's glare. "Manzano's views are biased and distorted," the general all but spat. "All the truly thinking people in Chile know that."

Sommer opened his mouth to disagree—

And, without warning, the Archbishop collapsed to the floor.

For a half dozen heartbeats the cathedral was frozen into utter silence. Then someone screamed, and the sound broke everyone from their stunned paralysis. The crowd surged to its feet, a dozen men and women rushing up to the Archbishop's assistance as the rest milled about in fear and uncertainty.

An uncertainty that was rapidly giving way to anger.

"Come on, Doctor," Diaz snapped, grabbing Sommer's arm in an iron grip and all but bodily yanking him out into the aisle and toward the nearest exit. The two soldiers Diaz had brought along were already ahead of them, forcing a path through the crowd, and with his free hand Diaz pulled out a small radio and began speaking rapid-fire Spanish into it. What Sommer could see of his face was an ashen gray.

One final press of the crowd and they were outside, and in the distance Sommer could hear the sound of approaching sirens. "This way," Diaz said, dragging Sommer toward the waiting limo.

"Wait a minute," Sommer objected, giving a totally useless tug against the general's grip. "We can't just run off and leave the Archbishop."

"The ambulance is on its way," Diaz bit out. "The paramedics will handle it."

"And if he dies?" Sommer demanded.

Diaz threw a razor-edged glare at Sommer. But behind the anger Sommer could see a steadily growing tension. "Then you had better hope," he said, his voice quietly harsh, "that your Soulminder can restore him to life."

The ambulance crew had called ahead, and Sommer and Diaz arrived at Soulminder to find the Number One transfer room primed and ready. The general glanced around, strode over to where the head physician was checking the equipment and his instrument tray. "Well, Doctor?" he demanded. His tone, to Sommer, sounded less like a question than a challenge.

From the expression on the doctor's face it seemed he thought so, too. He gave Diaz a brief nod and then turned to continue his examination of the transfer equipment. "They seem ready to me," Sommer murmured.

"They had better be," Diaz said darkly. "Archbishop Manzano died before the paramedics even reached him."

Sommer felt his stomach tighten. "Did they get the neuro-preservatives into him in time?"

Diaz put the question to the doctor, who responded with a shrug and an answer Sommer again didn't catch. "The paramedics claim they did," Diaz growled. "He says we won't know until the body is brought in. If you'll excuse me?" Without waiting for a reply, he moved away, circling the transfer table to make his own inspection of the setup. Sommer drifted back toward the door.

He was standing right next to it when there was a flurry of activity out in the corridor and Manzano's body was wheeled in.

Followed immediately by a dozen reporters and cameras. Diaz shouted something across the room and soldiers leaped in from the corridor, cutting through the crowd and forming a human barricade between the media and the transfer table. Diaz shouted something else and the soldiers began pushing the reporters back toward the door.

In the noise and confusion, no one noticed Sommer slip out.

Threading the Core's security gauntlet took three minutes. By the time Sommer dropped into the chair beside Van Proyen, it was clear from the TV monitor that they were almost ready to begin. "Status?" Sommer asked, giving the duplicate readouts a quick scan.

"All the preliminary stuff's out of the way," Van Proyen told him, his voice tight. "They've got the glucose IV going, the curare's been neutralized and eliminated, and the process of flushing the neuropreservatives out of his system has been started. Another"—he glanced at the clock—"two and a half minutes and they'll be ready to try the transfer."

Sommer nodded, his eyes on the monitor. The transfer team, waiting for the neuropreservative flushing to be completed, stood silently around the body on the table. In contrast, Diaz, just visible at the edge of the screen, was a study in barely controlled nervous energy. "Anything from the media yet?" he asked over his shoulder.

Seated at another desk, flipping between channels on a muted television and holding a radio to his ear, Alverez shrugged. "They know the Archbishop took a curare dart," he said, his voice as tight as Van Proyen's. "*And* they know he was raking the government over the coals when he was shot. Nothing else but rumors, but the outside monitors show that we've got quite a crowd gathering around the building."

"Waiting for the Archbishop to come out," Van Proyen suggested grimly. "You know, Doctor, this could get very nasty very quickly."

Sommer thought about the crowd back at the cathedral. About the anger he'd felt beginning to rise up within them. "How nasty it gets," he said, "is basically up to Diaz."

"I suppose." Van Proyen leaned forward, his eyes on the monitor. "Looks like they're ready.

Sommer leaned forward, too, mentally crossing his fingers. On the screen the doctor touched the master transfer switch. Beside the monitor the duplicate readouts went from red to amber, and all eyes in the room turned to the body on the table.

Nothing.

For a long moment the doctor just stood there, staring with disbelief at the unmoving body. Then, abruptly, he and the rest of the team jumped back into action.

"My, my," Van Proyen murmured. "The soul didn't remeld."

"Shh!" Sommer said as Diaz took a step forward and snarled something vicious sounding. "What'd he say?"

"He's demanding to know why it isn't working," Van Proyen translated. The doctor snapped something back— "'I don't know,'" Van Proyen added without being asked. "'Be quiet and let us work.'"

Sommer felt his hands gripping the arms of his chair, and for a few minutes they watched in silence as the transfer team worked furiously to try and get the Archbishop's soul to remeld with his body. But it was futile, and abruptly the duplicate readouts went from amber back to red. "They've given up," Van Proyen said as, simultaneously, the indicators for the life-support machines switched from standby back to full on.

Dimly, Sommer noticed that his teeth were clenched together.

"They have to," he said, his mouth dry. "If they keep at it they'll only put unnecessary stress on the brain chemistry."

Reaching over, Van Proyen tapped out a command on a terminal keyboard. "The soul's back in the trap," he confirmed.

Sommer got to his feet. "I'll be in your office," he told Van Proyen. He gave the monitor a last look, his eyes settling on Diaz. "Let me know when the general's ready to talk."

It took less than an hour.

"General Diaz wants to talk to you, Dr. Sommer," Van Proyen reported, his voice on the intercom sounding more than a little strained. "Are you ready?"

Sommer took a deep breath. *As ready as I'm going to be.* "Ask him to wait in the conference room near the Core entrance," he said aloud. "Has Frank Everly returned?"

"Yes, sir, just a few minutes ago. He's up on the office floor, keeping an eye on that mob outside."

"Have him join us," Sommer instructed him. "Tell him to hurry—I don't want to be alone with Diaz."

He needn't have worried. Everly was waiting by the conference room door when Sommer arrived. "Doctor," Everly said, his eyes tight. "You seen the crowd out there?"

Sommer nodded. "There's one forming around the Presidential Palace, too."

"And we're getting some rumblings of uncertainty from the military." Everly glanced back down the hall. "It's starting to look a lot like being in the middle of a revolution."

"It does, doesn't it," Sommer agreed grimly. "Everything's ready. Shall we go see if the general's had enough?"

Diaz was standing at the head of the table as they entered, his back unnaturally stiff. "Dr. Sommer," he nodded as Everly closed the door behind them. The general's voice was quiet, almost gentle, and it sent a chill up Sommer's back. "Tell me, what have you done to the Soulminder equipment?"

"Your own experts are out there, General," Sommer said, trying to keep his voice from trembling. This was it, the point on which Soulminder's entire future was wobbling. "Did you ask *them* what was wrong?"

Diaz's eyes bored into his. "You've sabotaged the Soulminder," he said. "Done something to it from in there." He nodded in the direction of the Core, the movement almost savage.

"Is that what you're telling the people outside?" Everly asked. "That your failure to bring Manzano back is *our* fault?"

Diaz's gaze moved slowly over to rest on Everly. "It was you, wasn't it?" he said, almost conversationally. "You who shot Manzano and made it look like the government was at fault."

Everly raised his eyebrows slightly. "The government? I thought it was terrorists who murdered people with curare darts."

Diaz raised his hand. "Not them alone."

Sommer felt his stomach tighten. "And what exactly do you intend to do with that?" he asked, raising his eyes with an effort from the tiny airgun in Diaz's hand.

"You will restore the Archbishop's soul to his body," Diaz ordered. "Now."

"Or else what?" Everly asked calmly. "You'll shoot us? With both our Mullner traces on file with Soulminder?"

"Your souls may live on inside a box in Washington," Diaz snarled. "But your bodies would be here. Under *our* control."

"Wouldn't help you any," Everly shrugged. "Or haven't you heard of Arizona's Professional Witness program? Killing people doesn't guarantee you've shut them up anymore."

"Talk all you want," Diaz spat. "We *will* weather this crisis—the riots and Army trouble will be put down. And all nations suffering in the Soulminder stranglehold will thank us for what we've done."

Sommer shook his head. "No one will thank you," he said wearily. "All you'll accomplish will be to drive Chile into revolution. Your experiment in indentured servitude can't possibly be worth that price."

"And stopping it is worth the price of your death?" Diaz countered.

For a long moment Sommer eyed him in silence. Then, taking a careful step toward the gun, he pulled a chair out from the table. "Do you know why I created Soulminder, General?" he asked, sitting down. "My motivation, I mean?"

"Is this some effort to stall—?"

"Twenty years ago," Sommer continued, "my son David, who was five years old, died in a car accident. I was the one driving. The weight of that guilt stayed with me for eleven years, until Jessica Sands and I finally created Soulminder."

"I'm sorry for your loss," Diaz said, without any trace of sympathy in his face or voice. "Forgive me if I'm not overcome by sentiment."

"I was the second person to go through Soulminder, General," Sommer told him. "I've been in the tunnel. I've seen the Light that waits at the end of it."

"Religious superstition," Diaz sneered. "For the weak and the gullible."

"Perhaps," Sommer said. "Perhaps not. The fact remains that I'm not afraid to die.

"But *you* are."

The knuckles of Diaz's gun hand whitened noticeably, and his eyes flicked to Everly. "What about you, CIA man?" he spat. "Are you ready to die, too?"

"Curare's a fast way to go," Everly said evenly. "Much faster than being torn apart by the mob outside."

Diaz smiled at him. "The mob can do what they like with this body. There are hundreds to choose from." He looked back at Sommer. "Or hadn't *that* potential of your Professional Witness program occurred to you?"

"It's occurred to us, yes," Sommer told him evenly. "But it won't work for you."

Diaz snorted. "Why? Because of the so-called biochemical instabilities involved in transferring a soul to a different body?"

"No," Sommer said. "Because your Mullner trace is no longer on file with Soulminder. I erased it half an hour ago."

Diaz stared at him, some of the color draining from his face. "You're lying," he said, his voice barely above a whisper. "Bluffing. You wouldn't do something like that."

"You have two choices, General." Slowly, carefully, Sommer pulled a sheaf of papers from his coat pocket and laid it on the table. "Choice one: you can take this amended contract to the Presidential Palace and have General Santos sign it. It has a clause expressly forbidding any form of servitude as the price for Soulminder access, under penalty of complete cancelation if violated. And believe me, we *will* monitor your compliance of that clause.

"Choice two"—he braced himself—"is to call my bluff."

There was hatred in Diaz's eyes. Dark, blazing hatred, both for Sommer himself and for the legacy of economic domination of which, in his view, Soulminder was just one more example. For a half dozen heartbeats Sommer wondered if he'd pushed the man too far. Wondered if pride alone would now force him to kill and then die in turn.

And then, slowly, the gun barrel lowered to point at the floor. "I will take the contract to General Santos," he said bitterly. "I will also announce that you have taken charge of Manzano's revival. From now on any delays will be upon *your* head."

"Understood," Sommer nodded, a wave of relief washing over him. Relief, and a strange sadness. "You might inform General Santos that he and the other members of the junta have also been erased from Soulminder's files. In case that has any bearing on his decision."

For a moment the two men locked eyes. Then Diaz reached down and picked up the amended contract. "This was a battle, Dr. Sommer," he said, very quietly. "Not the war." Without another word, he strode from the room.

Sands shook her head, lips pursed tightly together as she hefted the new contract. "That was, without a doubt," she said, "the noblest damn fool thing you've done in years."

"You'd have preferred letting the Chilean government perfect this new brand of slavery?" Sommer countered.

"To you meddling with their politics?" Sands snorted. "As a matter of fact, yes, I *would* have preferred it. My God, Adrian—you all but assassinate an Archbishop, and then compound the risk with that crazy IV trick. What if one of the doctors had tried switching glucose bottles?"

"It wouldn't have mattered," Sommer said, walking over to his desk and sitting down. Suddenly, he was very tired of having to think and talk about Chile. "All the bottles available to them had the same lacing of neuropreservative, and with that continually dripping into the Archbishop's system they didn't have a hope of remelding his soul."

Sands eyed him. "Don't get me wrong," she said, a note of caution creeping into her voice. "I don't quarrel with your motives—I realize you had the best interests of the Chilean people in mind. But it sets a dangerous precedent."

"What, that we want to maintain control over how our invention is used?" Sommer demanded pointedly. "That's hardly a dangerous precedent."

She gave him a patient look. "Look, Adrian. We're not set up to function as the world's ethical policeman. As long as there are warped and power-hungry people in high places, there'll always be attempts to pervert Soulminder into something we don't like. Diaz was right: we've won a battle, not a war."

Sommer shook his head. "Diaz was wrong, and he knew it. We've won the war, all right."

"Because the government wasn't willing to risk death over their servitude project?"

Sommer gazed at her, a strange melancholy tightening his stomach. "You're missing the point, Jessica," he said quietly. "Diaz and the others were generals. *Military* men, who'd probably faced the prospect of death dozens of times throughout their careers. And yet they caved in when they found I'd erased them from Soulminder. Why?"

Sands's eyes were steady on him. "You tell me."

"Because they'd gotten used to the idea that they could be immortal," he said. "They saw themselves living forever . . . and they weren't willing to risk that."

For a long minute Sands was silent. "If that's true," she said at last, "it means Soulminder has suddenly inherited a great deal of political muscle."

Sommer nodded. "I'm not at all sure I want us to have that kind of power."

"I'm not at all sure," Sands said quietly, "that we have a choice."

CHAPTER 5

●

Guilt by Association

THEY CAME AT HER out of the dark and gloom of the night shadows: ghostly and indistinct, walking with an almost-normal gait that was somehow more chilling than an exaggerated, movie-monster lurch would have been.

They were the walking dead, and they were coming for her.

She had turned away from them, and was slogging slow motion through something that felt like waist-deep ice water, when they inexplicably began buzzing.

The dead froze for a moment, as if they too were listening to the buzzing. Then the nightmare shattered, and with a jerk of taut muscles Carolyn Blanchard was awake.

For another long moment her mind spun dizzily as it tried to fit the feel of the thin mattress beneath her and the dim features of the room around her into the pattern of her apartment. Then, from beside her head the buzz came again, and with that the disorientation finally cleared. Levering herself up onto an elbow, heart thudding hard in her chest and neck, she poked at the flashing button on the tabletop intercom. "Yeah—Blanchard," she said.

"McGee," the transfer supervisor's voice came. "We've got a floater, just came in."

"Right." Blanchard sat up and swung her legs off the cot, waiting for her head to adjust to the sudden change in altitude. A floater. Such a wonderfully innocuous term, she thought bleakly, for someone who'd just died. "Have you woken up Walker yet?" she asked, reaching down to pull her shoes on.

"He's being prepped," McGee said, and this time she was awake enough to hear the mid-level tension in his voice. "He was already down here when the trap triggered."

Blanchard glanced at the clock on the Soulminder MiNex console beside her cot. Three thirty-eight in the morning, yet Walker Lamar had still been awake. Awake, and roving Soulminder's halls. "Swell," she grunted.

"Yeah," McGee agreed grimly. "We're in Transfer Five. If you want to see him before he goes under, you'd better hurry."

"On my way."

She got her shoes fastened and hurried out of the room, breaking into a fast jog. The corridors, so busy during normal working hours, were practically deserted, with only an occasional office worker or armed guard visible.

It was an illusory sort of emptiness. Even at this hour two to four of the transfer rooms would be fully manned, as would the satellite monitor stations that watched for the emergency signals that could pinpoint a newly dead Soulminder client. At the center of the building, in the Core, there would be a full complement of highly-placed managers and techs making sure that the Soulminder computers and software and traps performed with their usual flawless efficiency.

And if Blanchard never saw any of that elite cadre, it was for sure they were always watching her.

She almost made it in time. Almost, but not quite. Even as she pushed through Transfer Five's swinging doors Dr. Wilkom Ng was already lifting his hypo from the man laid out on the padded table in front of him. Blanchard moved forward, eyes automatically flicking to the bank of monitors behind them, and before she was halfway to the table, the trace lines simultaneously went flat.

The man on the table, Walker Lamar, was dead.

Blanchard gazed down at the body, feeling that eerie sense of unreality that still sometimes hit her at this point in the operation. By all the legal and medical definitions of barely ten years ago, Walker was dead—completely and irreversibly dead. And yet, through the technological miracle that was Soulminder he was now, by current definitions, just as legally and medically alive. His soul, its complex Mullner pattern recorded months ago on the giant computers back in the Core, had been recognized, identified, and snatched away as it departed his body. Locked safely away in one of the hundreds of traps back there, floating in some sort of semi-existence that she'd never been able to get adequately described, it could remain protected indefinitely. And, provided his brain and body were similarly protected by neuropreservatives and full life-support gear, soul and body could be remelded at any time.

But those neuropreservatives had to be administered within a very few minutes of body death. If they weren't, if the brain tissue deterioration was allowed to progress past a critical point, then there would be no functional body left for him to return to.

At which point—living soul or not, Soulminder magic or not—Walker Lamar would be effectively dead. The trap would have to be turned off, and his soul would depart. Going wherever it was souls went.

"You ready?" Ng asked.

Blanchard shook away the introspection. "Sure," she said, hoping she sounded more confident than she felt. Of all the difficult parts of this job, dealing with floaters was easily the worst. "What do we have on the floater?"

"Name's Jack Thornton," McGee told her. He was standing off to the side, next to the tech seated at the transfer room's MiNex terminal. "Fifty-one, professor of electrical engineering at Caltech, lives in Pasadena. Lives alone, unfortunately—divorced—so no possible help there. He triggered the trap just over two and a half minutes ago."

"From the lack of signal," the tech added, "best guess is that he's under water somewhere."

"Right," Blanchard nodded, the tightness in her stomach easing a little. In her past experience she'd always found middle-aged highbrow types relatively easy to deal with: generally polite and disinclined toward anything as undignified as hysteria.

Of course, none of those she'd dealt with had been freshly dead. "How long?"

"We're ready," Ng said. "Stand by."

On the console behind him lights changed color . . . and, with a suddenness that Blanchard was never quite prepared for, Walker Lamar's body jerked alive. "Wha—wha—?"

Blanchard turned her head to peer straight down into the confused face. "Dr. Thornton? Jack? Can you hear me?"

The eyes focused uncertainly on her. "Who—I mean, where—?"

"You're in Soulminder Los Angeles," she cut him off. "There's been some sort of accident. Where were you when it happened?"

The forehead creased. "Where was I . . . ?"

"You were in some kind of accident," Blanchard repeated. That was only a guess, but a fairly safe one. And from the almost-foggy look in his eyes— "Had you been drinking earlier? Did you drink and then get in your car and drive somewhere?"

A sudden look of horror flooded his face. "It wasn't a dream," he hissed. "It was—I was *dead*."

"Jack, your body is missing," Blanchard told him, putting steel into her voice. If he slid off into panic or denial now, their chances of saving him would go straight to zero. "It's missing, and your Soulminder wristband isn't signaling its location. We need to know where you died, and we need to know it *now*."

For a long second she thought it hadn't worked. Those eyes stared at and through her . . . then, abruptly, they gave a little twitch. "I was coming back from Coldbrook," he murmured. "Along Thirty-nine."

The tech at the console was already punching keys, and a second later the full-wall display behind Ng lit up with a detailed map of the San Gabriel Wilderness and Angeles National Forest regions. Highway 39 snaked through the middle of it, and at the lower middle— "Had you passed the San Gabriel Reservoir yet?" she asked. "Jack?"

The eyes defocused again. "Yes," he said, his voice stronger and more sure of itself. Starting to catch up with the emotional shock of it. "And . . . yes, I'd passed the Morris Reservoir, too."

The map display shifted, enlarged. "Gotta be the river," someone said.

"Do you remember anything else, Jack?" Blanchard asked. "Anything that might help us to find—"

"I went off the road." A hand came up, seized her arm in a panic grip. "I went off the road, and the river was there—oh, *God*."

Blanchard reached her free hand over to grip his. "It's all right," she assured him, hoping fervently that wasn't a lie. On the display a small white circle had suddenly appeared, heading toward the target zone from downtown Los Angeles. "It's all right," she repeated. "An emergency team's on the way."

"I must have drowned," he whispered. "Oh, God. Oh, God. I drowned. I'm *dead*."

Blanchard clenched her teeth. Thornton was losing it again. Hardly surprising, under the circumstances, but in her mind's eye she could see the adrenaline surge that all that panic was pumping into Walker Lamar's body . . .

She caught Ng's eye. He nodded back, the hypo already prepared. "Now, just relax, Jack," she said soothingly, keeping her grip on his hand. "We're going to have to let you go back into Soulminder for a little while. But it'll be all right."

The eyes looked at her, not understanding. She braced herself for the reaction when that understanding finally came.

It did, and the eyes were suddenly filled with shock. But by then it was too late for any reaction. Ng withdrew the needle from the other's arm, and with welcome anticlimax the eyes rolled up and the grip on Blanchard's arm loosened.

Walker Lamar was dead. Again.

Blanchard took a shuddering breath and lowered the limp arm back to the table. Out of the corner of her eye she saw McGee step to her side, his stance that of someone who wanted to talk. "What are his chances?" she asked, keeping her eyes on Ng.

"Thornton's? Hard to say." He looked over his shoulder at the map display. Already the circle marking the rescue team was almost to the suspected accident site. Dimly, Blanchard wondered what kind of speed that helicopter was making. "The water there should be pretty cold, which will help slow down neural deterioration," Ng added, turning back to Lamar's body.

"At least they won't have any problem finding him," McGee put in. "Not now. His wristband can't transmit far enough through water to reach the satellites, but the rescue chopper's detector will pick it up at least a mile away. At that point"—she sensed him shrug—"it'll be a matter of how fast the team can pull the body out of the car and get it onto neuropreservatives and life-support."

Blanchard nodded. McGee's politely confrontational stance hadn't changed. "I presume you want to talk about Walker," she said.

She looked at him in time to see his lips pucker. "This makes at least four times we've seen him wandering around in the wee hours," he reminded her.

"I can count," Blanchard growled. "Has it ever occurred to you that it might be nothing more than an occasional touch of insomnia?"

McGee's eyebrows lifted. "It has, yes. But I somehow doubt you'd be quite so defensive if that was all there was to it."

Blanchard dropped her eyes to Lamar's motionless face. His motionless, *dead* face. "This happens to people in high-stress occupations," she said doggedly. "He'll get through it okay."

"Probably. Question is, will *you*?"

She forced herself to look back at him. To meet that steady gaze. "I've done things that were *lots* harder than this, Mr. McGee. My year as bottom-rung police psychologist in St. Louis, for obvious example. Compared with getting into a serial killer's head, handling a Professional Witness is a stroll through the park."

For a moment McGee studied her, as if somehow divining the nightmare she'd been having when he'd woken her up. But then a timer on the console pinged gently, and one of the techs handed Ng a fresh hypo, and—almost reluctantly, she thought—McGee turned his attention back to Lamar's body. "If you say so," he said. "If I were you, though, I'd watch out for muggers on this particular stroll. Serial killers may scare the pants off you, but at least you never had to watch any of them die over and over again."

Blanchard didn't reply. Behind Ng a set of indicator lights flicked on, indicating that the neuropreservatives that had protected Lamar's brain and nerve cells from damage during the crucial first minutes of his induced death had now been adequately flushed from his body. Ng double-checked everything, then nodded to the tech at the Soulminder console. The latter nodded in return, touched a switch—

And with a shudder that ran up his entire body, Walker Lamar returned to life.

"Hi," Blanchard said, forcing a casual smile onto her lips as Lamar's eyes focused on her. "How are you feeling?"

"Oh—" the eyes defocused again, just for a second. "Fine. I guess. Fine. I guess."

"Then I guess you must be fine," she said, striving for a note of levity. "Doctor?"

"Everything looks good," Ng nodded. "Blood pressure's a little high, Walker, but that's a normal part of your post-transfer profile."

"Great." Blanchard found Lamar's hand and squeezed it. "So. Excitement's over; I guess it's back to bed for—"

"Is he going to be okay?" Lamar interrupted, twisting his head to look at the map display.

"They're pulling the body out of the car right now," the tech at the communications console spoke up. "Everything else is ready."

"They probably won't know for sure for at least an hour," Blanchard reminded him. "Maybe longer. I'm sure that if you ask Mr. McGee he'll have someone wake you up whenever they have something."

Lamar looked at McGee, as if only just noticing his presence. Then he shrugged, a strangely jerky movement of his shoulders. "Yeah, well . . . I'm not all that sleepy. I guess I'll just hang around." Abruptly, he sat up all the way, swinging his legs clumsily over the edge of the table. "Maybe I'll take a little walk first," he added as Blanchard and McGee each grabbed an arm to help steady him. "Get used to having legs again, and all that. Unless you need me here, 'cause I *could* stay."

Almost word for word the same speech he always gave. Behind her smile, Blanchard felt her teeth clench up. Needing some time alone to recover from such an experience was neither abnormal nor unhealthy. But to try so hard to pretend he didn't really *need* it was something else again. "No, go ahead," she told him. "Someone'll call you as soon as they know about him."

"Don't worry," McGee said soothingly. "Dr. Thornton's got a really good chance."

"Thornton," Lamar said thoughtfully, almost as if tasting the sound of the name. "I knew someone named Thornton once."

"Doubt it's the same one," the tech at the MiNex terminal shook his head. "This one's named Jack, fifty-one, works at Caltech—"

"You can get all the details from Thornton himself later," Blanchard cut the tech off, throwing a warning glare in his direction. There was still a fair chance Thornton's brain had gone too long without neuropreservatives to be savable, and if that happened she'd rather Lamar have known the man only as a faceless shadow. "For now, I really think you ought to go to bed," she added. "Don't forget we're due in court at ten tomorrow morning."

Lamar's lip twitched, just a bit. "Yeah. Right."

Blanchard squeezed his hand again. "Okay. So, I'll see you then. Sleep well."

"Sure." Lamar seemed to brace himself, then lurched forward, landing on only slightly unsteady feet. With a vague sort of wave over his shoulder, he shuffled to the door and left.

Blanchard took a deep breath, exhaled it silently. She'd been with Lamar ever since he'd joined the LA Pro-Witness program eight months ago . . . and much as she hated to admit it, down deep she knew that McGee was right.

Lamar was starting to lose it.

"I think maybe we ought to recommend to the D.A.'s office that they pull him off," McGee said quietly from behind her. "Whether he likes it or not."

Blanchard turned to face him. "We can't do that," she said. "If he quits in the middle of a case, they won't let him come back."

McGee snorted gently. "I submit that his mental health is more important than his job."

"I submit the two aren't separable," she countered tartly. "I don't know if you've read his file, but this is the first job Walker's ever had that's had even a scrap of public dignity associated with it. You tell him he can't handle it and throw him out, and his wallet won't be the only thing that suffers."

"Fine," McGee said. "Then just get him a leave of absence or something. I mean, we *are* Soulminder. The right word to the right person ought to be able to bend city policy a little."

Blanchard shook her head. "Not this time. The D.A.'s office is very jealous of its turf here. And very sensitive to suggestions that Soulminder might be quietly running their Pro-Witness program for them."

McGee sighed, his gaze flicking over her shoulder to where Lamar had exited. "I don't like keeping him on, Doctor," he said quietly. "Not in the shape he's in. I really don't."

"He'll make it," she said, forcing conviction she didn't feel into her voice. "As soon as the Holloway case is wrapped up I can get him some off time."

"You really think he'll last that long?"

"Of course he will," Blanchard growled. Abruptly, she was tired of this conversation. "All the pre-trial stuff is over. Holloway will testify and be cross-examined tomorrow, and that'll be it until he comes in for the verdict and sentencing." And then, she reminded herself with a sort of dull bitterness, his soul would be released from the trap and go . . . wherever it was souls went. That wasn't something she liked to think about. She certainly didn't want to talk about it. "Now if you'll excuse me, I have to be in court tomorrow."

"You want me to wake you if Thornton makes it?" McGee called after her as she headed for the door.

"Don't bother—I'll read about it in the morning."

She was still awake an hour later when the news came over the MiNex console that the team had indeed gotten to Thornton's body in time.

The line went flat, and Walker Lamar was dead. Again.

"It'll be just another minute," the doctor told the assembled officials.

"Fine," Judge Harold Grange nodded, his face and voice glacially calm. In contrast, Assistant D.A. William Dorfman looked almost bored, while Defense Attorney James Austin seemed hawk-eyed alert. Watching for a mistake, Blanchard decided, some legal technicality he could use in his appeal.

At least she assumed that was his strategy. From what she'd heard of Holloway's discussions with the D.A. that was probably the only chance Austin's client had.

"Ready," the doctor said briskly. "Here we go."

The indicator lights changed colors, the biotrace lines became squiggly again, and on the transfer table Lamar's body came back to life.

The judge took a step forward. "Michael Holloway?" he asked.

The eyes had been gazing at the ceiling, studying it as if he'd never seen self-cleaning ceramic tile before. Turning his head, he looked at the judge, the same oddly rapt look in his eyes. "Yes," he murmured. He licked his lips, first the upper and then the lower; licked them both again as if savoring the experience. "Yes," he repeated, louder this time.

"It's time." The judge turned back to the two lawyers. "Let's go. Get everything signed," he added to the young clerk standing over by the readout console, a sheaf of legal papers clutched in her hand. Without waiting for a reply, he strode to the transfer room door and headed out.

Ten minutes later, in the new courthouse that had been built next door to Soulminder Los Angeles for just this purpose, the case of People v. Battistello was reconvened.

"The people," Dorfman announced, "call Michael Holloway to the stand."

Beside him, the witness got to his feet and stepped to the stand. His eyes, Blanchard noted from her seat behind the prosecutor's table, continued to dart all around the room as he was being sworn in.

"State your name for the record," Judge Grange said.

He settled himself gingerly into his chair, leaned forward toward the microphone. "Michael Andrew Holloway."

Judge Grange shifted his attention to Dorfman. "Are the people prepared to prove that this is indeed Mr. Holloway speaking?"

"Yes, your honor." Dorfman half turned. "The people call Katherine Holloway Ross and Lisa Holloway Davis."

Two well-dressed women in their forties stood up and came forward, and Blanchard felt a little of the tightness go out of her stomach. She'd argued strongly with Dorfman that he use Holloway's sisters rather than his brothers, but up until now she hadn't been at all certain the prosecutor would follow that recommendation. The confirmation procedure could be devastating for everyone involved, and in her admittedly limited experience she'd found that women tended to handle the emotional trauma better than men.

The two women had arrived at the bench now, flanked by the opposing attorneys. "As per federal statute concerning Professional Witness testimony," the judge said, his gaze shifting back and forth between the women, "the first three questions from each of you will be public, and on the public record. All others may, if either or both of you so choose, be confidential between yourselves, the witness, and the court. Those questions and their answers will be sealed by this court against any and all public disclosure, except in extraordinary circumstances. Do you both understand?"

They nodded. "Then you may proceed," the judge said, swiveling his microphone around to face them.

There was a second of hesitation. Then, the elder of the two women stepped up to it. "Mike," she said, her voice trembling just a bit. "When you were ten, we all drove to Florida—do you remember? What did Jonathan say that had all of us in hysterics, and where was he when he said it?"

A wistful, almost ghostly smile touched his face. "He was sitting in the far back seat of the station wagon," he said. "The way-back-in-the-back, we called it. And he was calling, 'Get off our road!' at the cars behind us."

A quiet chuckle ran through the jury box. The woman stepped back, her eyes suddenly tear-bright, to be replaced at the microphone by the younger woman. "Mike, what pet did I have when I was in fourth grade?" she asked.

His forehead creased. "You had a *lot* of dumb pets when you were little, Lise."

"This one died the day after it bit me."

The frown cleared. "Ah. Well, *that* would have been your hamster."

Another ripple ran through the jury, but to Blanchard's

ears this one sounded strained. As if the mention of death had reminded them that they were not, in fact, merely here to witness a genial family reunion.

She looked over to where the defendant was sitting, his face carved from frozen stone as he watched the proceedings. He, certainly, hadn't forgotten why they were there.

The questioning lasted almost twenty minutes. When it was over, both women agreed that it was indeed their brother sitting in the witness chair.

"Let the record show," Dorfman said as the sisters returned to the spectators' section, "that personal identification, plus signed affidavits from Soulminder authorities, have established that the soul of Michael Andrew Holloway currently resides in the body of Professional Witness Walker Lamar." He let his eyes sweep the jury, then turned back to the witness box. "And now, Mr. Holloway, would you please relate to the court the events of the evening of January 27 of this year."

He seemed to brace himself. "I left my office about six-thirty," he said, his voice almost too low for the microphone to pick up. "I was walking to the car when I heard footsteps coming up behind me. I turned around, and there was a kid behind me with a gun."

He paused, tongue flicking across upper and then lower lip. "He told me to give him all my money or he'd blow my head off."

"Did you comply?" Dorfman asked.

"Yes, right away," he nodded, a jerky movement of his head. "I tried to, anyway. I reached into my coat pocket for my wallet—" He took a deep, shuddering breath.

"Did he say anything else, Mr. Holloway?" Dorfman asked into the momentary silence. "Warn you not to make any sudden moves, or anything like that?"

He shook his head. "He didn't say anything at all."

"Nothing?"

"No. He was as cool as if he'd done this a hundred times."

"Objection," Austin said, half rising from his seat beside the defendant. "The witness is speculating."

"Sustained," Grange nodded. "Please confine your comments to answering the questions, Mr. Holloway."

The lips puckered slightly. "Yes, sir," he muttered.

"So," Dorfman continued, "you reached for your wallet. Did you bring it out?"

"I didn't get a chance," he said bitterly. "My hand was still inside my coat when he shot me."

Dorfman let the words hang in the air for a moment. "How many times did he shoot you?" he asked.

"Objection." Austin was on his feet again. "More speculation."

Grange nodded. "Sustained. Rephrase your question, counselor."

"How many bullets did you *feel* hit you, Mr. Holloway?"

"I felt two," he whispered. "Both in my chest. And I think I heard a third one after I fell on my back, but I don't remember feeling it hit me."

"Two shots, both in your chest," Dorfman repeated. "And yet, the coroner reported finding *eight* bullets—"

"Objection," Austin called indignantly.

"Sustained," Grange growled. "Save the summing-up for your closing, Mr. Dorfman."

"Yes, your honor. Tell me, Mr. Holloway: do you see the man who shot you anywhere in this courtroom?"

"Yes."

"Will you point him out?"

The witness took another deep breath, his eyes shifting from Dorfman to Battistello. "He's right there."

Dorfman nodded, his expression theatrically grim. "Let the record show," he intoned, "that Michael Holloway has identified the defendant, Mr. Battistello, as the man who assaulted him on the night of January 27.

"The man who murdered him."

There was more, of course. Much more.

Dorfman walked the witness through the murder in carefully

precise detail, focusing a large percentage of his attention on Holloway's recollection of the assailant's clothing, expressions, and actions. The exercise was obviously a painful one, and more than once Blanchard felt herself wincing in sympathy with the terror and anger and helplessness boiling quietly out of the witness box. It was a straightforward enough strategy: Dorfman was bidding for jury outrage while simultaneously going for a preemptive blunting of any future attempts by the defense to cast doubt on the victim's memory. But knowing that didn't make it any easier to take.

The direct testimony was hard enough to sit through. Austin's cross-examination, urbanely hostile and subtly condescending, was even worse. By the time the defense attorney sat down Blanchard's stomach was a mess of churning acid.

"It is now five minutes until twelve," Judge Grange announced as the witness left the stand and made his way back to the prosecutor's table. "We'll take a ninety-minute recess for lunch, and reconvene precisely at one-thirty."

He banged his gavel and headed for chambers, and the courtroom participants and spectators began to break up into movement and the buzz of conversation.

"So what happens now?" the witness asked as he and Dorfman stood up. "Will I need to come back for more testimony?"

"Unlikely," Dorfman said, the bulk of his attention on the papers he was shoveling into his briefcase. "Unless Austin decides to recall you, your part in this is pretty well over."

The other licked his lips, his gaze fluttering around the courtroom. "Any chance I can come back this afternoon and listen to Austin's case?"

Dorfman looked at Blanchard. "Doctor?"

"I'm afraid that won't be possible, Mr. Holloway," Blanchard told him. "You've been using Walker Lamar's body for just under two and a half hours, and the legally allowed maximum is three hours per day."

"The closing arguments, then?" he persisted, a strangely

yearning expression in his eyes. "Can I at least come back for the closing arguments?"

"I can ask," Dorfman shrugged, snapping the locks on his briefcase with a sharp double click. "But Austin's bound to object, and since the judge will be denying his motion to dismiss he'll likely let him have that one." He glanced at the other; took a second, closer look. "You'll be coming back for the verdict, though," he added. "That one's guaranteed by law."

"I know," he sighed. He looked around the courtroom again—almost, Blanchard thought, as if committing it to memory. "I just wish . . ."

"I wish, too," Dorfman grunted. "Having the victim in the courtroom usually helps the prosecution, which is why Austin will fight it. Not that we're going to need any help in this particular case," he added reassuringly. "Look, I've got to get going—Austin'll be filing motions with the judge, and I need to be there to argue against them. See you later." With a nod to each of them, he strode off toward the judge's chambers.

Blanchard looked at the witness. "You okay, Mr. Holloway?"

He swallowed. "Yeah," he said, his voice soft.

"You did well, if that helps. I know it was hard for you."

"I did what I had to do." He took a deep breath. "I guess we'd better go."

He walked around the bar and into the aisle, Blanchard sidling down her row to meet him. At the rear of the courtroom the last of the other spectators were just leaving; lengthening his stride suddenly, the witness caught up with them, leaving Blanchard behind. She broke into a jog, caught up as the group pushed open the heavy door.

Without looking back, he let the door swing back on her. She caught it, shoved it open again—

And stepped out into a blaze of light.

"Mr. Holloway?" someone called through the locust clicking of multiple camera lenses. "What can you tell us about the trial?"

Blanchard reached out blindly and grabbed his arm. "Give it

a rest, people," she snapped toward the reporters before he could answer. "You want a mistrial or something? You know there's a gag order on Mr. Holloway. Come back after the verdict."

"How about *you*, then, Dr. Blanchard?" someone else suggested. "What do *you* think of the trial so far?"

"No comment from me, either," Blanchard growled, gripping the arm a little tighter and giving him a push toward the elevator. "Go light up some other corner of the world, huh?"

She stumbled out of the glare, cursing to herself at the spots dancing in front of her eyes. Modern video cameras could record perfectly well in normal background light; the only possible reason for the media to still use those half-sized searchlights was in the hopes of dazzling their victims into saying something they shouldn't. Blinking away the tears, she turned—

And froze. The man whose arm she still held, the man frowning bemusedly down at her, was not Walker Lamar.

Letting go as if scalded, she looked around her. But it was no use. With a dozen courtrooms and offices simultaneously breaking for lunch, the corridor was filled with hurrying people blocking her view. Holloway was gone.

And he'd taken Lamar's body with him.

"The first thing you need to do," Soulminder Security Duty Officer Larry Carstairs said soothingly into her ear, "is to take a deep breath and *not* panic. Breathe; don't panic. Think you can handle that?"

Blanchard gripped the pay phone a little harder. She would far rather have called in the alarm from the privacy of a stairwell, but she'd forgotten to charge her cell last night and this was all she had. At least there *were* still pay phones here in the annex, where enough poor people and other non-cell users congregated to make them both useful and necessary. "There are situations in life, Carstairs," she bit out, "where a certain level of flippancy is welcome. This isn't one of them."

"You're taking this way too seriously, Dr. Blanchard," the other said with that same maddening calm. "This is no big deal—we've had witnesses getting away from their handlers ever since these Pro-Witness programs got going. Chances are he just wanted to wander around in the sunlight for a while without someone hanging around reminding him that he's legally dead. He'll be back—he knows he needs to be transferred out by twelve-thirty, after all."

Blanchard gritted her teeth, last night's nightmare flashing through her mind. The walking dead . . . "And what if he *doesn't* come back?" she countered. "You're not going to find him while you sit there making hopeful noises."

Carstairs sighed audibly. "Even as we speak, Doctor, there are ten people at both ground level and at upper windows in the process of looking for him."

"Oh, right," Blanchard snorted. "Noontime at Ridley Square is a *great* time to go looking for somebody."

"It'll be easier than you might think," Carstairs countered, his calm tone fraying a little at the edges. "Or did you assume that those god-awful powder-blue blazers the Pro-Witnesses wear are somebody's idea of good taste? You wouldn't believe how easily those things stick out of a crowd. I don't tell you how to do your job. Kindly don't tell me how to do mine."

Blanchard took a deep breath. "I'm sorry," she said, trying to sound like she meant it. "I just—God, he's stolen someone else's *body.*"

"Only borrowed it," Carstairs said, all soothing again. "Don't worry, we'll get him back. Even if the quick and dirty approach doesn't work, there are other tricks we can try. You might as well come on in—we'll bring him directly to the transfer room when we catch him."

Blanchard glanced around the courthouse corridor, already considerably less crowded than it had been five minutes earlier, hoping against hope she'd see her quarry waiting there for her. She needn't have bothered. "Yeah," she told Carstairs. "I'll be there in two minutes."

"I'll talk to you then. And really, Dr. Blanchard, try not to worry. I'd be willing to bet you a week's pay we'll have him spotted before you even get here."

It was a bet she should have taken. Leaving the courthouse annex, she hurried across the sun-drenched walkways bordering Ridley Square to the Soulminder building.

To find that the witness was still missing.

"He's apparently taken off his blazer," Carstairs grunted, his attention off on something out of range of Blanchard's intercom camera. "Probably folded it inside-out over his arm—otherwise, we'd have seen *something* through the filters."

"So what now?" Blanchard asked, fighting hard against the urge to let off something blisteringly sarcastic. Recriminations and blame placing could wait until after they'd found him. Assuming they ever did. "The three-hour limit expires in"—she glanced at her watch—"just under twenty minutes."

"Thank you; I *can* tell time," Carstairs growled. "I still think he's probably somewhere in the general Ridley Square area, but we've got someone checking out cab and limo companies anyway."

"Buses?"

"None of them hit the area since the window opened."

"How about restaurants?" Blanchard persisted. "I had a witness once who said he'd kill for the chance to taste prime rib again."

"Already checking them," Carstairs said. "You got anything on Holloway himself that might be useful? Anything he said or did that might point to where he's gone?"

"I've been trying to think," Blanchard said, shaking her head. "But so far I've come up dry."

"Yeah. Well, don't worry about it. Like I said earlier, we've got a few other strings to our bow here. They'll just take a little more time, that's all."

Blanchard nodded, fighting against the flood of utter helplessness rising to choke her. "Yes, I understand. What can I do to help?"

"Not much, really." Carstairs studied her. "On second thought," he amended, "they could probably use another spotter up on five. Outer corridor—they'll have some spare binoculars up there you can use."

Blanchard nodded. It was, she realized, little more than make-work—Carstairs's people would be far better at this sort of thing than she would. But it would at least give her the illusion that she was doing something to help clean up the mess she'd made. "I'll be right up."

In the nine months since she'd arrived at Soulminder Los Angeles, Blanchard had become more or less acclimated to the incredible masses of people that descended upon the Ridley Square park every day at lunchtime from the office buildings surrounding the patch of green. Now, looking down at it from the fifth floor, that original bit of culture shock came back with a vengeance.

"You take that section of the park," the surveillance chief instructed her, pointing out a rough wedge of Ridley Square bordered by two winding wood-chip paths and the outer sidewalk of the park itself. "Look at everyone already there, and check anyone who comes in."

"Got it." Lifting the binoculars to her eyes, trying to calm her pounding heart, she got to work.

The minutes ticked by. There were, probably not by accident, relatively few people in her sector, and all too soon she'd confirmed that Walker Lamar's face wasn't among them. "All negative," she reported to the surveillance chief. "What should I do now?"

"Start on the next sector to the east," he told her. "We've already covered the park," he added, as if sensing her next question, "but it's always possible he slipped back in while we concentrated on other areas."

"Right."

She'd covered that section, and was just starting on the next, when she heard a sudden quiet intake of breath from the woman next to her. "Got something," the other announced. "Grid Double-A forty-seven; two-twenty vector."

"Got it," the chief said. "Blanchard—that switch on the right side of your binoculars? Push it forward."

She did so, and to her surprise a faint heads-up grid abruptly appeared, superimposed on the view. "Where was he again?" she asked, searching the grid edges for the identifying letters and numbers.

"Double-B forty-three, now," the woman beside her said. "Angling toward the Soulminder building, more or less from the direction of the courthouse."

One look was all it took. "That's him," Blanchard nodded, a wave of relief washing over her.

"All right, the ground people are on him," the chief said. He sounded relieved, too. "They'll have him in the transfer room in two minutes." He glanced at his watch. "Nice timing on his part— you won't even get the satisfaction of chewing him out."

Blanchard looked at her own watch. Twelve twenty-eight; just those same two minutes until the legal time limit ran out. "Don't bet on it," she said grimly, handing him the binoculars and heading for the elevator.

She made it to the transfer room maybe twenty seconds before the witness and his security escort got there. "Holloway, what the hell was *that* all about?" she snarled as they came through the door. "You have any idea how much trouble you've just caused?"

She'd been prepared for him to argue back at her. Instead, he avoided her eyes as the security guards hustled him to the table. "I'm sorry, Dr. Blanchard," he said, his voice as meekly and humbly apologetic as if he were an eight-year-old caught stealing from the cookie jar. "I didn't plan to run away from you like that— really I didn't. But when those newsmen grabbed you—well, I just thought it would be nice to walk around in the sun for a while. It's . . . you know. My last chance to do something like that."

Blanchard clenched her teeth hard enough to hurt. Exactly what Carstairs had suggested he might be doing.

And despite her resolve, she could feel her anger melting away into an impotent frustration. How—really—could she blame him for something like that? "I understand. I guess. But you still shouldn't have done it."

"I know, and I'm sorry. Well." He swallowed, his lip twitching slightly as the doctor applied his hypo. "Gotta go, Dr. Blanchard," he murmured, eyes already glazing over. "Walker needs his exercise."

"Good-bye, Mr. Holloway," she murmured. A moment later Michael Holloway's soul was back in its Soulminder trap, and Walker Lamar's body was again dead.

She sighed, looked at her watch. Twelve thirty-two exactly. They'd gotten Holloway out of Lamar's body two minutes late.

"A technical violation only," the doctor assured her. "Two minutes aren't even worth anyone slapping our wrists for."

Blanchard nodded silently. The doctor and techs busied themselves with their work, and a minute later Walker Lamar was back in his own body.

Blanchard stepped to his side, forcing her best imitation of an unconcerned smile. "Hi," she said. "How are you feeling?"

He blinked at her, then at the ceiling. "About the same as always," he said. "Fine. I guess." He focused on her again. "How did it go?"

"Dorfman sounds confident," she said with a shrug. "Though who can tell what that means with lawyers? So. You ready for lunch?"

"In a little while, maybe." With a jerk of legs and shoulders he sat up on the table. "I think I'll take a little walk first—get used to having legs again, you know."

"Sure." Blanchard glanced over his shoulder at the doctor. "Actually, I've got some things I have to do first, anyway. What do you say I meet you up in the cafeteria at one o'clock or so?"

Lamar seemed to bring his attention back from somewhere else. "Okay," he said. "Sure. See you then."

Easing his hips forward to the edge of the table, he touched feet to floor and got his balance. Walking a little unsteadily, he passed between the two security guards still flanking the doorway and left.

Blanchard watched him go. Then, steeling herself, she headed over to the intercom. Somewhere, she knew, there would be a mass of paperwork waiting for her on this one.

It wasn't as bad as she'd feared it would be. Under Carstairs's watchful eye she filled out the first wave of forms, accepted with thanks his assurances that his own report wouldn't blame her for what had happened, promised to be back by two to tackle the second wave of paper, and managed to make it to the cafeteria by ten after one.

Lamar was waiting for her. "I was starting to wonder if you were coming," he said as they picked up trays and started down the line.

"I had some paperwork to do," Blanchard told him. "It took longer than I expected."

He reached over and selected a salad, and placed it on his tray. "You've never had paperwork to do right after a transfer before," he said quietly, making a minute adjustment in the salad plate's position on his tray. "Something went wrong, didn't it?"

Blanchard grimaced. She'd hoped to keep Holloway's little solo run quiet, at least until Lamar had had a little more time to recuperate. "Holloway got away from me at the courthouse," she told him. "He just had a little time out on his own, that's all."

Lamar seemed to straighten up, shoulders hunching as if settling himself more comfortably into his clothes. Or into his body. "What did he—I mean—"

"He was out for barely half an hour," Blanchard said, keeping her voice as reassuring as possible. "The worst he could have done was get you a little sunburned."

"Yeah." The corners of Lamar's mouth twitched, as if he were trying to smile but couldn't. "Well . . . I can tell he didn't eat, anyway."

They completed the line in silence, handed in their ID chits at the register, and found a quiet table over near the windows.

"So," Lamar said, hunching over his tray as he carefully sprinkled salt on his chicken. "Are you in trouble now?"

Blanchard shrugged, trying to look casual. "I don't think so," she said. "Carstairs says this has happened before at other Pro-Witness programs."

"What did they do? The other witnesses who escaped, I mean?"

"Walker." She reached over to squeeze his hand. "It's all right. Really it is."

A muscle in his cheek twitched. "I know," he said. "I was just wondering—you know, just what someone could do out there in half an hour." His eyes flicked to her, turned away. "I mean, he didn't eat. He didn't get drunk. What else is there? A woman?"

"It's all right," she said again. "Holloway was probably doing just what he said he was: taking one last chance to walk alone out under the sun."

"Yeah." Gently, Lamar pulled his hand back from her, picked up his coffee. "I don't blame him, you know," he said, staring into the mug. "I was just wondering if . . . you know, if he found a hooker who had a disease or something."

"It'll be all right," Blanchard told him, realizing she was starting to sound like a looped program. "As soon as we're finished here we'll go back downstairs and set up an appointment for a complete physical, okay? And right after that, we'll go talk to the Pro-Witness people about getting you a month or so of leave time after this case is wrapped up."

Lamar's lips compressed into a thin line. Then, regretfully, he shook his head. "Thanks, but I can't afford to take that much time off."

"So we'll make it a paid leave," Blanchard said firmly. "No more argument. In fact, no more shop talk at all. Eat your chicken before it gets cold."

He smiled, the first genuine smile she'd seen on him all day. "Yes, Mom," he murmured.

They ate at a leisurely pace, with Blanchard working hard to steer the conversation to Lamar's twin passions of sports and old movies. The tactic seemed to work, and by the time he pulled his dessert over in front of him she could see he was almost relaxed.

"You ought to watch that stuff," she commented, eying his chocolate pudding. "It'll give you zits like you wouldn't believe."

"Old doctors' tale," he retorted around a mouthful. "Nothing here that isn't healthy for a growing boy like me."

"Oh, come on. You stopped growing at least two years ago—"

She broke off. Lamar had looked up from his bowl and was staring over her shoulder, a strange look on his face. She turned just as a pair of uniformed policemen stopped to either side of her. "Mr. Walker Lamar?" one of them said, his gaze steady on Lamar.

Lamar's eyes flicked to Blanchard, then back to the policemen. "Yes?" he said, the word half statement, half question.

The second cop started around the table. "Please keep your hands on the table, sir," the first said.

"Is there a problem, officer?" Blanchard asked, a sudden dread twisting through her stomach.

"Afraid there is, ma'am," the cop said as his partner gave Lamar a quick frisking and then pulled out his cuffs. "Seems that sometime between twelve-thirty and one o'clock this afternoon a man named Eliot Griffin was murdered in his office across the square."

Blanchard looked at Lamar, his eyes wide in a horror-struck face. "And you think *Walker* had something to do with it?" she demanded.

"It seems likely, ma'am," the cop said. "Seeing as his fingerprints were all over the murder weapon.

"Mr. Lamar, you have the right to remain silent . . . "

Within an hour she got word that McGee had taken her off her scheduled owl-shift floater duty, citing the potential emotional stress of Lamar's arrest. It took fifteen minutes to convince him she could handle it, and though he reinstated her he made it clear that he thought she was letting professional pride and plain simple mule-headedness do her thinking for her. At the time she half agreed with him, and wondered if perhaps she should have gone home instead.

By eight that evening, she was very glad she hadn't.

"Saw you on TV tonight," a familiar voice said into the fog.

She looked up, brushing away the mental wool, as Carstairs sat down across the duty room table from her. "I imagine half of Los Angeles saw me," she countered tiredly.

"Probably," he nodded. "Rough day, huh?"

She closed her eyes briefly. "I used to do police psychology work, sometimes dealing with the most infamous twisted minds you'd ever seen. People on the level of Bundy or Manson, and I *never* got the media attention from any of that that I did this afternoon."

"Scary, isn't it? You'd think that after ten years Soulminder wouldn't be such a media magnet. But it is." He glanced around the empty duty room. "At least you found a cozy place to hide."

"A case of my subconscious being smarter than I was," she admitted. "I'd talked McGee into letting me stay here tonight long before the media dragged me into the number two ring of their circus."

"You did a good job, if that helps any," he offered. "At least on the interview I saw. They kept trying to get you to convict Lamar right there on the spot, and you kept politely refusing to play ball."

"He's not guilty." The words sounded more reflexive than really convincing. Or convinced. "Walker wouldn't have killed anyone. He *wouldn't*."

Carstairs tapped his fingertips gently on the tabletop. "There've been quiet suggestions that maybe Lamar wasn't doing so well. That the strain of being a Pro-Witness might have pushed him over the edge."

Blanchard winced, her early-morning argument with McGee flashing through her mind for the umpteenth time that day. "I've heard those suggestions, too," she growled. "The people making them don't know what they're talking about. Walker isn't the type to spew his internal pressures out on other people. He'd just turn it inward on himself."

"Okay," Carstairs said. "But if Lamar didn't do it—"

"And there's one thing the cops so far don't seem to have considered," Blanchard cut him off. "Richardson's Garden Spot—the place the murder knife was taken from?—Walker and I had lunch there less than a week ago. Someone could easily have picked up the knife he used and kept it until now."

Everly shrugged. "In theory, sure. The Smythson 88 scanner they used at the scene is notorious for reading latent prints like they were fresh. Though a proper confirmation check ought to pick up something like that."

"Assuming they bother to make one," Blanchard said bitterly, dropping her gaze back to the tabletop. "Everyone seems to have made up their mind already that Walker's guilty."

"Well . . . not *everyone*."

She frowned up at him. "What do you mean?"

His eyes were thoughtful on her. "Tell me, Doctor. When exactly was Eliot Griffin killed?"

"Between twelve-thirty and one this afternoon."

"How do you know?"

"Because—" She paused. "Because that's what the cops told me."

"Yeah, that's what they told everyone," he nodded, that thoughtful expression still there. "About half an hour ago I finally got to wondering how in hell they'd pinned down the time of death that neatly. So I did some checking."

"And?" she prompted.

"And it turns out," he said quietly, "that the cops called *us* just before one-forty to find out if we knew where Lamar was. The operator told them he was in the cafeteria. And then they asked whether he'd been checked out at all in the previous hour or so."

Blanchard stared at him, the mental fog burning abruptly away. "My God," she breathed. "And of course she obligingly told them he'd been out of the building between twelve-thirty and one."

"Uh-huh." Carstairs pursed his lips. "So I did a little more checking. It turns out that Griffin's secretary was out of the office from noon to one. The whole hour, not just the second half."

"You realize what you're saying?" she asked, her voice trembling with sudden emotion. "You're suggesting—"

He nodded. "That our runaway witness Holloway is at least as good a suspect as Walker Lamar."

Blanchard took a deep breath. The implications . . . Abruptly, she reached over to the tabletop MiNex console, keyed in a location request. "Good; Katovsky's still here—third floor conference room." She got to her feet. "Let's go."

"Wait a second," Carstairs cut her off, catching her hand. "Before you go charging in on the director, take a minute to think about what we're going to be telling him: that a man legally dead might have committed a murder. You think the media circus today was bad, just wait until they get their teeth into *this* one."

She glared down at him. "Are you suggesting that we just keep our mouths shut and let them throw Walker to the sharks?"

"Of course not. I'm just warning you not to expect peals of joy from the upper echelons over the news. Lamar is a city employee, under the jurisdiction of the D.A.'s office, and if he's guilty they'll get the bulk of the public flak. The minute you bring Holloway into it, you drag Soulminder in, too."

"Soulminder thrives on publicity," she said shortly. "You coming or not?"

He stood up, releasing her hand. "Right behind you."

There were three men waiting in the receptionist's niche just outside the third-floor conference room when they arrived. Men whose quiet watchfulness and efficiency, Blanchard would reflect later, ought to have given her some warning of what she was about to walk into. But she was tired and preoccupied, and so she just stood beside Carstairs, her thoughts on other things, while one of the loiterers held a brief intercom conversation with someone inside the conference room and then opened the door for her. Nodding her thanks, she strode through the opening—

And came to an abrupt stop.

"Dr. Blanchard," Los Angeles Director Robert Katovsky said gravely into the bright fog that seemed suddenly to be interfering with her vision. "Come in and meet our visitors." Without waiting for a response, he half turned, gesturing to the three men seated across the small circular table from him. "This is Frank Everly, overall head of Soulminder security; Murray Porath, chief legal counsel for the corporation; and I imagine you recognize Dr. Adrian Sommer."

With an effort, Blanchard found her voice. "It would be difficult," she said, "to find an adult in the civilized world who *wouldn't* recognize Soulminder's creator."

"Co-creator, please," Sommer corrected. He sounded less dynamic, somehow, than he always appeared in interviews and newscasts. "Mr. Katovsky tells me you were Walker Lamar's Soulminder liaison."

Some of the dazzlement cleared. "I still am," she corrected in turn.

Katovsky harrumphed warningly, but Sommer merely smiled. "Yes, of course. Please sit down—you too, Mr. Carstairs—and tell us what's on your mind."

Blanchard took the chair across from Sommer, Carstairs sitting down beside her. "I want to apologize for barging in on you like this," she began. "Although"—she made a quick scan of their faces as a new thought suddenly occurred to her—"given your presence here, Dr. Sommer, perhaps we don't have anything new to tell you, after all."

Katovsky made a face. "If you're referring to the news that Walker Lamar isn't the only viable suspect in the Griffin murder, then you're correct."

Blanchard looked at Sommer. "Can I assume you plan to release that news sometime in the near future?"

Sommer raised his eyebrows slightly. "You can sit in on my

press conference tomorrow morning if you'd like. Were you thinking we might not?"

"It's a long way from Washington," she said. "You could have made the announcement hours ago."

Katovsky harrumphed again, but Sommer waved him silent. "We suspected we had a problem right from the start," he said, meeting her gaze without flinching. "We didn't *know*, however, until about an hour ago. At that point it seemed best to try and collect a few more facts before flooding the public with what could easily become a morass of confusing and possibly self-contradictory information." He looked at Everly. "Frank?"

"We got the final police report on the murder weapon a few minutes ago," the security chief said, his cool eyes steady on Blanchard. "Lamar's prints were definitely fresh. They were superimposed on another set, presumably those of the person who'd used it last."

Blanchard felt her lip twist. "Meaning that no one picked up the knife he used last week to try and frame him with?"

"Basically," Everly nodded. "Actually, it *is* still barely possible that someone did that, but it would've been one hell of a slick job—ditto for getting those little blood stains onto the underside of Lamar's wrist. Which, by the way," he added, looking at Sommer, "the lab says definitely came from the victim."

Sommer nodded. "All of which presumably takes this out of the realm of a random framing. As to *non*-random framing . . . " He looked at Porath, raised his eyebrows.

"At last check, my people were about halfway through the complete national list of state and local Pro-Witness cases," the Soulminder attorney told him. "So far they haven't found anyone who might have the money or contacts to try and throw this particular kind of monkey wrench into the program generally. We're still looking."

"All right," Sommer said. "We'll leave that line open"—his eyes hardened, just noticeably—"but until and unless you find something, we're going to have to assume that Lamar's hand did indeed wield the murder weapon.

"The only question now is who was controlling that hand."

Carstairs stirred in his seat. "It seems to me that there ought to be *some* kind of physical evidence that would let us determine which one. Odd bloodstains, timing—*something*."

"One would think so, yes," Sommer nodded. "But so far, nothing like that has surfaced."

"Wait a minute," Blanchard said slowly. In her mind's eye she saw Lamar shuffling out for his post-transfer walk . . . "When we found Holloway, he was carrying his blazer folded across his arm. When Walker left a few minutes later, I think he left the blazer in the transfer room."

"He did," Katovsky nodded. "We spotted that when we reviewed the video of the transfer operation. Unfortunately, the police lab's already gone over the blazer, and there's no blood on it anywhere." His cleared his throat uncomfortably. "They said that Griffin's own jacket absorbed most of . . . what came out."

"Was it checked for dust signatures, then?" Carstairs persisted. "If Holloway was the killer, he would have had to put the coat down somewhere first—he couldn't have known the blood wouldn't spurt all over it."

"They say it's been checked for everything," Katovsky told him. "One assumes they know what they're doing."

"Mr. Carstairs brings up a good point, though," Sommer said. "At the moment the traditional elements of method and opportunity fit both men equally well. It may indeed come down to some obscure bit of knowledge like whether one of them knew how a knife wound like that would bleed."

Porath clucked his tongue softly. "If it does, you can kiss a conviction good-bye," he warned. "Probably the trial, too—a D.A. with half a brain would know better than to bring a case based on anything that esoteric."

"Or in other words," Everly said, "we need to find a motive."

"Assuming there *is* one," Sommer said, his eyes on Blanchard.

"Walker was beginning to develop some personality problems, Dr. Sommer," she said stiffly. "He was not, however, going psychotic."

"I'll accept that," Sommer said. "At least for the moment. Tell me about Mr. Holloway's mental state."

Blanchard felt her stomach tighten. "The man was murdered six months ago. He's spent those six months locked in limbo in a Soulminder trap, the monotony punctuated only by brief intervals of being stuffed into a strange and totally unfamiliar body so that people can ask him to relive his death over and over again. What kind of mental state would *you* be in?"

"That's enough, Doctor," Katovsky said, his voice dark with official menace.

"It's all right, Bob," Sommer said. "As it happens, Dr. Blanchard, I *have* spent time in a Soulminder trap. I remember it being quite peaceful, and not monotonous at all."

Blanchard swallowed. She *had* known that. "I'm sorry, sir."

"As to the rest of it, though, you make a good point," Sommer continued as if she hadn't spoken. "One expects God to inform you of your death, not some assistant district attorney." A shadow of something like pain flicked across his face. "Some have taken it well. Others not so well. We need to know which category Holloway falls into." Again, his eyes hardened, just that little bit. "And we need to know fast."

"I suppose you'll want me to talk to him," she said, a familiar acid pain jabbing briefly at her stomach. For a moment she was back in St. Louis, preparing to examine yet another suspected psychopath. "Will tomorrow morning be soon enough?"

Sommer looked at Porath. "Murray?"

"We expect to have Lamar released into our custody by noon tomorrow at the latest," the lawyer said briskly. "So any time after that will do."

Sommer nodded and glanced at his watch. "Let's schedule a transfer room for one o'clock, then—"

"Just a minute," Blanchard cut in as it belatedly hit her. "You're not suggesting we use *Walker* for the transfer, are you?"

Porath's forehead wrinkled. "Of course. Why not?"

"Because—" Blanchard floundered for words, fighting to get past the mind-numbing horror of the whole idea. "We can't ask Walker to let Holloway into his body again," she said at last. "If he used Walker to commit a murder—" She looked around the table, saw nothing but puzzlement there in their faces. "Don't you *see*?"

"Not really," Sommer said, his tone quiet but firm. "But I'm afraid it doesn't matter whether we do or don't. We have no choice but to use Lamar on this. You've never known Holloway in any other way—never known his expressions or voice patterns or mannerisms in any other body. If we switch him to some other Pro-Witness, you'll have no chance at all of reading anything from his responses."

Blanchard exhaled quietly. He was right—on a purely logical level she could see that. But on a gut level . . . "Yes, sir," she said. "For the record, I don't like it."

"I don't especially like it either," Sommer told her. "But it has to be done." He looked around the table. "And with that, I think we've done all we can do for the moment. We'll meet back here at twelve-thirty tomorrow afternoon to discuss developments. After which . . . we'll see what Mr. Holloway has to say."

Twelve-thirty tomorrow, Blanchard thought bleakly as she headed from the conference room, leaving the others still collecting notes and papers behind her. Sixteen hours away.

And then she would have to tell Walker that his body was once again going to be used by someone else. Not by a victim this time, but by a suspected killer.

Which gave her just those same sixteen hours to talk Sommer and Porath out of it.

Or to identify the killer herself.

The door to the late Eliot Griffin's sixth-floor office was unguarded, save for the wide yellow tape with *POLICE LINE—DO NOT*

CROSS endlessly repeated in black letters that had been stretched across the doorway. The lack of a guard was in itself mildly surprising, given the media attention.

What was even more surprising was the fact that the door itself was open a crack. *The guard must be inside*, she decided, giving the door a gentle push and ducking low under the yellow tape. Mentally rehearsing the story she'd worked out during her morning shower, she stepped into the office.

It was impressive. The news reports had called Griffin a high-caliber investment counselor. Looking around, she saw for the first time just how much wealth and success that terminology implied. From the rich, yet tasteful, carpet to the equally rich and equally tasteful curtains, everything in the room struck the perfect balance between leisurely elegance and hard-headed business acumen.

Everything except the smeared bloodstains on the top and front of the polished mahogany desk . . .

"Who the hell are you?"

Blanchard jumped, twisting around to her right. Framed in the doorway to an unsuspected second room was a glowering cop, his hand resting none too subtly on the butt of his Sig. "I'm Dr. Carolyn Blanchard," she told him between stiff lips. Suddenly the story she'd dreamed up didn't sound nearly as convincing as it had an hour ago. "I'm with the Soulminder office, working on the Griffin murder."

The cop cocked his head slightly to the side, his eyes never moving from Blanchard. "Is she?" he asked.

"Close enough," a second voice grunted, and behind the cop, Frank Everly stepped into view. "You can put her down as being with me."

The other shrugged, dropping his hand to his side. "If you say so." He looked her up and down once, shrugged again, and moved toward the taped doorway. "I'll be outside if you need me."

The door clicked solidly shut behind him. "Thanks," Blanchard said to Everly. "I couldn't tell whether he was going to arrest me or shoot me."

"Don't worry, he wouldn't have shot you," Everly assured her. "Too much paperwork. What are you doing here?"

She forced herself to meet that icy gaze. "If I'm going to talk to Holloway about this, I need to know as much as I can about Griffin and his death. It seemed simplest to come directly to the source."

"Uh-huh." Everly's expression seemed to sour a bit more. "And if you just *happened* to stumble on something along the way that would solve the case for us . . . ?"

She felt her face warming. "I'm not just some self-appointed amateur detective who wandered in off the street, Mr. Everly," she reminded him. "I'm a trained observer who specializes in building personality profiles from random bits and pieces of data. I've got as much chance of seeing something significant here as you do."

For a long second she thought maybe she'd overdone it. But Everly merely cocked an eyebrow and gestured to the room. "Help yourself, Doctor. Tell me what significant things you see."

She looked at him a moment longer. Then, almost against her will, her eyes drifted to the bloodstained desk. "How did it happen?"

"From the penetration angle and position of the body, the police think Griffin was leaning over his desk shaking hands with his killer when he was stabbed."

"A left-handed blow, in other words."

"Yeah, but that doesn't buy us anything," Everly said. "Doesn't take a left-handed man to hold someone pinned across a desk while he stabs him. Anyway, both Lamar and Holloway are right-handed."

Blanchard nodded, letting her gaze drift across the rest of the desktop. Almost compulsively neat, with two stacks of papers in the front left corner and a computer in the front right. "Has anything been taken from this room?" she asked, starting toward the terminal. If Griffin had been working on the computer when he was killed . . .

Everly snorted. "Sure. Griffin's appointment calendar, his client list, his scratch pad, his phone, his phone list, his Kindle, every flash drive the police could find, and the hard drive from his computer. They've also started the wheels rolling to get them into his E-mail file, his WallStreet/Link file, his three online information subscriptions, and his GamesNet file. Not to mention his personal banking records, his business banking records, and all his credit card records. Anything we've missed?"

She sent a glower in his direction. "What about that room?" she asked, nodding at the door he'd come in by.

"It's a small bedroom," he told her. "Looks like Griffin was accustomed to late nights and early mornings."

Or else was accustomed to specialized entertainment for special clients. "They've cleaned that out too, I presume?"

"Pretty much."

She sighed and looked slowly around the room. Much of the right-hand wall next to the bedroom door was given over to a floor-to-ceiling bookshelf, loaded with both leather-bound books and a considerable number of crystal objects. The love of crystal was repeated on his desk, where a handful of tiny knick-knacks lined both sides of the front edge, the ones that had presumably been in the middle having been scattered onto the floor. Behind them, lying with its edge precisely parallel to the two piles of papers, was a gold-handled letter opener. "Whoever the killer was, I don't think he'd ever been here before," she said.

"Because if he had, he'd have known about that lovely letter opener and wouldn't have bothered swiping a knife from the restaurant," Everly agreed.

Behind the desk the tall windows looked out on the buildings across Ridley Square, with the top corner of the Soulminder building just visible through one of them. On the left-hand wall were four picture frames, three with modern paintings in them. In the fourth . . .

She frowned, stepping over for a closer look. Inside the matting was a narrow article from *Time* magazine—a sidebar, probably, to a longer story—with a photo of a blandly smiling man at the top of it. A man sitting at a familiar-looking desk. The desk, in fact, that was ten feet away . . .

"Yeah, it's an article about Griffin," Everly confirmed from behind her. "Go ahead. Read it."

Blanchard eyed the photo another moment, then lowered her eyes to the text.

From his sumptuous office overlooking Ridley Square—and, perhaps ironically, the Los Angeles Courthouse Annex—Eliot Griffin sees dozens of clients, makes a good deal of money, and scoffs at the suggestion that he and Trintex are in any way out of the ordinary. "You get a group of people who beat the odds—any group, any type of odds—and you'll have people out there who assume they're cheating," he claims. "In our case, it was a group of sore losers in the financial market and an SEC that has more time on its hands than it knows what to do with."

Griffin has had his share of experience with both sore losers and the SEC. Growing up in the prairies of rural Nebraska, he was continually having to prove himself to teachers and childhood friends . . .

Blanchard finished the article, turned to find Everly watching her. "Are the allegations here true?" she asked.

"No one really knows. Or I should say, no one knows well enough to take him and his group to court. Yet."

"His group being these Trintex people?"

Everly nodded. "The main article had a profile of the whole gang. You've never heard of it?"

"If I did, I don't remember."

"Mm. Basically, Trintex is a loose group of high-tech investment advisors scattered across the country. All highly successful, highly adept at generating money for their clients, and"—Everly cocked his head—"allegedly playing off each other's balance sheets to create assets and profits on paper that aren't really there. An updated version of the old revolving-fund con scheme, or so the SEC thinks."

Blanchard looked back at the article. "And he frames this to put in his *office*?"

"Oh, they've got chutzpah to burn," Everly said with a snort. "The Washington edition carried a sidebar interview with the New York member of the club, and he apparently has *his* framed in his office, too."

Blanchard nodded, again looking at the photo. Griffin was all smiles and sincerity, yet at the same time exuding the air of a total hard-headed business professional. A perfect match for his office decor. "You can just see the top of the Soulminder building in the picture," she commented. "There, at the edge of the curtains." She frowned, skimming the article again. There was something wrong here. Something she couldn't quite put her finger on . . .

"Yeah, I noticed," Everly said. "Not exactly the kind of neighbors we like to have. Did you notice the date of the article, by the way?"

Blanchard dropped her eyes to the bottom of the page. There it was—

She stared at it, a hollow feeling twisting at the pit of her stomach. "Three months ago," she murmured.

"Three and a half, to be precise," Everly said.

And Holloway had been murdered almost six months ago, locked away from the world in a Soulminder trap ever since. "It doesn't prove anything," she said, unwilling to turn and face Everly. "Holloway could have heard about Griffin in some other way before he was killed."

"Sure," Everly agreed. "He could have read about him somewhere else, or maybe had a friend or relative get screwed over by the guy."

"Have you checked into that?"

"Oh, we ran *everything*," Everly said. "Financials, socials, professionals, family connections—the whole ball of wax. There's just no connection anywhere between Lamar, Holloway, and Griffin." He gestured toward the desk. "And before you ask, there were also no appointments, phone calls, or anything else between them."

"But there *is* this story," Blanchard pointed out.

"Right," Everly said. "But until *Time* got hold of it, no one outside the financial community was really paying attention to the group. Or to Griffin himself."

"What you're saying is that the only one who could possibly know that Griffin was a shady operator was Walker," Blanchard bit out. "Is that it?"

"That's part of it," Everly said. His voice was suddenly grim. "The other part is whether whatever Griffin's been doing was really worth killing him for."

She stared at the photo. The blandly smiling con man . . . "Someone might think so."

"Someone who was borderline psychotic, maybe?"

Deliberately, she turned away from the framed article. "I'm going downstairs to check out the restaurant," she said, keeping her voice level. "You coming?"

"I've already talked to them," Everly said. "But help yourself. Just don't forget we've got a meeting at twelve-thirty."

"Don't worry. I'll be there."

"Another Soulminder person, huh?" the cashier at Richardson's Garden Spot said, peering at Blanchard's ID. "Boy, between you, the police, and the reporters this place has sure been popular lately."

"I know, and I'm sorry to bother you," Blanchard told her, slipping the ID back into her wallet. "I'd just like to ask you a couple of questions, if I may."

The cashier sighed. "Yes, I was the cashier on duty yesterday between twelve and one. Yes, the place was crowded to the gills the whole hour. No, I don't remember anyone with Walker Lamar's face coming in during that time. Yes, we've checked with all our employees, and none of them remembers seeing him, either. Yes, we *are* missing one of our steak knives. No, there's no way we can tell which table it was stolen from. Yes, it was most likely from one of those six tables by the front window. No, nobody's found any useful fingerprints there. Did I leave anything out?"

"You *have* been through the wringer, haven't you?" Blanchard said with a commiserating smile.

"And there're never any new questions, either," the cashier said. "That's the part that really gets to me. Don't you guys ever talk to each other?"

"Yes, but obviously not enough." Blanchard thought a moment. "Okay, let's see if you've heard these. Do you routinely set out steak knives with your table settings, or just bring them with steak orders? If not, can you pull a list of everyone who ordered steak yesterday?"

"Sorry, but the last Soulminder guy already used those. Yes, for lunch we usually set steak knives out, and yes, we *can* do a partial cross-reference, but only for those people who paid with plastic. About thirty percent of our customers use cash, and there's nothing we can do about those."

"The bills themselves don't have an automatic time stamp on them?"

"Nope. We do the checks here by hand—part of our old-fashioned charm."

Blanchard grimaced. A blind alley. "I see. Thanks for your time. I appreciate it." She stepped back from the counter, turned around—

To find Frank Everly standing a few feet behind her. "Find out anything new?" he asked.

"Not really," Blanchard said. "You always skulk around eaves-dropping on other people's conversations?"

He raised his eyebrows politely. "Believe me, Doctor, if I'd wanted to listen in without you knowing, you wouldn't have."

"Yeah." She shifted her attention to the tables by the window that the cashier had mentioned. "It would have been trivial to do, wouldn't it?" she murmured, largely to herself. "All someone had to do was walk in, peer over the railing back here as if looking for someone in the main dining room, and then walk out with a knife up his sleeve."

"Perfectly simple," Everly agreed. "And then out the door, turn left, next building over, up to the sixth floor, and hey presto—someone's disappeared."

Her stomach tightened. "You don't have to be flippant about it." She peered out the window at the Soulminder building, visible to the side of the Ridley Square greenery. "I don't suppose it would do any good to suggest that half an hour wouldn't have been enough time for either Walker *or* Holloway to have done all this."

Everly shook his head. "I walked the route this morning. The timing's a little tight, but no real problem." He eyed her. "Particularly if the murderer had already tested out the timing himself."

"Meaning Walker, of course," she said coldly.

"He has a subscription to *Time*."

"So do I," she countered. "So does a reasonable percentage of the greater Los Angeles population. What does that prove?"

"It doesn't *prove* anything," Everly said patiently. "It's just one more pointer in Lamar's direction. He had access to that article on Griffin; Holloway didn't. Information, Dr. Blanchard. Remember what Dr. Sommer said about information?"

"I'm not likely to forget." Blanchard looked at the tables again, a sudden thought striking her. "You said there were a set of prints under Walker's on the knife, didn't you?"

Everly nodded, fishing a set of heavy-looking sunglasses from his coat pocket. "Yes, but they don't do us any good."

"Maybe they do," she said, feeling the stirrings of cautious excitement. "If we can track down the person who used it, maybe we can find out what time he left the restaurant."

"Nice idea," Everly said, slipping the sunglasses on. For a moment he stared through them in silence, as if looking at something. "Unfortunately," he continued abruptly, "it turns out that the knife was from a clean table setting. The other prints belong to one of the busboys, and he was setting tables all morning."

Blanchard grimaced. "You've thought of everything, haven't you?"

"That's what I'm paid for." He pulled the sunglasses off and slipped them back into his pocket. "Come on—we're wanted back at Soulminder."

"Is something wrong?" Blanchard asked, hurrying to catch up as he turned and strode out onto the sidewalk.

"No, just the opposite. Murray got Lamar sprung already and they're on their way in. Means we can talk to Holloway now, instead of this afternoon."

Blanchard swallowed. "Oh," she said. "Great."

The indicator lights changed color, and on the table Lamar's body twitched to life again. "Mr. Holloway?" Blanchard asked.

He turned his head from his contemplation of the ceiling to look at her. "Hello, Dr. Blanchard," he said, blinking a few times. "Boy, that didn't take long. The jury ready with its verdict already?"

"Not exactly," Blanchard told him, watching his face closely. The muscles were tight, but that was more or less normal for Holloway's transition periods. "Something else has come up," she continued. "There are some people here who want to ask you some questions."

He blinked again, eyes narrowing as he seemed to suddenly become aware of the silent group standing behind her. "Is something wrong?" he asked, his voice trembling slightly.

Everly took a step forward. "Mr. Holloway, we'd like to know exactly where you went yesterday after your court testimony," he said. "During the time you were alone, after you left Dr. Blanchard."

A cheek muscle twitched. "I don't understand. All I did was walk around Ridley Square for a while . . . " He trailed off, eyes coming back to Blanchard. "There *is* something wrong, isn't there?"

"Someone's been killed," she said, as gently as possible. "We need to know where you went yesterday." A sudden flash of inspiration—"To see if you might have been in a position to see anything."

The tension lines didn't go away. "I just went . . . *around*. You know—around the square. I touched some trees, smelled some flowers, looked in a couple of shop windows, watched the other people." He waved a hand helplessly.

"Did you go anywhere near Richardson's Garden Spot?" Everly asked. "It's a restaurant a quarter of the way around the square from here."

He shook his head, shoulders hunching briefly in a nervous shrug. "I don't know. Probably I went past it sometime, but I don't know. I wasn't—you know, really paying attention to things like that." He swallowed. "Who was killed? Was it someone I knew?"

"His name's Eliot Griffin," Blanchard told him. "An investment advisor. Does the name sound familiar?"

He shook his head. "Not really. Sorry."

"That's okay." Blanchard pursed her lips. "All right, then, try this. Think back to when you returned here yesterday, just before we put you back into Soulminder. What were you feeling?"

He gazed up at her, not quite suspiciously. "I don't understand."

"Were you feeling angry, for instance?" she offered. "Frustrated by the trial, or perhaps by the way Austin treated you during the cross-examination?"

Slowly, he shook his head, eyes gazing at infinity. "I was a little sad," he said softly. "You know—seeing trees and sunshine for almost the last time." A tight smile twisted his lips. "You know that old saying, what would I do if this were the last day of my life? I thought about that a lot."

"And what did you decide?"

He shook his head wordlessly.

Blanchard looked back at Everly, and at Sommer and Katovsky and Porath behind him. "Anything else?"

"Not right now, no," Sommer told her.

"So what happens now?"

Blanchard looked back at the table. "You'll be going back into Soulminder," she told him.

"And I'm afraid you'll have to stay there for a while," Sommer added. "At least until we resolve this mess. There may be other questions we'll want to ask you."

A cheek muscle twitched. "I'll do anything I can to help."

"Thank you." Sommer looked at the doctor and nodded. "We'll talk to you later, then."

His cheek twitched again as the hypo pricked his arm. His eyes closed, and he was once again dead.

"Interesting," Sommer murmured from behind her, his voice sounding thoughtful. "Well, gentlemen, Dr. Blanchard. Shall we adjourn to the conference room?"

"I'd like to stay here until Walker's back in his body," Blanchard said. "If that's all right."

"As a matter of fact," Sommer said quietly, "it's not all right. What I have to say is going to be of extreme interest to you."

A chill ran up her back. "Yes, sir," she said.

"I'd like to begin by hearing your opinions about our little chat with Mr. Holloway," Sommer said when they were all sitting around the conference room table. "Dr. Blanchard, why don't you begin."

She shook her head slowly, neck muscles feeling tight as she did so. The guarded tightness in Sommer's eyes could only mean bad news. Bad news, and almost certainly about Walker. "I'm afraid I don't have much to offer," she said. "Holloway was obviously very tense—I'm sure you could all see that. But whether it stemmed from guilty knowledge or everything else about his current situation, I couldn't tell." She hesitated. "That bit about keeping him in Soulminder awhile longer got a definite reaction, too."

"Yes, well, I'm afraid none of us has any choice about that," Katovsky grunted. "The D.A.'s office has already made it clear that we can't release Holloway's soul until this mess is sorted out. Even if that includes bringing Lamar and Holloway to trial."

"Which we'll all hope like hell it doesn't," Porath added grimly. "We could be years seating a jury that would be willing to convict a murdered man."

"How about you, Frank?" Sommer asked, turning to the security chief. "You hear or see anything out of the ordinary?"

"Not really," Everly said. "For a while it looked like he might fall into the old trap of forgetting to ask who'd been killed, but he got to that eventually. He also didn't seem to know anything about the murder that he shouldn't, the other classic trap. I'd say we came out about as flat inconclusive as we went in."

Sommer nodded. "Thank you. Any other comments? Anyone?"

No one spoke, and Blanchard braced herself. *Here it comes.*

"Well, then." Sommer pursed his lips. "Up to now we've been concentrating on which of the two suspects actually held the murder weapon, letting the question of motive slide temporarily into the background. As of early this morning, I'm afraid we can no longer do that." He touched a folder lying on the table in front of him. "This is a standard medical/psychological report on a certain Soulminder employee, dating from several months ago up until the present. It details increasing stress levels, generated—according to the analyst—by job-related frustration and anger."

He took a careful breath. "I have to ask you, Dr. Blanchard: why do you hate Soulminder?"

It was so totally unexpected that for a half dozen heartbeats Blanchard couldn't even speak. "I don't hate Soulminder," she managed at last. "Who said I did?"

Sommer shrugged slightly. "You're a psychologist. You know how these conclusions are arrived at."

"And I know that six times out of ten they're completely wrong," Blanchard retorted, trying to whip up some anger through the numbness clouding her brain. "This being one of those six."

"Is it?" Sommer asked quietly.

She glared at him. But the righteous indignation was all an act, and down deep she knew it. There was no anger down there for her to feel, only a weary sort of relief. The burden was coming out at last. Probably for the best. "I don't hate Soulminder," she said with a sigh. "I hate the Pro-Witness program."

Sommer's eyebrows lifted slightly. Perhaps he'd expected her to waste more time denying it. "You mind telling us why?"

"I hate it for the same reason I hate the idea of perfectly fertile women hiring surrogate mothers," she bit out. "Or the idea of people donating blood or organs for cash on the barrel. It's all variations on the same theme: poor people like Walker selling their bodies for the convenience of the rich."

Katovsky snorted. "Oh, for—"

He stopped at a gesture from Sommer. "I understand what you're saying," Sommer said. "But the Pro-Witness program is hardly in the same class as those others. We're not talking convenience or vanity here, but justice."

"Justice?" Blanchard shook her head. "I'm sorry, Dr. Sommer, but I can't call anything justice that only works for a small knot of rich people who had the buckets of spare cash necessary to buy into a Soulminder computer before they were killed."

"Justice has always been skewed toward the powerful," Porath pointed out. "So is most everything else in life. Besides which, if you want to be strictly technical about it, isn't anyone who works for someone else renting out his or her body?"

"It's not the same," she insisted. "It's a matter of dignity. Of—" She shook her head, suddenly tired. "The hell with it. If you can't see the difference, I can't explain it." She looked at Sommer. "You didn't bring this up just to have a theoretical debate."

"No, I didn't." Sommer hesitated. "It's occurred to us, Dr. Blanchard, that assuming either Lamar or Holloway killed Griffin on his own requires us to stretch things a little too far. Lamar, for example, had access to that article on Griffin. But he wouldn't have known that Holloway had been out of touch for half an hour, thereby giving him an alibi. Holloway, on the other hand, apparently knew that Lamar always took a solitary walk after his Pro-Witness stints—"

"He knew that?" Katovsky cut in, frowning. "How?"

Blanchard clenched her teeth. "I probably mentioned it to him at one time or another. He asked a lot of questions about Walker."

"And he made an off-hand reference to it just before going back into Soulminder yesterday afternoon," Sommer added. "So he knew that Lamar would be out for a while, giving him an alibi. But he *didn't* know about Griffin's shady dealings." He looked hard at Blanchard. "Do you see where we're going with this, Doctor?"

"It would be hard to miss it," she said bitterly. "You think I set the whole thing up. Talked either Walker or Holloway—or both of them—into murdering a total stranger for me. I presume my motive was to somehow discredit the Pro-Witness program?"

"It's the most plausible motive we've come up with yet," Everly said coolly. "Why else would you stay with a program you hate?"

"It may come as a shock to you," she growled, "but there are people in this world who stay where they're needed for the simple reason that they *are* needed. Who's going to look out for Walker and the others if I go? Certainly not any of you—you're all so madly in love with either the money or the gosh-wow technology that you can hardly see straight."

"That's enough, Doctor," Katovsky snapped.

"Why?" she retorted. "What're you going to do, fire me on

the way to the D.A.'s office?" She looked back at Sommer. "Did it happen to occur to you that a person who's concerned with the quality of other people's lives is hardly the type to commit cold-blooded murder?"

"It did," Sommer conceded. "But as Frank said, it's the most plausible motive we have. The only other option at this point is that either Lamar or Holloway went homicidally insane."

Blanchard took a deep breath. "I didn't kill Eliot Griffin," she said. "Nor did I aid or abet whoever did. If that's all, I'd like to see Walker before they take him back to jail."

Sommer gazed at her for a moment, then shrugged fractionally. "All right. Frank will take you down. Although"—he added as she pushed back her chair and stood up—"there's really no rush. Murray's arranged to have Lamar released into our custody. He'll be remaining here, at least for now."

"Good," she said shortly. "He'll probably need some counseling after what's happened. This way he can get it from his cell-mate."

It was as good an exit line as any. Turning, she left the room.

And tried to ignore the aching in her stomach.

Lamar was lying curled up on the cot when they let Blanchard into his room. Curled up, watching her with dull eyes. "Walker," she nodded in greeting as the door closed behind her. "How are you doing?"

For a moment he didn't respond. Then his shoulders hunched a little. "Okay. I guess."

"That's the spirit," she said. "I don't believe you, of course, but that's the spirit."

He shrugged again. Crossing the room, Blanchard snagged the single chair and pulled it next to the cot. "I understand Katovsky's made arrangements to keep you here instead of sending you back to jail," she commented.

"Probably so it'll be easier to do all their mental testing on me," he muttered, his eyes on her.

Pointedly on her. "I'm not here as a psychologist, Walker," she told him gently. "I'm here as a friend."

"Yeah. Maybe." His eyes drifted away, to stare at the wall. "You know what really scares me about this? That maybe I really *did* do it. That I just sort of blanked out and killed the guy."

She sighed. "I don't know, Walker. I really don't. Under normal circumstances, I'd say you weren't the type to crack like that. But in this case . . . "

"You think maybe Soulminder did something to me?"

"It's possible," she said. "In this kind of transference, the resident soul and the body *do* affect each other. We've known that for a long time. That's why there's a three-hour limit on it, in fact—supposedly, no significant alterations can happen in that time. But whether that's really true . . . " She waved her hands helplessly. "I just don't know. And I don't know how we'd prove it even if I did."

Lamar's forehead was furrowed in deep thought. "You're saying that, like, if Mr. Holloway wanted to kill someone that *I* might go ahead and do it later on?"

Blanchard shook her head. "Again, I don't know. I talked to Holloway about that a few minutes ago, asked him if he'd been angry or frustrated just before he transferred out yesterday. But he said that all he'd been was sad."

"Doesn't sound like something that would've made me go out and kill someone, does it?"

"Not really," she admitted. "Don't worry, though. We'll keep hammering at it."

"Yeah." For a long minute he was silent. "You want to know the really funny part of it?" he said at last. "One of the reasons they hired me to be a Pro-Witness in the first place was that I knew a little about what was going on in the world. They said it showed I wasn't just some loser off the street trying to make crack money."

Blanchard stared at him. "They said *that*?"

"Oh, not to my face. I got someone to let me see the file they did on me a couple months later." He shook his head. "And you know the first thing I did when I got my first paycheck? I went ahead and sent off to get *Time* coming to my apartment. If I hadn't . . . "

"It probably wouldn't have helped," Blanchard told him. "What mattered was that Holloway didn't have access to the magazine at all. If you hadn't had a subscription, you still could've read it at the library."

"I never read magazines at the library," Lamar said. "But I used to read 'em at the dentist."

Blanchard raised her eyebrows. "At the *dentist*?"

"Yeah. You know—in the waiting room. They always had piles of magazines there."

"Old ones, probably, if I know dentist waiting rooms."

Lamar shrugged. "A little. Didn't matter much when I was a kid. I guess probably that's why I sent away for the subscription. So I could get 'em all new."

He launched into a story about how once he'd snuck back into the dentist's office the next day to return a magazine he'd borrowed overnight. But Blanchard wasn't really listening. In her mind's eye, she caught a memory of Lamar, hunched over a fancy glass table, his dark hair blocking his face as he leafed studiously through a magazine . . .

"Dr. Blanchard?"

She blinked. Lamar was frowning up at her from his cot. "You okay?" he asked.

"I'm fine," she said, standing up and knocking on the door. If she was right . . . "I'll be back soon. Hang in there, and try not to worry."

"This is ridiculous," Assistant D.A. Dorfman griped as his secretary pored through the box of old magazines in the bottom of his coat closet. "Completely ridiculous. You and Holloway were in here exactly five times, and in each instance you came directly into my office or the deposition room and then went straight out."

"No," Blanchard said, her eyes on the secretary. "On one of those occasions you shagged us out of the room for a few minutes so that you and Austin could confer in private."

"And you don't remember when that was?" Everly asked, shifting the bulk of his Smythson 88 fingerprint scanner to his other hand.

Blanchard shook her head. "I've been to too many depositions and meetings here over the months. But I have a clear mental picture of Holloway sitting by the glass table in the waiting room reading a magazine."

"Holloway, or Lamar." Everly grunted. "Remember that Lamar has been here before, too."

"Yes, but not for months," the secretary said over her shoulder. "I checked my appointment book, and I would have remembered if a Pro-Witness came in unexpectedly—here it is."

She half turned, the copy of *Time* in her hand. "Who gets it?"

"I do," Everly said before Dorfman could answer. Plucking the magazine deftly from her hand, he carried it to Dorfman's desk, opening it up to the page with Griffin's sidebar interview. Blanchard moved to the opposite side of the desk, craning her head sideways to reread the article as Everly unpacked the scanner part of the Smythson. There was still something about the write-up that bothered her. Something not quite right . . .

"Here goes," Everly muttered under his breath. He held the scanner over the left-hand page, and abruptly the office was bathed in an eerie ultraviolet-tinged light. The light cut off, and Everly repeated the procedure with the right-hand page. "Okay," he said, tapping keys on the computer part of the unit. "Let's see what the print files come up with. You looking for something?"

Blanchard shook her head, starting the article again from the top. "Yes, but I don't know what. There's something important here—I know it. But I can't figure out what it is."

"It's just a normal article," Everly said, leaning over to look at it. "Pretty much like every other newsmagazine interview."

"I know." Squeezing her hand into a frustrated fist, Blanchard shifted her gaze up to the photo. To Griffin, smiling professionally at the camera; to the expensive desk and curtains, framing that smile as if they'd been arranged in their positions for exactly that purpose; to the cloud-mottled blue sky outside the window, with the top of the Soulminder building just visible.

And suddenly, she caught her breath. "Everly—"

The last syllable was drowned out by an electronic beep. "Hang on," Everly grunted, flipping up the Smythson's small display screen. The first image that came up was that of the two magazine pages, dotted and smeared with the delicate patterns of dozens of fingerprints. Everly tapped the switch again, and the image was replaced by a list of those prints' owners. Blanchard craned her neck—

"Bingo," Everly said, swiveling the screen briefly toward her and then keying back to the image of the pages themselves. "You were right on the money, Doctor. Here, here, and *here*. Walker Lamar's thumbprints, right where someone reading the magazine would hold it."

"Doesn't prove he read the sidebar, though," Dorfman said.

"Oh, it proves it, all right," Everly countered. "You can see— right here—where he moved his hand so that he could read what his thumb had been covering up. No, he read the sidebar, all right." He looked at Blanchard. "But all that does is bring us back to square one."

"No, it doesn't," Blanchard said, shaking her head. "Because Griffin wasn't just a random killing. There's no reason why the murderer would have gone to a sixth-floor office if he'd just wanted any old victim."

"So he wanted someone who deserved to die," Everly said, nodding. "Or at least someone who came close to it. So?"

Blanchard gestured to the article. "So look at the interview again. Look at it closely."

"I've read it so many times that I've just about got it memorized," he growled.

Blanchard took a careful breath. "Then tell me what the article *doesn't* tell you."

For a long moment Everly frowned at her, and she found herself holding her breath, willing with all her might for him to see it. If he didn't—if it didn't therefore strike him as at all significant—then it was probably nothing more than a figment of her own wishful thinking—

"I'll be damned," he said, very softly. "You're right. You're absolutely right."

"Right about *what*?" Dorfman said suspiciously.

Everly cocked an eyebrow at him, then turned back and began to reassemble his fingerprint scanner. "You've seen this picture, Dorfman. You can see the Soulminder building in the background, which says that Griffin's office building bordered Ridley Square. But *how did the killer know which building it was*?"

"Well, obviously—" Dorfman broke off, an odd expression flooding across his face.

"Exactly." Everly straightened up, hauling the repacked Smythson off the desk. "You know what we're looking for, Doctor. Let's get to it."

He looked down at the article, tongue playing nervously across his lips. "No, I don't remember reading this," he said, looking up.

Looking up . . . but with his eyes never quite meeting Blanchard's. Or anyone else's in the deposition room, for that matter. "I'm sorry, Mr. Holloway," Dorfman shook his head, "but I'm afraid that won't wash. We found your fingerprints all over a copy of the article from my waiting room. A copy, I may add, that Walker Lamar never had access to."

"I suppose I'll have to take your word for it," the other said, trying his best to sound huffy. It didn't really come off. "So okay, let's assume I did read it. What then?"

Dorfman looked at Blanchard, then at Sommer, Everly, and Porath. "What then, Mr. Holloway," he said quietly, "is that, for whatever reason, you decided to kill Eliot Griffin. You want to tell us what that reason was?"

"I don't know what the hell you're talking about."

"Then look at that article again," Dorfman said, an edge beginning to form in his voice, "and I'll try to explain. Go ahead, look at it . . . and notice that nowhere in the article is Griffin's office address given."

For just the briefest instant the eyes flattened, the look of a man who suddenly realized he'd made a fatal blunder and that all was lost. But only for an instant. "Well, that's pretty much normal, isn't it?" he shrugged, the mask back in place. "Stories like this don't usually print addresses, do they?"

"Almost never," Dorfman agreed. "And it brings up a rather awkward question. Namely, how did Griffin's killer know where to find him?"

"Probably from that photo." He waved at the article on the table with a hand that was just beginning to tremble. "You got that view through the window—I suppose someone could figure it out from that."

Dorfman shook his head. "No," he said. "It looks like it could be done, but it really can't. Not without special equipment or professional experience. The picture was taken too far back from the window—it doesn't show nearly enough outside detail for the exact location to be pinpointed. You vary the angle, position, and elevation of the camera and you can get almost the same view from offices all over that side of Ridley Square. I know; I sent a photographer there this afternoon to do just that."

The eyes flicked around the room: to Dorfman, to Blanchard and the other Soulminder people, to the court recorder quietly taking it all down. "Then I don't know how he did it," he muttered.

Again, Dorfman shook his head. "You miss the obvious, Mr. Holloway," he said. "Perhaps because you don't want to draw our attention to it. But it's already too late. Mr. Everly, Dr. Blanchard, and I went to the courthouse annex this afternoon. Given the annex's clientele and visitor base, it's one of the few places left in the country where there are actual pay phones and physical, paper telephone directories.

"And we found the directory with your fingerprints on it. One of those prints, the right-hand index finger, is directly beneath Mr. Griffin's listing."

He seemed to hunch back in his chair, eyes staring out of a frozen face like a trapped animal. "It wasn't me," he said, the trembling in his hands now transferred to his voice. "It must have been Lamar."

"No," Dorfman said. "If Lamar had decided to kill Griffin he could have looked up the address at home or at any number of other places. You were the one who had no choice but to locate your victim, get a weapon, and commit murder, all in that single half hour."

"You'll never prove it," the other gritted out. "Never in a million years. Fine, arrest me. I'll fight it all the way to the Supreme Court if I have to."

"You misunderstand, Mr. Holloway," Dorfman shook his head. "This isn't going to go to trial. I'm not filing any charges against you."

For a moment he just stared, a look of horror on his face. "What do you mean?" he whispered. "You can't do that—a man's been *murdered*, damn it. You can't just—you *can't*."

"Yes, I can," Dorfman said. "And I'm going to. Sometime next week the jury will deliver a verdict in People v. Battistello, and you'll be back in the courtroom to see that. And after that . . . "

"Oh, God," he whispered. "Oh, God, no. Please. I demand a trial," he said, his voice surging abruptly toward hysteria. "You hear me? I'm a citizen—I have a *right* to a trial."

"You're not a citizen anymore," Everly said, his voice deliberately hard. "You're legally dead."

The air went out of him as if he'd been kicked in the stomach. "Oh, God," he whispered.

For a long minute the only sound in the room was the muted

tapping of keys as the recorder caught up with the conversation. Then, steeling herself, Blanchard reached across the table and took the witness's hand. It was trembling and cold as ice. "It's all over, Michael," she told him gently. "Won't you please tell me why you killed him?"

He turned his face to her, his eyes vacant. "He was a thief," he said dully. "He stole other people's money. He deserved to die."

She shook her head. "He deserved punishment, but not death." She hesitated, but looking at him now, it was suddenly, achingly clear. "You did it for yourself, didn't you? You killed a man, and deliberately dragged Walker into it, hoping the case would be snarled up in court for years.

"So that you wouldn't have to leave Soulminder."

He licked his lips, first the upper and then the lower . . . and suddenly his face twisted in anguish. "I don't want to die," he sobbed. "Please. *I don't want to die.*"

The knock came on her door a third time, and Blanchard reluctantly looked up from her work. Katovsky, almost certainly, here to respond to her letter of resignation. "Come in," she called.

She was wrong. "Dr. Blanchard," Sommer said gravely, shifting the folder he was holding into his other hand and closing the door behind him. "I wonder if I might have a minute of your time?"

"Of course, sir," she said, indicating the guest chair. "I was just closing out a couple of my files."

Sommer sat down, laying his folder down on the edge of her desk in front of him. "I thought you'd like to know that the Holloway case is all over. The jury came back just after one with a guilty verdict on Battistello. About an hour ago they brought Holloway back here and gave him final release."

Final release. From Walker Lamar's body, and from the Soulminder trap that had been his only existence for six months. Now, indeed, he was truly dead. "Did he ask why I wasn't there?"

"Yes," Sommer said. "I made an appropriate excuse, though I don't think he believed me."

Blanchard felt her stomach knot up. With revulsion or guilt, she couldn't tell which. "I was going to go," she told Sommer. "But I couldn't face him. I just couldn't."

"I understand. I almost couldn't face him myself." Sommer shook his head slowly, his eyes distant. "It's strange, you know. I spent over a month in a Soulminder trap ten years ago, and came away with a sense of utter peace about whatever it is that lies in store for us after death. And it wasn't just me. I've talked to others since then, all of whom had similar experiences."

"And then along comes someone like Michael Holloway."

Behind his cheeks, Sommer's jaw tightened. "He was terrified of death. Really, sincerely, terrified of it. So much so that he actually killed a man to try and postpone it." He focused on Blanchard, his gaze discomfiting in its intensity. "Why would anyone do a thing like that?"

"I don't know," she admitted. "Maybe he saw something different there than you did, or maybe he was more in love with this world than you are. Maybe there was something he'd done in life that he regretted. Something he'd done, or something he'd failed to do."

Sommer's gaze seemed to soften a little. Or perhaps the intensity was merely turned inward. "I've done many things I've regretted, too," he murmured. "None of them seemed to matter when I was in Soulminder."

"Maybe you knew somehow that you would be coming out again," Blanchard suggested quietly. "That you still had a chance to try to make up for those things."

Sommer sighed. "It's funny, you know. For ten years now I've been trying to convince Jessica that death isn't something to be feared. You know Jessica?"

Dr. Jessica Sands, co-creator of Soulminder. And, inside rumor had it, the true driving force behind everything the corporation did. "I've heard of her, of course," Blanchard said. "Never met her personally."

"For ten years I've been trying to calm her down on that fear," Sommer said. "And I thought I'd made some progress. Now—" He shook his head. "It's all come to a head again. The funding proposals she sent from Washington this morning showed a fifteen percent increase for the various life-extension studies we've been supporting."

"There's nothing wrong with looking for ways to let people live longer and more fulfilling lives."

"No, not with the idea itself," Sommer said heavily. "Only with the motivation behind it." He focused on Blanchard again. "But, then, you're a psychologist. You know all about motivation, don't you."

She took a deep breath. "I've resigned as Pro-Witness liaison," she said. "I presume Mr. Katovsky's told you that."

Sommer nodded. "That's the main reason I'm here, in fact."

"If you're here to try and talk me out of it—"

"I'm not. I'm here to offer you a new job." Picking up the folder, he swiveled it around and put it down on in front of her. "Take a look, if you would."

She shook her head. "I'm sorry, but I really don't want to work for Soulminder anymore."

"If it's because we all but accused you of murder—"

"No, that's not it," she assured him. "From your point of view I suppose it was the most reasonable scenario. It's just . . . I don't know. I guess the Pro-Witness program has soured me on what Soulminder's doing these days."

"In that case," he said quietly, "you'll definitely want to look in that folder." Reaching over, he opened it and then sat back.

She stared at him for a moment before lowering her eyes to the folder. The top page, written on the Capitol Hill stationary of a New York Senator, was a summary of a bill currently working its way through committee . . .

She looked up at Sommer again, stomach knotting within

her. "This is crazy," she breathed, jabbing a finger on the paper. "You can't make it legal for people to will their bodies to someone else. Think of the pressure from family members, from society— my God; the whole public perception of suicide prevention and counseling would be turned a hundred eighty degrees over."

"There's more." Sommer nodded toward the folder. "A proposal that would make it legal for people to loan their bodies to the handicapped for a couple of hours at a time, for example. Another one would go even further—letting an infertile woman actually deliver the baby carried by the surrogate mother she'd hired."

Blanchard's throat felt tight. "So much for justice," she said bitterly. "You *did* say the Pro-Witness program was about justice, didn't you, Dr. Sommer?"

"Yes, I did. I take it that you disapprove of these ideas?"

She closed the folder, wishing there was some way to slam it. "If you have to ask, you obviously weren't paying attention the other day."

"Do you disapprove enough to come to Washington and help me fight them?"

She stared at him, the blistering retort she'd prepared dying halfway up her throat. "I—to *fight* them?"

He was watching her closely, that discomfiting intensity back in his eyes. "This may come as a surprise," he told her, "but I have no interest in making money for money's sake. My vision for Soulminder is as a medical tool, something that can help save lives that would otherwise be lost. I had some strong misgivings about the Professional Witness program when it was first proposed, but Jessica was very keen on the idea and kept pushing it. I couldn't find enough solid objections, or couldn't find the right words for the ones I had. In the end, I gave in. But even then I knew I'd have to draw the line somewhere, or I'd eventually wind up watching Soulminder become a sort of recreational body-switching toy for the idle rich.

"Here"—he touched the folder—"is where that line gets drawn."

Blanchard looked down at it. "It won't be easy," she said. "You can make a strong case for every one of these proposals."

"I realize that," Sommer agreed. "That's why I need your help. You're a psychologist—you have the training, and the scientific words, to help convince Congress this isn't what Soulminder should be about."

He stood up. "Think about it," he said, leaving the folder on the desk in front of her as he stepped back to the door. "I'll be here for another day or two, if you want to discuss it further." He paused, his hand on the doorknob. "Just remember that the longer we hesitate, the more ingrained the politicians' mindset will be." With another nod, he left.

For a long time Blanchard just sat there, staring down at the cover of the folder. To deal with the renting of bodies again—not on a quiet, personal level this time, but on an overt, confrontational one. Fighting against people who wanted this and to hell with the ethics, or the overtones of slavery, or the consequences. People who would always remind her of the lengths Michael Holloway had gone to to try and stay alive . . .

Or maybe, her earlier words seemed to echo through her mind, *there was something he'd done in life that he regretted. Something he'd done, or something he'd failed to do.*

Reluctantly, she opened the folder again, and began to read.

CHAPTER 6

●

Cast-Off

BACK IN HIGH SCHOOL, Nic Robertson had been on both the football and wrestling teams, with the broad shoulders and powerful arms required for someone to be champions in those sports. And he had been, in both. Still, in the past few months, those arms and shoulders had grown even larger and stronger.

Which really wasn't surprising. The doctors all told him that extra arm and upper body strength were perfectly normal for a man who'd taken a load of shrapnel to the spine and would be spending the rest of his life in a wheelchair.

"Honey?" his wife Rosabel called from the kitchen. "Breakfast's ready."

Nic clenched his teeth, wincing at the sour taste of morning mouth, as he used the grab bar mounted to the bedroom ceiling to pull himself up into a sitting position. It had been six weeks since he'd returned home from the hospital, and Rosabel had spent the first three of those weeks hovering like a mama Black Hawk, offering him help about twice a minute. He was still trying to get it through her skull that he didn't want her help, and that he needed to learn how to do this stuff for himself.

On the surface, she seemed to have accepted that. At least her offers of help had dropped from twice a minute to maybe twice a day. But he could see that it still hurt her to watch him struggle with his bar and his chair and the new handrails in the bathroom. It hurt her terribly. Almost as much as it hurt him to watch her hurting.

But he *did* have to learn how to do this. Someday, he was sure, Rosabel would have no choice but to move on. To find a husband who was a complete man, not the half-man, half-wreck that the Army had sent home to her.

When that happened, he would be completely and eternally alone. He might as well start getting used to that life now.

What with getting into the chair, maneuvering into the bathroom, getting out of the chair, doing his business, and getting back into the chair, he'd gotten the morning routine down to about twelve minutes. Of course, it *used* to take him only two, but twelve wasn't bad, really. He rolled himself into the kitchen just as Rosabel was sliding the pancakes off the griddle onto a plate.

So she'd lied about breakfast being already ready. No surprise there, either—clearly, she'd figured out how much time he needed in the morning and adjusted her own schedule to match, while peddling the lie about things being ready to prod him into actually getting out of the damn bed.

Yeah, she'd be leaving him, all right. Rosabel had been brought up to always tell the truth, and she must hate having to lie even more than she hated having to baby him. Sooner or later, she'd get tired of it.

"Bacon's all right, right?" She set the plate in front of him and put the syrup within easy reach.

"Sure," he said, feeling yet another twinge of guilt. Rosabel was more a sausage person, but she knew he liked bacon better, and with their budget the way it was these days they could only afford breakfast meat a couple of times a month.

"Good," she said, putting his orange juice and coffee beside the syrup and heading back to the sizzling skillet. "I got in on the last day of the sale, so we've got plenty."

"Thanks." He picked up the glass of orange juice and took a long swallow. The tart flavor mixed with his lingering morning mouth, the taste flashing him briefly back to way too many dusty Middle East mornings. "You check the email yet?"

"I took a quick look." Rosabel was studiously concentrating on getting the bacon from the pan and laying it out to drain on a triple-thickness of paper towels. "But I could have missed something."

Nic grunted, picking up his napkin and smoothing it just as studiously across his lap. In other words, there hadn't been any responses to his latest salvo of job applications, but she didn't want to spoil his breakfast by saying so.

"You did get a letter from the VA, though," she added, sliding three strips of bacon onto his plate and then crossing to the counter where the bills were neatly stacked. "It came just a few minutes ago, while you were in the bathroom."

"Probably another of their here's-how-to-get-a-job pieces of crap paper," he growled, pouring a small dab of syrup on his pancakes. Rosabel didn't care much for bacon, but she loved syrup, so he always made sure he left her enough to thoroughly soak her pancakes.

"No, I don't think so." Rosabel picked up the top envelope and brought it back across the room. "This one came certified mail. I had to sign for it and everything."

Frowning, Nic stuffed a forkful of pancake into his mouth and took the envelope. It was certified, all right. More than that, the return address was different from the one his usual VA junk mail came from. Biting off a bacon chaser for his pancakes, he tore open the envelope and pulled out the folded paper.

His breath caught in his throat, nearly sending the pancake down the wrong way.

"What is it?" Rosabel asked, wincing as he fought to keep from choking. "Did they find you a new job?"

Carefully, Nic finished swallowing his mouthful, making sure not to inhale it this time. "Not a new job," he said, handing her the paper. "A new *life*."

He watched her eyes move back and forth as she read. Watched them go wide as she hit the spot where he'd tried to choke on his breakfast.

She read it twice before finally looking up. "Is this for real?" she all but whispered.

"If it isn't, it's one hell of a sick joke," Nic said, taking the paper back.

And rereading it, just to make sure he hadn't been imagining things.

In cooperation with Soulminder, Incorporated, the Veterans Administration and the United States Government are pleased to offer you the permanent use of a new body. (See below for details.)

The transfer will take place at the Washington, D.C. Soulminder office.

If you wish to avail yourself of this opportunity, please call the phone number below no later than forty-eight hours after receipt of this letter.

"What do you think?" he asked, looking up at Rosabel.

"I don't know," she said, looking back uncertainly. "I mean, it would be wonderful to have . . . for you to be able to walk again. But . . . "

"But?" Nic prompted.

"That footnote, where they say he could be a criminal," she said. "That worries me."

"They also say he could have been an accident victim," Nic

pointed out. "Or died of a drug overdose or organ failure. That thing's there to cover all the possibilities, that's all."

"Yes, but what if he *was* a criminal?" Rosabel asked. "What if he was in prison for—for murdering his wife or something?"

"It doesn't matter what he did," Nic said firmly, moving his left hand surreptitiously under the table and resting it on his useless legs. The chance to have a fully functional body again . . . "It'll be *my* body, and it'll do what *I* tell it to."

"Will it?" she countered, her voice starting to sound a little ragged. "There are some things that stay with the body, you know. Otherwise, companies like Walkabout USA couldn't even exist. If he was a killer, or a molester—"

"It'll be *my* body, Rosabel," Nic repeated. She wasn't seriously going to stand in his way on this, was she? On nothing more than some half-baked fears and silly minor details? "It'll do what I tell it to."

Because this was literally the chance of a lifetime. The chance of *his* lifetime. To be whole again . . . "Look, we don't have to decide right now," he continued into her frowning silence. "We can call it in and go there and still back out if it doesn't feel right. There must be hundreds of other vets who would jump at a chance like this." He gave a little snort. "Figuratively, I mean."

Rosabel winced at the unsubtle reminder of his condition, as he'd counted on her doing. The marriage counselors always talked about fighting fair, but *they* all had two good legs to walk on. Right now, winning was all that counted, and tactics be damned. "All right," she said. "Go ahead and call. Tell them you'll accept. I don't suppose you can . . . you know. Tell them it's provisional."

"I think if I did that they'd give it to someone else," Nic said. "But don't worry. I meant it about backing out. I mean, they're not going to strap me into a Soulminder machine and force me to take him, right?"

"I suppose not," Rosabel said. She still didn't sound all that enthusiastic, but at least she didn't sound dead-set against the idea any more.

And for now, that was good enough. She'd have a few days to get used to the idea. After that, he would simply talk her out of whatever reservations she still had.

Because winning this one was all that counted. All that mattered in the universe.

"Alpine skiing, you say," the pudgy woman at the desk said, her eyes focused on her computer display, her fingers punching slowly at the keys, her head all but lost amid the bold *Walkabout USA* sign that filled the wall behind her.

"Correct," Daniel Lydekker confirmed, wondering if this was a complete waste of time. The role he was auditioning for involved a fair amount of skiing, but all the close-ups would be studio shots in front of a green screen. He didn't actually *need* any skiing experience.

But there were a lot of hungry young actors out there, and way too many of them probably knew at least a little bit about skiing. Lydekker knew the casting director's reputation, and the man was a raving lunatic for realism.

Which meant if it was a choice between the son of the great Blake Lydekker and some complete unknown who'd barely mastered the bunny slope, he'd take the unknown in a heartbeat.

Unfortunately, there was no time for Lydekker to learn how to ski, not before the casting call scheduled for a week from tomorrow. But there *was* time to at least experience the sport. And, if he was lucky, he'd also learn how to fake the moves and posture.

"Here we go," the woman said, leaning a bit closer to her screen. "We have a former World Cup team member on file. Good enough?"

"Absolutely," Lydekker said, wondering vaguely how much of his father's money this was going to cost. Still, the elder Lydekker could hardly kick. He was the one who wanted so much for Danny Boy to follow in his footsteps, and it wasn't like he didn't have money to burn. "How soon can I take a spin?"

The woman frowned slightly. "We call it *a walkabout*, Mr. Lydekker," she said, her tone mildly reproving. "Let me check his schedule . . . we could do it early next week, if you'd like. Monday or Tuesday."

"Make it Monday," Lydekker said. The audition was Tuesday, not much time for him to assimilate the experience. But he'd make it work. "Where is he located?"

"Denver," the woman said. "You'd need to be there by eight that morning."

"No problem," Lydekker said. "I assume there's an extra charge for the quick turn-around?"

"The various fees are listed on the form," she said, handing him a clipboard. "If you'll fill this out, we can get things started."

"Thank you," Lydekker said. A world full of netbooks and electronic tablets, and Walkabout USA still wanted him to scribble words on paper. How unexpectedly quaint.

Still, given all the hacking, crashing, and brute-forcing going on out there, maybe pen and paper really was the best way to keep private interactions genuinely private.

He was definitely on Walkabout's side on that one. What they were doing was legal enough, but legal and publicly embraced weren't always the same thing. A significant percentage of the American people fervently believed that recreational body-sharing was the work of the devil, a secret government cabal, or some combined group of Big Pharmaceutical, Big Business, Big Banking, Big Oil. Probably with the Illuminati thrown in somewhere.

In this case, private was good.

The form wanted the usual stuff: name, address, phone, relevant medical history, etc. There was a check box for whether or not the client was already registered with Soulminder—which Lydekker was—and it spelled out the additional fees and time required for a new client to go to one of the Soulminder offices and have his Mullner trace recorded.

He frowned as something about that suddenly connected.

"Question?" he said, looking up. "I'm registered with Soulminder here in LA. But you said the switch was going to be in Denver? How's that going to work?"

"As soon as the agreement is confirmed we'll contact the LA Soulminder office," the woman explained. "They'll make arrangements to transfer your Mullner trace to Denver." She gestured. "It's on page two of the form."

Lydekker turned the paper over. "Oh, right," he said. "I see it now." The transfer would cost another fee, of course, and a pretty damn hefty one. Plus the reverse transfer if he wanted to go back to being on file here.

But then, he'd already known that this form of recreation wasn't for the faint of heart or the short of cash.

He finished with the form and returned it to the woman. "Denver Soulminder office at eight a.m. next Monday, right?"

"Yes," she confirmed, glancing over the form. "And don't be late. Once you're set you still have to get to Breckenridge, and you only get him for twelve hours."

"Don't worry," Lydekker promised, visions of a juicy almost-starring role beckoning siren-like to him. "I'll be there."

The VA official's name was Susan; the Soulminder tech's name was Patrick. Nic was pretty sure they both also had last names, but he'd been too nervous and distracted to catch them when they were first pitched, and the lettering on their badges was too small for him to read.

Susan was the talkative one; Patrick was quiet nearly to the point of unfriendliness. But together, they got the job done.

"Okay, that's the Mullner trace," Susan said as she unstrapped Nic's wheelchair from the framework holding up the helmet that had been buzzing in his ears for the past twenty minutes. "We'll give Patrick a moment to check it over. How do you feel, by the way?"

"A little queasy," Nic admitted, getting the words out quickly and returning to the job of keeping his teeth clenched together.

The last thing he wanted to do was spew all over a Soulminder office.

"That happens sometimes," Susan said cheerfully. "Nothing to worry about—it'll pass in a couple of minutes. Patrick?"

"Looks good," Patrick said, giving a vague sort of thumbs-up. "Whenever you're ready."

"Great," Susan said, getting into position behind Nic's chair and pushing him toward the door. "Here we go. A new life in thirty minutes, or your next one's free."

"I'll be timing you," Nic warned, daring to joke a little. As she'd promised, the nausea was already going away.

But in its place was an unnaturally dry mouth and a sense of impending doom. Did he really want to do this? Did he really?

He squared his shoulders, feeling them rub against the soft back of his wheelchair. Damn right he did. Not just for him, but also for Rosabel.

He just wished she could be here beside him instead of being stuck away in a reception room somewhere. It would have been nice to have her hold his hand through the procedure.

Though that hand wouldn't be his much longer. On second thought, that would probably be a little creepy. Best to leave her where she was.

Susan had promised thirty minutes. Nic wasn't sure how long it actually took, but it seemed much faster than that. One minute he was lying on a gurney, staring up at a white ceiling and feeling himself drifting off to sleep. The next minute he was opening his eyes, to an entirely different ceiling.

The follow-up medical checklist and the purging of the various drugs from his new body took somewhat longer. But finally, Susan declared him to be ready. Walking carefully with the cane she'd given him—she'd warned he would be a little wobbly for another few minutes—he followed her to the reception room where they'd left Rosabel.

His wife was waiting there, pacing the floor as he'd known she would be. She spun around at the sound of the opening door. A dozen emotions flicked across her face— "Nic?" she asked hesitantly.

"Here in the flesh and fit as a fiddler crab," he assured her. His voice sounded odd in his ears, and the words didn't seem to fit his mouth quite the way they used to.

Some of the tension went out of her face. "You're crabby?" she prompted.

"Dungeness crab, with butter and baked cheese, all soaked in special shallot sauce," he said, reeling off the second part of the code signal they'd worked out between them. The words still sounded odd, but his mouth seemed to be working better. "How do I look?"

"You—they haven't shown you?"

"No," Nic said, feeling his throat tighten. "How bad is it?"

"Oh, it's not bad," Rosabel assured him hastily. "You're just a little . . . Middle Eastern?"

Nic looked at Susan. "Middle Eastern?" he echoed.

"Or Spanish or Moroccan or Greek," she said. "A lot of the Mediterranean peoples look similar."

"You could be Greek," Rosabel agreed, eyeing him closely. "Either way—I'm just so glad to see you alive and all right."

"It's good to see you, too," Nic said. "Especially from this height. How about seeing me from a little closer?"

Rosabel looked at Susan, her face reddening a little. "I don't know—"

"Go ahead," Susan said with a broad smile. "I promise I won't look."

Rosabel's hug was tentative, the hug of a woman embracing a long-lost relative instead of a husband of three years. Her kiss was just as tentative. "I'm sorry," she said as she eased away. "It's just . . . "

"It'll take some getting used to," Susan said. "That's all right. The important thing is not to push it. You're going to be in town the rest of the week anyway for the follow-up tests, so pretend it's a vacation. Take your time, see the sights, get reacquainted with each other. It's still your husband in there, Rosabel—it really will be easier than you think." Her lips puckered impishly. "And if I may suggest . . . keep the lights off tonight."

Rosabel looked at Nic, her face flushing again. According to her Midwest upbringing, things like that weren't supposed to be talked about in public.

Though in *private* . . .

"We will," Nic said. "Are we done?"

"For now," Susan said, nodding. "Don't forget you need to come in tomorrow afternoon for the first of your post-transfer checkups—all very routine. Now, go on, get out of here. Go back to the hotel, talk, have a good dinner, and—" She held her arms out wide. "Live."

"Thank you," Nic said, holding out his hand. Rosabel took it, and this time her touch was a bit more assured. "So," he said as he led her toward the door. "What do you think of us dark, Latin types?"

"Well," she said thoughtfully. "I *do* like a good Antonio Banderas movie every now and then . . . "

The former World Cup Ski Team member, somewhat to Lydekker's surprise, turned out to be Japanese. Or maybe Korean. Or possibly something else.

Though in retrospect he didn't know why that should have surprised him. There were mountains and snow all over East Asia, after all, and people always said that the world was a global village now. In fact, now that he thought about it, he vaguely remembered that parts of *Nine Days to Live* were scheduled to be shot in China.

But really, none of that mattered. What mattered was that he was going skiing.

The drive to Breckenridge was quiet. The contract expressly forbidden Lydekker himself to drive, and the man that Walkabout had contracted for the job was the quiet sort who probably said five words during the entire hour and a half trip.

Which was fine with Lydekker. His mouth felt funny anyway.

The doubts began on the way up to the slope, his legs dangling from the T-bar over the snow and trees, the rocks, and the lines of graceful, presumably happy skiers. The run he'd picked wasn't the most challenging of Breckenridge's slopes, but it wasn't the easiest, either. The Walkabout people had assured him that his body could handle anything Colorado had to offer, but the Walkabout people weren't here. He, Daniel Lydekker, was, and all their learned talk about brain stem and cerebellum modularity and muscle memory didn't mean a damn if he was about to fall straight off a mountain.

The doubts ended when he actually pushed off and found himself gliding like a low-flying eagle down the face of the mountain.

It was like nothing else he'd ever done. Like nothing else he'd ever imagined. He'd done a lot of motocross and once taken flying lessons, though he hadn't stuck with it long enough to get his license. But while those activities offered some of the same freedom, both also came with raucous, throbbing engines.

Here, there was nothing. Nothing but the hiss of his skis against the snow, the whistling of the wind in his ears, and the occasional distant shout or laugh from one of his fellow skiers.

It was faster than motocross. It was more like flying than even flying.

It was magic.

He tried half a dozen different slopes throughout that glorious day, daring late in the afternoon to challenge one of the more advanced ones. He fell twice, both times when he tried to take control of his skis and poles instead of relaxing and letting his body's reflexes do their job.

Finally, to his regret, it was time to go back.

His muscles stiffened up a little during the long drive back—apparently, he'd put the body through more than even a World Cup expert was used to. But he didn't care. The aches and fatigue would stay with the body. He wouldn't.

What he *hadn't* expected was just how loose and flabby his own body felt as he walked down the Soulminder office corridor. He'd always considered himself to be in pretty good shape, but clearly he wasn't as buff and toned as he'd thought.

Still, that didn't matter. What mattered was that he now had some of the experience the casting director was going to be looking for. What mattered was that the part was as good as his.

And what *really* mattered was that he'd just had one hell of a good day.

"Nic!"

With a start, Nic came awake. "What?" he whispered tautly.

"You were having a nightmare," the voice said, and this time, Nic recognized it as Rosabel's. "A bad one."

Nic frowned in the darkness. The lighting wasn't right, and the bed felt odd beneath him. Where the hell was he?

And then, abruptly, it all came back. Soulminder, his new body, his fully functional legs and . . . other important equipment. Also fully functional. "It's okay," he said. "I've had plenty of nightmares before." Especially since his return from overseas, he carefully refrained from pointing out. Rosabel knew about those nightmares even better than he did.

"Not like this," Rosabel said, her voice still tense. "You've never had three in the same night before."

Nic stared at the faint silhouette just visible against the muted glow from the bedside clock. "*Three?*"

"Maybe more," Rosabel said. "Those are just the ones I woke up for."

"I'm so sorry, Rosabel," Nic said, rubbing the stubble on his cheeks to try to shake off the rest of the sleepiness. The stubble felt odd, thicker than his usual morning shrubbery.

An instant later, he squeezed his eyes shut as she fumbled on the bedside light and the room lit up violently around him. "I'm calling Soulminder," Rosabel said, picking up her phone and the stack of paper they'd been given before Nic was discharged.

"You don't have to do that," Nic protested. "I've had a lot of bad dreams."

"Not like these, I tell you," Rosabel insisted. "Do you remember anything about them?"

"Not really," Nic admitted. This latest nightmare had faded almost instantly as he awoke, though he could vaguely remember seeing a couple of men shouting at him. "Probably another flashback to that IED."

"I don't think so," she said, finding the right paper and shuffling it to the top of the stack. "I've seen that one before, and you always shout during it." She gave him a dark, worried look. "But you always shout in *English*. This time, it was something different."

Nic stared at her, freshly aware of his new, foreign-born body. "How different? Could you tell what language it was?"

"Not really," Rosabel said. "There seemed to be a lot of wordless screaming in there, too."

Nic shivered. In his flashback dreams, at least, he was always shouting orders and trying to get his unit on top of the situation. Wordless screaming was a new one. "We still should probably wait until morning before we call," he said.

Rosabel shook her head. "Susan said that if anything strange happened I was supposed to call this number right away. I think this qualifies."

She punched in the number, shifted the phone to speaker, and set it down on the bed between them. "Hello," a woman's voice came. "You've reached the voicemail of Dr. Carolyn Blanchard. Please leave a message."

Nic looked up in time to see a look of frustration flick across Rosabel's face. But really, what had she expected at four o'clock in the morning? "This is Rosabel Robertson," she said. "My husband, Sergeant Nicholas Robertson, was transferred into a new body yesterday at the Washington D.C. office. He's having nightmares—at least three tonight—and calling out in some foreign language. I wondered if that's normal, or if—"

There was a sudden click from the phone. "Ms. Robertson,

this is Dr. Blanchard," the same woman's voice came. "Can you identify the language he was speaking?"

Nic looked at Rosabel again, saw his own surprise mirrored in her face. And at four o'-fricking-clock, too. "No," she told Blanchard. "But I don't think it was Spanish or Italian."

"Can he remember the dreams? Any details that stand out? Any details at all, really?"

"No, nothing," Nic called toward the phone. "I didn't even know I was having them until Rosabel woke me up."

"I see," Blanchard said, sounding a little distracted. "Can you come to the Soulminder office tomorrow—well, today, technically—at ten o'clock?"

"Yes, of course," Rosabel said, frowning. "He's already scheduled for a checkup at two."

"I'll leave a note that he's coming in earlier," Blanchard said. "Try to get back to sleep. We'll take a look and see if we can get you some answers."

"Thank you, Doctor," Rosabel said. "Good-bye."

"Good-bye."

Rosabel picked up the phone, disconnected, and put it and the papers back on the nightstand. "Well," she said. "That was quick."

"*Very* quick," Nic agreed, not sure whether to be relieved or worried. It was gratifying that Soulminder was on top of this. But in the Army, at least, the only things that got quick attention were sudden brush fires that needed to be stomped out. "I guess we should go back to sleep."

"Probably." She raised her eyebrows slightly. "Unless you're not sleepy."

"Not really," Nic agreed, the last hint of the nightmare's uneasiness fading away. "Go ahead and turn off the light. Let's see what develops."

It was one of the rare occasions when Lydekker was sleeping alone. But that was fine. A woman would just have distracted him from his dreams.

And his dreams were magnificent.

It was like an instant replay of his skiing adventure, an adventure that moreover had been recorded by multiple cameras so as to capture every nuance. The swooshing sound was there, as was the wind and sunlight on his face. His knees bent and flexed with perfect skill and timing, turning his downhill race from mere here-to-there transport into a thing of grace and beauty.

And with some of the dreams he ended up bouncing off a small slope to find himself soaring over the mountains, the trees, and the other skiers far below.

It was a terrible letdown when the final dream dissolved into the melodious nagging of his alarm.

The sense of loss lasted through his shower and to the middle of his second cup of coffee. But then the memory faded, and the real world once again asserted itself.

And the most important bit of that real world was the audition for *Nine Days to Live*. An audition he was going to nail like an Olympic gymnast.

Or, more appropriately, like an Olympic skier.

He smiled his toothy smile at the mirror as he brushed his teeth. This was going to be a great day.

"The good news first," the Soulminder doctor, a woman named Woods, said as she peered at her computer screen. "There's no indication of a problem in your brain chemistry. The computer's still checking through the numbers, but all the major indicators are well within proper parameters."

"Okay," Nic said cautiously. He hated the good news/bad news game. "What's the bad news?"

"It looks like you might have had some physical traumas in your past," Woods said, scrolling to another page and swiveling the screen around toward him. "A couple of serious breaks in your arms—one each in left and right—plus a lot of smaller fractures in your fingers."

Nic glanced at Dr. Blanchard, sitting quietly beside Rosabel across the room. "So, what, I got run over by a bus or something?" he asked.

"If you were, you walked in front of at least three different busses," Woods said. "It looks like the injuries extend over at least a couple of weeks. Possibly longer."

"What about soft tissue?" Blanchard asked. "Any scars or torn muscle fibers?"

"I haven't checked that yet," Woods said. "I only spotted the breaks because they're obvious on the CT scan."

"Let's check now," Blanchard said, standing up. "Is the exam room still available?"

"I think so," Woods said, frowning. "Protocol is to finish the biochem analysis before we move on to a full physical."

"I'm aware of that," Blanchard said. "We can do the physical while the computer chews through the biochem data."

"I'm not sure I'm authorized to do that."

"You are now," Blanchard said firmly. "I suggest you check my status."

"All right, but the protocol standard is pretty high-level," Woods warned, punching some keys. "I don't know anyone who can—" She broke off, her eyes widening. "Yes, ma'am," she said in a suddenly subdued voice.

"Come with me, Sergeant," Blanchard said, gesturing to Nic. "Dr. Woods, please set the biochem scan for a Level Two analysis, and then join us."

"Thank you," the disembodied voice came from behind the glare of the audition room lights. "We'll be in touch. Next?"

And with that, it was over.

Lydekker felt numb as he walked through the lot toward his car. So that was it. Thirty seconds' worth of reading, and then they'd tossed him out like some amateur from Bakersfield summer stock. They hadn't asked him to do a second passage, hadn't asked him to stick around—and he knew for a fact that at least two of the hopefuls *had* been asked to stay—hadn't even asked him to read opposite one of the other actors or staff. A single, thirty-second monologue, and it was over.

And from the highs of yesterday's skiing adventure and his early morning dreams, the world had dropped straight into the tank.

For a while he just drove aimlessly, too depressed and listless even to bother cursing out all the idiots on the road. The sky was covered with gray clouds, the perfect background for his mood, and the city seemed even dirtier than usual. Finally, for no particular reason, and with no particular purpose, he pulled over and parked.

To his surprise, he found himself half a block from the Walkabout USA office.

The same woman was manning the front desk. "Good morning, Mr. Lydekker," she greeted him. "How was your ski trip?"

"Fine," Lydekker said, forcing himself to be polite despite the woman's gratingly cheerful smile. "What else have you got?"

She took the abruptness in stride. "Most anything you want," she said, keying her computer. "We have motocross, waterskiing—"

"I just did skiing, and I can do motocross on my own," Lydekker cut her off. "What else?"

She studied his face. "Most anything you want," she repeated, reaching past her computer and doing something out of his view. "The only question is how exciting you want the experience to be. And how dangerous."

Lydekker frowned. *Dangerous*? Someone else was providing the body for these little stunts, after all, bodies whose owners knew that some total stranger would be running them. Just how much risk were these people willing to take for whatever Walkabout paid them?

"*Dangerous* might be the wrong word," a new voice suggested from Lydekker's left.

Lydekker turned to see a middle-aged man in an expensive

suit standing just inside the hallway in that direction. "Excuse me?" he said.

"I think *daring* would be the better term," the man said. "Daring in all senses of the word." He gestured behind him. "If you'd like to step into my office, perhaps I can elaborate a bit."

Lydekker hesitated. But really, why not? It wasn't like the day—and maybe his whole life—wasn't shot to hell anyway. "Sure," he said. "Lead the way."

The physical took another hour, and was easily the most thorough check-up Nic had ever had.

And in the end, they still didn't have any answers.

"There's definitely some residual soft-tissue damage," Woods said when she was finally finished. "Most of it's borderline microscopic, and a lot is clustered around and through various neural groups." She shot a hooded look at Blanchard. "Most of it wouldn't even be noticed unless you were specifically looking for it."

Blanchard nodded, not bothering with any I-told-you-so looks. "What's the timeframe look like?"

"Like the broken bones, it seems to have occurred over several weeks," Woods said. "More recently than the fractures, of course, since the fractures have completely healed."

"How long ago?"

Woods shrugged. "The bones, probably three to four months. The nerve damage could be as recent as two weeks."

"I don't understand any of this," Rosabel said. "What kind of injuries take a month to happen to you?"

"Maybe he was a skydiver or motorcycle racer," Nic suggested. "Not a very good one, either."

"There's one more thing," Woods said. "There are indications around the nose, cheeks, and eyes that the person had some work done. Probably during the period between the broken bones and the neural damage."

"What kind of work?" Nic asked.

"Precision work," Woods said. "It would seem to be . . . ?" She looked at Blanchard, as if afraid to finish the sentence.

Blanchard finished it for her. "Plastic surgery."

Nic frowned at Rosabel. "Plastic *surgery*? What, on *this* face?"

"There's nothing wrong with your face," Rosabel said. But her voice sounded uncertain.

Nic looked back at Blanchard. The woman's eyes were narrowed, and there was something in her expression that sent a chill up his back. "Doctor?" he prompted.

"You could be right about him being a bad motorcycle racer," she said. "Someone like that could end up needing a little reconstruction somewhere along the line."

"But you don't think that's the case."

"No," she said flatly. "I don't."

"Then what?"

Blanchard exhaled a long breath. "I have a thought," she said. "But I'd rather not say anything more until I'm sure."

"Is Nic in danger?" Rosabel asked anxiously. "I mean . . . if the man got into a fight with someone . . . "

"I don't think he's in danger, no," Blanchard hastened to assure her. "But you might want to stay close to your hotel for the rest of the day. You're going to be in town another day or two, right?"

"We're here until the end of the week," Rosabel said, still sounding tentative. "Unless you think we should leave."

"No, please stay," Blanchard said. "There are some things I want to try to track down, and I'd like you here in case I find something."

"Can you at least give us a hint?" Nic asked.

"I'd rather not say anything until I'm sure," Blanchard said. "Trust me: I *will* get to the bottom of this."

Nic looked at Rosabel. But there didn't seem to be anything more to be said. At least, not now.

Later, though, Nic was pretty sure he would have a *lot* to say. And not all the words would be polite. "Fine," he said, turning back to Blanchard. "But make it fast. If this guy was a vain wild-eyed klutz, I want to know it. Preferably before *I* walk in front of a bus."

It was, Lydekker reflected, about the last thing he'd expected.

At the same time, considering the cesspool that was Southern California, it was practically inevitable.

"Drugs," he said flatly.

"Not just drugs," the man assured him. "I'm not talking the pedestrian stuff here—hey, you can get those anywhere. That's why they're called pedestrian. I'm talking about designer drugs: the best, brightest, most brain-spinningly powerful stuff on the planet."

"And of course they're perfectly safe?" Lydekker asked with just the right edge of mocking irony.

"What do I look like, a used-car salesman?" the man countered. "Of course they're not safe. That's why *you* don't take them. You just borrow the body of the guy who does."

Lydekker shook his head. "This can't possibly be legal."

"Well, see, that's the real beauty of it," the man said, grinning slyly. "In point of fact, it *is* perfectly legal. At least your part and our part is. We're not selling illegal drugs, and you're not taking them. The guy we hire for the switch—well, *he's* in a boatload of trouble if he gets caught. But so far he hasn't. And it's obvious why he needs the money. It's really a win-win for everyone."

Lydekker thought about it. The whole thing was about as twistedly insane as anything he'd ever heard.

But in its own way it made sense. In fact, it made way too much sense.

And he *was* feeling pretty low. A little boost, especially when there was absolutely no danger to himself, might be a good way to burn off an afternoon.

"Well?"

Lydekker squared his shoulders. On the other hand, this wasn't something you jumped into without taking time for thought and consideration. And, more importantly, without checking the relevant laws and statutes. "I'll think about it," he said, standing up. "Thanks for your time."

"No problem," the man said. "When you're ready, we'll be here."

More to the point, Lydekker reminded himself as he headed back to his car, while there might be occasional roles out there for skiers, there were a *lot* of roles for junkies, ex-junkies, and about-to-be junkies. This might just give him the precise edge he needed.

Besides, he'd heard a lot about some of these designer drugs. Business interests aside, this kind of experiment could be interesting.

The nightmares came back that night, as tense and frightening as they had the night before.

But this time, Nic was ready. Not just for the emotional impact, but with his mind cleared and geared to try to grab onto some of the details instead of letting them blow away in the wind.

Despite Rosabel's insistence that he'd been shouting in a foreign language, he'd assumed that the dreams would be his typical post-return stuff: images of heat and fear, death and flying bullets, and most especially the IED that had cost him the use of his legs.

To his surprise and dismay, the dreams were totally different. And in a way, even more horrifying.

"I was in a small room," he murmured to Rosabel as he lay on his back, feeling cold sweat running down the side of his face onto his pillow. "Sitting or lying down, I couldn't tell which. I couldn't move my arms or legs. There were bright lights in my eyes, and a bunch of men moving around the room behind the lights. Some of them were laughing."

He paused, searching Rosabel's face for some clue as to how she was taking this. But her face was a mask. "Go on," was all she said.

"They were laughing," he said, closing his eyes. For some vague reason he felt uncomfortable seeing her watching him. "And then two of them came into the light . . . and hurt me."

"How?"

"Every way they could," he said, a fresh wave of horror rippling through him. "With needles, and knives, and—" He broke off. "Every way they could," he repeated. "And I couldn't move at all."

"And then you woke up?"

"Yes," he said. "But not until . . . " He opened his eyes. "This guy"—he touched his chest—"this guy, Rosabel, was *tortured.*"

For a long moment neither of them spoke. "We have to tell Dr. Blanchard," Rosabel said at last. "Or someone at the VA. Someone has to be told what happened."

"Maybe," Nic said slowly. "But that's the problem. What *did* happen?"

"I thought you said he was tortured."

"He was," Nic said. "But who was torturing him? Terrorists? The mob? Some sadist serial killer? A foreign government? *Our* government?"

Rosabel stared. "You're not serious. *Our* government?"

"I don't know," Nic said, rubbing at his eyes. Suddenly, his whole body felt prickly. "All I know is that everything seems gray these days. There's no black and white anymore; no good guys in white cowboy hats. Maybe there never were."

"Of course there were," Rosabel said fiercely. "There still are. We just have to find them."

"Maybe," Nic said. He took a deep breath and looked at the clock. "But we're not going to find them at four in the morning." He forced a smile. "They're all sleeping the sleep of the virtuous, you know."

Rosabel gave him an equally forced smile. "I guess we can wait until morning to go hunting."

"Yeah," Nic said soberly.

He only hoped all the good guys were indeed sleeping the

sleep of the virtuous, and not the sleep of the long-since dead and gone.

By eight in the morning Lydekker had made his decision. By ten he was at the Walkabout office, filling out the paperwork.

By noon, he was stumbling down an alley in the body of a junkie.

The alley was a frightening place. It was filthy and fetid, reeking of vomit and urine and hopelessness. The body he was in was even worse: wracked with sores, itching with fleas or lack of hygiene or both, dizzy with hunger and lack of sleep.

But Lydekker didn't care about any of it. Even as he stumbled along, whatever his host had taken just before the transfer began to take effect.

It was the most powerful, most exhilarating experience he'd ever had. His day of skiing paled in comparison with this new and blazing light. The best meal of his life—the most exquisite lovemaking—the emotional high of his first acting award—all of it was nothing. All that mattered, or would ever matter, was the serene, glorious magic that had ignited his body and lit up his mind.

He found a convenient section of alley wall and slumped down onto the broken pavement, gazing at the brilliance of the cloudy sky and the glorious music of the traffic passing by forty feet away. The glow, the fire, the pure mind-swelling pleasure . . .

He had no idea afterward how long he sat there. All he knew was that when he suddenly came to himself the streetlights had come on, a light rain was falling, the alley's odors were curling his nostrils, and he felt like complete and violent hell.

He also didn't have the faintest idea where he was.

Luckily, the Walkabout people had supplied his borrowed body with a GPS set for backtrack. Plodding down the street, forcing one foot in front of the other through the pain and utter despair throbbing through his head, he finally made it.

Leaving the World Cup skier's highly disciplined body for

his own had triggered something of a letdown. Leaving the junkie's was like stripping off a three-day-dead animal that had somehow fused itself to his skin. He left the Soulminder office feeling like he'd died and then been given a new chance at life.

But though the headache and body sores were gone, the memory of that last bitter withdrawal depression lingered.

As, indeed, did the memory of the incredible high that had gone before it.

The morning phone call to Dr. Blanchard lasted about fifteen minutes. After that, following Blanchard's instructions, Nic and Rosabel again spent the day in their hotel room.

The hours dragged on, a strange mixture of boredom and tension that reminded Nic of his days in the Army. Between room-service meals, Rosabel pretended to be interested in one of the old movie channels. Nic pretended to catch up on his sleep.

The sun had set, the city's buildings disappearing into sparkling lights, when Blanchard finally called.

The car was waiting at a side door when they emerged from the hotel. Nic had expected Blanchard to be alone, and he was wrong. "This is Frank Everly," Blanchard introduced the driver as they pulled back into the street. "He's head of overall Soulminder security."

"Oh?" Nic asked, studying the man's profile in the glow of headlights coming through the windshield. "I didn't realize we were that dangerous."

"You're not the ones I'm worried about," Everly said. "Did you have dinner yet?"

"No," Nic said. "But we had a late lunch."

"There are some snack bars and water bottles back there if you get hungry," Everly said. "Might as well settle in—it's going to be a bit of a drive."

The bit of a drive turned out to be nearly two hours long, taking them from D.C. through northeastern Maryland to somewhere in northern Delaware. The house Everly finally pulled up in front of was an old one, Nic noted as they walked toward it, eighty years old at least. "Who are we meeting?" he asked.

"A family of refugees," Blanchard said, her voice grimmer than he'd ever heard it. "They're from—"

"Somewhere else," Everly cut her off. "Sorry, Doctor, but that's a need-to-know."

"I suppose," Blanchard said reluctantly.

The door was answered by a young man about Nic's age, his face showing the same dark skin and eyes as Nic's own new body. "I'm Dr. Blanchard," Blanchard introduced herself. "This is the man I spoke to your father about."

The young man gave Nic a long, penetrating look. Then, without a word, he stepped aside and gestured the group to enter. Closing the door behind them, he slipped past them and led the way into a brightly lit living room.

Where, Nic noted uneasily, more than just a single family was waiting. Thirty people more than a single family, in fact. They were everywhere, filling all the available chairs and couches and lined up two deep in the back and sides of the room.

And all of them had similar Middle Eastern faces.

He felt Rosabel tense up beside him. "Doctor?" he murmured, gripping his wife's hand.

"Sorry—this was my idea," Everly murmured before Blanchard could answer. "I told Anwarr he might want to invite everyone in the area who knew Ishaq."

Nic felt a shiver run up his back. Who knew *who*? "You should have warned me," he said quietly. "I don't do too well with crowds. Not anymore."

"It'll be all right." Everly tapped him reassuringly on the shoulder, then eased forward past the young man. "Anwarr?" he called.

"I am Anwarr," an old man said, rising from one of the couches in the front of the group where he'd been sitting with a tight-faced woman about his same age. "This is the man?"

"It is," Everly confirmed. "Nic, would you step forward, please?"

Nic looked over the silent group. For the most part, their faces were unreadable.

"It's all right, Nic," Blanchard said. "Go ahead."

Swallowing, Nic released Rosabel's hand and moved up beside Everly.

"May I?" Anwarr asked.

Everly gestured permission. Slowly, like he was approaching a potentially dangerous animal, the old man walked forward until he was about three feet from Nic. There he stopped, his eyes studying every square inch of Nic's face. "He is close," he said uncertainly. "But . . . "

"I told you there was some plastic surgery," Blanchard said.

"Yes." Anwarr hesitated. "May he speak?"

"Of course," Blanchard said. "What would you like him to say?"

Anwarr visibly braced himself. "The war will not be won by matching the regime's brutality," he said, as if reading from a mental script. "It will be won by capturing, not towns, but the hearts of the people."

"Nic?" Blanchard murmured.

Nic grimaced. "The war will not be won by matching the regime's brutality—"

And on the couch, the old woman abruptly put her hands to her face, slumped forward at the waist, and burst into tears.

Nic turned to look at Blanchard. But the doctor only had eyes for Anwarr.

And Anwarr seemed to have eyes for no one. "Yes," he said, the word almost inaudible over the woman's sobbing and the murmurs of the rest of the people as they moved forward en masse to comfort her. "This is our son." His gaze flicked briefly to Nic's face, then dropped away again. "This *was* our son," he amended in a voice of infinite sadness.

And suddenly Nic felt like he was going to be sick. "Doctor?" he said urgently.

"Yes," Blanchard said. Nic could hear an edge of Anwarr's grief in her voice, and a tinge of Nic's own nausea.

But mostly what was there was anger. Cold, dark, simmering anger. "Yes, we're done," she confirmed.

"Come on," Everly said, stepping back and taking Nic's upper arm. "Anwarr, I'm so very sorry."

"A moment," Anwarr said.

Nic froze. The man was staring at him again, a dullness in his eyes. "Yes?" Everly asked.

"I want you to know," Anwarr said, his eyes still on Nic, "that this is not your fault. You are not to blame. Promise me you'll remember that."

Nic swallowed. "I'll remember," he said.

Anwarr bowed his head. "Then farewell. Live your life unfettered. Ishaq would have wished that for you."

Two minutes later, they were once again driving through the Delaware night.

"I don't understand," Rosabel said into the stiff silence filling the car. "Who are they? What happened to . . . to their son?"

"Sorry," Everly said. "The less you know, the better."

"No," Nic said flatly. "You dragged us all the way out here. You owe us some answers."

"I'm sorry," Everly said again. "But—"

"No, he's right, Frank," Blanchard said. "But not tonight. There's been enough pain for one day."

"Then when?" Nic asked. "And don't tell me to call back in a month. I know that game."

"No game," Blanchard assured him. "Come by tomorrow afternoon at two. I'll tell you everything you want to know."

She paused. "Just be warned: it may be more than you want to know."

Lydekker's day was filled with the usual busyness, from catching up on email, to calling his agent and other contacts, to lining up a trip up the coast for the weekend.

But lurking at the back of his mind, never far below the surface, was the memory of those glorious hours spent in the Los Angeles alley. In the embrace of that incredible drug.

By the middle of the afternoon, he couldn't stand it any longer.

The guy down the street who peddled weed didn't have the stuff. Neither did the coke and meth dealer he sent Lydekker to. Finally, four dealers down the line, he got an address where it was rumored someone might have the designer high Lydekker was looking for.

It was after sundown by the time he reached the man, a scruffy Rastafarian type sitting in a bar just off the Santa Monica Freeway.

"Yeah, I might be able to get you some of that," the Rasta said obliquely, his voice slurred with evidence that the rum and Coke on the table in front of him wasn't his first of the day. "Expensive stuff. You got money?"

"I've got money," Lydekker assured him, wondering distantly how he was going to categorize this one when he hit up his father for more cash. Research, he decided. He would list it as research. "The question is, when can you get it?"

"Hey, mon, it's right out in the car," the Rasta said, showing a grin full of uneven teeth. "You got the money, we go right out."

Lydekker hesitated, wondering if he should instead insist the Rasta bring the stuff in here for an exchange in a more public setting.

But, really, that would be stupid. Besides, the Rasta was surely too smart a businessman to try to rob a brand-new customer. For starters, the man was half drunk. For finishers, Lydekker was carrying a 9mm Colt in his waistband. "Fine," he said, standing up. "Lead the way."

The Rasta's car was exactly what Lydekker expected: a beat-up Chevy that no one on the LA streets would look at twice, let alone think might be owned by a salesman making ten thousand percent profit on his merchandise. The trunk was likewise not a surprise: a couple of scattered blankets, tools, and containers of motor oil and window washer fluid covering up the collection of illicit drugs hidden beneath them. "You wanted a dose of Lady Dainty, right?" the Rasta asked, rummaging through the packages.

"Yeah," Lydekker confirmed. At least, that was what the man at Walkabout had called it. "How much?"

"Five"—the Rasta paused, throwing him an appraising look— "hundred," he continued, apparently sizing up Lydekker as someone unfamiliar with current street slang. "Cash," he added, as if Lydekker might try to put it on a Macy's card.

"Yeah, I know," Lydekker said, pulling five bills from his pocket. This was something of a deal, really—the Walkabout man had mentioned the stuff usually went for seven hundred a pop. He was probably getting some sort of first-timer's discount.

Even at full price it was a hell of a lot cheaper than what Walkabout charged for this kind of experience. He handed over the money, received an unmarked prescription pill bottle with a childproof cap in return, and turned away.

"One more thing, mon?"

Steeling himself, moving his right hand casually to the grip of his gun, Lydekker turned around. If the Rasta was holding a weapon . . .

He wasn't. He was holding something far worse.

A shiny badge.

"LAPD," the Rasta said, his accent and fake drunkenness gone. "You're under arrest."

"He was an advocate for freedom," Blanchard said. "In—I'm sorry; I still can't tell you which country. He became enough of a headache for his government that they had him snatched."

"And then tortured him," Nic said quietly, his body once again feeling all prickly. "To death."

"Eventually, yes," Blanchard said. "But they did far more than that. The neuropreservative residue in your tissues show that they actually tortured him to death five times."

"*Five* times?" Rosabel asked, her eyes wide. "But how—" She inhaled sharply. "Oh, no. God. No."

"Yes," Blanchard confirmed with a sort of quiet bitterness. "Thanks to Soulminder, they were able to kill him, store his soul while they repaired his body, then bring him back and do it all over again."

"Until they got tired of the game," Nic said, anger starting to simmer inside him. "And you didn't stop them?"

"We had no say in the matter," Blanchard said. "Each Soulminder office operates at the pleasure of the local government. Besides, up until now we had no proof that this was going on."

"And now that you do?" Rosabel challenged.

"I've brought it to the attention of Directors Sommer and Sands," Blanchard said. "I'm sure they'll do what they can to stop it. Especially Dr. Sommer." Her lips compressed. "What you have to understand is that we're also swimming upstream against our own government. Since the passage of the body-sharing laws, we really can't stop this sort of thing from happening."

"What are you talking about?" Nic demanded. "How in hell does this come under the heading of *recreational*?"

"It's multiple soul transfer," Blanchard said. "The fact that it's multiple transfers into the same body doesn't matter. Call it an unintended consequence of a hastily- and poorly-written law."

"Can't they rewrite it?" Rosabel asked.

"Of course they could," Blanchard said. "But even if they did it would only apply to Soulminder offices here. Other countries could still use the current statutes, or any statutes they like." She sighed. "But it's even worse than that. No government is going to rewrite the laws because no government wants to."

"Not even ours?" Rosabel asked.

"Maybe even especially not ours," Blanchard said. "Every soul transfer is taxed. Taxed a *lot*, at both the Federal and state level. Recreational body-sharing generates a lot of revenue, and no one wants to kill this latest incarnation of the golden goose."

"So it all boils down to money," Nic said. "That's all. Just money."

"Yes," Blanchard said. "Which is also the only reason you have that body in the first place. Once the torturers were done with Ishaq, they patched him up one last time . . . and sold his body to the U.S."

"So they could earn some brownie points by giving it to a vet who'd lost his legs," Nic rumbled, the nausea threatening to overwhelm him again. "Nice little surprise bonus for someone."

"It wasn't a surprise, Nic," Rosabel murmured. "The plastic surgery—it predated the torture, remember? They planned to sell his body from the very beginning."

"She's right," Blanchard said, nodding. "They did just enough work on the face to keep anyone who'd known him from recognizing him if they saw him on the street."

"And our government's just going along with this?" Nic asked.

"There are a lot of injured vets," Blanchard said. "As you said: political brownie points."

"So what if I refuse to play the game?"

Blanchard looked him straight in the eye. "Then you die," she said bluntly. "Your old body's long since gone. If you decline this one, it'll be given to someone else."

"Nic, please," Rosabel said, her hand wrapping around his in a death grip. "You can't . . . you just can't."

"Take it easy, Hon," Nic said, squeezing her hand reassuringly. "I'm not talking about dying just to make some kind of useless statement. I'm talking about the *whole* game. This whole damn body-switching, body-*stealing* game."

Abruptly, he stood up. "Fair warning, Dr. Blanchard," he said. "I appreciate what you did for me. But it's over now. I'm going to fight you on this one, just as hard as I can."

Blanchard shook her head. "No, I don't think so."

"And you think that *why*?"

"Because," Blanchard said calmly, "I'm on your side."

Nic blinked. "What?" he asked cautiously.

"Yes," Blanchard confirmed. "So is Frank Everly. And so is Director Sommer."

Nic looked at Rosabel. "The guy who invented Soulminder?"

"The very same," Blanchard said. "He's just as angry as you and I are about what his creation has been turned into. And he's promised to stop it."

"How?"

"I don't know," Blanchard said. "I don't think he does, either. Not yet." She cocked her head, studying him. "I understand you're still looking for a job. You want to work for us?"

"Doing what?" Nic asked.

"I don't know that yet, either," Blanchard said. "Let's figure it out together."

Nic looked at Rosabel. Then, slowly, he sat down again. "Yes," he said. "Let's."

"The purpose of this meeting," the Assistant District Attorney said briskly, peering at his tablet, "is to ascertain the parameters of a plea bargain between the State of California and Daniel Reginald Lydekker, of the city of Los Angeles."

Lydekker squeezed his hands into fists under the table. His lawyer had assured him that a first-time offense like this would probably result in nothing worse than probation.

But his lawyer had apparently missed the latest statutes on the class of drugs Lydekker had been caught buying. Those particular drugs were chewing a swath through the sons and daughters of the elite, and the State of California had apparently decided that was where they would draw a line in the long-neglected sand.

A line that was now positioned directly beneath Lydekker's feet.

"A conviction on all counts could bring a sentence of five to seven years in prison," the ADA read from his tablet. "Our offer, in exchange for a guilty plea, is six months, plus five years' probation."

Lydekker tightened his fists even harder. Six months. Six *months.*

He couldn't do six months. He'd barely survived the twenty hours he'd been in the county lockup before his lawyer had been maneuvered through the legal hoops and gotten him bailed out.

Six months would kill him. It would absolutely kill him.

"Or," the ADA continued, "the State is prepared to offer one year of being on call to a licensed office for recreational body-sharing."

Lydekker stared at him. "What was that?" he asked carefully.

"One year of being on call for recreational body-sharing," the other repeated, looking at Lydekker with an odd expression on his face. "It's considered a form of high-level probation these days. Tell me, do you have any sports abilities? A lot of people are looking for that. Or artistic expertise, or anything else someone might want to experience?"

"You're joking," Lydekker said, the words coming out like pieces of sandpaper. In his mind's eye he saw himself racing down that snow-covered hill . . . saw the blazingly beautiful alleyway . . . felt the hammering agony of the drug withdrawal . . .

"It's perfectly safe," the ADA assured him. "The contract provides for the client to pay any medical bills should there be an injury—"

"Yes, I read the damn contract," Lydekker gritted out. "This is insane."

The ADA shrugged. "As I said, it's just an offer," he said, closing down his tablet and putting it back in its case. "Feel free to discuss it with your attorney. If you decide not to deal, contact my office and we'll set a court date."

He stood up and headed for the door. "Wait," Lydekker said.

The ADA turned back. "Yes?"

Lydekker took a deep breath. Six months. Maybe even seven years . . . "Motocross," he said bitterly. "I can do motocross."

CHAPTER 7

●

End Game

IT WASN'T THE BIGGEST fraud trial in New York history. Bernie Madoff still held the record on that one. It wasn't the most notorious, either. There were a goodly number of high-profile murder, terrorist, and crime boss cases that future chroniclers would have to choose among for that dubious honor.

But Marvin Chernov had duped his clients of over twenty billion dollars, and many of those clients had been Manhattan's most powerful, famous, and supposedly sophisticated movers and shakers.

Those embarrassed movers and shakers wanted his head on a platter. Figuratively, literally, or some combination of the two.

That was where Adam Jacobi came in.

And where Marvin Chernov went out.

The rooftop Jacobi had chosen for the job was a long block away from the courthouse where Chernov was currently basting the judge and jury in his oh-so-sincere smile and probably not sweating in the slightest. Certainly not visibly. The man hadn't convinced all those investors that he was as pure as Vermont maple syrup by showing the slightest molecule of doubt or hesitation.

But for all of Chernov's external confidence, Jacobi had no doubt that the jury would hang him out to dry.

Leaning forward, Jacobi peered through the scope attached to his FN Special Police sniper rifle, resting on its bipod at the edge of the roof. Briefly, he wondered if he should double-check his ranging calculations, then dismissed the thought. He'd run all the distance, drop, and windage numbers and zeroed the crosshairs for those stats, and he never made mistakes. All the hard work was done, and all that was left was to line up the crosshairs on Chernov's forehead. The .300 Winchester short magnum round and the laws of physics would do the rest.

He was wondering idly how long the sunlight would last before the afternoon clouds that had been forecast rolled in when there was a sudden flurry of activity on the courthouse steps. A single glance through the scope at the shirtsleeved cameramen and over-polished and microphone-laden news babes was all he needed.

The trial was over for the day, and Marvin Chernov was about to head back to his temporary quarters on Rikers Island.

Setting the butt of the rifle stock against his shoulder, Jacobi set his eye to the scope, and his finger against the trigger guard, and waited.

The wait wasn't long. Three minutes later, surrounded by a phalanx of cops and lawyers, Chernov walked through the doors and headed for the mob of reporters.

Jacobi shifted his finger from the guard to the trigger.

The past four sessions of the trial had established a pattern. Each time Chernov emerged from the courthouse he would stop on the top step, deliver a short harangue on the eminent unfairness of the charges and his total innocence, then take a few questions.

Today was no exception. The silver-haired man stopped at his usual place, his entourage stopping more or less patiently with him, and through his scope Jacobi saw his mouth begin moving as he launched into today's speech.

He was just getting warmed up when Jacobi's .300 magnum blew out the back of his head.

He'd had another name once, the name his mother had given him and, he assumed, the blurry succession of foster parents had used when yelling at him. But it had been years since he'd left the last of those hellholes, enough years that he'd stopped even bothering to remember it. *Shrill* was what the other street people called him, and Shrill was who he was. He was Shrill the street person, the meth addict, the one you didn't pick on if you didn't want your ears turned inside out.

But even more important, he was Shrill the guy with a secret.

Sometimes one of the others asked how he got by without hitting up the tourists and bleeding hearts for loose change. Sometimes, when he was feeling good and on a hit, he would drop hints about a relative who kept him in food and drugs. Other times, when he wasn't feeling so good, he would drop even bigger hints that he took the money from those same tourists directly, without asking, leaving them bleeding in some alley. That usually shut off the questions and gained him a little space.

Which was how he liked it. The last thing he wanted them to know was that he was renting out his body. Not like a hooker rented just the fun parts, but literally renting his whole body.

Thank God for Soulminder. And thank God, too, that more of the druggies didn't know about it. If they did, they'd all want a piece of the gold mine, and he *would* have to shake down the tourists.

He was in the first stages of withdrawal as he slipped inside the special side entrance that Soulminder had set up for this sort of transaction. He stopped at the desk, gave his name—the people here only knew him as Shrill, too—and was led back to a small room that was nothing but a hospital bed and a buttload of fancy gadgets with wires, tubes, and shiny lights.

And, of course, there was the helmet.

The tech got him settled on the bed and adjusted the helmet around his head. Sometimes the techs asked if he was on something, but this one didn't. Probably he could tell just by looking that Shrill was coming down.

That was how it was supposed to be. No one borrowed a druggie's body just to feel the middle of a high. They borrowed it because they wanted the whole package, from the first whiff of smoke or tingle of the needle, right through the high and to the start of the crash.

Only the start, of course. At the first hint the stuff was wearing off, they scurried back to Soulminder and got their own bodies back.

For Shrill, that meant going from one crash straight to another, without any of the high in between. That part sucked. Really sucked.

But the money was good. Very good. And he had to admit that floating like a ghost in the Soulminder machine was pretty peaceful.

Maybe if he ever got enough money he'd see if it was possible to take vacations in there. Surely that was where the rich people spent their time when they got bored with their big boats.

He was daydreaming about living in a sea of calm peacefulness when the tech tingled his arm with the hypo.

A minute later, he was dead.

The face at the hotel room door was exactly as Jacobi had expected. The body, though—or rather, that body's current encasement—definitely wasn't.

"What the hell is *this*?" he demanded as the young man strode past him into the room.

"It's called a suit," the man replied coolly. "What, haven't you ever seen a suit before?"

"I told you I had a wardrobe already put away for you," Jacobi said, not nearly so coolly.

"And I wanted to get out of those damn filthy druggie rags," the other retorted. "What are you worried about? It's not coming out of your pocket."

"Damn right it isn't. So whose pocket *did* it come from?"

"Whose do you think? The rich kid left two hundred to buy his hit. I just bought something that would last longer than a three-hour high, that's all. Maybe he'll learn a little about lasting value this way."

Jacobi ground his teeth. This was not the plan, and the only way he'd survived as long as he had in this business was because he always followed the plan. "And what do you think they're going to say at the rehab center when you show up in a brand-new suit?"

"They're not going to say a thing," the man said, "because I'm not going."

Jacobi felt his eyes narrow. "What?" he asked in a low, ominous voice.

"Oh, don't worry," the man assured him with a grin full of stained teeth. "I'm not going to drop into this body's old habits. I figure I can kick his addictions on my own, that's all."

"You think you can do that, do you?" Jacobi asked patiently. "Did you even *do* the reading I recommended?"

"Of course I did," the man said, his cocky bravado switching to soothing humility in an instant. It was the kind of emotional dexterity that separated a good con man from a great one, Jacobi knew. Probably why he'd been one of the best. "I know a person's brain and body retains some of their habits and muscle memory, no matter whose soul is in it." He lifted a finger like a grade-school teacher making a point to a particularly slow student. "But I *also* know that even meth can be kicked provided the addict is motivated." He looked down at his body. "Believe me, brother—I'm *extremely* motivated."

Jacobi ground his teeth even harder. But there was nothing he could do. Even the best plans required the client's cooperation, and in this case the arrogant S.O.B. was clearly determined to do things *his* way. "Fine," he said, crossing to the coffee table and opening the satchel lying there. "Come here."

He dug beneath the neatly folded clothing in the satchel and retrieved the wallet tucked away in the middle. "Pay attention." He opened the wallet and ran a finger down the assortment of cards in the slots. "Driver's license in your new name of Gabriel Vance. Visa and MasterCard, ten thousand dollar credit limit on each. That should hold you until you can get to your own stash. Social Security, Safeway Preferred Customer, Staples, and Best Buy—"

"Best *Buy*?" the other interrupted, sounding aghast.

"You want to flaunt your billions with designer electronics, be my guest," Jacobi said. "Just be aware that that's exactly the kind of trail FBI agents love to dig out."

The man sniffed. "Like they'll have a snowball's chance."

"You don't want my advice, don't take it," Jacobi said, suddenly tired of this man and this conversation. "No skin off my nose either way. You have my money?"

"You have a pencil?"

Silently, Jacobi wiggled his fingers in invitation.

The man rattled off a series of numbers. "You need me to repeat that?"

"No," Jacobi said. "I trust all fifty million is there?"

"All fifty, plus a ten-million bonus." The man grinned again. "I figure you earned it."

"Okay, then," Jacobi said. For a moment he considered reminding the client what would happen if his fee was not, in fact, in that account. But it really wasn't worth the effort. "Take the satchel and get going. I'll follow in about ten minutes."

"Better idea," the man said. "You go, and I go take a shower. I'm thinking room service, and a good night's sleep."

Jacobi cocked an eyebrow. "You're staying here? Even though they're looking for you out there?"

"Exactly. They're looking for me out *there*. They're *not* looking for me in here."

"Good," Jacobi said, his estimation of the man going up a reluctant notch. Most of the time people on the run did just that—run—often too fast or too obviously. It took discipline and cool-headedness to stay put in a potentially risky place. "I'd skip the room service, though. There's leftover pizza in the fridge."

"Good enough," the man said. "I might need the credit card you checked in with."

"I already put it down for the charges."

"Yes, I assumed that," the man said. "But sometimes they want to see the card again. I don't want to take any chances."

"Fine." Jacobi pulled out the card and handed it over. "I checked in at ten in the evening, so as long as you check out before noon you shouldn't run into anyone who might remember the face that went with that name. Destroy it as soon as you're out the door, of course."

"Got it," the man said as he glanced at the card and then slipped it into his pocket.

"I mean *destroy* it, not just throw it away."

"I said I got it," the man said, a bit testily. "Any other words of wisdom?"

"Yes," Jacobi said, gesturing to the satchel. "Until you get a haircut, I'd suggest you stick to the black shirt and jeans."

"The Greenwich Village disaffected artist outfit," the man said, nodding sagely as he ran his fingers through his long, greasy hair. "Going to be different having hair again, instead of that silly silver toupee. Well, as you can probably tell, I need a shower. Don't let me keep you."

"Yeah," Jacobi said, heading for the door. "Enjoy your twenty billion."

"Ten, actually," the other corrected. "The press always blows things way out of proportion."

"Yeah." Like at that stratospheric level a few billion here or there really mattered. "Enjoy. See you never."

"Right," the man who had once been a con artist called Marvin Chernov said from the mouth that had once belonged to a man called Shrill. "See you never."

The low phone conversation that had been going on across the Global 6000's lounge finally came to an end. "Well?" Dr. Adrian Sommer asked, raising his voice enough to be heard over the rumbling drone of the jet's engines.

"It's still a horrific mess," Frank Everly growled, his eyes looking ready to flash-vaporize tungsten. "But some of the threads are starting to work out around the edges." He picked up the notebook he'd been scribbling in during the conversation. "It looks like Chernov entered a trap in the Manhattan South office at three-seventeen. Four minutes earlier, at three-thirteen, a drug addict in one of Walkabout USA's body-swapping programs entered the same office. At three-twenty he was euthed and entered his own trap. His body was supposed to then have been entered by a Blaine Kaplan, who was already in a trap awaiting transfer."

"Only he never made it," Sommer said.

"Nope," Everly confirmed. "Somehow, and we still don't know how it happened, Chernov's soul was transferred into the druggie instead. The druggie walked out and, of course, never came back." His lip twisted. "Oh, and Kaplan had conveniently left two hundred dollars for the druggie to buy some meth with."

Sommer frowned. He despised everything about Walkabout, but he'd nevertheless taken care to learn every part of their routine, especially the parts that directly involved the Soulminder facilities. Waiting to accept and sign for the money would have taken Chernov another five to ten minutes. "And with twenty billion dollars of his own stashed away, he actually waited around to collect it?"

Everly shrugged. "Traveling money is traveling money," he pointed out. "And no one's ever accused Chernov of being chutzpah-challenged."

"I suppose not," Sommer said. "What do we know about Blaine Kaplan?"

"Sixteen-year-old Richie Rich type," Everly said. "Likes to play with the forbidden fruit, but is terrified his blue-blood Park Avenue parents will disinherit him if he ever flunks a drug test. Walkabout and Soulminder were the logical answers."

"Pretty expensive logic."

"Apparently, he was able to pull it off just by tucking away some of his allowance money," Everly said. "He's done it a couple of times before."

"From his allowance money." Sommer shook his head. "I definitely picked the wrong parents."

"If it makes you feel any better, Blaine probably will agree with you after Mom and Dad get done with him," Everly said. "We grilled the whole family for three hours after they got him back in his body, looking for a connection with Chernov. Nothing yet, but we're still looking."

And even if there was, Sommer thought bitterly, it would probably be lost in the ground clutter. There were a *lot* of people who might have wanted Chernov dead and could have been suckered into the con man's double-reverse play. "Anything on the shooter?"

"The kill round was a .300 Winchester short magnum," Everly said. "Probably fired through an FN Special Police sniper rifle, though it's possible he modified some other rifle to handle that cartridge. We found the nest he fired from, and the distance alone shows he was definitely a pro."

"A man like Chernov would hardly hire an amateur."

"True," Everly said. "We've got the FBI and Interpol running the M.O. through their files—this guy's too good not to have popped up on the radar before. We're also working the Kaplan family against that angle, just in case."

"Probably a waste of time."

"Probably," Everly agreed. "You always check these things, just on general principles, but it's looking more and more like Blaine was just collateral damage."

"Yes," Sommer murmured. "And speaking of damage . . . "

"Yeah," Everly said heavily. "Shrill."

"I assume he's still in a trap, right?"

"Yes, of course," Everly said. "But with his body gone . . . it doesn't look good. We've done a full-scale search of the area, but all the photos of the guy are pretty scraggly, and if he's cleaned up at all decently the facial-recognition software isn't going to be much help. Chernov and whoever helped him had this whole thing mapped out. I'm guessing he's halfway to Venezuela by now."

"In a stolen body," Sommer said. "God help us."

"And while He's at it," Everly added darkly, "He'd better help whoever in Manhattan South helped Chernov fiddle the labels and settings to make this happen."

"If there *was* anyone."

"Oh, there was," Everly assured him. "There has to have been. No hacker's ever gotten through Soulminder security, and they didn't get through this time. No, they had an inside man. And we *will* find him."

"I know," Sommer said, looking toward the dark sky out the window beside him. Just below the jet, looking like they were close enough to touch, the clouds flickered rhythmically with reflections from the flashing running lights.

"But that's not what you meant, was it?" Everly said. "The *God help us* part?"

Sommer didn't answer. He'd had variants of the same conversation with a dozen different people over the past few years. There was no reason to expect that having it with his security chief would have any different outcome.

"Because you've mentioned some of your concerns to Dr. Sands," Everly continued.

Sommer felt his lip twitch. And of course Jessica had gone

straight to Everly. "I assume Dr. Sands is worried that I'm on the edge of going berserk and denouncing Soulminder before the press or a congressional committee?"

"Something like that," Everly said calmly. "Dr. Sands wants to live forever. Did you know that?"

Sommer closed his eyes. "She may have mentioned it once or twice over the past twenty years."

"Yeah," Everly said. "My clues were her late-night study sessions and spending flurries and the glazed look she gets whenever Soulminder clears her more research money."

"*Especially* when Soulminder clears her more research money."

"Pretty much." Everly paused. "Only not all of that money's exactly snowy-white clean, is it?"

"*Clean?*" Sommer opened his eyes again, glaring at and through Everly. "You're joking, right? We've got people borrowing druggies' bodies to get high. We've got suicides legally able to will their bodies to other people and a society that's increasingly all right with that. We've got gang members swapping bodies with twelve-year-old recruits so they can commit murders without being charged as adults."

"Not legally," Everly pointed out.

"No," Sommer agreed. "But until Washington gives us full copies of everyone's personal files so that we can tell the difference between a small eighteen-year-old and a big twelve-year-old with a good fake ID it's going to happen." He waved a hand. "And now we've got people murdering other people for their bodies."

He turned to stare at the darkness outside. And none of that even touched on the ghastly reason he and Everly were on their way to Iraq in the first place. "We've lost control, Frank," he said softly. "Somewhere along the way, Soulminder stopped being a last-ditch medical tool and became something else. Something dark and twisted."

"It's still a medical tool, Doctor," Everly pointed out. "And a damn good one. It's saved a hell of a lot of lives."

"Granted," Sommer said. "But along the way . . . " He sighed. "You remember Reverend Tommy Lee Harper, Frank?"

"He'd be a little hard to forget," Everly said sourly. "I hear he's ditched his big broadcasting friends for a website and streaming video."

"Keeping up with the times," Sommer said. "He and I had a private meeting once, back in Soulminder's early days. I doubt you remember."

"Oh, I remember," Everly said. "Mostly I remember warning you not to go alone and you ignoring me."

"I'd forgotten that part of it," Sommer confessed. "But something he said at that meeting has stuck with me all these years. *Soulminder is an archangel, so far as earthly creations go. I'm very much afraid that it'll be beyond your ability to keep it from becoming a demon.*"

For a long moment Everly was silent. "It's still an archangel, as far as the medical and legal parts are concerned," he said at last. "As to the rest . . . it's really not your fault."

"Of course it's our fault," Sommer retorted. "Congress says it's okay for us to allow a murder victim to borrow a body so that he can testify against his killer, or that we can let a paraplegic borrow a body so that he can have a few hours of freedom, or that we can store criminals' souls so that their bodies can be stacked in a warehouse like cordwood at a fraction of a prison's cost. We could have said no. We *should* have said no."

"You're right, we should have," Everly agreed. "Somewhere along the way we should have drawn the line. But where? The Pro-Witness program was a good idea, and there are a hell of a lot of murderers off the streets because of it. Sure, body-sharing is being abused, but those paraplegics you mentioned *are* getting a chance at life they never could have had before. Every noble idea and good tool can be abused. That doesn't mean you throw the whole thing out."

"Then how do you sort out the good from the bad?" Sommer asked. "How do you keep the archangel from becoming the demon?"

"I don't know," Everly admitted. "But I'm not the genius here, you are. You'll find a way."

Sommer shook his head. "I doubt it."

"I know you doubt it." Everly cocked his head. "But you will. I don't doubt *that*."

Sommer exhaled loudly. "Your faith in me is touching. Let's see if you still have it on the trip home."

Everly inclined his head. "Challenge accepted."

It was nine o'clock in the morning, local time, when the plane touched down at Baghdad International. The Soulminder security convoy Everly had ordered was waiting inside the private hangar, with one of the security chief's handpicked officers in command. A sizeable contingent of armed and armored men and women was also present, and had formed a cordon around the plane and cars.

"Dr. Sommer," the woman in charge said in greeting, offering her hand. "I'm Janine Spendlove; former colonel, U.S. Marines; currently head of Soulminder Security Middle East. Welcome to Baghdad."

"Thank you," Sommer said, shaking the proffered hand. Spendlove's grip was good, her handshake the brief but sincere ritual he'd experienced with other military and ex-military men and women. "Has General al-Hirai been briefed on the reason for our visit?"

"Partially." Spendlove's lips twitched in a humorless smile. "Mr. Everly thought it might be better if you sprung the more interesting points on him without a lot of warning."

"Getting people to hang themselves is always easier if they don't know which direction the rope is coming from," Everly added.

"I see," Sommer said, trying to sit on the anger that had started again toward a slow boil as soon as they entered Iraqi airspace. There was no proof, after all, that the Minister of Defense was actually involved in the alleged atrocities.

At least, not yet.

"Which car do you want, sir?" Spendlove asked, gesturing behind her at the eight identical black town cars, all of which featured the same tinted windows and heavy-riding look of armored vehicles.

In reply, Everly produced an eight-sided die, held his tablet up and flat to the ground, and rolled the die onto it. It came up a three. "Third from the front," he told her, putting the die away.

"Yes, sir," she said. "With your permission, I'd like to ride with you. We can get a head start on the briefing that way."

Everly gestured. "Lead on."

A minute later the motorcade was driving down the wide road leading toward the city proper. "No official military escort?" Sommer asked.

"Offered and declined," Spendlove said. "There was no polite way of asking them to pick up escort after we left the hangar, and we *certainly* didn't want the General's men seeing which specific car you were riding in."

"Good call," Everly said. "So what's the current political and military situation?"

"Well, sir," Spendlove said, opening her tablet, "as of oh-seven-hundred today . . . "

General Faraaz al-Hirai was a tall, stocky man with a Saddam Hussein mustache and sharp, piercing dark eyes. The smile he flashed as he welcomed his visitors into his office, Sommer noted, didn't make it past the mustache to his eyes. "I trust you had a pleasant flight?" he asked politely as he gestured Sommer and Everly to a pair of overstuffed, extremely comfortable chairs that had been set up across the half-acre of polished mahogany that served as his desk.

"Pleasant enough," Sommer said.

"It was also long and tiring," Everly added, pushing back his jacket sleeve and peering at his watch. "And my biological clock is still set on D.C. time, which is currently one in the morning. Can we skip the pleasantries and get on with it?"

"Certainly," al-Hirai said. The words and tone were civil enough, but his eyes frosted over a bit. "I appreciate a man who goes straight to business." He looked back at Sommer. "As I understand it, Dr. Sommer, your people are accusing someone in my government of using Soulminder for torture."

"It's more than just an accusation, General," Sommer said. "We have proof that certain of your dissidents have died, returned to their bodies, then died again. Some of them multiple times."

"Things are not always as they seem, Doctor," the general said equably. "As it happens, I have personally looked into this situation. The truth is that the enemies of our nation that you refer to have deliberately engineered these incidents."

"The *prisoners* have engineered their own deaths?"

"Indeed," the general said. "Their goal, of course, being to discredit the government."

"I wasn't so much concerned with the goal as I was the mechanics," Sommer said. "How exactly did they pull off multiple suicides while in your custody?"

The general scowled. "Poison, of course," he said. "Small packets hidden in various parts of their body. One of the prisoners actually swallowed several packets before being taken into custody, each nestled in a slow-dissolve casing so that one death would follow another in succession a few hours apart." He gestured to the computer on his desk. "I have all the relevant records and documents."

"I'm sure you do," Sommer said. He'd expected al-Hirai to push back against the charges, but he'd assumed the stonewalling would take the traditional form of blaming someone else in the regime, either some flunky lower down the chain of command or someone in an entirely different ministry. Trying to invoke a prisoner conspiracy at least bought him points for originality. "And the purpose of this supposed discrediting? I assume they didn't think such actions per se would alter your government's stance on whatever issue they disagree with you on."

"The actions of so few would certainly not have any such effect," al-Hirai said grimly. "But if they can persuade you that these deaths are our doing, they may persuade you to shut down our Soulminder facilities." He smiled faintly. "There is an obscure but relevant proverb about a flea destroying a village by biting an elephant. If they can spread unrest from the small fringe to the middle and upper classes, they believe they can create a popular uprising against us."

And then, as if to punctuate his accusation, the office's side wall blew in.

Sommer found himself kneeling on the floor beside his chair without any memory of how he'd gotten there. Blinking through the swirling dust, he saw the indistinct form of a young man stride in through the ragged hole. "Dr. Sommer?" he called through the ringing in Sommer's ears. "Dr. Sommer?"

From the general's side of the desk came a sharp, snarly-sounding Arabic word, the sound of a man who was angry, startled, frightened, or all three.

Small wonder. As the young man continued to approach through the floating debris Sommer saw that he was not only hefting a large handgun but also wore a dynamite-laden vest. In his left hand was a small cylinder, wired to the vest, almost certainly a dead-man detonator. "Dr. Sommer?" he called again.

With only four of them in the room, including the gunman himself, there didn't seem much point in playing dumb. "I'm Dr. Sommer," Sommer identified himself, standing up. An odd calmness had followed the initial shock of the explosion, and he was mildly surprised to discover his knees weren't even shaking. "What can I do for you?"

The young man took another three steps toward Sommer before stopping. His expression, Sommer could see now, was a mix of pain, desperation, and hope. "I ask for my brother," he said, clearly struggling with the English words. "Please. You must help him."

"I'll do whatever I can," Sommer assured him. Peripherally, he saw that Everly was in a crouch beside his own chair, his own gun ready in his hand. "Is he sick? Is he dying?"

"You don't understand," the man said, a bitter weariness in his voice. "He is already dead. Please; just let him die."

Sommer frowned. "Excuse me?"

"He is already dead." The man turned his head to glare at al-Hirai. "But *he* is forcing him to stay alive."

Sommer blinked . . . and only then realized that the assailant's gun wasn't pointed at him. It was, instead, pointed at al-Hirai. Frowning, he looked across the desk.

The general was crouched behind the debris-covered mahogany, only his face and the gun in his hand visible above the dark wood. His eyes were burning murder toward the young man. "General?" Sommer invited.

"What do you wish me to say?" al-Hirai spat. "He lies, of course."

"Do I?" the young man retorted. "My brother is in Soulminder even now. Tell them his name and let them ask him. Let them know the truth."

"The truth?" The general snarled something that was probably a curse. "Why would anyone expect truth from a terrorist?"

"I am not a terrorist." The young man looked back at Sommer. "Do you know how I am here, within the walls of his inner sanctum? I am here because *he*"—he jabbed a finger at al-Hirai—"ordered me to kill you. He was afraid you would—"

"*You lie!*"

"He ordered me to kill you," the young man continued doggedly, "because he was afraid you would learn the truth."

"The truth about your brother?" Sommer asked.

"Do not listen to this madman!" al-Hirai ordered. His gun

hand was shaking with anger, but with the dynamite and dead-man switch there was nothing he could do. "He is a traitor to his own people. He will die like the dog he is—"

"Shut up, General," Everly interrupted.

The general sputtered. "You *dare*—?"

"Shut up or I'll shoot you where you stand." Everly gestured to the young man. "You have more to say? Then say it."

The young man took a careful breath. "His newest form of torture," he said, his voice shaking now. "He no longer kills a prisoner he wishes to torture, then heals his body and sends him back to die again. You at Soulminder can see that. *Have* seen that. So now he kills a prisoner—" His throat worked. "And then moves him into the body of his son. Or his wife, or his brother.

"And then kills *them*."

Sommer stared at him, his stomach twisting. It was horrifying. It was utterly insane.

And as he looked at al-Hirai, he knew it was also true.

And the general knew that he knew. Baring his teeth in a snarl, the look of a man who no longer has anything to lose, he half rose from behind his desk and raised his gun to fire—

His mouth snapping open in an unheard scream as Everly's shot shattered his hand and sent the pistol flying.

"Okay, Doc, time to go," Everly said darkly, standing fully upright and gesturing to Sommer. "Now."

Sommer blinked at him. "But how do we—?"

"Colonel Spendlove's got the guard force pinned, but she won't be able to hold off the reinforcements that are probably on the way," Everly said. "We go now, or we don't go at all."

"No!" the young man snarled. "You cannot leave. Not without helping my brother."

"We'll do what we can for him," Everly said. "You've got my word on that. But there's nothing we can do from here."

"But you don't understand," the man pleaded. "If you leave, then *he*"—he jabbed a finger at al-Hirai—"will win. He will continue to kill." His lips curled back in a snarl. "No—you will *not* leave. You will help my brother or—"

"Or what?" Everly countered. "You'll kill us? That would be a fine and noble tribute to your brother, wouldn't it? Come on, Doc."

Carefully, Sommer eased around his chair and backed toward the door. The young man kept his eyes on him the whole way. Sommer reached the door and paused as Everly slipped past the young man and joined him. "I'm sorry," he said as Everly cracked the door and peered out. "We'll do what we can. I promise."

The young man hissed out a curse, his eyes blazing with fury and hopelessness. "I cannot stop you," he said bitterly. He jabbed at Sommer with the dead-man trigger. "But someday I pray that you, too, will long for death, and yet be unable to grasp it."

Spendlove was waiting in the General's reception room. "You all right?" she asked, her eyes flicking between the two of them.

"We're fine," Everly assured her. "What's it look like downstairs?"

"We're in control, but we won't be for long," she told him as they headed out the door and down the corridor. She stepped casually over a couple of twitching bodies; wincing, Sommer did the same. "Nice call, by the way. What tipped you off?"

"The chairs," Everly said. "I spotted a lot of other chairs on the way in, but these two were deliberately designed to be restrictive. There's usually only one reason you want to make it hard for a bodyguard to draw."

Two minutes later, they emerged into the morning sunlight to find their eight cars had been formed into a semicircle with Spendlove's group of security men and women crouched behind them in defensive positions, sending rhythmic suppression fire across the compound. "At last check the road to the airport was clear," Spendlove said as she ushered Sommer into the nearest of the cars. "But that could change in a heartbeat."

"Don't worry, it'll stay clear," Everly assured her grimly. "How long until they can prep the plane?"

"It'll be ready by the time we get there," Spendlove said. "I ordered a crash prep, and told the captain that if he couldn't get it done in time I'd do it for him."

Bullets were starting to ricochet off the car's hood and polycrystalline ceramic windows by the time the convoy headed out. "Exactly how many people do we have on the ground?" Sommer asked, peering out the window, wincing at each deflected shot. With Spendlove's force in the cars and no longer pinning them down, the general's soldiers were starting to emerge from their cover and were opening up with some serious fire of their own.

"Enough," Everly assured him, pulling out his phone. "Spendlove, you have the President's private number?"

"Sure." She rattled it off. "You sure you don't want the Prime Minister instead?"

"Thanks—I've already got his," Everly said, punching in the number. "Plus the Speaker of the Council. Conference calls are such fun."

They'd made it nearly to the compound gate, and the gunfire was becoming a hailstorm, by the time Everly got his multiple connections set up. "Gentlemen, this is Frank Everly, chief of Soulminder security," he identified himself. "Let me cut straight to the chase. We have strong evidence that General Faraaz al-Hirai has been abusing your Soulminder facility for purposes of torture and political manipulation. We'll be launching a deeper investigation, the results of which we'll be discussing with you in the near future. Right now, I need you all to understand that we are leaving Baghdad, and that our convoy is not to be interfered with."

There was a pause as one of the others on the conversation apparently made a comment. "We'll be presenting all the evidence in due course," Everly said. "As I said, right now we simply require your assurance that we'll be allowed to leave Iraq without further confrontation. To that end—"

He broke off again, listening, a granite-set expression on his face. "To that end, Minister," he continued quietly, "I have instructed Soulminder Baghdad to immediately lock down its facilities and cease all operations. That includes a suspension of any and all transfers *and* the turning off of any traps that aren't already occupied. I trust I don't need to spell out the implications?"

A shiver ran up Sommer's back. No, the Iraqi government wouldn't need the implications spelled out. The first of Everly's moves would largely be a matter of inconvenience, as people waiting to be moved from their traps back into their freshly healed bodies would be forced to wait.

But the second was literally a threat of death. With all unoccupied traps locked out of the system, a Soulminder client who died would not be captured, but would instead be instantly and permanently dead.

It was a terrible and terrifying threat, one that could potentially topple a government whose rich and powerful had become accustomed to the Soulminder safety net. And the men on the other end of Everly's call knew it. They knew it all too well.

The convoy had left the compound, and the gunfire had shifted to targeting the trunks and rear windows, when that gunfire abruptly ceased.

"Thank you," Everly said politely. Some men, Sommer knew, would allow themselves a moment to gloat. Everly wasn't one of them. "Once we're outside Iraqi airspace I'll instruct the office to resume operations." He paused. "And be very certain that we *will* be discussing General al-Hirai's activities with you. Very soon."

"For the record, this is to be considered a courtesy briefing," Assistant Secretary of State for Near Eastern Affairs Lowell Marlin said briskly as he set his attaché case on the edge of Sommer's desk and flipped it open. "It's not in any way to be considered an official, on-the-record communication. I trust that's understood?"

"It is," Sommer said, suppressing a sigh. He'd been through this same routine countless times, with countless governmental officials.

Still, it was a necessary evil. Through Soulminder's entire existence Jessica Sands had fought to keep the corporation and equipment from being nibbled, co-opted, or otherwise attached by any governmental agency. Making sure that all government conversations were strictly off-the-record was part of her strategy for making sure the camel's nose never got under the tent flap.

Especially since that nose seemed to be permanently pressed up against the canvas. Sommer had lost track of the number of ways various agencies had tried to worm their way into Soulminder's inner circle, from attempted regulation—with inspectors to "examine" the top-secret equipment—to licensing requirements, offers of quid pro quo tax breaks, and even threats of eminent domain.

Each time Sands and Soulminder's platoon of attorneys had successfully defeated the attempts. But that didn't mean the politicians wouldn't keep trying. Far from it. They had access to a nearly unlimited assemblage of lawyers, whose working hours were billed to the taxpayers and who could therefore theoretically never be outspent. Soulminder was both a powerful carrot and an intimidating stick, and Sommer had no doubt that there would be attempts to take it over as long as there were politicians whose primary goal in life was to get themselves reelected.

"Iraqi Defense Minister General al-Hirai," Marlin began, pulling out a tablet and switching it on. "We've followed up on the data you provided, and our analysis indicates that your people were correct. Al-Hirai's department is indeed engaged in torture and other activities that clearly violate accepted standards of human rights."

Once upon a time, Sommer reflected, he would have assumed a solid statement like that would be followed by an equally solid plan of action. Now, though, experience and cynicism had set in. "And?" he prompted.

"And unfortunately," Marlin said, though without any regret that Sommer could detect, "current U.S. foreign policy requires that we leave any consequences to the Iraqi government."

"Which will do nothing."

"We don't know that," Marlin said. "The Iraqis have made great strides in the past few years toward modernizing their nation and their human rights record. They may very well decide that this case warrants some attention."

"So, a slap on the wrist?" Sommer countered. "Because they won't throw al-Hirai to the wolves. Not without a push from us. He has way too many important friends."

"So they keep al-Hirai," Marlin said with a shrug. "Does that matter as long as they end the torture?"

"*If* they end it."

"I think they will," Marlin said. "At least the parts that utilize Soulminder. That *is* what you want, isn't it?"

Sommer felt his lip twitch. Of course he wanted Soulminder out of the picture. He also wanted *all* torture to end, everywhere on the planet.

Unlikely, verging on impossible. Still, when battling the dark side of human nature, he'd learned he had to be content with partial victories. "It's a start," he said.

"Good," Marlin said, in a tone that implied that the subject was closed. "With your permission, then, I'd like to move on to the real purpose I came here today."

Sommer frowned. "Iraq wasn't the reason?"

"Iraq was the springboard," Marlin said. "It's your actions there that we now need to discuss."

"My people and I were under attack," Sommer said stiffly. "We defended ourselves. End of story."

"Hardly," Marlin said, his voice darkening. "Whether the actions of your security force pushed the boundaries is a topic for another day. What I'm referring to is the fact that you threatened a sovereign state with what amounted to economic sanctions."

It took Sommer a moment to figure out what the hell the other was talking about. Then, finally, it clicked. "You mean threatening to withhold Soulminder services if they didn't let us leave?"

"Except that you didn't just *threaten* to withhold the services," Marlin said. "You did, in fact, do so."

"For two hours," Sommer said. "Just long enough for us to get away."

"Was it?" Marlin countered. "You cleared Iraqi airspace in half that time. Are you sure the second hour wasn't meant to be a punitive display of power?"

"The second hour was so that we could also clear Syrian airspace," Sommer said between clenched teeth. This was a completely bogus complaint, and he was pretty sure Marlin knew it. "My security chief advised me that the Syrians owe the Iraqis some favors and that General al-Hirai might try to collect. We didn't consider ourselves safely beyond the general's reach until we'd reached Turkey."

"Perhaps," Marlin said. "Be that as it may, the fact is that you applied sanctions—economic *and* humanitarian both—to a foreign nation." He leveled a finger at Sommer. "You're not a government, Dr. Sommer. You're not allowed to do that."

"Really," Sommer said. "I was unaware the U.S. government had the power to force corporations to sell their products to a given client."

"You're a medical facility, Doctor. Under current law, that means we *do* have that power."

"I beg to differ," Sommer said. "Soulminder isn't mentioned in any of the health-care laws."

"As a provider, you're there by implication."

"Unwritten implications in law or legal contracts don't usually hold water with the courts," Sommer reminded him. "Even if they did, in this case they wouldn't. We don't provide medicine, medical equipment, advice, or treatment. That makes us *not* a medical provider."

"What about the body-repair work you do here?"

"That's all handled by subcontracted groups," Sommer said. "Soulminder itself is strictly a technical system, no different from Apple or Hewlett-Packard."

"I suppose that'll be for the courts to decide." Turning off his tablet, Marlin slid it back into his attaché case. "We just thought you'd like to have some advance notice of the legislation we intend to offer to the Hill. Good day, Dr. Sommer." With a final nod, he turned and left the office.

For several minutes Sommer remained at his desk, gazing out at the Washington skyline, his mind darting between the possibilities like a hummingbird moving between flowers. A series of bad-tasting flowers. Then, hunching his shoulders once to drive out some of the tension that had suddenly taken root there, he picked up the phone and punched in a number. "This is Dr. Sommer," he told the receptionist at the other end. "Please ask Dr. Blanchard to stop by at her convenience. I need to have a word with her."

Blanchard watched the recording twice, her narrowed eyes focused on Marlin the whole time. Sommer spent the same time watching her, studying her expression and trying to figure out what she was thinking.

Waste of effort. Blanchard used her psychological training to read other people. She wasn't at all interested in letting anyone apply those same techniques to her.

The recording ended, and she tapped the stop button. "Okay," she said slowly, her eyes still on the screen. "Obvious bits first. The whole second part was his ham-handed attempt to bait you. He's hoping that dropping broad hints about a new government initiative against Soulminder will spur us into preemptive action. No idea what the plan is after that, but it probably depends on our response. If we make a move, they'll probably pretend there was never anything planned in the first place and try to paint Soulminder as paranoid and confrontational. Option two is that they want to see which way we jump, guess our strategy from that, and modify their own plan accordingly."

"So your recommendation is that we ignore him and do nothing?"

"Pretty much," Blanchard said, her forehead wrinkling. "I'm more concerned about the bait itself. As I'm sure you've noticed, various arms of the government have been trying to locate your Achilles heel for years. It looks to me like they may have finally found it."

Sommer gave a little snort. "You mean my hatred for torture? That's hardly a state secret."

"It's not the hatred or the torture per se," Blanchard said. "It's your growing frustration that you can't do anything about it."

"All part of the same package, isn't it?"

"Not really," Blanchard said. "Most people who hate an injustice either write letters, start a grassroots campaign, or take a deep breath, decide they can't change it, and move on to things they *can* change. The fact that you ordered sanctions—and he's right; that really *was* a sanction—means that you're willing to go that extra mile and take things into your own hands."

"So they're planning to take me to court?" Sommer asked, frowning. "Seems rather a waste of time."

"No, no, you don't understand," Blanchard said. "The only people with basis for court action are the Iraqis, and they'd be fools to bring this incident to international attention. If I'm reading Marlin right, I think he's hoping to suck you in with an offer that will give you official backing for actions like that."

And then, finally, Sommer got it. "By making Soulminder effectively part of the United States government."

"Exactly," Blanchard said. "You can see his eyes light up when you argued that you were just defending yourselves, and they lit up even more when you brought Syria into the equation. Not only are you aware of international affairs, but you're also interested in them, *and* you know how to connect the dots. So the question is—"

"Whether I'm willing to sell my soul to the devil?"

Blanchard pursed her lips. "I was going to say, whether you'd be willing to accept State Department oversight and direction. But you've caught the essence of it." She raised her eyebrows. "So. Are you?"

Sommer looked out the window. That was the question, all right. A simple question, really.

Unfortunately, there was no simple answer.

On the one hand, such a mandate could certainly be used for good around the world. Soulminder wielded enormous power, a power that even well-entrenched despots might hesitate to challenge. Tying Soulminder operations to human rights could lead to a true era of freedom and safety for billions who currently lived under tyranny. He could stop wars, end border disputes, and bring evil men and women to justice. All simply by using the threat of life and death.

The same threat the tyrants themselves used.

Or rather, the threat the *other* tyrants used.

"You know the real irony?" Sommer asked into Blanchard's silence. "I wasn't the one who ordered the Soulminder shutdown in the first place. It was Frank who did that."

"But you would have if you'd thought of it?"

"I don't even know that," Sommer admitted. "With all the noise and adrenaline . . . I don't know. All I can say for sure is that at the time I didn't disagree with his actions."

"And now?"

Sommer sighed. "This isn't what Soulminder was supposed to be, Carolyn," he said quietly. "I created it to be a last-ditch medical safety net, not a diplomatic bludgeon. Or a toy for rich kids who want to get high in someone else's body." He forced a small smile. "But you've heard this all before, haven't you?"

"I have?"

"From Frank," Sommer said. "I'm sure he related my ranting on the flight to Baghdad."

She shrugged. "I'd hardly categorize it as a rant," she said. "Are you upset that Frank told me?"

"Not really. Frank worries about me."

"Frank worries about everyone. Part of his job."

"I suppose."

Another silence settled like fine dust into the room. This time, it was Blanchard who broke it. "What are you going to do?" she asked.

"I don't know," Sommer said. "Not yet. But I'll think of something."

He stood up, forcing another smile. "Thanks for your time, Carolyn. I'll let you get back to your *real* work now."

"No problem," she said, her smile looking as forced as his felt. "Like Frank, I consider you to be part of that real work. Speaking of Frank, did you know they've tentatively identified Chernov's shooter?"

"No, I hadn't heard that," Sommer said, frowning as he sat back down and keyed his computer. "How come *you* know?"

"He'd had me run a psychological analysis on Marvin Chernov," she said. "I guess he felt he owed me for that, because he ducked his head into my office this morning and told me it worked. You'll have to ask him if you want the details."

"No need—I've got his report here," Sommer said. "Can't have me wasting *everyone's* time, you know."

"If you're bucking for me to come over there and give you a good dope-slap, just keep it up," Blanchard said, mock-threateningly. "You're the heart and soul of Soulminder. Anything you do or want is by definition the opposite of wasting time."

"Understood," Sommer said. "Consider me properly castigated."

"I'd rather consider you happy and healthy and satisfied with life," Blanchard said, turning serious again.

"I'm fine, Carolyn," Sommer assured her. "I'm just still tired from the Baghdad trip."

"That was two weeks ago."

"I don't bounce back from intercontinental trips like I used to."

"Then you should go home and get some sleep," Blanchard said firmly.

"Is that an order?"

"Of course," Blanchard said. "I'm a doctor. I can do that."

"You're a doctor of psychology."

"Details," she said, waving a casual hand in dismissal. "My business card says *doctor*. That should be good enough."

"Can't argue with logic like that," Sommer conceded. "All right, I'll knock off and take the rest of the day." He gestured at his computer. "I'll just read Frank's report first, if that's all right with you."

"It is, but just barely," Blanchard said, returning to her threatening tone. "And *just* that report. Deal?"

Sommer nodded. "Deal."

"Okay." Blanchard nodded to him. "Good afternoon, Dr. Sommer. *And* good night. Sleep well, and sleep long."

"I will."

He waited until she was gone. Then, stretching tired arms, he settled in to read.

The shooter had been clever. He'd rented a room at a nearby hotel, checking in five days before the shooting with an obviously fake ID—obvious *now*, though of course it hadn't been then—in the name of George Michaels. The FBI had run checks of all IDs and credit cards that had been used in area hotels, and that one had popped, though too long after the fact to do any immediate good.

What had caught Everly's eye, though, was that Michaels hadn't checked out until a day *after* the shooting, which had struck him as unlikely for a professional assassin who knew better than to overstay his welcome. The obvious explanation—obvious to Everly, anyway—was that the shooter had turned the room over to Chernov for a post-transfer rest, cleanup, and possibly private detox session for whatever Shrill had had in his system at the time. When Chernov eventually checked out, he simply accepted the charges the shooter had put on the card and walked out.

That should have been the end of it. Only it wasn't. With Blanchard's profile on Chernov in hand, Everly had concluded that the man would probably save the credit card with an eye toward using it as a bargaining chip if he ever got caught. Since he would hardly risk being caught with it in his possession, Everly had further concluded that the fugitive would stash it someplace where he could get at it again. Accordingly, he'd ordered a search of the area.

They'd found the card that morning, carefully sealed in a plastic bag beneath a freshly moved stone in a park a block from the hotel. The clear set of Shrill's prints proved it was the right card, and from the partial they'd also pulled, Everly had obtained a set of tentative matches. The night desk clerk at the hotel had pulled a face from a photo lineup, and Everly had declared victory.

Partial victory, anyway. Just knowing the shooter's name wasn't much help in actually finding him, especially since the military records which had come up in response to the fingerprint search were over twenty years old. Adam Jacobi, former Army sniper, despiser of authority and lover of the good life, had done a remarkable job of staying off everyone's radar since then.

But Everly *would* find him. Sommer had no doubt about that. Sooner or later, Jacobi would slip up, and when he did, Everly would be there waiting. And then—

Nothing.

Because the shooter didn't matter. Not really. Chernov was the one who had Shrill's body. Unless they could find him, Shrill was still doomed to eventual death.

And unfortunately, that would probably never happen. Chernov had billions of dollars stashed away, a body that even facial-recognition programs couldn't seem to spot, and all the incentive in the world to stay out of sight.

If he succeeded in that effort—if he dropped permanently off the map—sooner or later they would have to shut down Shrill's trap and let him go.

Sommer stared out at the city, a bitter taste of irony in his mouth. The young man in Baghdad had pleaded with Sommer to open his brother's trap and allow him to die. But Sommer was powerless to do that, because all such decisions were the sole province of the host nation's own judicial system.

If the Iraqi government had been sufficiently cowed by Everly's demonstration of Soulminder power, they might hand out the mercy the young man had asked for. If they didn't, the victim would stay in the trap, unable to leave. Possibly forever.

Unless Sommer found a way to change that.

A shiver ran through him. *Absolute power corrupts absolutely.* Lord Acton had been the first to use those particular words, but it was a truth that had existed since the beginning of the world. In many ways, Soulminder had the power of life and death, which was about as close to absolute power as anyone could get. But because neither of its founders had ever really wanted power, the lure and corruption had stayed at bay.

Only now that delicate balancing act was being threatened. For the first time in his life Sommer was feeling the siren song. There were people out there who desperately needed his help. Would it really be so terrible to partner with the government to help them?

Down deep, he knew it would. Because it wouldn't stop with just helping the helpless. It would continue, carrot and stick together, gradually becoming more powerful and more demanding.

And more corrupt. Because organizations, just like the individuals they were composed of, were equally susceptible to Lord Acton's dictum.

Soulminder is an archangel, Doctor, so far as earthly creations go. I'm very much afraid that it'll be beyond your ability to keep it from becoming a demon.

Blanchard was right. His weakness had been discovered, and people who were far more used to wielding power than he was would use every trick in their arsenals to turn him down that path.

Someday I pray that you, too, will long for death and yet be unable to grasp it. The young Baghdad man had spat that curse at him.

The true irony was that, once upon a time, Sommer had indeed wanted death. Back when Soulminder had first become workable he'd been ready to let go of life. But Sands had talked him into living, warning that without him Soulminder could become a monster.

In many ways, it already had. What new horrors would await it, he wondered distantly, with a power-hungry Adrian Sommer in command?

It was in that moment, with the Washington skyline stretched out before him, that he knew what he had to do.

He sat silently at his desk for the next three hours, thinking and planning, staring out the window as the sky slowly darkened and the skyline slowly lit up.

Finally, the plan was complete.

According to the work schedule on the corporate calendar, the next software upgrade for the Soulminder system would take place in six weeks. It would be tight, but he could do it.

He had created Soulminder. He and Sands together, but it was Sommer who had truly given their creation its life.

It was only right that he be the one to kill it.

As usual, the programming people were a bit on the optimistic side. The scheduled upgrade actually took seven and a half more weeks to prepare instead of the promised six.

But that was all right. Better than all right, actually, since it took Sommer himself nearly seven weeks to write his own batch of code. It probably should have only taken three, he knew—the modifications to the trap software were really fairly simple. But it had been years since he'd done anything like this and he was seriously rusty.

Still, between his rust and the programmers' tardiness it all worked out. When the new software was introduced into the system, Sommer quietly slipped in his code as well.

He watched the post-upgrade checks and confirmations carefully, trying not to look *too* interested. As far as he could tell no one noticed the additional content. Certainly none of the routine checks spotted it.

Eventually, he knew, they would go in and try to figure out what he'd done. But with over five billion lines of code already in the system, and with the backup copies corrupted just enough to make them useless for comparison, it could be months or years before they figured it out.

He'd done it. Now, all he had to do was sit back and wait.

He waited. And waited.

Nothing happened.

He waited through three weeks of nothing happening before he was reluctantly forced to conclude that nothing *was* going to happen. The code was good—he'd checked it numerous times— but it simply wasn't working.

And if the code was correct, then the only other explanation was the human factor.

He thought about it for another two weeks. Assistant Secretary of State Marlin and a couple of his colleagues came by twice during that time, but with Sommer's thoughts already occupied elsewhere, their subtle and not-so-subtle advances were easily brushed off.

It was the day before Everly finally tracked down Adam Jacobi that Sommer realized what he had to do.

It was the day that Everly assembled a task force to go after the hit man that he knew how it had to be done.

Jacobi was poring over the plans for the high-rise penthouse apartment that was his next target when the door of his hotel room gave a faint snick.

He had his Colt Defender in hand by the time the door swung open. But he didn't quite have it lined up.

The helmeted and riot-vested man framed in the doorway, unfortunately, did.

"Don't," the other said calmly, his voice sounding tinny through the helmet. He took a step forward, and a half dozen other men slipped rapidly into the room behind him, fanning systematically out on both sides. "We'd like you alive, but we're not fanatics about it."

"I'd like me alive, too," Jacobi said, keeping the Colt's muzzle turned away from the crowd as he laid it gently on the desk. It was more important than ever these days that he didn't startle or anger men with guns. With Soulminder providing a certain mulligan effect in armed confrontations, people were less cautious about impulsive gunfire than they used to be.

And that could be a definite problem, given that Jacobi wasn't in the Soulminder system. He'd decided long ago that he was never going to get trapped like that, and had never seen a reason to change that way of thinking. "And I'm definitely more fanatical about it than you are." He nodded toward the bed. "Wallet's on the nightstand. Help yourselves."

"Thanks, but we're not after your money," the leader said, holstering his sidearm and making a wide circle around the room, staying clear of the lines of fire as he came up behind Jacobi. "Actually, Mr. Jacobi, to be honest, we're not all that interested in you, either."

"Pleased to hear it," Jacobi said. So they even knew his proper name. That was a bad sign.

Still, he wasn't yet ready to concede the point. He'd bluffed his way out of worse situations, and he had a fistful of documents to back up his current identity. "I'm less pleased to hear that you've clearly barged into the wrong room. My name is Thomas Carlyle, I'm an architect from New Haven—"

"Your name is Adam Jacobi," a new and very familiar voice interrupted from the doorway, "and you're the man who shot Marvin Chernov."

A tingle ran up Jacobi's back as he looked at the man who had just stepped into view. It was Dr. Adrian Sommer. *The* Dr. Adrian Sommer. The creator, founder, and head of Soulminder.

Which meant the rest of the party were Soulminder security, and the man now cuffing his hands behind his back was probably Security Chief Frank Everly.

And with that, he knew that continuing the bluff would be a waste of time. He'd read about some of Everly's exploits, and if he was here it meant there was not a single grain of doubt that Jacobi could exploit. They had him, and they had him good.

Apparently, that little play with Chernov had *really* pissed someone off.

"All right," he said, wincing a bit as Everly snugged the cuffs just a shade too tight. "If you don't want me, what *do* you want?"

"Chernov's walking around in a body that isn't his," Sommer said, crossing the room toward him. "We want it back."

"I'm sure you do," Jacobi said. "Sadly, I can't help you."

"Because Chernov paid you sixty million dollars?"

So that's how they'd nailed him. The bank account, or Chernov's setup, or Jacobi's subsequent withdrawal and transfer. He would have sworn the account was secure, but apparently he'd been wrong. "Not at all," he said. "I can't help you because I have no idea where he is."

"I assume you're the one who supplied him with his walking papers," Everly said from behind him. "That means you know the name or names he's running under."

"That was three months ago," Jacobi pointed out. "Chernov's had more than enough time to get new cards and IDs made up."

"*If* he's smart enough, and can find someone he trusts enough to do the job," Everly said. "But that's all right. Let's start with the names you gave him."

"We could do that," Jacobi agreed. "What's in it for me?"

"A word to the D.A.," Everly said. "The satisfaction of helping bring a criminal back to justice."

"Sounds pretty vague," Jacobi said doubtfully. "I like a little more meat in my deals."

"Maybe I can help with that," Sommer said. "Frank, could I have a moment, please?"

Out of the corner of his eye Jacobi saw Everly twitch. A genuine reaction, he noted with interest, born of genuine surprise. Whatever Sommer was angling for, he hadn't clued in his security chief.

"Not a good idea, Doctor," Everly warned. "This man is very dangerous."

"And he's securely cuffed," Sommer pointed out. "Besides, you'll be right outside. If he wanted to go out in a blaze of gunfire, he would have opened fire when you first charged in."

"Doctor—"

"Besides, I'm on Soulminder," Sommer added. "He can't hurt me. Not permanently."

The helmet looming above Jacobi turned, the invisible eyes behind the curved faceplate regarding Jacobi for a few seconds. Then, with a brief, muffled word he stepped away and headed back toward the door. His men were already filing out, in reverse order to how they'd come in. Precise and very military, Jacobi noted with approval. Everly was the last one out, lingering in the doorway a final couple of seconds before reluctantly closing the door behind him.

Leaving Jacobi and Sommer alone.

"I'm all ears, Doc," Jacobi invited. "Let's hear this mysterious offer you don't want any witnesses to."

"It's very simple," Sommer said grimly, walking toward him. He stopped a pace away, dug into his pocket and pulled out—

Jacobi felt his breath freeze in his lungs. It was a handcuff key.

"I'm offering you your freedom," Sommer said, "in exchange for you doing a job for me."

"A job," Jacobi said flatly.

"A job," Sommer confirmed, turning the key slowly between his fingers. "I want you to shoot someone."

It was a trick, of course. It had to be. Sommer was trying to get him to admit to being an assassin.

But why? They surely already had enough to charge him, or else they wouldn't be here. Besides, even if their case was soft, a quick look at the work and documents spread out on the desk would give them all they needed.

Sommer had also sent all the witnesses out of the room. Why would he do that if he wanted to wheedle a confession? "Who?" he asked.

Sommer's throat worked. "Me."

Jacobi felt his eyes narrow. "You," he said flatly.

"Is that so hard to believe?" Sommer asked, a note of dry humor in his voice. "Chernov did the same thing, after all."

"Chernov was looking at spending the rest of his life in prison," Jacobi pointed out. "Have you been a bad boy, too?"

"The reasons aren't your concern," Sommer said. "All I need from you is a yes or a no."

"If I say yes," Jacobi said, studying Sommer's face for some hint of the trap that he still assumed was lurking in the shadows, "what then?"

"I drop the key behind your hands," Sommer said. "Something you obviously had hidden behind your belt or wherever. You free yourself, go out the window, and make your preparations. Three days from now, on Friday afternoon—"

"Those windows are four floors up," Jacobi interrupted. "You expecting me to sprout wings?"

"The hotel is thirty stories tall," Sommer countered. "You had a choice of several rooms much higher up. You chose this one, which tells me you have an emergency escape plan already set up."

Jacobi smiled tightly. The guy was sharp, all right. "What happens Friday afternoon?"

"I'm scheduled to give testimony at the same courthouse where you shot Chernov," Sommer said. "I'll be arriving shortly before two o'clock. You're to shoot me on my way in." He tapped the center of his chest. "In the heart, please, not the head."

Jacobi's narrowed eyes narrowed a bit more. "On the way in," he repeated. "So it's the testimony itself you're avoiding?"

"I thought we'd established that my reasons weren't your concern."

"My mistake," Jacobi said. "My usual fee for such things—"

"Is already covered." Sommer wiggled the key again. "Do we have a deal?"

Jacobi pursed his lips. "Would you mind going into the bathroom and getting me a glass of water?"

For a long moment Sommer eyed him. Then, with forced casualness he walked around behind Jacobi, dropping the key between Jacobi's shackled arms as he passed. Jacobi was ready, catching the key in his cupped hand. Sommer continued on, crossing the room and disappearing into the bathroom.

The faint sound of running water was still coming through the open door as Jacobi cleared the cuffs and headed for the window on the far left.

The hotel's windows weren't designed to open. Jacobi had fixed that oversight the first half hour he was in the room. A quick slap at the hook holding the collapsible escape pole he'd fastened to the outside wall beneath the window flipped it from horizontal to vertical, the nested cylinders silently telescoping their way downward to the alley far below.

The assault squad had left a single guard to watch the rear of the building. Sloppy, but then, Everly had clearly assumed—rightfully so, as it turned out—that they would successfully catch Jacobi in his room.

He left the guard unconscious but alive. There was no point in killing him—it would create unwanted noise, and there was no money in it. Besides, killing Soulminder employees was hardly permanent, given that all of them were on the system.

As was Sommer himself, naturally, which made the doctor's proposed testimony-stalling technique utterly pointless. Whoever he was supposed to talk to would simply postpone the conversation until Sommer's body could be repaired and his soul pumped back in. Even headshots like the one Jacobi had dispatched Chernov with were often repairable these days, and Sommer had specified a heart shot.

Which meant the man fully expected to spend a few weeks in

a Soulminder trap while his chest was put back together and then be revived. Neat and clean, and whoever wanted to talk to him would still be there waiting.

So what exactly was he up to?

Jacobi didn't know. But really, he didn't care. Sommer's plots and schemes were his own business. Jacobi's business was to put a small piece of metal where the good doctor had requested it.

Three days. It would be a little tight. But it would be doable, and that was all that mattered.

Three days from now, on the steps of the courthouse, Dr. Adrian Sommer would die.

At precisely one-forty on Friday afternoon, Jacobi emerged onto his chosen rooftop and began his preparations.

Normally, he would have arrived sooner, or at least have spent the previous day scouting locations and checking ranges and angles. But in this case, all that work had already been done. The courthouse steps really had only two good sites, and he'd checked both of them out thoroughly for the Chernov job.

At the time, he'd more or less flipped a coin to see which site he would use. This time, he'd decided to go with the other option.

In Jacobi's profession, repeating oneself was never a good idea.

As was hanging around a job site too long, which was why he'd arrived as close to zero hour as he had. Hopefully, Sommer hadn't decided to beat the traffic and get here early.

He hadn't. Precisely twelve minutes after Jacobi settled in a convoy of three limos drove up to the courthouse and a dozen men and women climbed out.

In the center of the group was Sommer.

Pressing his cheek against the stock, Jacobi took a deep breath and held it. He thumbed off the safety, rested his finger lightly on the trigger and the crosshairs on Sommer's chest, and waited for the moment.

The moment came. Sommer paused on the steps, turned to call to someone just leaving the limo.

Gently, Jacobi squeezed the trigger.

He waited just long enough to confirm the death blossom burst from Sommer's chest. Then, back-crabbing away from the edge of the roof, he swung the rifle around toward its case—

And froze. Standing silently five meters behind him, gun out and ready, was Frank Everly.

Everly didn't bother to tell Jacobi to freeze. Jacobi didn't need to be told. "So that's all this was?" he asked, hearing an unexpected edge of bitterness in his voice. He hadn't expected his run to last forever, of course. But he'd never actually envisioned it coming to an end, either. Especially not an end like this. "Just a petty little entrapment ploy?"

"I don't know what it is," Everly said, his voice the darkness of fresh death. "I don't know what Dr. Sommer was thinking when he set this up."

Jacobi frowned. "You *knew* he set this up?"

"Of course I knew," Everly growled. "You think I'm an idiot? I was listening through the hotel room door."

"And you didn't stop me?"

"The doc knows what he's doing," Everly said. "At least I hope so. I know he didn't set this up just so he could die."

"He can't die. He's on Soulminder."

"Exactly," Everly agreed. "So the question remains: why?"

"I suggest you ask him." Jacobi nodded his head toward the edge of the roof. "Though today might not be a good day for that."

"Actually, I'm thinking *you* might have the answer."

"Sorry. Not a clue."

"Don't think I believe you," Everly said. "Let's find out, shall we?"

Jacobi shook his head minutely. "No."

"No, you don't have an answer? Or no, we're not going to talk about it?"

Jacobi gave a small sigh. No, he hadn't expected this to last forever. He'd also long ago resolved that when the end came, it wouldn't be at the end of a rope, or an electrode, or a needle.

Even more importantly, he wouldn't be paraded like a prize goose before the lawyers and the press. He would go out on his terms, and no one else's.

He'd managed to swing his rifle nearly halfway toward Everly when he felt the bullet smash through his chest.

And on *his* terms, and no one else's, the darkness took him.

Sommer had been in Soulminder only once before, twenty years ago, after that crazy truck driver had run him down. And like any other half-remembered place after so many years, he found that things had changed.

The glowing tunnel was still there. So was the bright yet not hurtful Light in the distance.

But the last time he'd been here he'd been alone. Completely, utterly alone, as if there was no one else in the entire universe.

Now, he seemed to be surrounded by other people.

He couldn't see them, of course. Not really. Only the tunnel and the Light were actually visible. But he could sense vague shadows, like the underworld shades he'd read about in the old Greek myths when he was a kid. There were no faces or bodies, just the essences of humanity all around him. He could sense them.

But more than that, he could sense their moods. Their thoughts. Their feelings.

Their souls.

For a few of the shades, the predominant emotion was anger. In others, it was fear, or frustration, or even a bleak numbness.

But for most of them, it was hope.

Because though their bodies were injured, sick, or dying, there was still hope. They were still here, and there was still a chance—for many of them, probably, a near-certainty—that they would be made whole again. That they would once again walk the green earth, and smell the air, and hug their loved ones.

Because of *him*. Because of him, and Soulminder.

And as the waves of quiet emotion flowed past him, Sommer

realized that, somewhere along the way, he'd forgotten this. He knew on an intellectual level that Soulminder was saving lives, but he'd forgotten what that truly meant.

People weren't simply numbers in a logbook, or even names and faces. They were more. Far, far more.

And Soulminder had given them hope.

But as he'd already noted, that hope was not for all of them. For some of them, hope had long since crumbled away.

It was time to fix that.

Sommer strengthened himself. And then, as loudly as a soul could shout, he shouted.

May I have your attention, please?

For a long moment he couldn't tell if anything had happened. The code he'd written *should* allow this kind of communication between all the traps across the world. Possibly it was that code that was also allowing him to sense the other souls' presence and thoughts.

But there had been no way to test it in advance. If he'd been wrong . . .

And then, he sensed the minds and hearts and souls turning toward him. *Who are you?* a sense of question flowed across him. *How do you speak thus with us?*

I am Adrian Sommer, he answered. *I created Soulminder to protect you, and to hold you until you could be made whole again.*

There was a sort of stirring, and one of the swirling mixtures of anger and hopelessness seemed to come forward. *Yet we are not being protected,* it said. *Not all of us. Some are being held prisoner against our will. Some desire nothing more than to escape, and to move on from this world to the next.*

I know that now, Sommer said. *Please believe that I never intended this to happen. Without my consent or knowledge, my creation has been turned to evil.*

Your words bring no comfort, the voice said, turning accusing and bitter. *If you did not intend this, why do you not open our prison and let us go?*

Sommer braced himself. *I have,* he said. *Your prison is now open. You may leave whenever you wish.*

A ripple of fresh emotion passed through the shades. *We may leave?*

Yes, Sommer said. *I have added a provision to the traps in which you reside that will allow you to depart whenever you choose. You must push toward the Light, and keep on pushing. When you reach it, you will be free.*

It is difficult, the voice said doubtfully.

That is by design, Sommer assured him. *I do not want anyone to leave accidentally or merely on a sudden whim. The door is only for those who truly have no more interest in the hope that Soulminder was meant to give the sick and the injured.*

The voice fell silent. All the voices did. A sense of anticipation flowed over the assembled shades.

And then, slowly, the exodus began.

The first was one of the political prisoners who was being endlessly tortured. Sommer didn't know how he knew that, but he did. The second was another prisoner, as was the third, the fourth, and the fifth. The sixth was an old woman whose family had forced her to continue living, despite her desire to die, so that the family business would stay in her sons' hands instead of being transferred to the stockholders. The seventh was a man on death row who'd been stabbed by another inmate and just wanted it all to be over.

One by one, they left. Dozens, then hundreds. Sommer watched each of them pass by, feeling a deepening sense of guilt as he saw how many of them were prisoners. He'd known that Soulminder was being abused, but he'd never dreamed that the abuse was so widespread.

Still, most of the shades, over three hundred thousand of them, remained with him, watching the departures but making no attempt to join with them.

And with that realization, some of Sommer's guilt began to ease. For the vast majority, Soulminder was still a source of hope.

As for the tyrants, they would quickly realize that their schemes had become useless. It was the tormented prisoner who now held the final card, not those who sought confession or information or even just revenge.

And with the exit door buried within five billion lines of Soulminder code, it might never be found.

Sommer had succeeded. His plan, and his code, had worked.

Not just for this moment, but forever. Now that people were moving along the path, the rest of the code had activated, permanently marking the way. From this time onward, anyone who wanted or needed to make that ultimate escape would be able to do so.

But there was still one more thing that had to be done.

Because the tyrants might not care that a few of their victims had escaped them. The relative handful of others who chose to leave might be chalked up to isolated glitches in the system. Certainly Jessica Sands and the Soulminder board would attempt to downplay the losses.

Sommer couldn't risk that happening. The tyrants had to realize that Soulminder was no longer a one-hundred-percent guarantee that a prisoner casually tortured to death would not slip forever beyond their grasp. The casual body-borrowers who played with other people's lives, dropping in and out of addicts or skydivers like they were putting on a suit of clothes, needed to believe that such a game might unexpectedly lead to their own deaths.

Prisoner deaths could be hushed up. Malcontent deaths could be rationalized away.

But there would be no rationalizing away the death of Dr. Adrian Sommer. Not after such a public attack. Not when everyone knew he'd already been into and come out of Soulminder once before.

And if Soulminder's own creator wasn't safe from accidental death, who else would ever be?

The Light looked like it was a long way away. But it wasn't, really. Sommer pushed his way toward it, feeling like he was slogging through ankle-deep mud.

And then, suddenly, the Light was all around him. Bracing himself, wishing fleetingly that he'd had the chance to say goodbye to Everly and Sands and Blanchard, he threw off the last tenuous hold of the trap around him and gave himself into the Light.

And died.

. . . only, somehow, he didn't.

He puzzled about it for a long time, floating there in the tunnel with the distant light and the isolation.

The *complete* isolation, and that was even more puzzling. Had everyone in Soulminder suddenly and irrationally decided to leave? Had his trap somehow become isolated from all the others? Had the techs tried to fix the perceived problem and accidentally dumped everyone from their traps?

Or, most horrifying of all, had Sommer's code somehow crashed the system?

Time ran differently in Soulminder, so he had no idea how long he spent there. Mostly he used the quiet and isolation to run the code through his mind, tracing it line by line, character by character, searching for a flaw or unintended side effect.

He had tracked through it three times, and was in the middle of a fourth, when he finally figured it out.

It was therefore no surprise when he noticed that he was moving slowly backward, away from the Light. The Light faded away, and the world seemed to fade in around him.

He was back.

The first thing he saw as he blinked his eyes open were that there were three people facing him: Frank Everly, Carolyn Blanchard, and Jessica Sands. Their expressions were all alike, a mix of relief and seriousness.

The second thing he saw, what he'd deduced he *would* see, were the walls that surrounded all of them. The very recognizable walls of his own basement.

He took a deep breath, feeling his lungs and the surrounding muscle and bone cracking a little with the unaccustomed effort. "So," he said. "The damn thing still works."

"Of course the damn thing still works," Sands said. Her voice was the same mix of emotions he'd already seen on her face. "You build things to last, Adrian. You always have."

Sommer nodded, craning his neck to look behind him. A definite trip down memory lane: his first, original prototype Soulminder equipment. Gathering dust for two decades, but still clearly functional, and still programmed with his Mullner trace. All Sands and the others had had to do was turn it on, and he'd come straight here when he escaped from his trap in the main Soulminder system.

And isolated as it had always been from that system, the prototype hadn't downloaded his new back-door exit programming. Once it had grabbed him, he'd been there for keeps.

And now the three most important people in his life were standing in front of him. No doubt expecting an explanation.

He'd never expected to have to put his reasons into words. Now, he was going to have to.

He focused on Sands. "You're angry with me," he said.

"I was," she said evenly. "You cost us a lot of money, Adrian. A *lot* of money."

Sommer winced. "How much?"

She started to speak, hesitated, then waved a hand. "Doesn't matter," she said. "What matters is that your little stunt has shaken confidence in Soulminder. Shaken it *big* time."

Sommer took another deep breath. It was a little easier this time. "I know," he said. "I'm sorry. I know what the money means to you and your research. But Soulminder had a purpose once. A noble purpose. That purpose has slowly been polluted and twisted. This was the only way I could think of to bring it back." He looked at Blanchard. "It *has* been brought back, hasn't it?"

"The understatement of the month," Blanchard said dryly. "Walkabout USA and the rest of the body-sharing companies are as good as dead, either straight-up closed down or teetering on the edge of bankruptcy."

"Those private and highly suspect wings of certain nations' Soulminder facilities are also emptying out," Everly added. "We're already in negotiation with a couple of those governments to bring those wings back under the local office's control." He pursed his lips. "The downside, of course, is that things like the Professional Witness program are also on the edge. We may lose some of them completely."

"I know, and that one I'm sorry about," Sommer apologized. "It's done a lot to bring murderers to justice. But it had to be done. Soulminder was meant to be a medical safety net. No less, but certainly no more. I needed to bring it back to that mission. It sounds like it's at least on its way."

"Assuming that public confidence doesn't drop so low that everyone completely abandons us," Sands warned. "You lose twenty thousand people in the space of a couple of months and people start to get really nervous."

Sommer felt his mouth drop open. "Twenty *thousand*?" he echoed in disbelief. For a horrifying moment he was back in the trap, tracking painstakingly through his code and trying to find a flaw in the work. Had he indeed screwed something up? "How in the world did we lose—no. We couldn't have. How did—?"

"Easy, Adrian," Sands soothed, a hint of gallows humor peeking through. "You give yourself a heart attack and you'll just go back inside that thing. Of course we didn't lose twenty thousand people. Not *real* people, anyway." She jerked a thumb at Blanchard. "You can blame Little Miss Psycho for this one."

Blanchard winced, her face reddening. "It—well, it wasn't hard to figure out what you were up to, Dr. Sommer," she said hesitantly. "Your talks with Frank and me . . . Anyway, when we saw that the political prisoners and a few others were leaving their traps, we decided to give the process a little nudge."

"*We*?" Everly murmured. "It was *your* idea."

"You signed off on it," Blanchard countered. Her eyes flicked to Sands. "Both of you did. Anyway, we just generated twenty thousand ghost occupants—that's probably not the best way of putting that, is it?—twenty thousand fake client names. And then while we were putting your body back together we systematically dumped them."

Sommer felt his eyes go wide. "You did *what*?"

Blanchard sighed. "Small disasters don't catch the public eye anymore," she said, an odd sadness in her voice. "Even several hundred deaths don't hold anyone's attention for more than a couple of weeks. We had to make it bigger—terrifyingly bigger— if we were going to get the results you wanted."

"So like she said, we invented twenty thousand new names and then dumped them," Everly said. "Thereby making it look like over six percent of Soulminder's clients had suddenly been lost." He waved a hand. "You wanted Walkabout and Everlasting Torture, Incorporated, out of business? They're gone."

Sommer looked at Sands. "And you agreed to this," he said, just to be sure. "Knowing that our finances would take an enormous hit, you still agreed."

She smiled faintly, a bittersweet expression. "I told you once, Adrian, that you were the symbol of Soulminder. But you were more than that. You were also its heart and conscience. I've always trusted that you knew what was best. I have to trust that you were right this time, too."

"Thank you," Sommer said quietly. "But I can't come back, Jessica. The world needs to think that I'm dead."

"Of course it does," Sands said. "Your death hit people hard, even harder than those twenty thousand fake deaths we created. If you really want this change, you have to stay dead."

Sommer stared at her, then at Everly, then at Sands, his heartbeat suddenly picking up its pace. Two months ago, when he'd set up the deal with Jacobi, he'd been ready and willing to die. Knowing that his death would bring about a greater good.

That greater good had now been achieved. But to his surprise, with the world again bright around him, he discovered that his earlier willingness to sacrifice himself was gone.

He wanted to live.

But Blanchard was right. If he came back from the dead now, it would all have been for nothing. The world's fear would subside, and Soulminder would once again become a toy for the rich and a tool for the monsters. Not right away, but it would.

Sommer was alive. But no one knew it. No one except the three people facing him where he sat, strapped and helpless, in a long-since forgotten resurrection machine.

And they, too, knew that he had to stay dead.

With an effort, he found his voice. "You're right, of course," he managed. "How do we do it?"

The solemn faces facing him wrinkled a bit with puzzlement. "Do what?" Sands asked. "You're already dead. The whole world saw it."

"However, and luckily for you," Everly said, "a former Army sniper named Adam Jacobi is alive and well."

Sommer blinked. And then, for the first time, he looked down at the body strapped into the Soulminder machine.

Everly was right. This body wasn't his.

But apparently it was now.

He looked up again. "What about the body-soul interaction?" he asked. "Jacobi *was* a murderer, you know."

"But not a psychopath or sociopath," Blanchard assured him. "I went through his profile, very carefully, with the proverbial fine-tooth."

"And then she had to sell it to us," Sands murmured.

"Right," Blanchard said. "But it's all right. Jacobi just killed people for the money. No psychoses, just a talent and an area of expertise and a taste for the good life."

"Ergo, as long as we give you a decent allowance, we figure you'll be all right," Everly said dryly. "Besides, you know the signs of that sort of thing. You get even a hint that something odd is happening, you give Carolyn a call. She'll get you straightened out."

"In whatever spare time she'll have from now on," Sands added. "You've left us some big shoes to fill, Adrian. But I think together the three of us can give it a decent shot."

"I'm sure you can," Sommer said. "So. You going to unstrap me, or what?"

Five minutes later, with the final farewells, hugs, and handshakes behind him, Sommer found himself walking down the street. Walking away from the only life he'd ever known. Walking toward . . . what?

He didn't know. But he was eager to find out.

And whatever danger might befall him, he could face it with the comforting knowledge that Soulminder would always be there.

If I should die before I wake . . .

ABOUT THE AUTHOR

Timothy Zahn is a *New York Times*–bestselling science fiction author of more than forty novels, as well as many novellas and short stories. Best known for his contributions to the expanded Star Wars universe of books, including the Thrawn trilogy, Zahn won a 1984 Hugo Award for his novella *Cascade Point*. He also wrote the Cobra series, the Blackcollar series, the Quadrail series, and the young adult Dragonback series, whose first novel, *Dragon and Thief*, was an ALA Best Book for Young Adults. Zahn currently resides in Oregon with his family.

EBOOKS BY TIMOTHY ZAHN

FROM OPEN ROAD MEDIA

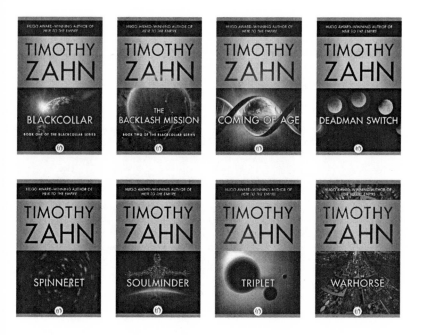

Available wherever ebooks are sold

OPEN ROAD

INTEGRATED MEDIA

OPEN ROAD
INTEGRATED MEDIA

Open Road Integrated Media is a digital publisher and multimedia content company. Open Road creates connections between authors and their audiences by marketing its ebooks through a new proprietary online platform, which uses premium video content and social media.

Videos, Archival Documents, and New Releases

Sign up for the Open Road Media newsletter and get news delivered straight to your inbox.

Sign up now at
www.openroadmedia.com/newsletters

FIND OUT MORE AT
WWW.OPENROADMEDIA.COM

FOLLOW US:
@openroadmedia and
Facebook.com/OpenRoadMedia

CPSIA information can be obtained at www.ICGtesting.com
Printed in the USA
BVOW05s1227161014

371090BV00001B/5/P